FASTBALL FARI

A NOVEL

ALSO BY MICHAEL CRUIT

Nuclear Mission

Phillip Moonfire Shot-to-pieces

Invitation to Globalogy: An Alien Perspective
(with Pat Lauderdale)

FASTBALL FARI

A NOVEL

MICHAEL JOHN CRUIT

SUMMER
GAME
BOOKS

ISBN: 978-1-938545-29-0 (pbk)
ISBN: 978-1-938545-30-6 (ebook)

For information about permissions, bulk purchases,
or additional distribution, write to
Summer Game Books
P. O. Box 818
South Orange, NJ 07079
or contact the publisher at
www.summergamebooks.com

to Frances Irene Rasmussen

ACKNOWLEDGEMENTS

Bradd Johnson from Aquila de Osa went over the manuscript page by page and offered valuable suggestions. Several people read various versions of the book and offered new insights: Pat Lauderdale, Jim Haidos, Jeff Andrusesky, Tracie "the bug lady" Stice, Susan Cameron, Kathy Klehr, Colleen Cruit. All lines of poetry were written by Nikole Andrusesky Madrigal. Carolyn Fireside contributed powerful insights and helped convert a good story into a great story.

I appreciate the help and support of the Herbert Blumer Institute for Applied and Creative Science and Art, Peninsula de Osa, Costa Rica.

FASTBALL FARI

A NOVEL

ONE

A baseball rolled across the smooth grass, ricocheted off Chet Macquire's foot, and bounced into the dugout. Macquire stood on a vast field of green grass surrounded by forty thousand empty seats. This was Target Field, home of the Minnesota Twins professional baseball team. Men wearing white uniforms threw baseballs, caught baseballs, pitched baseballs, hit baseballs. Some exercised alone, others worked in groups. Their annual salaries ranged from four hundred thousand dollars to ten million.

Macquire was the pitching coach. He had been with the Twins for ten years, the first six years as a starting pitcher, then, after his injury, as pitching coach. In the past four years he had built up a solid pitching staff. Last season the Twins had made it to the playoffs primarily on the strength of their pitching.

Mac jumped into the dugout, picked up the stray ball and threw it onto the field. It was cool in the dugout and the darkness suited his mood. He sat on the bench and stared into the outfield. Tomorrow he would have a birthday; he'd be thirty-eight. Was that old? It sounded old. He saw himself crawling over the rounded peak of life and now facing the *down* side. From now on he'll slide irrevocably into old age, infirmity and death.

And I promised to live with you, Jennifer, until death do us part, but you're already gone and I'm still here.

The cell phone jerked him away from the perverse comfort of self-pity. "Hello?"

"Hi, Mac." It was JD Johnson, General Manager of the Minnesota

Twins.

"Hi, JD."

"Anything new?"

"Nope, not yet. The farm teams are picked over. There's no one left. We gotta go for free agents."

"The season starts in seven days!" JD chewed cigars and his words came across wet and mangled.

The Twins were in trouble. Two weeks earlier, one of their best pitchers had been injured in an auto accident. The young man was in stable condition, but it would be months before he pitched again. This hurt the team, since he had been the linchpin in their rotation; an ERA of less than 3.00 and 19 wins. "What about free agents?" Mac asked again.

"We're short on cash, as Howard is forever reminding me. We can't pay what a free agent wants."

"Well, hell, JD, they're forcing us to look for quality at a bargain price." Mac and his assistants had looked at many pitchers during the past two weeks, but no one had caught their attention.

"How about Japan?" JD asked.

"We got Japan covered. Also, Puerto Rico, Cuba and the Dominican Republic."

"I got another call, Mac. It's Howard again. I'll talk to you later."

Mac laid the phone on the bench, leaned back and took off his cap. His long, thick, auburn hair showed streaks of silver. Fine lines radiated from the corners of his mouth and eyes. His face presented a pleasing symmetrical arrangement, except for a thick nose that pointed slightly to the left. He smiled as he recalled the birthday card he had received that morning from his daughter, Kimberly. Inside the card were two tickets to the circus. Kimberly was thirteen, a beautiful little girl, and he loved her until his heart ached.

Inside Kimberly lived her mother, his wife. God rest her soul.

The cell phone went off again and Mac scooped it up. "Yeah?"

"Hi, Dad." It was Kimberly!

"Hey, I was just thinking about you. What's up, darlin?"

"You gotta see this, Dad. A YouTube video. A girl pitcher!"

"Ah, c'mon, Kim, you know I don't look at that stuff."

"You better look at this one, Dad. This girl pitches *hard*. She's in the

Dominican Republic."

Mac didn't use the computer much. He majored in physical education, and they never bothered too much with computers. He used it occasionally to look up information, peruse the latest news, or download movies. He stayed away from the social networking sites, preferring his human contacts to be flesh and blood encounters. Kim, however, spent most of her waking hours on the computer – Facebook, Twitter, Myspace, YouTube – she was everywhere.

"C'mon, Dad," Kim shouted. "You need a pitcher and this girl is blowin' 'em away! She pitches in the nineties!"

This caught Mac's attention. "How do you know that?"

"They had a radar gun. You better hurry before the other coaches find out."

Is it possible a girl can pitch in the big leagues? Mac didn't think so. On the other hand, he felt a sudden a tingle along his spine; sometimes positive surprises arrive from unlikely sources. "How many hits does it have?"

"Not many, only about six thousand. YouTube gives me an early alert for things I like."

"What's the name?"

"It's called 'girl with a fastball.' It was posted by someone called Omarcastrobooks. Doesn't give the name of the girl."

"Omar Castro? Are you sure?" Mac knew Omar. They had played together for a while when Omar was with the Twins. Omar returned to the Dominican Republic about six years ago and they had kept in touch over the years.

"Yeah, I'm sure. I'm lookin' at it right now."

"Okay, baby. I'll take a look. Where are you?"

"Outside. We're having free period. My next class is gym."

"You're a sweetheart, darlin'. I love you. See ya later at the house."

"I love you too, Daddy. Bye."

Mac ducked through the dugout door, climbed upstairs and made his way through the maze of corporate offices. In the early afternoon, most offices were abandoned and Mac appreciated the quiet and privacy. He knew several scouts involved in the Dominican baseball leagues; most US coaches and managers did. Many good players in the major leagues came from the Dominican Republic, a country as crazy about baseball as the US. How come no one called him about this girl?

He sat at his desk, fired up the computer and went straight to YouTube. He typed in the name and the video appeared. He enlarged the image and sat back. The camera looked through a mesh fence directly behind home plate, about ninety feet from the pitcher's mound. Mac saw the umpire, catcher, batter and pitcher. He heard the distant shouts of the crowd.

The batter stepped up to the plate, the catcher went into his crouch and so did the ump. Now Mac had a clear view of the pitcher's mound and the pitcher standing on it. He saw a tall, wiry body with long arms and legs. He saw few details from this distance, but he discerned a definite female shape.

The pitcher stepped back, reared high off the rubber, cocked her left leg and hurled her body toward home plate. The ball moved in a blur.

Strike! Right down the middle! The batter never moved!

Mac leaned closer, his interest piqued. He liked the smooth, fluid motion of this kid and the power behind the pitch. A black object appeared in front of the camera and Mac recognized a radar gun. The digital numbers read, "94 MPH."

"Wow." *How can a woman throw that fast?*

The batter stepped up to the plate, and the catcher and ump squatted down. Mac watched the pitcher go into the same smooth, coordinated motion, the high kick and forward explosion of the body. This time he noticed a long ponytail flying out behind the pitcher's cap.

Another lively fastball and the ump shouted. "Strike!" The crowd cheered louder and Mac heard the name "Fari." This must be the pitcher's name.

The radar gun appeared again: "96 MPH."

"Ninety-six!"

The batter had stood as before, with the bat cocked to swing, but he never moved. Mac wondered if the radar gun had been modified; he knew about that trick. On the other hand, he had seen enough pitches in his life to recognize the snap and blur of a quality fastball, and this kid had it.

The batter moved up to the plate and Fari went into her delivery.

The batter circled his bat, getting cocked. Fari flew forward and released the ball. "Pop!" The ball hit the catcher's mitt and the batter swung. Strike three.

Ninety-seven MPH!

The office phone rang and Mac punched the "hold" button. He stepped across the office and slammed his door shut. He made it back to the computer just in time to see the next batter step up to the plate, a left-hander. Fari went into her smooth delivery and threw the ball. Whoa! This time the ball came in slow and fat, then broke to the right. The batter started to swing, then checked, but it was too late. Strike one.

Mac could not make out Fari's facial features, except that her skin was dark. She wore her cap with the bill pulled low. She stood motionless on the mound, waiting for the batter to step into the batter's box. Her right hand rotated the baseball rapidly.

The batter stepped up to the plate. Fari immediately went into her wind up and threw the next pitch. The ball floated in, then dipped away. The batter let it go. Ball one.

"Fari's setting him up," someone shouted in perfect English. "This next pitch is gonna be a *zinger.*"

Mac watched closely as Fari went into her wind up. Some pitchers, when they're ready to unload a fastball, will give it away by a certain emphasis in their movement. He could detect no such changes in Fari's motion.

The ball sped like a rocket and blasted the outside corner. The batter stood frozen, his feet stuck to the ground. The ump's right hand stabbed the air. "Strike two!"

The crowd cheered wildly and so did Chet Macquire. He jumped to his feet and clapped his hands. "Now a breaker to the inside!"

Fari went into her wind up and released the ball. It came in fast down the middle, then broke down and in. The batter swung, but missed by a mile. He swung so hard he turned in a complete circle and wound up kneeling in the dust.

Mac swept up his cell phone, went into "contacts," and clicked on Omar Castro.

*   *

Mac knocked on JD's door. "It's me."

5

"Come on in."

Mac stepped into the office of Jack Daniels Johnson, General Manager of the Minnesota Twins. JD was seventy-two years old, with fifty years in professional baseball as a player and coach. The Twins' coaching staff and players regarded JD as a sort of baseball wizard, and gave him their total respect and loyalty.

However, like all wizards, JD was considered eccentric and maybe even a little insane. For example, everyone knew about the dozens of tropical plants filling his office – growing from pots or hanging from the ceiling. It was a running joke that people have gotten lost in there and never heard from again.

Mac looked around, but didn't spot JD at first; too much foliage. He heard water and saw the GMr bent over in the corner, watering can in hand. Mac stepped into the office, carefully pushing aside branches and leaves.

JD's body was short and round. He wore one of his home-made smocks, or "robes," as he called them. He made these simple garments on an old, pedal-driven sewing machine. They came with one triangular hole for his head, two arm holes (long-sleeve and short-sleeve versions) and hung loosely to his ankles. He claimed they were the only clothes he could wear comfortably.

"Hi JD," said Mac. "The plants look good. I gotta go to Santo Domingo."

JD looked up. An unlit, stubby cigar stuck out from one corner of his mouth. The round, smooth skin of his head shone like the full moon. A neat white beard and mustache covered the lower half of his face. But his pale blue eyes commanded the most attention; behind the thick eyeglasses they appeared magnified to an absurd size. He had the look of a demented Santa Claus. During seven years with JD as GM, the Twins had won two World Championships and four league titles.

"Ouch!" Mac was stopped by a fern brandishing two-inch needles. "I found a pitcher, JD, a real *fireballer!* But the pitcher's in Santo Domingo and we gotta act fast."

JD's cigar jumped up and down. He had heard the excitement in Mac's voice and he trusted his pitching coach completely. "You sure about this?"

Mac looked straight into JD's enormous eyes. "I gotta go *now*. Give me the jet. Let me have Hagerty. We'll be back tomorrow."

JD reached up and jerked out the cigar. "Go!"

Mac rushed down the stairs, out the dugout, and onto the field. He took a deep breath and his lungs filled with the stale, chemical debris of popcorn, peanuts and beer. He called out. "Hagerty! Hey, Hagerty!"

A tall, well-built black man peeled away from a nearby group of players and trotted over to Mac. Cleo Hagerty stuck out his right hand and they went through Cleo's hand-shaking routine, which included rubbing elbows and ears.

This always got Mac laughing and he laughed now. "Ever been to Santo Domingo, Cleo?"

"No, sir. What they got down there?" Cleo stood six feet, four inches and weighed two hundred and twenty pounds. He presented a handsome figure – shaved head, delicate facial features, golden hoops hanging from each ear, wide shoulders, narrow waist. Last year Cleo had finished second in the league in batting average. It had been his first season with the Twins, who had signed him as a free agent. He was a switch hitter and strong from both sides of the plate.

"They've got a pitcher that pitches like a friggin' *storm*," answered Mac, still laughing. "You got anything planned for tonight or tomorrow?"

"Yeah, man. Me and Betsy are goin' out." Cleo's voice trailed away when he saw Mac wave his hands and shake his head.

"I talked to the old man, Cleo. We're goin' to Santo Domingo. We're takin' the jet. We'll be back tomorrow."

Cleo danced backward, his eyes round. "Whoa, man. You mean *now*?"

"C'mon, buddy, you know how important this is. We gotta find a starter."

Cleo smiled, revealing a tiny diamond embedded in one front tooth. "You want me to go down there and bat against this guy, huh?"

Mac smiled back. "I bet a hundred bucks that in six at-bats, this pitcher strikes you out four times."

Cleo danced and laughed. He stuck out his right hand and again they went through the hand-shaking routine. "I'll call Betsy and cancel.

You owe me one, Mac."

"Yeah, I do. Thanks, Cleo. Go get ready. We leave in fifteen minutes."

Cleo jumped into the dugout and disappeared. Mac turned his back on the field and pushed a special button on his cell phone.

His daughter Kimberly answered immediately. "Hi, Daddy."

"Hey, honey. How ya doin'?"

"I did a flip in gym. *Two* flips."

"Really? That's great."

"Yeah. You were right. The practice on the mattresses helped a lot."

"I'm proud of you, baby. Where are you now?"

"Going home on the bus. Where are you?"

"Still at the stadium. Listen, you were right about that pitcher. She's amazing. I'm leaving right now for the Dominican Republic."

"What? You think she's that good?"

"Ah, Kim, this girl is snap, crackle and pop!" They laughed together at this private joke, comfortable with each other, loving each other.

"What's her name, Daddy?"

"Fari. That's why I'm callin', darlin'. I have to leave right now. We're takin' the jet."

"But tomorrow's your birthday. Will you be back in time for the circus?"

"I'll try, honey. But you know how important this is for us. I wouldn't leave unless I had to." They had talked about this before, their obligations and responsibilities to each other now that Mama was gone. Their relationship has changed radically and they had become far more than father and daughter: They were a nation of two.

"Okay, Daddy. That's your job and you know best. Call me tonight when you get to Domi . . . Domi . . ."

"Dominican Republic. Listen, I talked to Mrs. Olsen and she'll be waiting at the house. You be a good girl and I'll see you tomorrow afternoon."

"Okay. Call me tonight, Daddy. I love you."

"I love you too, honey."

Mac turned off the phone and stepped back into the shadows. Kim had sounded disappointed. She didn't like it whenever they were separated for more than a few hours. He remembered the same disappointed tone in Jennifer's voice whenever he came home late or the team went on the road. He had never paid too much attention; baseball was a *job*. Besides, he had assumed they'd be together forever, with plenty of time for love and romance.

A burst of laughter poured over him like cool water. He looked toward center field. A group of players horsed around before their afternoon break. Directly above the players hung the giant scoreboard, with its video screens, lights, sirens and explosions. The board lay dormant now, presenting a blank and silent face.

Just like me, Mac thought; the light has gone from my life. But not all the light, he reminded himself. Kimberly was a shining sun inside his dark little universe. And now there's this kid, this Fari, who pitches like a dream!

*　　　　　*

The flight to Santo Domingo took four and half hours. The jet had plenty of room, with a galley, lounge and bathroom with shower. It was leased to a corporation controlled by the Twins owners. They respected and trusted their manager, JD Johnson, and allowed him to use the jet for "urgent business." Mac and Cleo were accompanied on the flight by one of the team's doctors, Skipper "Doc" Harris, an orthopedic specialist.

Cleo and Doc played chess in the forward cabin, while Mac sat alone in the galley. He felt more like a business executive than a baseball coach – flying in a corporate jet on a mission to check out a valuable asset. In fact, professional sport in America has evolved into a corporate enterprise, with the *sport* side of the equation subordinate to the laws of marketing and profits. Quality players no longer played for the team or the town; they played for money. Like gunslingers for hire, they roamed the free agent range until someone came up with the cash.

Mac closed his eyes and listened to the hum of the jet's motors. Not too long ago he didn't dare close his eyes because every time he did he saw Jennifer lying in bed, skin and bones, cheeks caved in, hair all gone. . .

His eyes snapped open and he sat up quickly. He poured a glass of ice water and drank it slowly. The western horizon appeared as a straight black line against the orange flash of the setting sun.

Mac had met Jennifer in high school in Montgomery, Alabama. He was a junior at Robert E. Lee High School, and Jenni was a sophomore at Sidney Lamere High School. Mac had been quarterback for the *Generals*, while Jenni was a cheerleader for the *Poets*. They were just kids and neighbors, but they liked each other and started "going steady." On the night of the homecoming dance, when the Generals trounced the Poets, they taught each other how to make love.

Mac had always been good at sports and earned a four-year scholarship to a local community college. In his senior year, when his true talent turned out to be as baseball pitcher, he had met with a representative of the Atlanta Braves. In June of that year, just after graduation, he and Jenni had gotten married. That was sixteen years ago.

"Hey, Mac!" Cleo yelled from up front. "Get on the phone. Pilot says you got a call."

Mac reached over and lifted the receiver. "Macquire here."

"Mac! This is Omar. Everything's set up for tomorrow morning."

"Hey, Omar, that's good. And it's secret, right?"

"Yep. Fari won't say a thing. She's excited as hell. I got a little park picked out, but we should get there early. A couple other scouts are lookin for Fari."

"Okay. The earlier the better. We don't want witnesses. Has Fari got an agent?"

"Not really." Omar was silent for a moment. "Fari's father pitched in the majors. He pitched for Baltimore in the seventies. He died about two years ago. A farming accident."

"Who was he?"

"Jose Madrigal. He was before our time, but twice he won the Rolaids Relief Award for best reliever of the year. Anyway, Frances, Fari's mother, will represent Fari for the time being." Omar paused again, then spoke softly. "I was real sorry to hear about Jennifer, Mac. I didn't know her that well, but I thought she was a fine lady."

Mac couldn't respond right away. Finally, he said, "Yes, she was a fine lady."

"I lost my mother not too long ago and it still hurts like hell."

More silence. Cleo and Doc burst into laughter. The jet bounced and shook, going through turbulence. Now Mac heard Omar laughing. "What?" he shouted. "What are you laughing at?"

"Ah, Mac, you're in for the surprise of your life. You, the Minnesota Twins and the whole sports world!"

"What're you talking about?"

"Fari, Mac. *Fari!* You'll find out tomorrow. Hold on to your hat, buddy – life will never be the same."

They landed shortly after ten p.m. local time. The air felt wet and warm and smelled of sea. They checked into a ground floor suite with three bedrooms. After a quick shower, Doc and Cleo visited the casino, but Mac remained in the room and mixed himself a stiff drink. It was nearly ten in Minneapolis, but Kimberly would still be waiting for his call. First, however, he had to talk to JD.

"Yeah?" JD sounded awake and alert.

"We're here safe and sound, JD. Everything's set for tomorrow morning."

"I watched that video." JD's voice reflected his Scottish heritage. "There's something you didn't tell me about this Fari."

"I know. I'm sorry. I couldn't bring myself to say it. Does it matter that she's a woman?"

"Not when she pitches like a whirlwind. Does she have an agent?"

"Not yet. For the time being the mother will speak for her. Did you know Fari's father? Jose Madrigal. He pitched for Baltimore in the seventies."

"Jose Madrigal was Fari's father?"

Mac detected the quick beat in JD's voice and wondered about it. "Yeah. He started in the American League and wound up with the Orioles. He retired and went back to Central America."

"He died about two years ago," said JD. "He was a pretty good reliever."

"Well, I guess he taught his daughter how to pitch."

"I guess he did."

They remained silent for a moment, the comfortable silence between two people who know and like each other. Finally, JD heaved a sigh. "Ah, Mac, life is truly marvelous. Sometimes we think we know what's going on, but we don't know crap. Shiva dances, Mac. That's all we can say. Shiva dances."

Mac hesitated, not sure what this meant. JD often spoke in parables and metaphors, or quoted poetry and Eastern philosophy. JD was the wisest man Mac knew, but sometimes he didn't get the spacey comments and obscure references. He brought the conversation back to business. "What about money?"

"I asked Howard the maximum he would allow."

"Which turned out to be the minimum."

"Right. He says Fari's a rookie, untested in the majors. Also, he's thinking this Fari is poor and hungry."

"Does he know Fari's a girl?"

"Not yet. We'll offer a one year, standard contract with an incentive clause."

"Okay. That's the most she can expect. We don't want to get into a bidding war."

"God, no. We need Fari, but don't make promises we can't keep. Just be enthusiastic."

"Oh, I am that, JD. I like this pitcher. I've got an intuitive feeling."

"That's good, Mac. It's good to see you excited, more animated."

Mac didn't answer. They listened to each other breathe.

"Well, just remember this," said JD. "The fires of new passion rise like the Phoenix from the ashes of the old."

*   *

Mac went back to the bar and poured himself more scotch. He thought about what JD had said. He didn't recognize the reference, but he understood the meaning; no matter how bad it hurts right now, life goes on and the pain will fade. This was a rational view, logical, like the beat of time itself. But the heart marches to a different beat; it doesn't think, it *feels*.

Now it was time to call Kim. He added more ice to his glass and punched in the numbers.

"Hi, Daddy."

Mac laughed. "How did you know it was me?"

"I have a feeling about you."

"Oh, yeah? What's that?"

"You're in this hotel room having a drink, feeling lonely, thinking about your loving daughter."

"My lovely, loving daughter." They laughed together at another inside joke.

"What's up, honey?" asked Mac. "What did you have for dinner?"

"Pizza. Super Supreme."

"Wow. Now you made me hungry."

"It was great. Cheese in the crust. Mrs. Olson said grace in Dutch."

"Yeah, I know. I've heard her."

"You and I don't say grace in any language."

Mac recognized another variation on his daughter's current intellectual interest - religion. Kimberly was a smart girl and considered questions of great import, such as life and death. Mac had lost his wife; Kim had lost her mother.

Mac chose not to respond, thinking Kim had tried to provoke him. He didn't want any more philosophy tonight.

"You remember that priest, Daddy? The one at mother's funeral? Father something."

"Father Schultz."

"Yeah, Father Schultz. He said God works in mysterious ways."

"That's right." Mac closed his eyes, held his breath.

"He said we can't ask *why* God took Jennifer to heaven. Yes, she was a good person and we all loved her, but God works in mysterious ways. It must be part of His great plan."

"Kim, honey . . ."

"So what *is* God's plan?"

TWO

Tuesday: March 25

Mac sat on a deck chair on the outside patio and watched the dawn approach. The ocean crashed against the rocks only a few yards away. He leaned forward and inhaled deeply. The new day smelled of sea, roses and rot.

Greeting the dawn has become a recent ritual for Mac, mainly because he had been going to bed earlier. The hospital psychologist suggested the earlier bedtimes might be a faster escape into unconsciousness, to avoid pain and boredom. Mac said if that was the case, then it wasn't getting him anywhere; now he *rose* earlier and had the same amount of torment every day.

Nevertheless, he enjoyed these dawn encounters, when the darkness fled before the light. The freshness and sense of renewal appealed to him.

The patio door slid open and Cleo Hagerty stepped out. "Morning, Mac."

"Good morning, Cleo. Come on over. It's beautiful out here."

Cleo's bare feet slapped the stone tiles. He wore a bathrobe provided by the hotel, but it was much too small; the sleeves ended halfway up his forearms. He looked around and breathed deeply. "It's nice here."

"Yeah. I found this place on my last trip. I love the ocean."

The ocean lay dark and restless beneath a white sky. Cleo shivered and pulled the robe closer. "It gives me the creeps. I can't swim."

Mac laughed, a free, spontaneous outburst. "Oh, come on! A million-dollar sports hero on the cover of all those cereal boxes, and you can't swim?"

Cleo's soft, dark lips curled up. He liked Mac and felt pleased to see him laughing. He could hardly imagine the horror Mac must have endured the past few months during Jenni's sickness and death. It changed Mac completely, but Cleo had just seen a glimpse of the old Mac. "You ought to teach me to swim, Mac," he said, and nodded toward the marina next door. "I'm gonna buy one of those yachts."

"Shoot, Cleo, you don't know a rudder from a head."

Meanwhile, inside the suite, Doc Harris crawled out of bed with both hands holding his splitting head. The throbbing hangover carried the bitter memory of losing over a thousand dollars at the blackjack tables. In fact, Doc believed it was time for a serious painkiller. He poured a cup of coffee and added a generous shot of tropical rum. He picked out a pill bottle from his suitcase, shook out a red capsule and washed it down with the rum-laced coffee.

Doc was forty-nine, but looked older. His gray eyes and cheeks drooped from a lifetime of gravity and abuse. Once a week he tinted his hair and every night he performed a series of facial contortions that were supposed to smooth-out the wrinkles and lines. Doc battled death and death lurked in the passage of time.

Cleo and Mac returned to the room and Doc composed himself. During breakfast Mac told them about Fari's father Jose Madrigal and Fari's fantastic fastball. Cleo was impressed and came up with a new name: "Fastball Fari."

"I remember Jose Madrigal," said Doc Harris, wiping his lips incessantly. "He wasn't too bad. I even have his card."

Doc collected baseball cards and took any opportunity to boast about his collection. He was known secretly as "Doctor Bubble Gum."

"That was before my time," Cleo said. "But his son, this Fari, doesn't sound too bad."

Mac smiled to himself and kept his secret. The hotel phone rang and he grabbed it. "Hello?"

"You ready, Mac?" It was Omar. "Ready for the biggest surprise of your life?"

"I'm ready, but I don't know about Doc and Cleo."

Omar continued. "In fifteen minutes a blue and white Chevy will pull up in front of your hotel. The driver's name is Gomez. He doesn't know who you are and can't speak English. He'll take you to the ballpark. See you soon."

*   *

Senor Gomez sported an impressive crop of dreadlocks, with tiny silver bells hanging from each braid. His eyes were hidden behind purple sunglasses, which went nicely with his banana-yellow suit coat. He wore shorts, but no shirt or shoes. He might not speak English, but he tried. He looked at Doc, who sat in front. "You book peoples?"

Doc looked at Mac in back and raised his eyebrows.

"Omar sells books," whispered Mac.

"Oh, yeah, we're book people," Doc told Gomez. He hooked his thumb at Cleo in the back seat. "This big guy here is our number one bestseller. He writes *romance* novels."

Cleo slapped Doc on the arm. "I'm gonna put you in my next book. You'll be the villain."

Doc laughed. He felt great, completely numb from the neck up. If his foot should burst into fire, he'd never know or even care. "Just make sure there's plenty of romance."

The driver turned off the main road and approached a small school. "Here the place," he announced.

It was a "colegio," a high school. They sped through the entrance to the parking lot behind the school, where they saw a baseball diamond. Mac leaned forward and looked it over. The fences in the outfield were not very deep, but Cleo loved to hit home runs, so that was fine. He saw three people; one person sitting on a bench and two others standing on the field.

Senor Gomez stopped at the curb, fifty yards from the field. "You get out here."

Mac gave Senor Gomez an extra tip. "Thank you, sir," said Gomez and he sped off in a cloud of exhaust and dust.

Cleo had brought a bag of his favorite bats ("the tools of my trade") and threw it on his shoulder. As they approached the field, Mac studied the person on the bench. It appeared to be an older woman; in her fifties, maybe. He focused on the two playing catch and recognized one as Omar. He wore a catcher's shin pads and a chest pad. The other person must be Fari.

Cleo and Doc froze in mid-stride and their jaws dropped. "No," whispered Cleo. "It's not possible, is it?"

Mac laughed. "Surprise! Fari Madrigal is a girl."

"Hey, Mac," Omar shouted. "Come and meet Fari and her mother."

Fari Madrigal stood near the pitcher's mound, her head tilted toward the ground, her face hidden by the bill of her cap. She wore a loose, gray T-shirt, gray sweat pants and baseball shoes. Her long, black hair hung in a ponytail, just as Mac had seen on the video. She was tall, built solid, with long arms and legs, but also the gentle curves of a feminine shape.

"Why didn't you tell us, Mac?" Cleo asked, still whispering.

"More fun this way," Mac whispered back. Suddenly, Fari's head jerked up and she looked straight into his eyes. A soft explosion detonated in the middle of his brain.

"Mr. Macquire?"

Mac stood stunned for a second, then heard a voice next to him. He turned and lost the vision of Fari. It took a moment for his eyes to refocus.

"A pleasure to meet you, sir. I'm Fari's mother, Frances."

The older woman stood before Mac, holding out her hand. He saw the resemblance immediately; a handsome woman with smooth, dark skin and big, penetrating eyes. He took her hand and hesitated, wondering if he should kiss it.

Frances tugged Mac onto the field. "Come and meet my daughter, Mr. Macquire."

Fari stood slightly taller and Mac had to look up to connect with her eyes. But he couldn't connect. She wouldn't look at him. They shook hands and Mac noticed the strong fingers and skin like velvet.

"Con mucho gusto," Fari said softly, her eyes still hidden.

Mac smiled and nodded. He knew a little Spanish; about half the guys on the team were Latinos.

Omar walked over and slapped Mac on the back. "What's the matter, Mac? Can't talk?"

"Hi, Omar." They shook hands, but Mac couldn't keep his eyes off Fari. She was the most beautiful woman he had ever seen. He wanted her to look at him again.

Cleo stepped forward and stuck out his hand. "Hiya, Fastball Fari.

I'm Cleo Haggerty." He pumped Fari's hand.

Mac noticed Fari didn't look at Cleo either, but Cleo certainly looked at her. Doc Harris acted gracious toward Frances, but tentative and hesitant with Fari. Mac had felt the same awkwardness, as if a female baseball pitcher somehow challenged his own identity. *What kind of mystery do we have here?*

During the commotion and embarrassment, Fari made a quick assessment of these men. She saw how they looked at her, their eyes lingering in predictable places. She decided that Chet Macquire and Cleo Hagerty were all right, but the doctor was dangerous.

She felt an affinity toward Macquire, a pitcher like herself. However, she sensed he felt deeply troubled. *Maybe because Fari Madrigal is a woman?* It didn't matter that she was a woman; he had come here to see her *pitch.*

Omar took over leadership of the proceedings and got them organized. "We should begin soon, Mac, before the kids arrive for school." He put on the catcher's mask and walked toward home plate.

Cleo stood near the batter's box, wearing a batting helmet and holding a bat. Frances had wandered to the first-base side of the pitcher's mound. Fari stood on the mound, her body facing home plate but her face turned toward third base. Once again, Mac wondered about her strange behavior. He walked over to Cleo. "What's your plan?"

The big center fielder and batting champion looked at Mac like it must be a trick question. "I'm gonna *bat*, man."

"Don't hurt her, Cleo. I'm worried about liners. We don't have a pitching shield."

Cleo danced in place and rolled the bat behind his back. "If she was a man, would you say that? Besides, I don't see why you're worried; a liner improved *your* looks."

"Yeah, but nothing could improve Fari's looks." They stared at each other for a second. Finally, Mac said, "We'll do fifteen or twenty at-bats. Start off left-handed. I'll tell you when to switch."

"Okay." Cleo looked over at Fari and lowered his voice. "You know what, Mac? I hope she's got it. You and I and the team would be a part of history."

"Yeah, we would. But let's see how she pitches. Be serious. We need a hit!"

Mac jogged out to the mound. He wanted to stand behind Fari and watch the trajectory of the pitches. She had turned as he approached, but kept her face averted. She spoke softly. "Que quiere que hago?"

Mac barely heard her, but he didn't understand. He looked at Frances.

"What would like Fari to do?" Frances answered with a smile.

Mac turned back to Fari. Her big, dark eyes glanced at him for one split second, then slipped away. He saw a profound, untroubled confidence inside those glorious orbs, as if Fari lived deep within herself, watching something she had already seen. He looked down at the turf and kicked it. "Cleo will start left-handed. Pitch fastballs. Try to go low and inside."

Frances translated. "Cleo empezara por la izquierda. Manda bolas rápidas, por abajo y adentro."

Fari nodded. She sensed Mr. Macquire's discomfort. Maybe he's shy, she thought. That's all right; shy people were less likely to be pigs. She spun around and looked at Cleo Hagerty, one of the best baseball hitters in the world. Finally, it hit her: *This is my dream and it's happening now!*

She inhaled deeply, wiped away the tears and blinked until her vision cleared. She dug her right foot into the rubber and leaned forward. The pitch formed in her mind and she wound up and threw.

Mac watched Fari hurl her body toward home plate, her right arm snapping down and following through. Pow! The ball hit the catcher's mitt right over the inside corner, just above Cleo's knees.

Cleo just looked at it. He stepped back, took off the helmet and flashed his teeth. "Strike one!" He shouted and bowed toward the mound.

Fari bowed back, her face hidden, but Mac saw she was smiling. He watched her for a moment and finally she glanced at him again. This time her eyes penetrated to the secret corners of his heart. His mouth went dry. "More fastballs," he croaked. "In the same place."

"Otra vez!" Frances shouted.

Pow! Pow! Cleo swung twice. On the second pitch, he ticked the ball, but Omar caught it. Strike two. On the third pitch, he swung way too late. Strike three. Now he backed away from the plate, no longer smiling.

"She's good, huh?" said Omar, squatting next to Cleo.

Cleo lifted the helmet and wiped his brow. "That fastball is *fast*." He would not have believed this if he hadn't seen it with his own eyes. A girl pitcher with a killer fastball! He had faced the best pitchers in both leagues and he put Fari right up there. She was no longer just a good-looking woman, she was a *baseball pitcher*. She was Fastball Fari.

Adrenalin raged through Fari's veins. *This is Cleo Hagerty and I struck him out!* Her emotions exploded. She covered her face with her glove and laughed and cried. She heard Mama clap and shout. "Go Baltimore Bananas!"

Doc Harris watched from behind home plate, holding a radar gun in one hand and a pair of binoculars in the other. His blood ran hot and thick. He was stunned at Fari's beauty and every time he looked at her, he saw her *naked*.

"How about a breaking ball?" Mac asked.

Frances translated. "Quiere una curva."

Fari stared at her feet and spoke toward the ground. "Okay. Como?"

"Cleo likes outside stuff," said Mac. "Throw it outside, then try to break it down and in. He's a sucker for it." He saw Fari nod even though Frances had not translated. How much English does Fari know?

Fari turned to face Cleo Haggerty. She thought about it; slightly outside, then down and in. She had several variations of this pitch for left-handed batters and decided to throw a variety to Cleo.

She threw the ball and pulled back on the speed. Cleo swung and missed, way out in front of the ball. Strike one. The next pitch started way outside, then broke in and over the outside corner. Cleo didn't move. Strike two. Now she threw what she called a "splitter"; this pitch came in waist high, then dropped and split home plate. Cleo swung wildly and missed. Strike three.

A beautiful pitch! Fari hopped on the mound in celebration. Mac felt moved by this joyful, private expression. *This woman loves to pitch!*

Unlike Doc, Mac had focused on the trajectory of the pitches and noticed they were essentially the same pitch, each one going in at a different angle. He wondered if this was a coincidence, a stroke of luck, or did Fari actually have that much control?

She stood loose and relaxed on the mound, waiting patiently for his direction, but again looking toward third base. Mac turned toward home plate and shouted. "Switch to the right, Cleo."

Cleo backed away from the batter's box and trotted over to his bag of bats. Fari's head whipped around and she laughed loudly. "Quiere cambiar el bat!"

This outburst startled Mac and looked at her, but she had already turned toward third. He looked back at Cleo and gave him a hand signal; swing away! Cleo nodded and stepped up to the plate.

*　　　　　*

After fifteen at-bats, Cleo had struck out eight times, walked twice, hit three weak bloopers and two solid hits. When Cleo got the first hit, Fari had turned toward Mac and spoke quietly. "El esta muy bien, verdad? Era un buen pitch."

Mac shivered. *Fari was impressed that one of the best hitters in the world had hit her pitch!* She had the best movement and control of any pitcher he had ever worked with. He felt ecstatic, anxious, terrified. He knew now that the game of baseball, including him, would never be the same.

He called time-out. Doc walked out from the behind the backstop and pulled Mac to one side. "Those kids know who Fari is," he whispered. "And I think they recognize Cleo."

Mac tried to think straight. He had seen enough of Fari's pitching to know she could definitely pitch in the majors. This, coupled with her youth – she was twenty-five – made her an outstanding candidate for a successful career in the big leagues.

But she was a *woman*. And this, Mac knew, would cause a media frenzy.

"What we need now is secrecy," said Doc and he put on dark sunglasses, as if demonstrating.

"That's what I think too." Mac leaned closer and whispered. "I need some help here. Tell Omar to call a taxi. You and Cleo go back to the hotel and pack. Pack my stuff too, please."

The sunglasses looked straight at him. "What are *you* gonna do?"

"I'm going with these people and talk business. Maybe Fari can return with us on the plane."

"You mean today?"

"Yeah, why not? The season starts next week!"

Doc smiled, showing all his perfectly capped teeth. "Don't you think I should give her a physical? I'm up for it."

Mac laughed. He couldn't help himself, a welcome release of tension and shock. "Oh God, Doc, what are we getting into here?"

"We're getting into one of the biggest sports stories in decades." Doc's face composed into a frown. "But what's that gonna do to *her*?" He nodded toward the bleachers where Fari stood with her mother.

Mac wondered about that. "I don't know."

"She acts weird," said Doc, still staring at Fari. "It reminds me of autism." He looked at Mac. "Maybe she needs a guardian. You know, someone to watch over her."

Mac answered sharply. "Well, it ain't gonna be you. Hurry up. We gotta get out of here."

Doc trotted toward Omar and Mac strolled over to Cleo. "Well, what do you think, Cleo?"

Cleo rolled his eyes. "Ain't seen nothin like it, Mac. She pitches *hard*, man. She pitches *sneaky*."

Mac laughed. "Yeah, she does." He noticed several kids staring and pointing at Cleo. "You'd better get out of here. Go back to the hotel with Doc. And for God's sake, keep quiet about this."

"Don't worry. I know we're about to get hit by a shitstorm." He hefted his bat bag to his shoulder. "We gotta help her, Mac. She's a tremendous pitcher, but I don't think she has any idea what's gonna happen in Minneapolis."

"You're right. It's gonna be a media free-for-all. She needs a bodyguard, and for the moment that's *your* job."

*   *

Omar drove Mac, Frances and Fari to his office, which was nearby and private. Mac rode in back with Frances, while Fari sat up front with Omar. They rode in silence, spellbound by the sobering prospect of stepping into the pages of history.

As they drove, Fari's upper body jerked back and forth in quick rhythmic beats while she spun a baseball furiously in her pitching hand. Pinwheels of fire lit up her heart. *Papa*, she called in her mind, *puedes ver lo que esta pasando?* She and papa always spoke Spanish to each other.

Jose Madrigal appeared as a shadow in her thoughts. He looked straight at her, his eyes brimming with love. *Ah, mi amor, estas llegando por los grandes!*

Si, Papa. Llegaremos juntos.

Mac noticed Fari's repetitive movements and stared at the back of her head, trying to look inside it. Cleo's right, he thought; she doesn't recognize the significance of being the first woman to play in the pros. The significance for Fari was personal; she simply loves to pitch! It's almost as if her physical identity has no significance, at least to her. Yet, he had rarely seen such a big person move with such grace and coordination. And though she acted distant and cool, her eyes, when she looked at him, reflected warmth and openness, as if the Fari inside those eyes was much different than the Fari appearing on the surface.

Mac shook his head and tried to gather his wits. He went over in his mind the terms of the contract. After watching Fari pitch, he knew she could get more than what the Twins offered. He didn't want to lie to her about this, but he didn't want to lose her either.

Frances tugged on his sleeve and whispered in his ear. "I ask for your help, Mr. Macquire. Fari is going into a world she knows nothing about. She just wants to pitch, but I think there's more to it."

Mac shuddered and Frances felt it. She continued. "The media here in Santo Domingo became rude and intrusive very quickly. What will it be like in the United States?"

Mac had an idea what it might be like, but he didn't want to say it. "I don't know. They'll be excited." He cringed inwardly at this wild understatement.

"Fari speaks English, Mr. Macquire, but she's a little shy." Frances looked at him and smiled. "She's a very special person. Please have patience."

Have patience? What did that mean? Mac almost asked, but at that moment they arrived at the office building. Omar escorted them to a large, corner office and addressed Mac. "I'll leave you to talk in private. Call me when you're through." He winked and left the office, closing the door.

Fari and Frances sat on a sofa set against one wall, while Mac sat in a chair facing the sofa. Fari had taken off her baseball shoes and wore only white socks. The baseball rested motionless, cradled in both hands. She kept on her cap, which provided a barrier for hiding and peeking. Mac saw only the lower half of her face. He studied the wide, curvy mouth – the lips full in the center, then tapering gracefully and decorated with perfectly shaped dimples. Her strong, square jaw swept forward to a plump chin punctuated by a soft cleft. The symmetry was classic and stunning.

Omar told him earlier that Fari felt uncomfortable around strangers, avoided journalists and sometimes wore disguises. She had "Asperger's Syndrome," Omar had said, which he described as a form of autism. Mac knew enough to know this should have no effect on Fari's competence as a person or as a baseball pitcher. Still, did she think differently? Did she feel differently?

Mac had read somewhere that great events were often preceded by a psychic energy wave. He felt such a wave pressing in on the room right now. I'm like Alice in Wonderland, he thought; I fell down the rabbit hole and all I can do is hang on for the ride. He felt more comfortable speaking to Frances, but this was Fari's moment and he should address her directly. Frances said Fari spoke English, but he had not heard much. He cleared his mind and got his speech ready. At that moment, Fari lifted her head and looked directly at him. Mac forgot his speech and could only say two words. "Fastball Fari."

Frances and Fari laughed.

"You are still bothered Fari is a woman?" Frances asked. Fari's eyes were hidden again.

"Yes," answered Mac. "But I'm most impressed by her pitching."

Fari's face bloomed. That was the nicest thing Mr. Macquire could have said. In her brief career in the Dominican Republic most of the coaches had tried to get personal with her immediately, but she could tell Macquire was different.

Mac leaned forward and tried to look under the bill of her cap. "We want you to pitch for us and we offer you a standard, first-year contract, with a generous incentive clause." He sat back and waited for a reaction.

Fari glanced sideways and spoke to her mother. "Quiere que yo lanzo para los Twins?"

Mac shifted sideways and looked at Frances, who translated. "You want Fari to pitch for the Minnesota Twins?"

Mac smiled and nodded. "I sure do! But this is the most we can offer a first year rookie. The incentive would be paid as a bonus, based on performance." Now he spoke directly to Frances. "If Fari has so many strike outs, so many complete games, or a certain level of ERA, she'll be paid more." He turned back to Fari and almost caught her looking at him. "It could mean an additional three hundred thousand dollars." This was an exaggeration, but he wanted to see her reaction.

Fari's upper body began to jerk back and forth in a slow, steady rhythm. The baseball spun quickly in her right hand. Her eyes were hidden, but she seemed to stare at the baseball as she spoke in a soft, musical lilt. "Estas hablando de las ligas minores?"

Mac felt enchanted by the sound of her voice, but he didn't understand. He looked at Frances.

"Are you talking about the minor leagues?" Frances asked.

Mac laughed. "The majors! We need a starter and maybe you can help us!"

Fari's body stopped moving and the baseball stopped spinning. She looked him full in the eyes and spoke English. "I will pitch for the Twins? Against the Yankees?"

"And against the Tigers and White Sox!" shouted Frances. She threw her arms around her daughter and they hugged each other fiercely. "You'll pitch in the big leagues, honey! *The big leagues!*"

Fari buried her face in her mother's neck and sobbed. They held each other tightly and rocked back and forth.

Mac heard muffled whispers: "Papa" and "Jose." He decided it was a good time for a phone call. He stood up and excused himself. "I'll be right back." Fari and Frances didn't seem to notice as he left. Omar loaned him a phone and he called JD.

"Hey, JD."

"Mac! I've been waiting like a maid in bloom."

Mac laughed. "Talk about maids in bloom!"

"Well, how is she?"

"We were blown away. Doc's got the shakes."

"Good looking, huh?"

"Oh my God!"

"Keep Doc away from her!"

"Fari can handle herself. Also, I made Cleo her bodyguard."

"Good idea. He's a good man."

Mac hesitated a second, thinking about Fari. "JD, this is a very remarkable woman." He said this with more force than he intended, prompting silence from the other end. He rushed to fill it. "She struck out Cleo eight times in fifteen at-bats. He used five different bats."

"That's not much to go on."

"It was enough for me. She's got great speed and control, hits the corners with everything. Also, she's a big person, over six feet, about one sixty-five or seventy, perfectly proportioned. Big hands, long fingers. Cleo says she was born to pitch. That's what I think."

More silence from the other end. Mac imagined JD roaming among the plants in his office dressed in a brightly colored robe, the cigar in his mouth jerking up and down rapidly.

Finally, JD asked. "Who knows about this?"

"Just us."

"And everyone knows to keep quiet?"

"Oh yeah. That's why we left early. The kids knew Fari and Cleo."

"We gotta keep this secret for now."

Mac felt anxious and looked for leadership. "She wants to pitch for us, but we need a plan."

JD didn't answer right away, but Mac heard his brain spinning. Finally, JD answered. "A car will be waiting at the airport. Come directly to my place on the lake."

"Good. It's quiet there, private."

"Also, I want you and Kim to move in for a while. I'll call Kim and have her come over here."

"Okay. Is it a problem if Fari's mother, Frances, comes with us? She's Fari's agent."

"Of course not. I'm expecting her. But the main thing is speed, Mac. We have to move *quickly*."

*   *

"Today?" Frances' eyes were still red and wet. She clutched both hands to her chest.

"I know it's sudden, Mrs. Madrigal," answered Mac. "But we don't have much time."

Fari and Frances had composed themselves, but they were unable to sit still. Frances tapped her feet on the floor, while Fari paced back and forth, the baseball spinning quickly in her right hand.

"The season starts next week," Mac continued. "We open Sunday against Chicago. There's not much time to introduce Fari to the team, or teach her our system." He paused and smiled. "Plus, we're bound to have special problems."

Fari and Frances looked at each other.

"I'll leave if you need privacy," said Mac.

"No, no." Frances waved her hands in the air. "Mas bien, we need your help. I have been to the States, pero Fari no lo conozce!" She looked at Mac, her eyes pleading.

He stared back at her. Did she ask a question?

Fari stopped pacing and stood next to Mac's chair, her face turned to one side. "Empezaremos la próxima semana," she said and flicked a quick glance toward Mac. "I am on team?"

Mac smiled, feeling more comfortable in her presence. "Not legally. Not until you sign the contract. But in my heart and in your heart, you're on the team."

Fari suddenly bent over, grabbed Mac's upper arm and hauled him to his feet. He was surprised at her strength.

"Papeles no significa mucho." Fari transferred the baseball to her left hand and stuck out her right hand. "Tome la mano."

Mac laughed and shook her hand.

"How much time do we have?" asked Frances.

"It's a four or five-hour flight," answered Mac. "We should leave within the next two hours."

"Y que tal el numero?" Fari asked. She bounced on her feet, her eyes on the floor.

"What do you mean?" Mac realized he still held her hand. He loosened his grip and stepped back, but she wouldn't let go.

"She asks about the number," said Frances.

"Que tal el numero?" Fari asked again, her face still averted. She squeezed his hand tighter and laughed with genuine delight.

What was she talking about? Mac felt sweat break out on his palms. *What* number?

"Can I pick any number for my uniform?"

THREE

Fari and Frances stared at the sleek corporate jet squatting on the tarmac. They watched the pilots walk around the plane slowly, inspecting it.

"The ultimate in status and prestige," whispered Frances.

Fari shook her head. So like Mama to frown on symbols of corporate power. Yet they're giving us a free ride.

Frances read her daughter's mind. "I know they're giving us a ride. I meant we're going somewhere we've never been."

Fari looked at her. "I thought you went to Minneapolis once with Papa."

They spoke Spanish to each other. Frances wrapped one arm around Fari. "I'm not talking about places. I'm talking about a lifestyle you and I can't imagine. You know how crazy it was with the media here? It'll be worse in the US."

Fari shivered and snuggled closer to her mother. "We expected that, Mama."

"Yes, but how long do you think you can take it?"

Fari had no idea what to expect during the next few months. Here, in the Dominican Republic, her life had changed very quickly. She had pitched in only three games, but their house and phone had been invaded by people pleading to Fari for interviews, or to appear on TV, or on radio, or a press conference, or photo sessions, or public relations, or product endorsements, or charities, church groups, civic clubs and schools. Then there were the love letters, hate letters, fan letters, pornographic letters and marriage proposals.

Fari shivered again. Although she loved to pitch, she regarded everything else with distant suspicion. This leap into the United States would take her into unknown territory, but one thing was certain; the Eyes and Ears were everywhere, and she would become the target for

29

money, lust and fantasy. "Let's see how it goes, Mama. At least one year. Is that enough?"

Frances smiled. "One or two no-hitters would certainly help."

Fari laughed. "Not if all the batters are like Cleo."

"Oh, there's not many like Cleo."

"You're right. He's one of a kind. I like him."

"I like him too."

They heard men's voices behind them. Mac and the others loaded baggage onto a trolley. Mother and daughter looked at each other with hope and terror. Frances smiled bravely. "We'll do fine, honey. We have our plan and we'll stick to it. You do the pitching and I'll do the business."

Cleo escorted Fari to the plane. He tried to teach her his special handshake, but his hoop earrings caught in her hair. Mac watched and laughed. Cleo was the perfect protector for Fari; he has a quick mind, a gentle soul and muscles galore.

Doc escorted Frances with warmth and charm, but acted cool and formal toward Fari. Mac was reminded of a lion on the prowl; Doc purring at the mother, while holding Fari in the corners of his eyes.

The pilot estimated they'd arrive in Minneapolis at seven p.m. local time, too late for the circus. Kim would be disappointed, but she'd forget about it quickly when she met Fastball Fari.

Cleo gave Frances and Fari a quick tour of the plane. Doc trailed along behind, his eyes on Fari, waiting for his chance. When they returned to the main cabin, Frances and Fari made a point of sitting together, with Fari on the inside next to the window.

Obviously, this was a defensive position. Fari had mentioned to Cleo that this was "only my third time flying in a jet airplane." Maybe she didn't like flying, or maybe she didn't like being confined with strangers. In any case, she did not appear accessible.

Doc sat across the aisle from Frances, and Cleo took the seat directly in front of Fari. He turned around, leaned over the backrest and talked loud and fast, comparing Fari with other pitchers he'd faced. Fari still wore her cap and did not look at Cleo, but he didn't seem to mind. She listened and nodded, but did not speak.

Mac watched from his favorite place in back. He remembered what Omar had told him about the death of Fari's father, Jose Madrigal.

He died in a farming accident two years ago. It had been big news in the Dominican Republic because of Jose's fame as a former major league player. Then, only two weeks ago, exactly two years after Jose's death, his daughter Fari appeared suddenly on a semipro team in Higuey, on the eastern peninsula.

A few days later the media in Santo Domingo picked up on the story and sent reporters to Higuey. However, Fari refused to grant interviews or answer questions; instead, the journalists concentrated on Fari's recent history. According to the locals, Fari was greatly affected by her father's death and went into seclusion on the family farm, located in a remote jungle environment. During the next two years there were several "eyewitness accounts" of Fari Madrigal running naked and wild in the rainforest.

Mac didn't think she looked like a deranged woman from the rainforest. Just the opposite. Her coordination, elegance and careless beauty came straight out of the pages of any glamour magazine – except for the defensive body language and troublesome eye contact.

Fari wore her traveling clothes; a baseball cap, grey T-shirt, light-blue jacket, black sweat pants and white tennis shoes. She carried a baseball. Mac had detected no make-up or jewelry, not even a watch. Frances, by contrast, wore a carefully tailored, color-coordinated outfit, including earrings, bracelets and rings. She had told him earlier that Fari started throwing a ball when she was three years old.

Suddenly, Mac remembered that today was his birthday! Immediately, he recalled the birthdays from his past – the warm, carefree days when a birthday meant a special, joyous event. Those were the *early* birthdays, the ones he could count on his fingers. But time was a thief, as he knew well. Time consumed everything. It took Jennifer. It takes away birthdays. Now, with a birthday in the high double-digits, Mac felt sorry for himself.

The steward appeared and motioned for Mac to pick up the phone. He grabbed it and growled. "Yeah?"

"Yeah yourself," said JD. "Pilot says you'll be here in about three hours."

"Yeah."

"Good job, Mac."

"Yeah."

"What's the matter? Waiting for someone to wish you happy birthday?"

"What?"

"Happy birthday, Mac!" JD laughed and quoted his favorite poet. "'As I walk the paths of life, full of joy, full of strife, I gather wisdom and woe.'"

"Bullshit. How did you know it was my birthday?"

"I didn't, the computer did. Lights flashed, the siren went off, it's Chet Macquire's birthday."

This got Mac smiling. "What's up, JD?"

"I told Howard we found a pitcher and now Stephen wants a press conference for tomorrow morning."

"Tomorrow?"

"Yeah. We've taken a beating about the delay in finding a pitcher. Stephen hopes to get the media off our backs."

Mac laughed. "It'll do just the opposite!"

"God, I love this."

"Obviously, he doesn't know Fari's a woman."

"Hell, no."

"Be careful, JD."

"Don't worry. They need me more than I need them. I asked Stephen to hold off on the media until after he's met Fari, but he's a sneaky bastard. By the way, I talked to Kim and she'll be waiting here when you arrive. Mrs. Olson will stay at your house."

"Thanks, JD." Kim enjoyed staying at JD's house. Shortly after Jenni died, Mac and Kim had lived with JD for two months until they found a new house.

"Where's Fari?" asked JD.

"On the starboard side, sitting next to Frances. Cleo is telling her about the physics of baseball flight. Fari listens, she doesn't speak."

"Where's Doc?"

"Sitting across from Frances, turning on the charm."

"Is it working?"

"No."

"Good."

Fari laughed suddenly and Mac looked at her. She took off her cap, undid the ponytail and her hair fell like a black, silky curtain.

"Are you still set on Ferguson to start on Sunday? asked JD.

This caught Mac's attention. "Yeah. I thought we already agreed."

"Well, we did. But remember, Chicago is vulnerable to right-handers, and they're not so good with hard throwers fastball."

"That's right, but . . ."

"See ya later, Mac. Happy birthday."

JD was gone, but his final words echoed around inside Mac's head until the light went off: *JD wants to start Fari in our season opener!*

Mac sat up and thought about it. The Minnesota Twins announce that rookie phenomenon, Fari Madrigal, will be their starting pitcher for Sunday's season opener against Chicago! Forty thousand people will cram into Target Field, millions more before TV screens across the country, the *world*, watching the historic debut of the first woman to play in the major leagues. (Or, as Cleo said, "She's also African and Hispanic.")

The media will go *crazy*. Mac suffered a seizure of excitement, jumped to his feet and clapped his hands.

The others looked at him in surprise. "Good news, Mac?" Cleo asked.

Mac composed himself. "Today's my birthday."

Cleo didn't believe it. "Aw, come on."

"No, really. Today, March twenty-fifth. I'm thirty-eight."

They clapped and sang "Happy Birthday." Frances and Fari sang in Spanish, and Mac received his first present; Fari looked him straight in the eyes for one full second.

*   *

They were three hours into the flight and it was quiet and dark inside the jet's cabin. Cleo and Frances sat a table and played chess. Doc Harris sat off by himself and contemplated the ruins of his life.

Fari leaned back with her eyes closed, but she wasn't sleeping. She had entered her "cocoon" – a quiet place inside her mind where she could think and dream. Also, it was a great way to escape reality or painful and confusing circumstances. For example, she felt the doctor's eyes and sideways looks. The man was a pig, for sure, but she had detected something more; a faint aura of doom and disease.

She liked Cleo. He treated her with respect and didn't try to flirt.

Also, she respected him for being an expert at hitting a baseball. It was informative to hear a pro talk about watching a baseball come in at ninety miles an hour. It gave her a new perspective on pitching and she believed it would help her.

At one point, Cleo said something that surprised her. "The ball is moving so fast I can't follow it with my eyes, I *imagine* where it's going." Fari liked this insight; she imagined the pitch, then threw it; Cleo didn't see the pitch, he imagined it!

She remembered when she was younger and pitched baseballs in the backyard of their home. She dreamed she pitched for the "Baltimore Bananas." It was always a crucial game and thousands of fans squeezed into the stadium.

Fari pitched for hours under the shade of nearby banana trees, dreaming of pitching in the major leagues. Sometimes she'd throw a particularly nice pitch and hop on the mound. The fans in the stands jumped to their feet and cheered.

But there were no stands and no fans. She was always alone. Sometimes Papa joined her for one of their fantasy games, but usually she was accompanied only by the home-plate target, a department store mannequin.

Papa had taught Fari everything he knew about pitching, and as Fari grew bigger and stronger he knew she might be a great pitcher some day. "My dream is to pitch in the majors," she told him, and he believed her and encouraged her.

Now the dream was coming true.

Yes, but the dream carried unknown dangers and terrors. She could feel it in her heart, and the feeling grew stronger the closer they approached the United States of America. She hated confined spaces and crowds of strangers, and Minneapolis was full of confined spaces and a million strangers.

As a young girl, even before she could talk, she sought open spaces and familiar faces. The doctors noticed these anomalies in her behavior and later confirmed they were symptoms of Asperger's Syndrome. At six years old she absolutely refused to enter the crowded schoolroom in town, and Jose and Frances arranged for a private tutor. As Fari grew older and her social phobia continued, the doctors suggested new drugs that might "suppress" the anxieties. To please the doctors and her parents, she tried the drugs for a while, but they made her feel slow and stupid, and she quit.

Eventually, the anxiety attacks became less intense as Fari learned strategies in coping – like inventing her "cocoon" – and to how to avoid threatening situations. When she was sixteen, they moved to the farm in the Dominican Republic, in Higuey, which offered wide-open spaces and total privacy. Within this lonely jungle space, Fari's social phobia almost disappeared. She and Papa continued to pitch their fantasy games and Fari earned an on-line degree from Santo Domingo University.

However, two years ago, when Papa died suddenly, the farm was invaded by groups of journalists, baseball fans and neighbors – all strangers. Already devastated by Papa's death, Fari lost control. She fled to the little cabin on the beach, where she lived alone for the next two years. Mama visited occasionally, bringing food and books. Fari read books, walked in the jungle, sat on the beach at night and watched the waves lap at the moon and stars. She grieved for her father.

On one of those nights Papa appeared in her mind, wearing his old Baltimore Orioles uniform. They spoke to each other. Fari knew this conversation must be her own creation, but Papa looked so real and sounded so clear, she wasn't really sure. They talked all night, and by morning Fari was convinced that she could fight her phobia and become a baseball pitcher, a major league pitcher!

Now the dream was really happening, but it was happening much too fast. She hadn't the time to prepare mentally or emotionally and now she wondered if she had the strength to go through with it. Even riding in this little jet with these strangers – one of them dangerous – took a great effort. But it was too late to back out now; when you reach for your dream and your dream reaches for you, you're trapped. She was going to Minneapolis, Minnesota, as the new starting pitcher for the Minnesota Twins!

Fari shifted sideways and looked at Chet Macquire. He sat by himself with his eyes closed. Today was his birthday, thirty-eight years old, but he looked much younger. She found him attractive. While waiting at the airport, Omar had told them about Mr. Macquire's terrible ordeal with his wife, Jennifer. Fari had been hurt profoundly to hear this story. It reminded her of when Papa died and brought a lump to her throat.

This was the sadness she had seen in Chet Macquire; he has lost his wife, the mother of his little girl, and he has a right to be distant and angry. But as time goes on, he will learn that life can still be beautiful.

*   *

The neurons inside Mac's brain fired off a familiar nightmare.

He entered the bedroom, which was now a hospital room and it made him sick. Jennifer sat up in bed with several pillows propped at her back. Her wasted body barely made an impression under the covers.

This was his wife, the woman he loved, but this bedridden person did not look anything like his beautiful Jennifer. This face was gaunt and pale, with only a few wisps of hair clinging to the scalp. Her eyes no longer reflected the light, but absorbed it.

Mac turned away, his heart bleeding. His eyes focused on a shoe box in the corner. He hadn't noticed it before. It held a new pair of tennis shoes.

"I bought those shoes in August," said Jenni. "You remember; I signed up to play basketball at the club."

Mac nodded and looked at her, but Jenni continued to stare at the shoes. Tears filled her eyes. "I never had a chance to put them on."

The cancer had hit so hard and fast, Jennifer didn't even have time to try out her new shoes!

Tears rose hot in Mac's eyes. He doubled over, his mouth flung open.

"Mr. Macquire?"

Mac opened his eyes and saw Fari's lovely face hovering over him.

"Perdón, pero estabas soñado." Fari stepped back and looked away. She folded her arms across her chest, still holding the baseball. "You were dreaming."

"Thanks for waking me." Mac looked at his watch. "We'll land soon."

"Estas bien?" Fari kept her face averted, but glanced at him from the corners of her eyes. "You like water?"

Mac smelled lilacs and realized the scent came from her. "I'm fine. We're almost there. Are you excited?"

Fari leaned back against the bulkhead and her mouth twisted into a grimace. "Tengo miedo. I feel like Alice in Wonderland."

Mac laughed, remembering his recent reference to that very same story. "And I'm the Mad Hatter?"

Fari cocked her head and a frown flashed across her face. She looked at him sideways. "You are the rabbit, Mr. Macquire, leading me into a dream."

A hollow *zing* shot up Mac's spine. He tried to read her expression. She *did* look a little scared. "Please call me Mac. Only my mother calls me 'mister.'"

Fari nodded and looked down. Her face darkened, as if embarrassed. "Me llamo Fari."

She seems so shy, thought Mac, and more than a little naïve, like a little kid. Yet she's so big and strong, and pitches like a tornado! He regarded her as a total mystery.

At that moment, they heard the pilot's voice. "Ladies and gentlemen, please find a seat and fasten your seat belts. We'll be landing shortly."

*   *

They passed through customs with no trouble and gathered by the exit doors, their luggage stacked nearby. Mac pulled Doc and Cleo to one side. "Be sure to stay quiet about this. We need a few hours of peace."

They both nodded. "What happens now, Mac?" asked Cleo.

"We all go home. I appreciate your help. I'll see you tomorrow at the stadium. Will you be there, Doc?"

Doc flicked his eyes at Fari. "I wouldn't miss it for the world."

They laughed and shook hands. Cleo and Doc said their good-byes to Frances and Fari. Doc offered to be their guide around the city, just give him a call. They thanked him politely.

Mac led Frances and Fari through the exit and the warm air pushed them into the cool, dark evening. Frances and Fari cried out, dropped their bags and hugged each other. Mac laughed. He thought it was fairly warm for the end of March.

Fari shook with cold and apprehension. Out here in the open, Minneapolis seemed particularly alien – dark, cold, strange. More than this, she sensed powerful waves of conflicting energies; some joyous, others wicked. A sudden bolt of panic passed through her and she shivered even harder.

"Look!" Frances pointed up the sidewalk. A young man stood next to a black limousine, holding up a sign: "F. Madrigal."

"That's us." Mac hefted his bag and led the way to the limo. He chose to sit on a jump seat facing the rear, while Fari and Frances sat next to each other in the deep back seat, their arms interlocked. They inspected the plush interior with wide eyes. This was another perk from the corporation.

Mac asked the driver to take the scenic route along Minnehaha Parkway. The Parkway followed the meandering path of Minnehaha Creek as it wound its way through south Minneapolis toward Lake of the Isles, where JD lived. Mac noticed Frances searching the interior panel of the door. "Are you looking for something?"

"Yes, I want to open the window. I want to smell Minneapolis."

Mac laughed and pressed the buttons for both windows. Fari leaned toward her mother, into the cool wind, her long black hair blowing back. He noticed her face held a mixture of curiosity and dread. Her eyes appeared troubled and her fine fat lips had compressed into a severe line.

Fari knew Minneapolis was a "medium" sized city, but to her all cities seemed big. She inspected the endless rows of houses, each different in design, but similar in size. She felt grateful for the darkness, and riding hidden inside this luxurious limousine, while the people in those houses lived in electric light and a morass of consumption. "Casas bonitas," she said. "Aparecen fuerte."

"Nice houses," Frances translated. "They look strong."

Mac nodded and answered. "They need to be strong to keep out the cold."

"How cold does it get?"

Mac smiled and looked at Fari's dark profile. She was focused on the neighborhood, her eyes reflecting the street lights.

"We have about five months of winter. Sometimes it gets below zero. Lots of snow. Do you know snow?"

Frances nodded, but Fari pulled in her shoulders and shook her head. "No, pero quiero conocer."

"She wants to know snow," said Frances.

Mac wished for snow immediately, but not likely tonight. They passed Fiftieth Street, less than a mile from Lake Harriet, still following Minnehaha Creek. The homes along here were two and three stories, each sitting on a vast landscaped lot.

"Is this the affluent area?" Frances asked.

Mac thought about that; not the question, but the word "affluent." "I guess it's a wealthy area," he said carefully. "Minnehaha Parkway is a desirable place to live."

"Me gusta el nombre," said Fari.

"She likes the name," said Frances. "So do I."

"It's an Indian name. It means 'laughing waters.'"

They were enchanted by this name and the name of Minneapolis; "city of waters." As they traveled around Lake Harriet, Frances and Fari slid over to the other side for a better look. They exchanged short, staccato sentences in Spanish, excited by all that water inside the big city.

The limo swished quietly around the lake, but less than a minute later it approached the great liquid surface of Lake Calhoun. Beyond Calhoun, only a few blocks away, was Lake of the Isles, on the shore of which was JD's house.

"We'll stay at the manager's house tonight," said Mac. He looked at Frances. "We'll try to guard our privacy as long as we can."

Frances nodded and smiled. "Jack Daniels Johnson."

Mac looked at her sharply, wondering what this meant. The limo slowed, turned hard and rolled into a lighted garage.

"Here we are." Mac opened the door and climbed out.

"Daddy!" Kimberly ran across the concrete floor.

Mac bent and scooped his daughter into his arms. "Hiya, honey. How ya doin?"

"Happy Birthday, Dad!" Kim planted a wet kiss on his cheek. She was tall and thin, with the budding signs of adolescence. Like her mother, she had blond hair and a white, creamy complexion. She got her blue eyes and strong, Roman nose (minus the bend) from Mac.

As Frances and Fari stepped from the limo, Kim's eyes flew open. She stepped back and wrapped an arm around her father.

Mac indicated the visitors. "Kim, this is Frances and her daughter Fari."

"Hi," said Kim with a shy smile. "Nice to meet you." She looked up at Fari. "Wow, you're really big!"

They all laughed. Kim turned to Mac, her face bursting with excitement. She whispered loudly. "Will Fari pitch for the Twins?"

Mac looked at his daughter, loving her, and a sudden thought occurred to him: Tonight is the beginning of my new life, *our* new life. He wasn't sure where this idea came from, but he felt it might be true. He squatted next to his daughter and gestured toward Fari. "Kim, honey, this is our new pitcher. This is Fastball Fari."

Kim listened carefully with her mouth wide open. "*Really?*" she whispered.

Mac looked straight into her eyes and nodded.

Kim's face flushed and she jumped in a circle, punching the air with her fist. "Yes! A girl! Pitching in the majors! Yes!" She stopped in front of Fari and hugged her fiercely, burying her face in Fari's stomach. Fari seemed surprised and her body stiffened, but she reached out one hand and squeezed Kim's shoulder.

Mac looked away and saw JD standing in the doorway. He wore a long-sleeve shirt, dark slacks and leather slippers. He had trimmed his beard and gotten rid of the cigar. "Hi, Mac," he said. "Hello, Frances."

Frances' cheeks turned dark. "Hi, Jack Daniels."

JD skipped lightly across the floor and stood in front of her. He held both her hands and bowed. "Nice to see you again. You're as beautiful as you were twenty-five years ago."

Frances laughed and blushed. JD turned to Mac. "I was at their wedding in Costa Rica."

JD and Frances knew each other! Mac was stunned. JD had attended Frances' wedding in Costa Rica and now we're here in Minneapolis twenty-five years later with her daughter, the new starting pitcher for the Minnesota Twins!

JD turned to Fari and threw his arms in the air. "My God, you're wonderful!"

Fari smiled shyly and submitted herself to JD's bear hug. The top of his head barely came to her chin. JD pushed Fari at arm's length and looked her up and down. "You are a *pitcher.*"

*　　　　　*

JD's house was built on a small hill overlooking Lake of the Isles.

It was three stories high, with six bedrooms, an enormous kitchen, a library, a study, an entertainment center and a gym.

JD ordered two large pizzas and they stood around in the kitchen, eating, talking, drinking wine. JD and Frances reminisced about old times, while Kim told Fari about her school. Kim seemed tiny standing next to Fari.

Mac stood off to one side, marveling at the odd surprises life sometimes offers. He still coped with one jarring experience, Jenni's sickness and death, and here comes another – Fastball Fari. He had to admit, however, that this new shock felt pleasant and exciting – so far, anyway. He had an uneasy feeling that tomorrow his life would change in ways he can't imagine.

He watched as Fari spoke to Kim in her low, soft voice, gesturing with her long arms and big hands, the right one still holding the baseball. She spoke English and seemed to favor Kim with more frequent eye contact. What did that mean?

After a tour of the house, the travelers were tired and jet-lagged and JD escorted everyone to their respective bedrooms. Kim and Mac shared a corner room on the second floor. Fari and Frances stayed in a third floor bedroom.

Kim crackled with excitement. "Fari's really cool, Dad. She can do a flip."

"Oh yeah?"

"We went to the gym. She's got a great bod. Nice muscles."

"She's in good shape." Mac suppressed the lurid images flashing through his mind. He could just make out the white smear of Kim's smile. He was touched at the way Fari and Kim had warmed to each other. Kim had dragged Fari through every corner of JD's house.

"We went to the sun room," said Kim. "I played Metallica. Fari liked it."

"Fari liked Metallica?"

"Yeah. We danced." Kim let out a sigh of admiration. "But she acts a little quirky, you know? You said she had Asper . . . Asper . . ."

"Asperger's Syndrome."

"Right. I looked it up."

"What is it?"

"It's a form of autism. They don't know what causes it. It's like a kink in the brain or something. Nothing serious. They say people with Asperger's have some problems socially, but are usually highly intelligent and skilled at their chosen profession."

"Well, that certainly describes our lovely Fari. You two got along okay, huh?"

"Oh, yeah. She's really *present*, Dad."

In current school lexicon "present" meant cool. Earlier, at dinner, Mac had noticed how Kim's mouth hung half open whenever she looked at Fari. This introduced him to a new perspective on this situation; little girls need heroes too. He imagined Kim's reaction on a grand scale, among all the girls and women in America. Once again, the enormity of this event made him shudder.

He rolled over and tried to force himself to sleep. Suddenly, he realized he hadn't thought about Jennifer all day (except for the nightmare, which didn't count). He summoned her now and she joined him under the covers. He hugged his pillow and whispered into her ear. "I hope you're watching, Jenni. Tomorrow the world will change."

*   *

Frances and Fari lay in bed together under layers of blankets. Their third floor suite faced Lake of the Isles. Frances heard music from somewhere, but very faint. "Cleo will find me a computer specialist," she whispered into Fari's ear.

Fari shifted further under the covers. Like Mac, her pillow was for hugging. "Will you keep the plan secret, Mama?"

"I don't have to. We'll let the cousin surf, while I do the business." Frances moved closer against the broad back of her daughter. She laughed softly. "First, we'll get everyone's attention, then we'll hit 'em hard!"

Fari closed her eyes, but her brain flashed brightly with expectations and anticipations. Just two days ago she slept at home in the jungle; now she was in a strange bed in strange country. For years, she and Mama had studied the United States of America and Fari had come to regard the US as a giant conundrum of opposites – with a culture of freedom hitched to the yoke of consumerism, with a passion for peace coupled with a willingness to war, with compassion for the poor overwhelmed by a race to become rich.

She didn't understand it, nor did she understand most of social reality. She knew pitching and she knew the jungle, but everything else was a challenge and not really relevant, unless it created an obstacle.

Her new life has begun here, in Minneapolis, USA, but she was the same person. And this created an obstacle. A new life meant change, which meant *she* would have to change. To perform in this culture, to move successfully among these strangers and still maintain her peace and dignity, she would have to overcome her phobias.

Can I really do this? She snuggled closer to her mother. *With Papa's help and Mama's guidance, I have a chance.*

*   *

JD sat alone in his study on the third floor. Dozens of plants grew from pots sitting on the floor or hanging from the ceiling. Inside a small, round space in the middle of the room, like a clearing in the forest, sat a black, cast-iron sewing machine. Mozart issued from speakers hung on the walls.

JD sat with his eyes closed, waving his arms, conducting the orchestra. The tempo increased as the music built toward a finale; violins screamed, horns howled, the kettle drums pounded. JD jumped to his feet and waved his arms wildly, his whole body shaking. The music rose to a thunderous frenzy and exploded into silence.

JD stood with his arms flung out in the final gesture of the last note. Gradually, he relaxed. He reached out and touched a nearby plant. "Fari will go down in history," he whispered. "We'll all become famous – Fari, me, Mac, the Minnesota Twins."

He wandered through the room, caressing the plants. He stopped before an ornamental banana tree just beginning to flower. Bright, purple buds peeked out from under the shiny green leaves.

"I know what to do, my little pet." JD stroked the leaves and laughed. He twirled in a circle, his robe swishing like a cape and addressed all the plants at once. "The signs are clear, my pets. There's only one possible way to go. Should Fari be our starting pitcher for this Sunday's season opener?"

He cocked his head and listened. His potted audience responded with a resounding "Yes!"

FOUR

Wednesday: March 26

Fari slipped out of bed, tip-toed to the windows, and got her first good look at Minneapolis. Lake of the Isles lay like a dull silver platter, with small, bushy islands floating on cushions of fog. A strange, enchanted place. She saw no traffic along the Parkway, but there was one early jogger running around the lake.

Fari whirled around, opened her luggage and dressed quickly; sweat pants, two sweat shirts, socks, running shoes and a baseball. Mama was still sleeping soundly and Fari left the room quietly. She tiptoed downstairs and opened the front door. The sudden cold felt like a slap in the face. She was fascinated by the bright, crystal puffs of her breathing. The grey light revealed a quiet, motionless world; Minneapolis still slept. Fari knew this was the best moment in any city – before people woke up and invaded the landscape.

An asphalt path circled Lake of the Isles and Fari broke into a fast trot. It felt good to move and stretch her body. She saw the lone jogger moving now in her direction. She passed a flock of geese floating serenely on the lake's surface and slowed for a better look.

The path sloped uphill and over a stone bridge spanning Minnehaha Creek. The sky appeared lighter and the tips of trees glowed with sunlight. The branches bent with fat, green buds and Fari recalled what Mr. Macquire had said the night before. "April is when everything comes back to life."

Her intuition about Chet Macquire has shifted into the positive zone, or, as they say in Dominica, "El mi cae bien" – he falls good to me. She and Mama agreed; Mr. Macquire seemed like a good man, definitely not a pig.

The other jogger was much closer now, moving more slowly in a plodding, tired gait. Fari recognized Mac! She stopped. "Ola, Mac."

Mac slammed on the brakes and looked up. His nose and cheeks glowed pink and he breathed heavily. "Hi!" He smiled broadly, surprised to see her.

Fari turned and looked at the lake. The baseball spun quickly in her right hand. "Yo vi una persona corriendo." She flicked her eyes at him and smiled. "I wanted to run."

Mac straightened up and caught his breath. "You like to run in the morning?"

"A veces." Fari kept her face averted, still looking at the lake. A sheen of sweat coated her forehead and the front of her shirt. The baseball continued to spin. "At home I run on beach." She glanced at him briefly. "We have farm on ocean."

Mac saw a spark of passion in her eyes, the same spark he saw when she talked about pitching. "What do you grow on your farm?"

She looked away and sighed deeply. "Muchas cosas. Piñas, bananos, limones, papaya, yucca." The baseball stopped spinning. "I love it there."

"It's on the ocean?"

Fari nodded, turned sideways and faced the lake. "Running on sand is hard work."

She hadn't worn a hat this morning and hiding her eyes meant moving her head. Mac smiled and gestured at the lake. "This sure isn't the ocean."

Fari nodded and pursed her plump lips into a silent kiss. "No, pero es muy bonito." She glanced at him from under the long, thick eyelashes. "It is laughing waters."

Their eyes locked for one brief second. Mac felt himself go numb and his ears burned, the world closed up like a cocoon and there was just he and Fari. He smiled and shook his head; was this an intimate moment, or his imagination? "C'mon," he said. "I'll race you home."

*　　　　　　*

Kim taught Frances how to make waffles on JD's antique waffle iron. Frances and Fari had never eaten waffles and were intrigued by all the holes. JD regaled the breakfast table with a long discourse about "baking evenly everywhere at the same time."

After breakfast, they reviewed their agenda for the day. At eight thirty, they had a meeting with Stephen Rains, vice president for public relations. At nine, there would be a team meeting and Fari would meet her teammates.

At the mention of these upcoming events, Fari slumped in her chair, her face and eyes rigid. Her upper body began moving in quick, rhythmic beats.

JD turned to Frances. "Stephen wants a press conference this morning, to introduce Fari to the local media and the fans."

"Does he know Fari's a girl?" Kim asked.

All eyes turned to JD. He shook his head and smiled. "He knows we have a new pitcher, but that's it."

They all laughed, except Fari who sat hunched over in her chair, her face tilted toward the table, her body still jerking. Frances recalled the look on Mac's face when he first saw Fari. She reminded him of this.

"Hey, that's right." Mac smiled happily and looked at JD. "Stephen might have a heart attack."

Stephan Rains, the PR executive, was on the opposite side of the organization; Mac and JD were on the *team*, StephenStephen was in the *corporation*.

"Will he go ahead with the press conference?" asked Frances.

"I don't know," answered JD. "Most likely he'll call the owner, Howard Sikes, and Howard will take over."

"Is that good or bad?" she asked.

JD gave her a shrewd look. "Howard likes a lot of publicity. Fari will be great for business."

"Oh yes." Frances' eyes narrowed. "Good for *profits*. Well, StephenStephen and Howard will have to understand that only *I* speak for Fari. Her English is not so good, huh? Also, she's shy and afraid of crowds."

JD's eyelids dropped halfway. "Afraid of crowds? What about Target Field? I guarantee a *crowd*."

Frances laughed. "That's different. When Fari pitches, she doesn't notice anything around her." She looked at Fari. "Right, *querida*?"

Fari nodded and blushed. She twisted sideways on her chair and faced her mother, her eyes averted from the others.

Mac admired her profile and the long, luxurious eyelashes. Again, he felt charmed by the peculiar symmetry of her features – lovely, yet unique. She wore the same outfit as yesterday; loose sweat-shirt, sweat pants, tennis shoes. She had taken off the cap for breakfast and the baseball disappeared. Mac and JD had dressed similarly in their uniforms. Only Frances and Kim displayed variation and color.

Mac identified a few more quirks about Fari Madrigal. For example, the only concession to a "feminine" presence was the light scent of lilacs – a smell he was beginning to love. She favored baggy, athletic clothing, displayed no trace of make-up, and wore no jewelry. She carried a baseball instead of a purse. She spoke a mixture of Spanish and English. And despite the astonishing beauty of her eyes, she kept them hidden. Apart from these oddities, she displayed a sharp intelligence and a strong personality.

"What's this business about not speaking English?" he asked her.

Fari glanced at her mother. "Is it dishonest?"

Frances rolled her eyes. "Don't worry about deceiving the media. They're *experts* at it!"

*   *

While they rode to the stadium in the limousine, Kim gave a verbal tour of landmarks and points of interest. Fari hardly listened. Her body moved back and forth and the baseball rotated constantly. The further they traveled into the heart of this city, the more intense the human activity and the more acute her anxieties became. She felt the familiar tightness in her chest, the dryness in her mouth, the quick uptick in her heartbeat. She compensated by imagining the limousine as a private spaceship flying through an alien environment. For the moment, she was safe. But when they landed and disembarked, she would be exposed and vulnerable.

They cruised slowly through downtown Minneapolis. Frances commented on the clean, formal look of the citizens, but was most impressed with the order. "Everyone obeys the street lights and lines!" She looked at Mac. "At home, traffic is *dangerous*."

The limo approached a squat, round building; Target Field. It sat alone surrounded by empty parking lots and office buildings.

"There's the office!" shouted Frances.

The limo glided to a stop next to the staff entrance. They climbed out and stood on the vast parking lot, all but Fari. She sat motionless in the back seat, breathing deeply, trying to control the commotion in her chest.

After a moment, Frances leaned into the limo and held out her hand. "Come on, honey. We can do this."

Fari's heart hammered wildly. This strange place gave off an intense energy, and like most energy, it attracted and repulsed. She concentrated on the attraction – the baseball stadium, a *major league* baseball stadium, and inside the stadium lay her life's dream. But dreams can also turn into nightmares.

She reached out, grabbed her mother's hand and stepped out of the limo. She smelled the asphalt, heard the distant rush of traffic and went into her cocoon.

Frances held Fari's hand tightly as they walked toward the building. The security guard knew JD, Mac and Kim, and they greeted each other. He looked curiously at the two women, but no one offered to explain their presence. Obviously, they were with JD. "Hi," he said, but the women didn't respond.

As JD led them through the reception area, Fari walked close to Frances, leaning into her and gripping her hand tightly. Mac was reminded of how Kim had behaved on the first day of school – full of skittishness and dread. Yet, Fari was taller than Frances – taller than Mac – with broad shoulders and a perfectly proportioned body. *Why does she act afraid?* He remembered the personable, almost friendly Fari he met jogging by the lake this morning, but this was a different Fari. *Who is this woman?*

When they reached JD's office, Frances and Fari were immediately delighted with the plants. They recognized several tropical varieties, and JD gave them a tour.

Mac stood by the door and watched them move slowly through the indoor forest. He felt struck by how absurd it seemed: Upstairs, around the corner, at any moment, history will be made and pandemonium set loose on all their lives. And here we are tiptoeing through the tulips.

The lights on JD's office phone blinked; two lines, three lines, four

49

lines. Mac wondered about Cleo and Doc. He hoped they hadn't given away the secret. He looked at his watch; they were six minutes late for their meeting with StephenStephen.

JD introduced Frances and Fari to a plant with slender stalks and huge, rounded leaves. He told them the formal name, and Frances and Fari giggled at each other.

"In Costa Rica," said Fari. "Llamamos aquella mata cari mula."

"We call that plant 'cari mula,'" said Frances.

"Cari mula," repeated JD slowly, as if committing it to memory.

Frances smiled. "It means 'mule face.'"

JD stepped back and looked at the plant from a different angle. He laughed. "You're right! It has the exact shape of a mule's head." He looked at Mac. "No wonder they're so stubborn."

They heard a soft knock on the door and JD shouted. "If that's you, Stew, don't knock again!"

Mac heard footsteps retreat rapidly. Stewart Finn, the staff secretary, was foiled again.

JD continued with the tour. Mac looked at the clock; fifteen minutes late. JD took this time to allow Fari and her mother to relax to distract them from the coming media explosion. Also, it was an excellent opportunity to make fools of the corporate boys in the ongoing political poker game. JD held *all* the aces; he had Fari Madrigal.

Finally, JD judged it was time. "Well, let's go upstairs and meet with Stephan."

As they left the office, Stew handed Mac a note. It read, "Stephan called a press conference for 8:45, but now he's pissed off because you don't have a pitcher."

JD read the note and laughed. "He's boxed himself in. He can't call off the media."

"Yeah," answered Mac. "But do you know how many reporters will be there? Only about six or seven."

JD laughed again. "Well, those few are the lucky ones. They're about to get the sports scoop of the decade."

They made their way through the maze of corporate suites. Fari moved behind Frances, one hand holding onto the back of her mother's suit coat, the other holding the baseball. They entered the reception area where they found Doc and Cleo. They all greeted each other loudly, except for Fari, who stood apart, stiff and silent.

Stephan's secretary watched this noisy show with a sour expression. She picked up the phone and punched a number. "They're here," she announced. "But no pitcher." She slammed down the receiver and stood up. "Excuse me, Mr. Johnson," she called out, addressing JD. "Mr. Rains will see you now."

"Thank you, Ms. Ferris."

"We'll be here as witnesses," said Doc. "In case Stephen needs convincing."

"I'll convince him fast enough," said Cleo.

Mac turned to Kim. "You have to wait here, honey. I'll see you in the press room." He bent down for a kiss.

Kim gave him a quick peck and said, "Good luck, Daddy." But her last words were for Fari. She shook Fari's hand and said, "Give 'em hell, buddy."

The secretary opened Stephen's door and they filed into the office; JD, Frances, Fari and Mac. Behind them, the door closed a little too hard.

Stephen's office resembled a piece of pie – two walls set at a ninety degree angle, with the opposite wall conforming to the rounded shape of the building. Photos arranged on the walls presented the glowing testimony of a public relations executive; Stephen with local TV and sports personalities, Stephen with local politicians, Stephen with an astronaut or two, Stephen with the vice president.

Stephen Rains stood up with a careful smile on his face. Owing to office politics (and his own lofty pride) he could not acknowledge that they were twenty minutes late. But he was furious, and not because they were late, but because he had called a press conference to introduce the new starting pitcher and now there was no pitcher!

Stephen stepped from behind his desk to greet his visitors. He wore a dark suit with a white shirt and sky-blue tie. His physical features tended toward circles and curves; a short, round body and a round, moon face. "Good morning, JD," he said, still smiling politely. "Good morning, Mac." They shook hands.

JD turned to indicate Frances and Fari. "Stephen, this is Frances Madrigal and her daughter Fari." He turned to the women. "Ladies, this is Stephen Rains, vice president in charge of public relations."

Stephen shook hands with Frances, but when he turned toward Fari, his smile wavered. He bent backwards to look up at her. "How do you do?" He stuck out his right hand.

Fari recoiled at this white, pudgy hand reaching toward her, but her mother tugged on her sleeve. "Honey," Frances whispered a soft warning.

The energy inside this office bombarded Fari with images of "consumer goods." At a lower frequency, however, she heard the cries of Mother and her Children, cut down and killed. Although StephenStephen could not know it, he was the enemy. She transferred the baseball to her left hand, took Stephen's hand and squeezed hard. "Con mucho gusto."

StephenStephen's face twisted sideways. "Oh!" He dropped Fari's hand quickly and backpedaled to safer territory behind his desk. "Please sit down." His adjustable chair had been set at maximum height and now he was level with his visitors. He flexed his right hand a few times, then focused on Mac. "Well, Mac, how was Santo Domingo?"

Mac smiled pleasantly. "Much warmer than here, a lot greener." He wondered how this might look to Stephen; an older woman dressed in a business suit and a stunning beauty dressed like a playground rat.

Stephen kept his face composed and pulled his eyebrows together, as if carefully considering Mac's answer. "How was the trip? The *jet* was comfortable?"

"Very comfortable, thank you." Mac could barely keep his face straight. He wanted to scream with laughter. Frances and Fari sat quietly, watching and listening. JD also sat quietly, his hand to his mouth, hiding a smile. As a birthday present, he had graciously allowed Mac the honor of introducing Fastball Fari to Stephen Rains.

Stephen's upper lip twisted and his smile became more of a snarl. He glanced at Fari again. Who is that woman? Is she some movie star? Is that the big joke here? He addressed Mac again. "Did you, uh, find a pitcher?"

"Oh yeah." Mac leaned forward and looked Stephen in the eyes. "We found a pitcher with a fastball consistently in the nineties."

Now Stephen's smile displayed more substance, but still tentative. He glanced at JD, expecting some trick or joke, but JD remained silent. Stephen's face relaxed slightly. "That's great, Mac," he said with enthusiasm. "So, where *is* this pitcher?"

Mac composed his face and adopted a dead serious tone. "Right here in front of you, Stephen." He turned and gestured toward Fari. "This is Fari Madrigal from the Dominican Republic, our new starting pitcher."

Stephen's smile collapsed. A second later, he forced a laugh and shook his head. "You really had me there, Mac." He chuckled again, then looked at Fari. "Excuse me, miss, but what are you and your mother doing here?"

Fari flicked her eyes at him and shifted sideways in the chair. "Me gusta lanzar la bola."

Stephen flinched and turned toward JD. "What's going on here, Jack?" His voice issued with more snap. "Where's this pitcher? What're these people doing in my office?"

JD stood up, leaned on Stephen's desk and pointed at Fari. "Stephen, this woman, Fari Madrigal, is our new starting pitcher."

Stephen held himself erect in his chair. His mouth moved, but made no sound. He searched JD's face for humor, but saw only serious intent. His cheeks flushed. "You'd better explain yourself, Jack. There's a press conference in five minutes."

JD stared right back at him. "That's your problem. I asked you *not* to call a press conference." He spun around and walked across the office, unwrapped a new cigar and looked out the window.

Stephen seemed to deflate. He fell back into his chair and rolled his eyes toward Mac – hoping for redemption, waiting for the punch line.

Mac stared back silently, concentrating on every second and detail of this meeting. He knew it would become legend.

Frances leaned toward Stephen. "Excuse me, Mr. Rains."

Stephen jerked his startled eyes toward Frances.

"Mr. Rains, my daughter has been pitching her whole life. She pitched three games with a team in Santo Domingo. She won every game. You can verify this easily.

"I'm Fari's spokesperson. She doesn't speak English too well. I'll represent her to the media and in any business negotiations. Please don't worry about the press conference. I'll handle it." She sat back with a satisfied smile, as if that cleared up everything, now let's move on.

Stephen's hands moved in small circles, but still he made no sound.

"Well, we'd better get going." JD pointed to his watch. "The reporters are waiting."

At this, Stephen woke up. He pushed himself higher in his chair. "We'd better wait on that, JD. We need more time. This is too, uh, too . . ."

"I'm sorry, Stephen, we don't *have* time." JD walked back to the desk. "There's a team meeting at nine. We have fifteen minutes to introduce Fari to the media, or call off the press conference."

"Wait a minute." Stephen held up one hand. "I'd better talk to Howard. This is just too, uh, too . . ."

"Okay, we'll wait outside." JD guided Frances and Fari toward the door. "Come, ladies. Let us flee the darkness and seek the light."

They gathered in the hallway. Doc and Cleo begged to hear the story, but JD beckoned everyone to silence. "We have to move fast. Stephen's talking to Howard right now. There're only a few media guys waiting. It's the perfect time to introduce Fari." He turned to Fari. "Are you ready for this?"

Fari nodded and looked at the floor. She hung onto her mother and the baseball spun furiously.

They hurried down the stairs, through another hallway and into the press office. Once again, they assembled into a huddle, enjoying their conspiracy, Fari standing slightly behind Frances. Beyond the next door was the conference auditorium where the sports reporters waited, nibbling on doughnuts and rolls, slugging coffee, bored and restless.

JD looked at Mac. "You want to say anything?"

"Hell no, but I want to watch."

"No problem, Mac," said Frances. "JD and I will do the talking."

"Let's go." JD opened the door and led them onto a small stage facing rows of empty chairs. The room was big; a hundred feet by fifty feet. Off to one side, below the stage, a group of men sat around a table. Nearby, cameras and lighting equipment lay on the floor.

JD walked to a podium in the middle of the stage. Frances and Fari followed him, Fari hanging onto her mother. The media people dropped their rolls and wiped their faces. Mac recognized the sports reporters from the area's biggest newspapers, and the others were from local TV and radio stations. The newspaper and radio guys had recorders; the TV people carried video cams and lights.

Mac, Cleo and JD exchanged greetings with the journalists. Doc was also known to these people, but of less interest, unless there was an injury. However, within five seconds every journalist stared at Fari.

The Eyes and Ears found their target and zeroed in with savage instinct. She hid behind Mama and offered only bits and pieces. Still, the intensity of their attention evoked a corresponding increase in her anxiety. Her teeth chattered, her stomach clenched, the baseball spun rapidly.

JD switched on the microphone. "Good morning. Stephen Rains asked me to introduce our new starting pitcher." He paused and looked at one of the TV reporters. "You guys ready?"

"Ready, JD. Go ahead."

"As you know, we've had problems finding a quality starter to fill the hole in our rotation. Part of the problem was a late start; most free agents had already been signed, and the farm teams were picked over.

"A few days ago, our pitching coach, Chet Macquire, found a pitcher on one of the pro teams in the Dominican Republic." Eyes and cameras looked briefly at Mac, then back to JD.

"Mr. Macquire flew to Santo Domingo the day before yesterday and returned last night with our new pitcher." JD paused and gathered his wits. This would be his role in the historical drama; introducing Fari to the world.

The reporters seemed eager to know about the new pitcher, but where was he? They knew Cleo was an outfielder. What about those women? Who were they? The younger one held a baseball! Two reporters turned around to look *behind* them.

JD stepped over to Frances and Fari and ushered them toward the podium. Frances took Fari by the arm and pulled her forward. Fari walked in a stiff shuffle, her eyes on the floor, the baseball clasped tightly in both hands. "Gentlemen," JD began. "Allow me to introduce Fari Madrigal, our new starting pitcher."

The silence fell like a ton of foam rubber. The reporters reacted like puppets on a string; all jaws dropped at once. Before anyone could react further, JD continued. "Fari is a right-hander with a blazing fast-ball and great control. She'll be a valuable addition to our pitching staff and we're confident we can win many games with Fari."

The reporters broke out of their shock with shouts and uncertain laughter. The cameramen jostled each other for the best shots of Fari. Someone shouted "Bullshit!" A few reporters pulled out cell phones and whispered furiously. Others expressed disbelief. "Come on, JD, what's the joke?"

JD held up his hands. "I know you have questions, but Fari doesn't understand English that well. Her mother, Frances, will take your questions and translate her daughter's answers. Please be brief, we have to leave in four minutes."

Four minutes! The reporters begged for more time, shouting questions, shoving their cameras and recorders closer toward Fari. Mac thought of a pack of hungry dogs. Fari moved closer behind her mother.

Frances stepped up to the podium, Fari right behind her, hanging onto her suit jacket, bending her knees to stay hidden. "Hey!" Frances shouted and everyone shut their mouths. "Excuse my rude manners, but with everyone shouting at once, we'll get nowhere." She pointed at one sweaty young man with pudgy cheeks. "You, sir. Do you have a question?"

"Yes!" He leaned sideways, trying to look around Frances at Fari. "Uh . . . Uh . . ."

Someone else shouted. "How long have you been pitching?"

"Fari started throwing balls when she was three," Frances answered. The reporters waited for more, but she waited for the next question.

More shouts and hollers. The pudgy young man had thought of a question. "What team did you pitch for in the Dominican Republic?"

"The Sanchez Tigers in San Sanchez." Frances answered quickly. "You have three minutes."

Three minutes! They yelled into cell phones. Get on the line to the Dominican Republic! Fari Madrigal, a woman! A pitcher! Yeah, a *girl*. She's gonna pitch for the Twins!

Meanwhile, Fari crouched behind Frances. The cameramen scrambled further along the stage, trying for straight-on shots of Fari, but she kept shifting sideways. Mac felt thrilled she might actually put her back to them!

Frances waved her arms and pointed at someone else.

"Has Fari ever been a model?" the journalist called out.

Frances cocked her head. "A model what?"

The journalist looked at his cameraman and wagged his tongue. "A swimsuit model."

Someone else shouted. "How does Fari feel about being the first woman to play in the major leagues?"

This time, Frances turned and spoke to Fari in Spanish. "Estara la primera mujer en la historia para jugar en las ligas grandes. Que piensa de eso?"

The room fell silent, all eyes on Fari, the cameras and recorders held high.

Fari stood straighter, but kept her face to one side. She shrugged her shoulders. "No se. Simplemente, me gusta lanzar."

Frances turned back to the gaping newsmen. "Fari recognizes the significance and honor of being the first woman to play in North American professional baseball. This is an achievement for all women everywhere, and demonstrates once again that there is no field of endeavor a woman cannot excel in." She looked at her watch. "Thank you for your kind attention. Fari and the others have to leave now . . ."

Frances was interrupted by a chorus of shouts. She turned and placed Fari's hand on JD's jacket. "Go with JD," she said quietly.

JD turned for the door, pulling Mac and Fari with him. The reporters followed, running alongside the stage, shouting questions. Someone bumped into a chair and several men stumbled and fell. Microphones and recorders clattered to the floor. JD, Mac and Fari disappeared through the door.

The journalists picked up their things and ran back to Frances. They shouted at her and into their cell phones. Hurry up! Get on it quick! Here they come! CNN! FOX! ABC! NBC! CBS! ESPN!

FIVE

Fari Madrigal became a nationwide celebrity within hours. The videos taken during the short, boisterous press conference hadn't been all that great, and although Fari seemed to hide behind her mother, there were enough close-ups and full-body shots to cause a rush of sighs in newsrooms across the country.

Frances, as Fari's spokesperson, also became instantly famous. She had answered reporters' questions for half an hour. Where was Fari born? Where did she grow up? Where did she learn to pitch? What message did she have for little girls, for all women? Does she have a boyfriend? (This last question was asked three times, but Frances ignored it.)

People with only a mild interest in baseball became very interested in Fari Madrigal. After one hundred years of male domination, here was a woman who can play with the pros. Commentators compared Fari with Jackie Robinson and Willie Mays, famous ethnic pioneers in professional baseball.

Women and girls around the country took immediate note of *Fastball Fari*. Most didn't care about baseball, but Fari Madrigal was a girl smashing through another all-male barrier. She was also African and Hispanic. This ethnic, sexual mix made Fari attractive to millions.

Not all the focus was on history-making. The media devoted almost equal attention to Fari's appearance. Although she had worn a baggy sweat suit, it was obvious she possessed an uncommon beauty and shape. These observations ranged from respectful comments to crude tongue-wagging. Also, Fari's odd behavior engendered comment and speculation. Several cameras had focused on the baseball spinning in her right hand.

The YouTube video of Fari went viral quickly, with over a million views. A TV station in Miami paid one hundred thousand dollars to a media outlet in Santo Domingo for photos and video footage of Fari wearing a bikini. She had been filmed running through the surf and lying on the beach, seemingly unaware of the camera. (When this video had first appeared in the Dominican Republic, Fari had been inundated with frantic pleas to mate.)

Although the photos and news about Fari blew across the country like a hurricane, the center of the storm remained relatively calm. The principal players did not yet know their identities had been thrust into the public glare. They engaged in their own personal drama of introducing Fari Madrigal to her teammates.

All players had been asked to attend the team meeting, and please arrive completely dressed – no towels, jock straps or underwear. Of course, the players had heard about Fari, and they gathered in an atmosphere of excitement. Several players asked Mac if it was true; do we have a *woman* on the team? He answered with silence and a smile.

Finally, JD and Fari entered the room from the stairway. Conversation ceased and all heads snapped up. JD and Fari stood arm in arm, Fari straight and tall, towering over JD. She wore her cap low over her eyes, with her right arm behind her back. Mac wondered if she held the baseball.

The eyes hit her like a physical blow and took her breath away. The fantasies tugged at her clothes, stripped her naked. Hands and lips reached for her breasts, always her breasts.

Fari's breasts were secret weapons. The extra weight and muscle added speed, power and momentum to the forward thrust of the delivery. However, the cost of this advantage was examination, evaluation, fascination and, no doubt, masturbation.

JD talked loudly into the restless silence. "Gentlemen, this is Fari Madrigal from the Dominican Republic. She's a right-handed pitcher with a mean fastball, and we're gonna try her out in our rotation." This announcement was followed by more silence. Mac watched the players' faces as they struggled to accept and believe. He saw surprise and disbelief, but also the sideways smiles of butchers appraising a quality piece of meat. They turned to each other and whispered. Someone shouted. "Are you serious?"

JD shouted loudly for everyone to shut up. "We'll all go out on the field *right now* and watch Fari pitch to our best hitters!" As he said this, he guided Fari toward the dugout tunnel. It was a dramatic gesture, and JD the baseball wizard was fond of drama and magic.

The players laughed and whooped and Mac heard a few nasty variations on locker-room jokes. It was clear most of them couldn't believe Fari was a baseball pitcher. Mac cringed at this rude display of testosterone and bad taste. At the same time, he felt smug because he knew Fari could *pitch.* Yes, these boisterous boys of summer were about to be humbled and kicked in the balls.

As Fari stepped onto the field, she stopped and turned slowly in a circle, inspecting the huge spaces and thousands of empty seats. She felt small and unrecognizable, which gave her hope; she can get lost within this vast expanse. "Nada que ver, Baltimore Bananas," she whispered. "It's not the Baltimore Bananas anymore."

Cleo escorted Fari to the pitcher's mound. As she approached the mound, it felt like coming home. Until now, the morning had passed as a tumultuous blur – the whirl of noisy activity outside her cocoon – but this pitcher's mound offered safety and comfort.

Cleo stepped back and squeezed her arm. "Blow 'em away, buddy."

Fari's eyes filled with tears. She remembered a time many years ago when Papa had said those same words to her. Then, as now, she had stood alone on the pitcher's mound, aware only of herself and the empty, silent space around her; the *cocoon.* The space inside her, however, fluttered wildly with electric butterflies.

She controlled herself by focusing on the details around the mound. Everything had been cared for meticulously. Of course, this was the *pros.* She planted both feet on the rubber and faced home plate. Adrenaline pumped thick and fast through her chest and limbs, delivering power, energy, magic.

The men threw their hats into a bag and JD pulled out nine, one by one. These batters would face Fastball Fari. Their shortstop, Tony Rikes, a .300 hitter, was first up. The rest of the team stood restless on the sidelines, no one inclined to sit or miss a single detail. Most still believed it must be some trick or joke.

Fari bent down, picked up a new baseball and focused on home plate. It glowed fat and pale in the morning light.

Tony cocked his bat, glanced at his teammates and shouted. "I'm gonna cream the first pitch!"

The boys laughed and chattered, watching Fari, but when she went into her wind up, they fell silent. Fari reared back and flew forward in her characteristic explosive delivery. The ball moved in a blur and split the center of home plate. Tony Rikes did not move a muscle.

"Strike!" shouted the catcher.

"Ninety-eight!" shouted a coach with a radar gun.

A sigh of awe and disbelief issued from forty throats. Tony stood at the plate with his mouth hanging open. Finally, someone shouted. "Do that again!"

Rikes went into his crouch, no longer smiling. Fari wound up and POW – another smoker. Rikes swung too late. Strike two.

Tony stepped out of the batter's box and shook his head. "*Carumba!*"

Now the boys burst into cheers and applause, slapping at each other and Mac. Fari stood motionless on the mound, her face turned toward third base. Tony stepped back into the box. "C'mon!" He shouted. "Once more!"

Everyone fell silent, all eyes on Fari. This time she threw a wicked curve ball! Rikes swung and missed by a mile. He looked at his bat as if it had a hole in it. The boys hollered at him. Get the hell out of there! They danced and clapped and laughed – the joke was on them! Fari was a *pitcher*.

Donald Reynolds, their first baseman and a home-run hitter, swaggered toward the plate, his biceps and forearms bulging. He sliced his bat through the air in a savage display of speed and power.

Fari stood motionless on the mound, waiting patiently for Reynolds to finish his intimidation routine. Finally, Reynolds stepped into the batter's box and Fari went into her wind up.

Whoa! She pulled the string on it! Donnie swung viciously two beats before the ball hit the catcher's mitt. Strike one! The players and coaches erupted into cheers and whistles.

*   *

At the end of twenty minutes, during which Fari threw forty pitches, she was very definitely *on the team*. Pitch by pitch, the players found themselves turning into professionals, judging and observing one of their own. Now the comments had little to do with breasts and butts: "Shit, man, that's *fire*." "Look at that! It broke a mile!" "Hoo, buddy, *strike three!*"

Fari struck out seven batters, four of whom were their best hitters (including Cleo, who laughed so hard he could hardly hold his bat). Two players had hit the ball. Their second baseman, Brent Shiner, swung quickly at a Fari fastball and sent a crackling grounder through the hole between second and first.

As Fari had done with Cleo, she saluted Brent and bowed slightly from the waist. The guys razzed at Brent, a shy, staunch family man, until his ears burned. Soon everyone scrambled and shouted for the privilege of batting against Fastball Fari.

Some players, however, liked Fari a little *too* much. She was besieged with requests for dates by all the single guys and most of the married ones. These romantic opportunities were shouted from the sidelines in a sorry demonstration of male group behavior.

JD and Mac issued a stern warning: No dating among team members! This led to more shouts and rude noises.

"Listen!" JD shouted. "We all regard Fari as a companion and teammate, *nothing more.*"

Including me, thought Mac. He looked around and saw Howard Sikes had appeared on the field.

Howard was Chairman of the Board and majority owner of the Minnesota Twins. He was a trim, dapper man in his early sixties. His father had made a fortune building a chain of supermarkets, and Howard had inherited this fortune and made another. Seven years ago he bought the Minnesota Twins.

At that time, the Twins were struggling. They suffered from an aging staff and players, with no money to pay for anything better. Howard turned the company around by injecting enough money to attract quality players and coaches. He persuaded the city government to help him build a new stadium downtown. ("Imagine," he had argued, "Thousands of people coming into the area regularly, *spending money.*")

To get the fans riled up and increase attendance, he introduced more promotional campaigns and gimmicks. There were more "bat days," "helmet days," "T shirt days," "free hot dog days." In fact,

Howard had been putting together a special promotional effort for this Sunday's season opener. And now, as he watched Fari Madrigal, a lovely heat wave rolled through his belly. Here was a *woman* on his baseball team! He hardly considered the historical or social consequences; he thought about the profits.

Mac greeted Howard, who appeared in a good mood – smiling, shaking hands, remembering everyone's name. Finally, JD escorted Fari to the sidelines to meet Howard.

Howard oozed charm and called Fari "my darling." Fari favored Howard with one split second of eye contact, but smiled graciously and answered his questions with one or two words. When Howard invited her to dinner, JD pulled Fari away by claiming they had work to do.

Howard had to yield since JD ruled on the field. But Howard didn't mind; this golden goose was in *his* hen house. The calculator in his head displayed numbers with marching zeros, but then he remembered Fari was not actually signed yet. This threw a little wrench into his happy works. Although it was common for unsigned players to play while still negotiating their contract, Howard knew he had to get Fari's signature on a piece of paper *very soon*.

*   *

For the rest of the day, Mac and the pitching staff – including Fari – reviewed game plans for their opening series with Chicago. Fari experienced another emotional moment when Mac announced she would start in Sunday's season opener. Opening the season was an honor and the other pitchers gave her their endorsement and support, including Doug Ferguson, who had been the original choice. He offered graciously to tell Fari about the strengths and weaknesses of Chicago's batters.

Mac noticed the men behaved differently. Usually, these gatherings were characterized by horseplay and obscenities, but now the men acted subdued and anxious, careful with their language. He saw the subtle competitive byplay as each man vied for Fari's attention.

However, Fari favored no one. She kept her cap on and her face and eyes averted at all times. She sat back from the table, keeping her distance, her back against the wall, with her arms crossed over her chest and a baseball in her right hand. Occasionally, her upper body jerked back and forth. She answered questions with a minimum of words – usually in English, sometimes in Spanish – and smiled at the attempts at humor.

These were the hardest moments for Fari, when she was required to step out of her cocoon and present herself to strangers. She felt the excited wavelengths of these men, their interest and curiosity – mostly prurient, occasionally plutonic. She kept her breasts covered, her legs crossed and her eyes well hidden. An uneasy pressure expanded in her chest and belly, but the presence of Mac provided a source of stability and strength.

Two of the men, natural leaders, did most of the talking, but they could not capture Fari's eyes. They threw puzzled looks in Mac's direction, but he ignored them. Fari's behavior was odd, or "eccentric," but never inappropriate. Ironically, the strangeness seemed to highlight her beauty and poise.

At four o'clock, JD called it a day. Before leaving the field, each player stepped up to Fari and welcomed her to the Minnesota Twins. Mac stood off and watched Fari manage these clamorous sentiments. She shook hands or slapped high fives, but her movements seemed stiff and contrived. The *real* Fari was hidden, Mac decided.

Each physical contact set off an alarm, but she held her breath, clenched her teeth and managed to go through the motions. On the inside, however, she burned and squirmed. The eyes still appraised her, still flicked down to her breasts, but now they held a measure of respect.

Doc Harris waited until the players had paid their respects, then stepped quickly in front of Fari. He smiled broadly. "Well, Fari, you're a long way from home."

Fari looked briefly into his eyes. She saw friendly interest on the surface, but just beneath was the flat, cool passion of the predator.

"Are you enjoying Minneapolis?" Doc blinked his eyes.

Fari almost blinked back. She had an urge to measure the depth of this man's weakness. With his eyes and body language he had communicated one clear message; he would do *anything* to please her. "I like Minneapolis," she told him. "But it is too crowded."

"You're right!" Doc bounced on his toes. He glanced down once quickly and registered the presence of her perfect breasts. He pushed his smile into megawatt range. "I'd love to show you Minneapolis. Anytime you want. A *private* tour."

Fari stepped back and looked toward center field. "Thank you, Dr. Harris. And please bring your wife and children." She turned and trotted toward the dugout.

Mac watched this encounter with curiosity. He saw Fari turn and run away, leaving Doc Harris with a stunned, painful expression.

"Hey, Mac, c'mere!" JD sat on the infield grass talking on the phone. "Stew says there's quite a crowd outside. He sees at least three satellite trucks."

At first Mac drew a blank, then it hit him. "Fari," he said. "They're here for Fari."

JD nodded. He held up the phone. "Here, listen."

Mac took the phone and put it to his head.

"One news guy told me they're hoping to catch a glimpse of Fari as she leaves the stadium," Stew said. "Also, they're putting lots of pressure on Stephen and Howard for another press conference."

"We're going home, Stew," said Mac, careful not to mention *what* home. "No press conference."

"Well, all right, but I think you'd better have a plan, Mac, or you'll get mobbed. There're a lot people out here."

"Okay, Stew. Thanks." Mac didn't have a plan, but Fari and Frances did.

JD hurried into the locker room and asked the players to hang around for another minute. Meanwhile, Fari had gone to JD's office, which had a private dressing room and shower. JD appraised the players of the situation outside the stadium, then reminded them of their traditional policy to refrain from speculating or commenting to the press about other teammates. Finally, he dismissed everyone.

Mac and Cleo accompanied JD to his office, where they found Fari standing by the windows. She wore a flannel, long-sleeved shirt, blue jeans and walking shoes. The shirt had been tucked into the jeans, which accentuated her shape. Her hair was still wet and gathered in a long ponytail. No sign of the baseball.

It was the first time Mac had seen her wear something other than a sweat suit. He took one look and his heart shuddered. He looked away quickly, vowing not to stare like those nasty boys downstairs.

Cleo fought his way through the forest of plants. "Damn, JD, next time I'm bringin a chainsaw."

JD heard these sorts of remarks all the time. "I do make trails," he answered. "But the plants keep *moving*."

They all laughed, except Fari. She stared out the window with her shoulders pulled together, a frown marring her lovely features.

Cleo weaved through the plants to her side and wrapped an arm around her shoulders. "Don't worry about that," he said, gesturing toward the crowd. "We'll be all right."

Fari flinched at his touch, but then leaned into him. Cleo's warm, solid body offered protection from the Eyes and Ears, which were *everywhere*. They poked and probed and lied and corrupted. It was technological rape; her image captured and violated.

JD skipped behind his desk and rubbed his hands together. "Now we go into the escape plan." He lifted a bag onto his desk and pulled out two pairs of baggy overalls. He looked at Fari. "Your mother sent these here about an hour ago. One for you, one for Cleo." There were also two caps that said "Maintenance," and a small plastic bag containing two fake mustaches and a pair of eyeglasses.

"I don't believe it!" Mac shouted and laughed. "It's a disguise!"

Fari stepped back from Cleo and flicked her eyes at Mac. "Mama esta preparada."

Cleo hopped into the overalls and pressed on the bushy mustache. Fari turned away from the men as she pulled on the overalls. She pressed a thin, brown mustache above her lip and pinned her hair up under her cap. As a final touch, she put on the glasses.

Mac and JD jumped with laughter. JD held up his cell phone and took a few photos. "For history!" He turned to Cleo. "Follow Stew down the back stairs to the maintenance area. A security van will be right outside the door. At the same time, Mac and I will walk out the front doors."

When Cleo and Fari left the office, JD announced that he and Mac were about to leave. In the ensuing scramble to *get the story*, the journalists and cameramen congregated at the front doors, while Cleo and Fari left quietly out the back.

Mac and JD ran the gauntlet of journalists waving microphones and shouting questions. At one point, they were jostled and shoved. The security guys closed in and they became an island surrounded by a sea of media.

Doc Harris was also in this crowd. He too carried a camera. He had hoped to get into position for a dead-on shot of Fari's butt. However, when he saw Mac and JD come out alone, he knew they had been fooled. Fari went out the back; she's long gone.

I wonder where she's staying?

*　　　　　*

JD ordered take-out meals from one of the city's most popular vegetarian restaurants, *The Mud Pie*. Fari wondered about the phrase "mud pie" and asked if it was related to "cow pie." Kim laughed so hard she had to excuse herself briefly.

Frances entertained the table with her description of the press conference. JD, Fari and Mac had missed the part when the reporters fell to the floor. Kim promised to bring a camera to the next press conference and *film the media*.

Mac sat across from Fari and watched her interact with the others. She had taken off the cap and her long, black hair was pulled back. He noticed her ears stuck out slightly, and he was enchanted by this. Also, she had loosened up among this close, familiar company and spoke more often, offered more eye contact.

After dinner, JD announced he and Frances had found a condo for Fari over by Loring Park, close to downtown. "Most reporters know where I live. They're searching for Fari and soon they'll look here." He looked at Mac. "Mrs. Olson says a couple of media guys are parked in front of your house."

Mac looked at Kim. "No journalist has *ever* been to our house."

Kim beamed a big smile. "Now we're famous!"

"She's right, Mac," said JD. "The media is hot on our trail."

Mac glanced at Fari. She had moved sideways in her chair with her face averted, almost as if she was embarrassed. We're under siege by the media because of our association with *her*.

"I want to ask you a favor, Mac," JD continued. "I rented another condo next door to Fari's. I'd appreciate it if you and Cleo stayed there for a while. It's a big place, completely furnished." He glanced at Kim.

"Kim has volunteered to stay with Fari, if that's all right with you."

"Whoa!" Mac was taken aback by this sudden shift in events. Fari and Kim living together? He and Cleo next door?

"Please, Daddy," begged Kim. "Uncle Jack says there's an interior connection between the condos. We can meet *in secret*."

"When the going gets weird," said JD. "The weird get going. Frances will be in the spotlight, so she has to stay here. We want the condos to stay secret."

Kim leaned toward her father. "There's a bus from school that stops only two blocks from the condo."

Mac was overwhelmed and he knew it. He nodded. "Okay."

*   *

After dinner, Frances retired to what she called "the Command Center," which she had established in one of JD's libraries. She had hired Cleo's cousin, Alfred, to help her on a project for the University of Santo Domingo. Alfred was fifteen years old and a computer whiz. Frances told him where she wanted to go, and Alfred flew through the internet and landed on the exact spot.

Kim and Fari went up to the "entertainment room" to watch a movie – *The Wizard of Oz*. Fari had heard of it, but had never seen it. JD retired to his third floor study and "sewing room" to review a mountain of phone messages.

Mac found himself alone in the kitchen, so he volunteered to clean the table and stack the dishes in the washer. He clicked on the kitchen TV and tuned to the evening news. The first thing he saw was himself – a short video clip of he and Fari standing together during the press conference. He turned up the volume.

"She was discovered by Chet Macquire, the Twins' pitching coach," said the broadcaster. "An hour ago, Stephen Rains, spokesperson for the Twins, announced that Fari Madrigal will be the Twins' *starting pitcher* in their season opener this Sunday against Chicago." The video of Fari and Mac disappeared and was replaced with a photo of JD Johnson. Below it were the words, "By phone from Minneapolis."

JD's voice boomed into the kitchen. "Fari Madrigal will be our starting pitcher this Sunday. This decision was made by me and our pitching coach, Chet Macquire. . We're confident Fari will give us a good effort in our season opener, and throughout the season."

Good for you, thought Mac. Short and to the point.

Back to the announcer. "That was JD Johnson, general manager of the Minnesota Twins, talking to us earlier by phone. Since this morning's surprise press conference, the Twins' new starting pitcher has not appeared in public, nor has she issued any statements, except those made by her mother, Frances Madrigal. Despite several requests for interviews, the Twins remain tightlipped about Fastball Fari and her whereabouts."

Mac clicked off the TV and poured himself a glass of wine. He went into the front living room, turned off the lights and sat on the sofa. He stared at the liquid shadow of Lake of the Isles and sipped the smooth wine. Occasionally, a car passed slowly along the parkway, the headlights creating a hazy cone of light.

He thought about Cleo and Fari in their disguises and laughed. When they had arrived at the house earlier and stepped from the security van, Kim had gone crazy. Mac was afraid she'd wet her pants.

Cleo shoved his fake, bushy mustache into everyone's face. He had agreed readily to move in next door to Fari, and seemed enthusiastic about having Mac and Kim as roommates.

"Every safe house needs guards," Kim had told Cleo. "I'll be the eyes, you'll be the muscle."

In some ways, Kim seemed more mature than Fari, more subdued and in control, while Fari's emotions played over her face constantly. Kim approached most situations with eagerness and confidence, while Fari seemed hesitant and terrified. Tonight, however, Fari appeared more relaxed in this private setting.

Mac heard voices in the kitchen, and in a few seconds Kim and Fari found him in the living room. They joined him on the sofa. Kim sat on his lap, Fari sat a few feet away.

"How was the movie?" he asked.

"Great!" they both said at once.

"Me gusta," said Fari. She had taken off her shoes and lost the baseball. Her hair hung long and loose. "But I did not like flying monkeys."

Mac laughed, recalling the first time he saw that movie. The flying monkeys had terrified him. They chatted about the movie a while, then Mac told Kim she'd better get ready for bed. Tomorrow was a school day.

She protested only weakly. It had been a long day for her too. She said good night, kissed Mac on the cheek, shook hands with Fari and skipped upstairs.

The living room filled with shadows and silence. Mac felt acutely aware of Fari sitting next to him, three feet away. He felt her warmth and smelled the lilacs. He glanced at her profile. She had leaned back on the sofa with her hands folded in her lap and her face toward the window. "I am like Dorothy," she said suddenly, speaking almost in a whisper.

Mac smiled at her. "You mean Dorothy from Kansas?"

She nodded. "Yes. After tornado, when house lands, she opens door and says, 'I don't think we are in Kansas anymore.'"

Mac laughed. "That's a famous line."

"Justamente como Dorothy, I flew over rainbow and landed next to laughing waters."

Mac saw she was smiling. This was yet another Fari. She seemed almost comfortable, sociable. Speaking more English than Spanish. "Does that make me a Munchkin?"

She shook her head. Distant street lights sparkled in her eyes. "No, not Munchkin."

"The Tin Man?"

Immediately, her face changed and she glanced at him briefly. The darkness allowed for more overt eye contact. "No, Mac. Very definitely, you do have a heart."

For some reason, this statement, and the way she said it, hit Mac deep inside that very same heart. He leaned back, his eyes blinking.

Fari's upper body moved back and forth, not a jerky movement, but precise and controlled. Mac felt a sudden heat wave and deflected the subject slightly. "What about JD? Who would he be?"

Fari shifted sideways and faced him directly, but kept her face averted. "JD is wizard."

"Sometimes he does work magic." Mac remembered many times when JD's sense of intuition had led him to the right decision at the right time.

The world turned and the moon peeked above the trees. It was only a few days past the new phase and resembled a thin, disembodied smile.

Mac had met Jenni in high school and she was the only woman he's been with intimately. During their marriage, he had had fantasies about other women, but it never occurred to him to do anything about it. But now Jenni was gone and he was a single man.

What did this mean, to be single? Mac knew it was part of his new identity, but what *role* did it imply? "Single" meant alone, but it also meant available. He looked at Fari and wished he knew what to say. He felt his ears burn.

Fari had never felt threatening sensations from Mac. His evaluations seemed genuinely focused on her pitching, not her breasts or butt. At least, this was the rational view, what she tried to tell herself, but her anxieties grew out of irrational fears. She deflected these fears by searching for something to say. Her eyes landed on the moon. "When moon shines on ocean, it glows on waves like stairway. Have you seen that? Like those things in skyway. What are they?"

"Escalators."

"Yes, escalators."

Mac liked that image, and knew it to be true. He recalled when he and Jenni had visited Hawaii. The full moon had sat low on the horizon and unrolled a long, reflective path atop the ocean's waves. They had fantasized about skipping up that brilliant staircase and jumping into the wide, pale mouth of the moon.

Fari rested her head on her arms and sighed softly. "On our farm, we see dawn in morning and sunset in evening. Very peaceful."

Mac felt touched by the purity of emotion clutching at her voice. Also, this was the most words she had ever spoken to him. He felt in awe of this woman. Everything about her – the way she pitched, the way she looked and acted – evoked majesty and mystery. He wondered about the *real* Fari, the one deep inside those gorgeous eyes.

At that moment, Fari glanced at him and caught him staring at her. "On first day I wear a disguise." She leaned back and looked away. "Los bastardos. They steal my identity and sell it!"

Her voice issued sharp, edgy. No clowning around now. Mac knew she talked about "those bastards," but what about her identity? It sounded like a verbal snippet of an interior conversation. Was this another quirk?

Fari's body began its rocking movement. "You are anchor in storm, Mac." She glanced at him and spoke quickly. "You, JD, Cleo and Kim. I appreciate your help." This was true. These people protected her from the Eyes and Ears. Her body stopped moving and she sighed deeply. "I could click my heels together and go home."

This broke the tension and Mac laughed. He found something to say. "There's no place like home."

"Mama and I have job to do, then we go home."

She said this in a deadly serious tone and Mac's antennae perked up. "What do you mean?"

Fari sat up quickly and glanced at him. "Remember Glenda, good witch?" she asked, referring again to the movie.

Mac nodded.

"That is Mama, the good witch." She paused and held herself still. "*I'm* her magic wand."

A blinding flash went off from the other side of the window and Fari screamed. Mac rolled to the floor and pulled Fari with him. They crawled quickly to the front hallway, turned the corner and scrambled to their feet.

"Que fue eso?" Fari whispered hoarsely.

Mac flicked a switch and a tiny electric motor closed the front curtains. He leaned against the door and peered through the eye-hole. Parked on the street was a truck with a satellite dish.

"They found us," he whispered.

*   *

Doc Harris sat alone in the trainer's office just off the locker room. The last player had left several minutes ago and Doc wrote his report. Half his brain was on the job, while the other half thought about Fari's snub that afternoon on the field. "Bring your wife and kids." What kind of smart-ass remark was that? Fari was beautiful as long as she kept her mouth shut.

No matter, thought Doc. In another week, he'd be lying in the tropical sun, a free man. The escape plan had been in the works for several weeks, ever since his wife's private detectives caught him in full-color action at a "paper-bag party" (leave your clothes in a bag by the door).

Sherry had gone ballistic. She forced him to shut down his social life and insisted he see a psychologist twice a week. This was supposed to help him "get in touch with himself" and "make positive changes."

The humiliation cut deeply, and inside his secret heart Doc entertained hatred and revenge. He was vulnerable to Sherry's power; the building housing his clinic was owned by Sherry's father, Sherman Lansing, and the house they lived in was in Sherry's name. Doc owned a little Mercedes sports car and the clothes on his back.

He had a little money in the bank, about one hundred and thirty thousand, but he hoped for a little more. He had made contact with an underground friend and arranged for the Mercedes to be "stolen," his only possession worth anything. Doc would make fifteen grand on the deal. Soon after this "theft" occurred, he'd board a jet for Central America and disappear forever.

He felt so pleased by the progress of his plan, he decided to reward himself. He closed the office door and prepared a little hit of morphine. He shot it home and immediately the drug thudded through his veins like hot molasses. He closed his eyes and savored the delicious warmth.

SIX

Thursday: March 27

Mac entertained the breakfast table with a description of the media invasion the night before. He had called the police and they arrived within three minutes. They shooed away the media vehicles; no parking on the parkway. This morning, however, several journalists stood on public land across the street from the house, tending their cameras and microphones.

JD reacted with scorn toward this "gang of Peeping Toms." Frances delivered a three minute discourse on what she called the "diabolical union" between the corporate world and television. Mac recognized the vocabulary of higher education.

The discussion turned back to practical matters: how to evade the journalists camped across the street. ("Maybe they're in back too," Kim shouted. "We might be *surrounded*.") Frances suggested they try the same trick as the day before; she and JD would step out the front door, while Kim, Mac, and Fari escaped out the back.

JD called the office secretary, Stew, and asked him to come to the house as soon as possible. "Drive down the alley and stop beside the back gate."

Kim jumped and laughed, enjoying this game of cat and mouse. Also, it looked like she might miss half a day of school. "And you know how I *hate* to miss school, Dad."

Mac rolled his eyes. Fari wore a floppy hat, huge sunglasses, a heavy sweater and loose trousers. She looked like a fugitive movie star. She held a baseball and rotated it rapidly. He remembered what she had said the night before, about being the focus of such intense

74

scrutiny. It can't be healthy to live in constant fear of an invasion on your person. Maybe notoriety and fame induced a kind of insanity in some people – they wanted to be near it, they wanted to touch it.

This morning, however, Fari appeared relaxed as she kidded around with Kim, emphasizing the humor in the situation. Meanwhile, Mac wondered about the invasion on *his* person, and that of Kim. They too had been caught in the media spotlight. They had been forced (urged?) out of their house!

"Get ready." Kim folded her cell phone. "Stew's only two blocks away."

They said their good-byes to Frances and JD. After dealing with the journalists, Frances would stay on at the house. Later this morning she had a meeting with Howard Sikes, the Twins' owner.

Stew's car appeared in the alley behind the house. "Go!" yelled Kim.

Frances and JD opened the front door and stepped outside. Instantly, the journalists came alive, grabbed bags and cameras and ran across the street, shouting questions. "Where's Fari? Is Fari coming out?"

Mac jerked open the back door and he, Kim and Fari ran across the yard to the fence. Kim tugged on the gate, but it wouldn't open. "Hurry up," whispered Mac. Fari held his forearm and leaned against him, delivering lilacs and body heat. Mac nearly swooned. Finally, the gate swung open and they bolted for the alley.

"Hey!" A man stepped out between two garages, holding a camera. "Hey!" He ran toward them, holding the camera high.

Kim was first to the car and yanked open the back door. Fari dove onto the seat, followed by Mac, then Kim jumped in and landed on Mac's legs. Stew stomped on the gas and the wheels kicked up gravel. The camera guy skipped neatly out of the way, stooped low and pointed the camera into the car as it sped by.

Mac lay lengthwise on the seat, pressed backwards by the acceleration. They all laughed wildly. He caught his breath and looked up into Fari's face. His head rested on her thigh and he felt the solid warmth of her.

He twisted around quickly and fought himself upright. Kim squirmed over the top of the seat and plopped down in front. "Keep an eye on your mirrors, Stew," she said. "He might follow."

Fari's body moved in quick, small jerks; an agitated movement. A paid gunslinger lay in ambush, pulled out a camera and shot them several times – more pieces of her identity stolen, soon to be sold "to the public." She whipped off the hat and sunglasses and brushed her fingers through the black softness of her hair. She glanced at Mac and gripped his arm, her body still moving back and forth. "El tenía una camera."

Mac couldn't answer; his mind was elsewhere. We're sitting too close together, he thought. Her upper body rubs and bumps against me. Our legs are touching and she's holding my arm. And those lilacs!

Take it easy, he told himself. It's the Latin culture; they like to be close and they like to touch. He decided to regard these intimacies with passive acceptance. Still, he felt nervous sitting this close to Fari, and he hoped Stew and Kim wouldn't notice.

"Hey, he's after us!" cried Kim. She had twisted around and looked out the back window. "He's on a motorcycle."

"She's right, Mac," said Stew, checking his mirrors. "He had a dirt bike stashed between the garages." He glanced into the back seat. "Now what?"

"Lose the sucker!" shouted Kim.

"Drop us off downtown," said Mac. "We'll get lost in the skyway system."

*   *

Howard Sikes, owner of the Minnesota Twins, and Frances Marchena, mother and agent of Fari Madrigal, sat side by side on a wooden bench next to Lake of the Isles. The bench was shaded by a nearby Willow tree. The feathery branches drooped under the weight of bright green buds.

Howard wore a cashmere pinstripe suit, white shirt, silk tie and custom-made shoes. Frances had dressed for more athletic activity; a gray sweat suit and black tennis shoes. She had been working at JD's house and had jogged halfway around the lake to arrive at this meeting.

Howard glanced over his shoulder at his long, black limousine parked next to the curb, so far away. Pedro, his chauffeur, had opened the window and watched from the driver's seat. Howard felt reassured, but it did not quell the fluttering in his stomach. He felt vulnerable and out of his element.

Frances glanced at Howard and instantly saw his discomfort. It was she who had suggested this secret meeting next to the lake. "It's a beautiful day, Mr. Sikes," she had said on the phone with breathy cheerfulness. "Maybe we should meet by the lake. Yes, let's meet by the lake and have a friendly chat." And here they were, alone together, in a place where no one could hear them or interfere.

"This was a good idea, Mrs. Marchena," Howard said with a smile. "The hot sun and cool air is refreshing."

Frances wondered if Howard was wired and recording this conversation. She didn't think so; he didn't seem that devious, or not likely to be devious around her. She reached into her jacket pocket and turned on a tape recorder. "Let's talk about Fastball Fari."

Howard's heart jumped and he looked at her. "Is this a business meeting?"

"Oh yes, Mr. Sikes. Do you mind?"

Of course I mind, he screamed inside his head. I'm out here in the cold, with no lawyers, no board, no advisors, all alone! He forced himself to keep smiling. "What did you have in mind, Mrs. Marchena?"

Frances had a lot on her mind. She had learned that Howard and his family controlled a fortune estimated at over nine hundred million dollars. Besides owning the Minnesota Twins and a chain of supermarkets, they held a controlling interest in three local high tech companies, plus stock in many blue chip companies on the New York Stock Exchange. Also, the family was reported to maintain cash reserves of about fifty million dollars. She had learned all this with Alfred's help.

Further, she was aware that tickets for every Twins home game will be sold out by later today, thanks to the addition of Fari to the team. Also, the games in other cities where the Twins will play were expected to sell out. , With Fastball Fari on the Twins, Howard stood to reap a huge windfall.

Frances looked at Howard and on sudden impulse, she asked, "Mr. Sikes, how much money do you think one person should have?"

Howard turned toward the lake, hiding his expression. What the hell kind of question was that? He knew he was on the weaker side of this negotiation. He very badly wanted Fari, *needed* Fari. The games were selling out and he was about to squeeze the TV guys for all he could get. *But Frances has Fari.*

"Well, Mr. Sikes, what do you think?"

"I'm not sure I understand. Do you mean how much does one person need?"

"Yes, sir, that's exactly what I mean."

Howard looked away and thought about it. What was the angle to this question? Maybe the hidden meaning was how much does Fari need. In that context, the question made sense and he was on familiar ground. He chose a philosophical approach. "I suppose it depends on what one wants. A human being actually *needs* very little. Food, shelter, clothing." He looked at her and smiled. "But sometimes our wants exceed our needs."

"That's right, sir. In that case, should one be allowed to accumulate as much as possible?"

This was a different question altogether and Howard had no desire to explore it. He felt tight in the chest and hot behind the ears. He was a busy man and had many important things to do! That's right, but there was nothing more important in his life right now than Fari Madrigal. He decided to let his irritation show. "Mrs. Marchena, I don't get your point here. How much does *Fari* want?"

Frances heard the sudden change in tone and smiled to herself. She couldn't resist this opportunity to make Howard squirm. She had never been this close to such a wealthy person and was genuinely curious as to what made him tick. She looked into his eyes. "Are you satisfied with nine hundred million dollars, Mr. Sikes? Or do you want more?"

Despite the chilly air, Howard felt beads of sweat sticking to his two hundred dollar shirt. That question had been personal and very bad manners. He saw the moral high ground and jumped. "Pardon me, Mrs. Marchena, but my personal finances are none of your business." He paused and looked at her with a frown. "Besides, I don't know where you got that number, but you're completely wrong." And that's true, he thought. As of this morning, the family had only eight hundred ninety-four million, nine hundred and forty-seven thousand.

Frances felt heat on her face. How *dare* this man assume a righteous attitude! She wondered if Howard held stock in United Brands Company. At that moment, a vision of Felipe crossed her mind: He lay dead in the dirt, his blood soaking the roots of banana trees. A black wind rose up from her soul and she spoke through clenched teeth. "Mr. Sikes, there are billions of people on this planet who do *not* have the basic needs of survival. *They do not have the basic needs!*"

Howard leaned back and blinked. "What?"

Frances shut her mouth and took a deep breath. She did not want to get emotional at this meeting, nor did she want to preach. She knew Howard could not see the great sin he committed every day. Only when he sees with his heart will his eyes come open.

Meanwhile, I'm going to open his wallet!

She assumed an attitude of contrition. "Excuse me, Mr. Sikes. You're right, sir. Your personal finances are your business." She paused and looked at him from under her eyebrows. "I suggest we return to our more immediate business. Fari and I made a verbal agreement with Mr. Macquire for a standard, one year contract with a basic incentive clause. Is that your understanding, sir?"

Howard had seen fury in Frances' eyes just a second ago, but now they were back to words like "contract" and "salary." *What was wrong with her?* "I believe that was the understanding," he answered cautiously. "I don't know the details."

"Well, sir, whatever the details, we wish to stick to this agreement. You may go ahead and draw up this contract and Fari will sign it."

Howard leaned back and thought about it. Fari will sign for minimum? A standard contract? He felt a burst of glee, but quickly suppressed it. Something's wrong here. Surely Frances knows Fari is worth more than that. "Mrs. Marchena, are you saying that you and Fari are willing to sign a standard, minimum wage contract?"

Frances almost rolled her eyes, but maintained patience and answered slowly, bordering on sarcasm. "Yes, Mr. Sikes. We will sign a minimum wage, standard contract under the terms as previously understood among Fari, me and Chet Macquire."

Howard felt a warm glow as he contemplated all those millions about to fall his way. But he wouldn't let himself believe it until he had the contract in hand, signed and legal. For now, he was satisfied with a firm commitment from Frances. He smiled and stuck out his hand.

"Mrs. Marchena, will you shake my hand on this agreement?"

Frances sensed Howard's relief and saw the fire in his eyes. He thinks he got everything he wanted, she thought, but he hasn't heard yet what *I* want. She shook his hand and smiled sweetly. "We have a deal, Mr. Sikes."

Howard's smile seemed more genuine, a little less guarded. He could sense no sneaky tricks in this business discussion, apart from the strange comments about "basic needs." He allowed himself a brief shiver of good cheer. He smiled with benevolent tolerance, the smile of the *owner*, the Patron, the guy in charge. "Mrs. Marchena, I'll have the contract drawn up immediately and you can sign it this afternoon. In any case, I must leave now. I have an appointment in fifteen minutes. Perhaps you'll ride with me back to JD's house and we'll make arrangements for later."

Frances watched Howard adjust his coat and tie, a busy man on his way to the next Big Deal. I give him everything he wants and he doesn't even have the decency to thank me. Well, that's all right. I don't want his gratitude. I want his money! "Before you go, Mr. Sikes, I have one more little detail to discuss."

*   *

JD arrived at the stadium later than usual. He had delayed his arrival until he was sure that Mac and the others had settled safely and secretly into their new condos. A crowd of journalists hung around outside the stadium, much greater than yesterday. There were also crowds of fans hoping for a glimpse of Fastball Fari. JD was reminded of the kind of passion ignited by rock stars or Hollywood celebrities.

Fari's presence on the team would be worth millions in extra revenue for Howard Sikes. Yesterday, shortly after the famous press conference, there was a run on Twins season tickets, and by now every home game had sold out. Especially prized were tickets to their season opener this Sunday. Stew told him about offers on the Internet for up to five thousand dollars!

Further, there were runs on tickets in other cities where the Twins would play. According to media reports from these cities, "everyone wants to participate in history."

Maybe so, thought JD, but he had a more cynical view. There was more than history being made here; cash registers everywhere sang and grew fatter.

As he walked into the reception area, Clara, his personal secretary, jumped to her feet and smiled brightly. "Good morning, JD. Call Howard."

"Good morning, Clara. Screw Howard." They smiled sweetly at each other. "You're here early this morning."

Clara gestured toward the windows. "I wanted to avoid the crowds, but there're already quite a few people." Clara was fifty-nine years old and had been JD's secretary for twelve years. As he moved from team to team, she had moved with him. She was tall and slim, with soft, blue eyes. Thick strands of black and gray hair lay piled on top of her head.

"It's gonna get worse too." JD walked over to the windows and looked out. It was rumored that Clara and JD were lovers. They had never admitted this, nor would anyone have the bad manners to ask. People merely assumed it. JD had never been married and Clara had been divorced for twenty years. Publicly, they treated each other with a mixture of respect and intimacy.

JD busied himself with his morning ritual – watering the plants, greeting them, quoting his favorite poet: "'Rain is to flowers as tears are for pain.'" He listened to their advice, praise and complaints.

Howard called again, but Clara knew better than to interrupt JD's morning routine.

"Where's Jack?" Howard wanted to know. "I know he's in the building, Clara. Where is he?"

"He's in the bathroom, Mr. Sikes. I'll have him call as soon as he comes out. Excuse me, sir, I have another call." And she put Howard Sikes on hold! Of course, the Chairman of the Board holds for no one, but Clara felt pleased to cut him off before he could hang up.

JD finished with the plants and settled himself behind his desk. He unwrapped a fresh, fat cigar, stuck it between his teeth and picked up the office phone. "Okay, Clara, connect me with hell."

Clara made the connection and Howard was on the line. "Good morning, Jack!" He sounded cheerful.

JD was immediately on guard. "Hello, Howard." He decided to fire off the first shot. "I think we'd better get ready for a lot more people today. What's the policy on that?"

"The policy?" Howard was caught off guard and tried to make a joke. "We might have to call out the National Guard!"

JD kept silent as Howard laughed by himself. In seven years, JD had never called Howard about anything, except to return Howard's calls. They rarely consulted, yet they had to work together to keep the Twins a prosperous and winning team, and, so far, they had been successful. However, their individual approach to this common endeavor came from two wildly different philosophies.

"As you can imagine, Fari's stirring up a lot of interest." Howard still spoke in an upbeat, cheery tone. "The phones in the PR office have been jammed for hours, and now all those people in the parking lots. How can we control it?"

"We can't."

"Where's Fari right now?"

"I don't know."

Howard took a second to absorb the indignity of this obvious lie. When he spoke again, the bounce was gone from his voice. "I assume she'll be here for practice."

"I assume she will." JD suddenly felt impatient. "Did you have something specific, Howard?"

Howard had rehearsed this conversation, but JD wasn't playing the way he imagined. Also, he was still in shock from his lakeside meeting with Frances and the horrifying prospect of losing all those millions. He hated being in the position of needing something from JD, or from anyone, but he had no trouble humbling himself if the price was right. He began. "We're getting enormous pressure from every news organization in the country, from around the *world*. They say this is of historical significance." He paused and waited for a reaction.

JD held the phone closer to his mouth and chewed loudly on the cigar.

Howard pretended not to notice. "As you know, Jack, we still have two more hours committed to 'field access,' and one press conference where we introduce the whole team."

"I'm aware of that. What's the point?"

"Well, I know we agreed to do the two hours on Saturday, but could we break that up a little?"

"We've already made up the schedule." JD wondered what Howard was getting at.

"Yes, I know. But maybe instead of two hours on Saturday, we could have one hour today and one hour on Saturday. It would help take off the pressure."

JD didn't really care when they had their media "field access" day – when members of the media were allowed into the stadium during practice. He smelled something rotten in Howard's motives behind this suggestion, but he didn't have the time or stomach to figure it out. On sudden impulse, he once again quoted his favorite poet. "'Change arrives suddenly, like a strange world, like a green cat found.'"

"What?"

JD spoke again quickly. "Okay, Howard. It's all right with me if we change the schedule, but you'd better be careful with security. Make sure only licensed journalists get in. Also, I'm going to be strict about this; *one hour.*"

Howard ignored this impertinence. In fact, he had to fight to keep from laughing. He had done it! The media boys had promised him a hefty bonus on top of this year's royalty contract if he could produce Fastball Fari by today. Already, this phone call has netted him a nice profit. Now for a little more. "Just one more thing, JD."

JD sat up straighter. Howard never called him "JD" unless he was on his knees begging.

Howard continued. "I think we have to respect the larger issue here. That is, the *historical* circumstances. It's our duty to allow more access to Fari."

JD allowed a little sarcasm into his voice. "Should we call the news people and tell them where she's staying?"

"Oh no, of course not," Howard answered quickly. "We've got to respect her privacy." Actually, he was delighted with Fari's reluctance to appear in public. It added to her mystique and increased her value. "I was thinking of a special news conference. The public could meet with Fari face-to-face, so to speak, and get to know her. Then maybe they'd leave her alone."

This was so patently absurd that JD could not respond immediately. He looked at his plants and rolled his eyes. They shared his disgust.

He did not want to give in to Howard, but now was not the time to reject him completely. He had the perfect solution. "You'd better take that up with Frances," he said in his I-want-to-get-off-the-phone voice. "She's Fari's spokesperson. Was there anything else?"

"Uh, no."

"Okay, Howard. Here's your thought for today: 'In the darkness, I stop to think on this; be or not be, that my question is.'" JD hung up laughing. He glanced at his watch; a quarter to ten. The media would start coming in at about eleven. He'd better warn the team and have a little talk with Fari Madrigal.

*   *

The Minnesota Twins practiced under a battery of white, artificial suns. Players ran, jumped, worked out. They knew their careers (and paychecks) depended on strong, healthy bodies and a positive performance.

Fari worked out with serious intent, not so much because she needed it, but to demonstrate she was willing to work. At the moment, they engaged in twenty minutes of free style calisthenics, accompanied by hip-hop music blaring from the loudspeakers. Each player did whatever he (or she) wanted.

Most players did aerobics, Fari noticed, but she stuck to running in place. Aerobics was too much like dancing and she didn't feel like dancing in front of all these men. Also, she stayed close to the other pitchers, with whom she felt camaraderie. She tried to be included in the fun without being the object of it.

She had spent a few private moments with each of these men. Some were quiet and shy, others more outgoing, but they all behaved toward her with formality and respect. Now, however, gathered together in a group, they tended to act like pigs.

Her body was a lightning rod for eyes and minds. It didn't matter which direction she faced; she was the only female among many males, most with primitive passions. She felt the electromagnetic sexual energy of males competing for mating rights. Some stared at her openly, others from the corners of their eyes, but to all she was the secret star in their fantasies, playing a lurid interlude on the inside of their skulls.

Fari looked at Mac. He was a few yards away doing a complex aerobic routine, keeping perfect time with the music. He was obviously in good shape. His eyes were closed and occasionally his hands reached out for an invisible partner. Fari studied those strong hands and long, broad fingers – pitcher's hands. Sudden warmth spread through her belly and she looked away.

After the exercise routine, JD called the team together and explained the change in schedule, without mentioning why. "The media people will be let in at eleven o'clock. Fifteen minutes from now."

He was interrupted by shouts and whistles, everyone looking and pointing at Fari. They had seen the crowd of journalists outside the stadium and knew they were here to see one person, Fastball Fari.

"The same rules apply," JD continued. "The journalists can take their photos and scream to their heart's content, but they're not allowed on the field. For your part, you're not obliged to grant an interview, but as a courtesy to the fans, you're encouraged to do so. At noon it's all over and we'll break for lunch."

JD pulled Fari and Mac aside for a private conference. He asked Fari if she would pitch to a few batters in front of the journalists. "I know you're not comfortable with all this hysteria, but we gotta deal with it. The fans buy the tickets and the media is our connection to the fans."

Fari understood and consented graciously. She looked at the ground and hunched her shoulders. "No interviews, please."

JD squeezed her arm. "No problem. Just put on a little show for the cameras." His eyes sharpened. "Baseball is a *spectator* sport."

Fari laughed loudly, surprising Mac and nearby players. To Mac, her laughter sounded genuine – a glimpse of the real, inner Fari.

The media people crowded into the areas around third base, home plate and first base. Already there were more journalists than anyone could remember and more arriving. Mac recognized the principal members of the local media, but most of the others were strangers.

Fari walked toward the infield with her head down, her face hidden by her cap. She glanced up once quickly and could hardly believe her eyes. People scrambled on top of the dugouts, stood on the seats, grappled and shoved each other. The lenses of their cameras appeared like a sea of black holes.

She gasped and looked away. Her heart banged against her rib-cage like a trapped animal. One thought filled her mind; turn and run!

Fari, Papa whispered. *Fari.*

She stopped, stood still and closed her eyes. She concentrated on her breathing; inhaling deeply, exhaling slowly. Gradually, her heart slowed and she discovered the entrance to her cocoon. Immediately, she found herself walking along the seashore, the sand soft and hot beneath her feet. She opened her eyes and watched the waves roll in and smash against the beach. She walked up the mound and stood on the rubber. A batter stood at home plate, crouched over, waving his bat.

In the silence between waves, she heard the cry of a sea bird, a cry of joy and triumph. She saw the pitch form in her mind, reared back and unloaded a fire ball.

The batter blinked and the catcher fell back on his butt. Journalists behind home plate shouted and jostled with each other, training their cameras on the radar guns. Others shouted into microphones or cell phones. "We're watching history in the making!"

However, after ten pitches the journalists became noticeably quieter. They even forgot about their cell phones and cameras. They realized that Fari Madrigal was a phenomenal pitcher!

Mac stood off to one side and watched this awesome display of talent and power. His phone vibrated. "Yeah?"

"Hey, Mac, it's me." It was Stew. "I'm out here in the parking lots. You wouldn't believe it, man. Now there're *six* satellite trucks. Also, lots of other people are showing up. High school kids mostly, but adults too. A little while ago, a minivan pulled in with a girl's little league team. They unfolded a big banner that says, 'Farmington for Fastball Fari.'"

"Farmington?"

"It's a little town about sixty miles southwest. The girls are hanging out by the portable hot dog stand. There's also an ice cream truck and a coffee truck. A little while ago I saw some kid selling T-shirts with Fari's face on the front. Can he do that?"

"I dunno," answered Mac. "But it sure is happening fast. The circus is on!"

"Oh, yeah. Great shots for the media guys, but what they really want is Fastball Fari."

"Damn."

"Yeah. Howard called a security firm and they set up barricades. But he likes the commotion. It stirs up more drama and interest."

"Right. Well, thanks, Stew. We'll have to come up with a new plan." Mac folded the phone and looked at Fari, the object of all this frenzied attention. How will we get home, he wondered. Do I have to wear a mustache and wig?

SEVEN

Howard Sikes stood at the window of his office and admired the crowds in the parking lots. His stomach still felt in turmoil from this morning's encounter with Frances and the prospect of losing all that money. However, the sight of those fans provided comfort.

"She'll be on the evening news all over the country," said Stephen Rains, public relations whiz. He sat in a chair in front of Howard's desk. "More publicity than we could ever want."

Howard turned away from the windows. "Yeah. It's amazing." He walked back to his desk and sat. His office was larger than Stephen's, but more austere. He didn't need symbolic expressions of power. Today he had worn his new, dark-blue pinstripe with a flashy silk tie. He had already been interviewed by two of the local TV stations, and later he would appear on NBC! He made a note to call his wife and tell her.

"Is there anything special you want me to do?" asked Stephen. They had been running commercials for the last two weeks, promising a massive giveaway of Twins paraphernalia for the season opener.

Howard laughed and his stomach unwound a little further. "Pull the commercials, Steve."

"Pull 'em?"

"Yeah. The contracts are daily, right?"

"Yes, sir."

"Pull 'em. We don't need to promote anymore. The media is doing it for us." He laughed again, pleased to see someone else getting screwed in this deal. "Now they'll lose the fifty grand a day they charged *us*."

Stephen laughed with his boss because this was expected, but he also saw the beauty in this double-cross.

"As far as promotions go," Howard continued. "We don't have to give away anything for the rest of the season. All home games are sold out!" Reminding himself of this was good therapy. For example, they would save on the promotional budget, and he could raise the concession prices – tack another fifty cents on hot dogs and beer.

Stephen leaned closer to Howard's desk. "Hey, I just thought of something. We'll have a special uniform made for Fari. We'll have it made at *Victoria's Secret!*"

Howard laughed. "Yeah! A sheer negligee with pin stripes."

"We'll give her number *sixty-nine.*"

"Ha! And on the front, right across her tits, it'll say 'Twins.'"

They laughed with their shoulders hunched up, like little boys being naughty in the bathroom. Howard's phone rang. He composed himself, picked it up, then covered the mouthpiece. "Will you excuse me please, Steve?"

"Oh, sure." Stephen jumped up and headed for the door. "We'll talk later."

As soon as Stephen left the office, Howard hung up the phone. He had told his secretary to call him so he could get rid of Stephen. He needed to think in peace. His scary encounter with Frances this morning still commanded his attention, but he needed to concentrate on his next visitor – CEO of Midwest Productions (two television stations, five radio stations). Howard had to figure out how to squeeze more money from the local media, and yet maintain a good relationship. This was crucial in stirring up interest for the Twins in a regional market saturated with competing professional sports.

But now he had Fastball Fari, who, at this very moment, was quickly becoming the most celebrated sports personality in the country, in the world! He had scored a big coup today by giving the media an early look at Fari. At the same time, he had arranged for the local media to enter the stadium ahead of their competitors, giving them first crack at the best locations.

Howard knew, however, that the media would not stay content for long. Several local and national media people had requested interviews with Fari. Howard could not say "no," but how could he force a player to grant an interview? He couldn't, but he could *entice* a player. Indeed, this was Howard's overall, fundamental belief regarding business and life in general: Everyone had their price, whether it was fame, fortune or fantasy.

Would this work with Fari?

He thought about all the different ways Fari could exploit her image. If *he* were Fari's agent, he'd arrange public appearances, product endorsements, TV shows, the movies! He thought of a series of posters and calendars (Fari posing in her little negligee uniform). They could license clothing, lunch boxes, cups, backpacks, notebooks, everydamnthing! Or how about her own line of perfume and cosmetics? Big money in cosmetics. He saw a mountain of millions off in the distance, growing higher by the second.

He flashed on a brilliant idea. *Fastball Fari dolls!* How many girls in America would want an official Fari doll? Millions! And the Twins would get royalties on every doll.

Howard liked this idea so much, he made a note. Immediately, however, he sank back to reality with a hollow thud; he did not have Fari. Frances has Fari.

Frances and Fari were not good candidates for enticement. Apparently, they didn't care about the money. This attitude was far beyond Howard's experience, his *ken*. This made Frances a very dangerous character.

Howard had a policy of never agreeing to first proposals; he'd rather fight and negotiate and make the best deal for himself and his companies. Although he told Frances he'd "think about" complying with her demands, no way would he give up eight million dollars without a fight.

Howard pulled out his cell phone and called his favorite private investigation agency. He wanted to know more about Frances Madrigal.

*   *

Frances and Alfred worked inside the Command Center, monitoring two computers and four cell phones. Alfred took care of the Internet and e-mail, while Frances worked the phones.

Alfred didn't look at all like his bigger cousin. He was short, thin and round-shouldered. He wore a black T-shirt, black jeans and black tennis shoes. A shadow across his upper lip announced the struggling birth of a mustache. The most striking thing about him was his hair; it hung loosely in long, ropey dreadlocks.

Frances loved Alfred's hair. Dreadlocks were common in the Dominican Republic. She complimented him and got his permission to touch it.

When they first started working together, they immediately developed a comfortable relationship. Alfred preferred to work in silence, which suited Frances just fine. When they did speak, the conversation resembled the staccato urgency of commanders in battle.

For the last two hours, the rush of in-coming messages overwhelmed their ability to monitor them. Alfred devised a program that scanned the text of each message, identified key words and separated the messages into categories.

"How many have the word 'agent?'" asked Frances.

"One thousand four hundred and eighty-two."

"Get rid of them, please. How many with the word 'love?'"

"Wow, over six thousand!"

"How do we work with that?"

"How about if we scan for words like 'sex' or 'fuck?'"

Frances laughed and punched him on the shoulder. "*There* you go, Alfred! Also, look for all those other nasty words. We'll send those to the trash heap."

In this way they worked out a system. They also monitored a special e-mail address Frances had sent to the promotional departments of corporations across the United States. This address had accumulated three hundred and fifty-four responses and grew steadily. It was this correspondence that most interested Frances. Occasionally, she asked Alfred to roam through these messages. They found clothing and shoe manufacturers (especially in sports apparel), soft drink makers, hamburger and pizza empires, eye-wear, cosmetics, automobiles, furniture, liquor, even a national hardware chain. There were several messages from Hollywood producers and agents.

Frances had her eyes on one particular corporation; United Brands Company, formerly known as United Fruit, but so far United Brands had not responded.

The red cell phone rang. Only five people had the number to this phone. Frances picked it up. "Empresas Marchena. En que puedo servirle?"

"Hello? Uh, excuse me, but is Frances Marchena there?"

Frances recognized Howard Sikes. "Un momento, por favor." She put Howard on hold and had no doubt he would stay there. She turned to Alfred. "Is there any movement on those bank accounts?"

Alfred punched a few keys and waited three seconds. "Nope. Not yet."

"Thanks." Frances flicked a button on the phone. "Hello? This is Frances Marchena."

"Hello, Mrs. Marchena. How are you? This is Howard Sikes. I would like to . . ."

"Excuse me, Mr. Sikes, but I notice you have not yet made the deposits."

"Uh, yes, that's right. It takes time to get that kind of money together. In the meantime, I expect to meet with you and Fari tomorrow afternoon, as we agreed. We'll go over the terms of the contract. You and Fari can read it and maybe she'll sign before the game on Sunday."

Frances had plenty of experience in academia, but very little in the world of business. However, she knew that the essential ingredient in any negotiation was *power*, and the only power she needed was her daughter Fari. Howard Sikes badly needed Fari Madrigal and he would pay – one way or the other. "Mr. Sikes, Fari and I will meet with you at your office tomorrow afternoon. Good day, sir."

She cut him off and laid the phone on the table. This was rude, but thinking about United Brands had put her in a black mood. She turned off all the phones and stood up to stretch. "I need a break, Alfred. The phones are off. I'll be back in a little while."

"Cool." Alfred plugged in ear buds, switched on the music, and waved goodbye.

JD's house was dark and quiet in the late afternoon. Frances noticed only two journalists standing across the street. She went into the kitchen for a glass of juice and returned to the front room.

Lake of the Isles appeared as cold and hard as steel. There were no ducks or geese in the water and all other birds had gone home, hunkered down against the chilly wind. Frances was struck at how gray and lifeless it looked, with the trees still bare and the grass and bushes brown.

She remembered a time when she and Jose had traveled to a town close to the Haitian frontier. It was a startling sight – the Dominican side was green and alive, while the Haitian side lay black and twisted, as if it was the outer boundary of some catastrophic event.

Frances had felt a great urge to *do* something, to help somehow, but she did not have the resources. Now, however, she *does* have the resources, thanks to Fari, bless her heart. A sudden rush of affection swept through her. Since Jose died, she and Fari had become more like sisters than mother and daughter.

Ah, Jose, my love. She closed her eyes and felt her husband's strong arms wrap around her. She laid her cheek on his shoulder and smelled the clean, soapy scent of the shirt and the musky odor of the man.

She shivered. I'm so cold, Jose, and so alone.

I'll warm you, my love, he answered. And you know you're never alone. He rubbed his finger on the secret place behind her ear.

Frances shivered again, this time with pleasure. Help me, Jose. Guide me. The interest in Fari is *overwhelming*.

"Frances?"

Her eyes snapped open. "Hello, JD."

"Sorry if I surprised you." JD stepped into the room carrying a briefcase, still dressed in his Twins uniform. He saw the tears on her cheeks, but did not comment. "I'm taking a dinner break." He smiled around the stubby cigar. "I have to get back to the stadium later."

Frances smiled back. "What's for dinner? The cigar?"

They both laughed. He dropped the briefcase and sat heavily in a nearby chair. "I had a very productive day. Three hundred and fifty emails, seventy-five phone calls, eight interview requests."

"You should see how it is in the Command Center."

They looked at each other for a second and the humor faded. Frances wrapped her arms around herself. "I'm sorry to bring such chaos into your life, JD. You've been very kind to help us, but maybe I should move on."

"Aw, nonsense." He waved his hand in the air. "You're no bother. It's all those peeping Toms." He laughed. "Besides I don't mind a little chaos, as long as I come by it honestly. You and Fari are a very pleasant surprise in my life and I'm honored to have you living in my house. Please stay."

Frances heard the sincerity in his voice. "Thank you, JD. I believe I will stay, for a while longer anyway." She looked out at the gray, rainy day. "I had no idea the response would be so heavy. Poor Fari. She's living in a hurricane."

"Yeah, but the eye of the storm is usually calm. She'll be all right with Cleo and Mac."

"Yes. I feel much better knowing they're together in a secret place. I guess *we're* the ones caught up in the storm."

JD laughed and stood up. "That's right! As for myself, I love every minute of it. If you'll excuse me, I'll take a shower. Are you hungry?"

"Yes, I am, come to think of it."

"Okay. I'll be right back. I make a great veggie sandwich." JD left, heading for the elevator.

Frances sat back on the sofa and stared at the sleeping landscape. Once again, she pictured the devastated hills of Haiti. She imagined those hills green again, breathing life back into the earth and into the Haitian people.

Reforestation in Haiti. Reforestation throughout Central America.

She wondered who should have that honor, but the answer was obvious; in fact, poetic justice demanded it. We'll give that job to Ronald McDonald.

*   *

Doc Harris sat alone in the study of his suburban home, eating a pizza and watching TV. He had been to the stadium earlier, but raced home to watch the media free-for-all that occurred that morning in the stadium. Fari pitched in front of the cameras for over fifteen minutes.

He ate the pizza with one hand and worked the remote with the other. There! He saw the unmistakable form of Fastball Fari. The camera angles kept changing as Fari threw pitch after pitch. Doc noticed she worked quickly, every ten or twelve seconds she unloaded a pitch. Her movements appeared precise, fluid and smooth. He saw an additional movement around her chest and leaned closer to the TV. It looked like she wasn't wearing a bra!

The segment on Fari was over and they moved on to other news. Doc continued surfing channels, chewing mindlessly on the pizza. As the brightly colored images flashed before his eyes, a fantasy appeared in his mind: Fari sat on a towel wearing a skimpy bikini, her brown skin smooth and wet. Doc came into the picture wearing his bathing thong, showing off the bulge at his crotch. Fari looked into his eyes and he grew hard . . .

"Skip?"

Doc choked on the pizza and almost spit cheese on the TV. He turned around quickly, gagging into napkins. It was Sherry! "Jesus," he gasped. "You scared the hell out of me."

"Sorry. I didn't know you were here." Sherry stood tall and thin, with the wiry musculature of a fanatic exerciser. Her lips appeared as a slash of bright red; her dark eyes peered out from shadows. She stood with her back slightly bowed, as if ready to fight or flee.

Doc jumped up abruptly and flicked off the TV. Is this really a coincidence, or did she know he was here? He searched his head for something to say and his eyes fell on the pizza. "Want some pizza?"

She regarded him silently for a second. "No thanks." Her voice issued flat, without inflection.

Doc wiped his hands and walked to his desk. He searched through his files, looking for something, then found it. "Here it is!" He held up the folder for her inspection. "I just stopped by to pick this up. I have to get back to the office."

Sherry merely stared at him.

Doc felt her eyes like hot pokers. For one spilt second, he recalled the incredible scene inside this very room almost two months ago when Sherry had confronted him with the hard, cold evidence of his infidelity.

She had told him divorce was out of the question, for the moment, then dictated the terms and conditions of their future life together, concluding with these words: "And if you don't like it, or can't make an effort, then I and my family will *crush* you! *Do you hear me?*" Her voice had risen to a piercing shriek. "*We will crush you!*"

Doc had not doubted it one bit. From then on his life hung by a thread and Sherry held the scissors.

*　　　　　　　*

Kim stirred a big wooden spoon inside a steaming pot. "These noodles are ready, Dad."

"Okay. Put 'em on simmer, then see how the sauce looks." Mac stood at a rectangular island in the middle of the kitchen, slicing to-matoes for the salad. He wore a long, gaudy apron over his clothes. Tonight they were having Macquire's special tuna fish spaghetti.

They were in Mac and Cleo's condo. Kim had crossed over earlier through the connecting door. Fari was still next door and expected soon for dinner. Cleo had a prior engagement this evening, co-hosting a charity dinner sponsored by the Minneapolis Athletic Club.

Mac didn't like this condo. It reminded him of a hotel – strange furniture and decoration, strange appliances, strange sheets and pil-lows. It gave him the unsettled feeling of being on the road. The only reflections of his personal identity were the clothes on his back.

He had to admit, however, that JD's choice of these condos made sense. They were surrounded by a hundred other condos, all exactly the same. As long as they kept off the street and kept the condo a secret, they should remain hidden to the media's eyes and ears.

All in all, it wasn't too bad. The main problem was transportation. Kim and Mac, both avid readers of spy novels, came up with sever-al clandestine routines. Minneapolis' famous skyway system figured heavily in their strategy. The skyways offered so many twists, turns, entrances and exits, it was almost impossible for anyone to follow them.

Mac finished with the tomatoes and started in on the peppers. At that moment, they heard a soft knock on the connecting door.

"That's Fari!" Kim skipped down the hallway and opened the door. "Hi, Fari, come on in."

Mac looked up, but when he saw Fari, he held the knife still and moved his fingers away. "Hi."

"Hi." She gave him a brief flash of eyes. She wore a white silk blouse and gray slacks, revealing a graceful, hourglass figure. Her hair hung long and loose, slightly curly. She held a baseball in her right hand. "Tengo hambre," she announced. She sat on a stool next to Mac. "I heard about Macquire special."

Immediately, Mac noticed the light scent of lilacs and his ears buzzed. "That's right. Macquire's special spaghetti dinner."

Kim turned down the flame on the sauce. "We're about ready." She looked at Fari. "Would you like a little red wine?"

Fari glanced toward Mac. "Sera bien?"

"Sure. Pour me one too, Kim."

Fari noticed a difference in Mac tonight, but she wasn't sure what. She too felt different. She had passed a crucial test this morning in front of all those journalists. Despite the panic, she had maintained the integrity of her cocoon. Of course, the real test would come this Sunday when the stadium would be jammed with forty thousand people.

"I propose a toast," said Kim, handing them both a glass of wine. She had also poured herself an inch or two. She raised her glass and announced, "To a *safe* safe house!"

They laughed and clinked glasses. Fari asked if she could help with anything.

"Naw," answered Kim. "We got it together. The special noodles are ready, the special sauce is ready and now we're making the special garlic bread."

Fari nodded. "Sounds special." She toasted the special dinner.

Mac and Kim argued good-naturedly about how they should warm the bread. Kim argued for her mother's method, but the second time she said "Mama," her voice stuttered and stopped. She stood motionless in the center of the kitchen, head lowered, tears rolling down her cheeks.

Mac stepped over to his daughter and folded her gently into his arms. Kim buried her face in his chest and sobbed.

Fari looked away, uncomfortable in the presence of such private passion. On the other hand, this was the stuff of life – at the very heart of Mac and Kim – just as her father was at the heart of her. She swung her legs off the stool, stepped into the center of the kitchen and wrapped her arms around this family of two.

EIGHT

Friday: March 28

"Excuse me, Mr. Sikes, but Mr. Chuck Osborne is on line two."

Howard felt a jolt of excitement; Chuck was the top detective at the Sloan Investigative Agency. He had called Chuck yesterday with the info on Frances. "Thank you. I'll take the call."

"Hello? Mr. Sikes? Can you hear me okay?"

"Good morning, Chuck. I hear you fine. How's the Dominican Republic?"

"Hot and green. I have a few facts about Frances Marchena."

"Go ahead, Chuck."

Five minutes later, as Howard dropped the office phone in the cradle, his heart grew wings and flew to the heights. He was shocked, scandalized and ecstatic. How should he properly exploit this information?

He knew he was at a disadvantage in his negotiations with Frances. For one thing, she wasn't interested in money, and for another, she controlled Fari. Although Howard and Frances had shook hands on the contract, they had not agreed on the *informal* contract – that is, the additional eight million dollars!

Howard had to tread very lightly here. He knew he had little power in this transaction. Also, he could do nothing that might jeopardize Fari's association with the Twins. Yet he did not want to pay out this extra money!

Now, however, he held a potential piece of power, even though it bordered on dirty and underhanded. He wasn't averse to using such methods, especially faced with the potential loss of eight million bucks. He decided it was worth the try, even though it went against his own premonitions.

*　　　　　*

Fari stood in her bathroom wearing only a thick cotton robe. Droplets of water clung to her eyelashes and her hair hung wet. She looked at herself in the mirror and listened to the rhythm of her heart. She felt the warm afterglow of throwing good pitches, getting strike-outs, and hearing the praise of her teammates.

However, there was also a measure of dread. When she had walked off the mound yesterday, the sound of the surf had been replaced by the screams of journalists. It had sounded like a wail of savage urgency, as if she had something they desperately needed.

She shivered at the memory. Mama was right; the media here were much more intense.

JD had given her, Cleo and Mac the rest of the day off today, allowing them to get away safely and settle into their new home. Later this afternoon, she and Mama would meet with Howard Sikes.

Fari and Mac had left the stadium inside the back of another delivery van. There were no windows in back and Fari had not seen the crowd in the parking lots. Mac described it to her. They had laughed at the presence of hot dog trucks and the boy selling "Fastball Fari" T-shirts. (Fari remembered what Mama had said: "You'll create opportunities for all the big and little capitalists. We'll go after the big ones.")

Fari padded into the bedroom and sat on a sofa facing a large, ornate window. Over the roofs of nearby condos, she saw the sparkling blue surface of the ponds in Loring Park, four blocks away. People gathered along the shore, cars moved in the background.

She looked into the sky. There were no trees around the condo, no birds singing or flying. The piece of sky she looked at could be anywhere in the world. She focused on that thought and allowed herself to meditate.

Mac had mentioned a girl's little league team had arrived in the stadium parking lot, along with a lot of other people. These were not journalists, they were *fans*, and they had come to see Fastball Fari.

She remembered the same thing had happened when she first

started pitching with the Sanchez Tigers. Suddenly, a lot of people wanted something from Fari Madrigal. At first, she had been surprised by these offers, but even more shocked by their aggressive manner. People called on the phone and rang the doorbell at all hours of the day and night.

Fari was not comfortable around strangers in the first place, but to imagine facing crowds of strangers, with everyone staring at her, wanting to talk to her, wanting to touch her – the mere thought of it made her blood freeze. However, there had been one young man who had not been aggressive; a Catholic priest who worked at a nearby orphanage. Fari had decided to meet with this man because he hadn't offered money, favors or love.

He had asked Fari to visit the orphanage. The children had heard about Fari and were excited about her prospects of pitching in the Dominican pro leagues. "You're their hero," he had said.

"What's a hero, Father?" Fari had asked.

The priest had laughed. "I'm not sure exactly. My hero is St. Frances of Assisi. I guess because he *inspires* me. He makes me want to be a better Christian and a better man."

Fari had thought this over. In that case, her father was her hero, along with Whitey Ford, Sandy Koufax and Nolan Ryan. However, the priest had referred to a religious figure within a moral context. "I like to pitch a baseball, Father. How can that inspire anyone?"

"You worked hard to become a pitcher, didn't you? You had to learn and practice and work at it, right?"

"Yes."

"Well, these kids need to know that. If you believe in yourself and work hard, you can be a success. This is very important for these kids to know. They've lost everything, but you can give them something they need more than anything else: hope."

Fari had agreed to visit the orphanage, but only in secret – no media, no cameras. She had enjoyed meeting with the kids. They had been shy and polite, but she had seen the excitement in their eyes, and something else as well – a sense of pride that Fari Madrigal would favor them with this personal visit.

The priest had seen this too and whispered to Fari. "The wellspring of hope is a feeling of self-worth."

And now, as Fari remembered this, she felt disappointed she couldn't meet with the girls' little league team. Those girls saw her as a "hero," an inspiration, but how could she walk through those crowds without being shouted at or grabbed? She was a prisoner of her own anxieties, and "fame" made the prison even stronger.

*   *

Howard Sikes sat on the armchair in his office, while Frances and Fari sat across from him on the sofa. Between them was a small, glass-topped coffee table holding a silver tray with a coffee pot, cups and pastries. Howard sipped coffee and munched on a cinnamon roll, but Fari and Frances had declined refreshment.

Fari wore a long-sleeved flannel shirt, jeans and walking shoes. Her hair hung long and loose; she hadn't worn a cap and did not carry a baseball. Frances wore her customary business suit and carried a shoulder bag. Inside the bag were her cell phones and a small cassette recorder, now turned on and recording.

They had already reviewed the standard contract and Frances had approved, although she advised Fari in Spanish not to sign it just yet. Howard continued to exhibit an expansive mood, smiling and chomping on the pastry, and sneaking secret looks at Fari. Frances had wanted Fari at this meeting to distract Mr. Sikes, but he seemed different today – too self-assured – and this worried her.

Howard swallowed, patted his lips and spoke. "Well, Mrs. Marchena, will Fari sign the contract today or tomorrow? We'd love to announce your formal association with the Minnesota Twins, preferably before the game on Sunday."

Fari sat quietly, motionless, her eyes on the floor. Her role in this encounter was merely aesthetic. Mama dangled her in front of Howard Sikes like a bright light, obscuring his vision and thinking. Fari endured this violation because it was part of their plan, and the plan was worth the pain and discomfort.

"As I told you earlier, Mr. Sikes, Fari will sign the contract when you've made the donations."

Howard leaned back, crossed his legs and lost the smile. "Eight million dollars is a lot of money, Mrs. Marchena. You're asking me to gamble too much. Fari is untested in the majors. I don't make business decisions based on faith. Besides, we shook hands on a deal."

Frances nodded. "That's right. We shook hands on the *contract*, not the donations."

"Yes. So why should I throw away eight million dollars?"

"Excuse me, sir, but you're not throwing it away, you're making *donations*. You'll get most of it back on tax breaks. Plus, you get Fari Madrigal. You might lose three million."

Howard was sipping coffee and almost choked. "*Three million?* Is that all?"

Frances smiled and shook her head. This man is worth hundreds of millions. She looked at it this way; if she had nine hundred dollars and had to pay three, would this hurt, especially if she was paying for Fastball Fari? "You exaggerate, sir. With Fari on the Minnesota Twins, you'll recover that money and make even more."

Howard admitted to himself that this was probably true, but beside the point. Why pay more when he might get a better deal? Besides, he was the expert here; he was the *capitalist*, she was the *communist*. He leaned forward, looked Frances in the eyes and spoke softly. "Here's the deal. I'll donate three million, domestically, and I promise not to mention your conviction for second degree murder." He sat back and savored the shock on both their faces.

Fari felt waves of fury and sorrow emanate from her mother. In a reflex, to her own surprise and shock, she reached out and grabbed Mama's arm. How did Mr. Sikes know about the Red Gang?

In an instant, Frances was transported in time to a series of momentous events in her life. She remembered it very clearly; the workers on strike, Felipe killed, his funeral, and the rage of the families and workers. She had almost lost her mind from grief and hatred. Five days later, she and four friends ambushed one of the private security guards who had fired on the workers. They had waited on a small hill in the plantation, and when he passed on his bicycle they threw a barrage of rocks. Two rocks hit him square on the head, knocked him into a coma, and he never recovered.

The strikes, the violence and the trial of the "Red Gang" – three girls and two boys – had captured the country's attention for one long summer. The "gang" members were sons and daughters of plantation workers and all were juveniles. Frances and her friends were found guilty of second-degree murder, but they never spent much time in jail. To the authorities they had been juvenile delinquents, but at home on the plantation they had been heroes.

Frances had long since made peace with herself and with the family of the security guard. Also, she knew this news would eventually surface, but she was surprised Mr. Sikes could be the culprit. And now he wanted to use this secret shame as a weapon. She answered him calmly. "You talk about handshakes as if it's an honorable procedure, and yet you threaten me with events that happened when I was sixteen years old. What do you call that?"

"Business," Howard answered immediately.

"Extorción!" Fari exclaimed in a loud voice.

Howard's eyes flew open and he leaned back in his chair. He studied Fari for a moment, but she continued to stare at the floor. It was the first word she has said since entering the office.

"Fari's right, Mr. Sikes. I admit I don't know much about business, but I know about dirty tricks and power politics." She paused, leaned forward and spoke firmly. "I have three pieces of power, Mr. Sikes, while you have *none*. First, your threat of exposure doesn't bother me because the news will come out anyway. Second, Fari and I can walk out of this office and talk to the New York Yankees, handshake or no handshake." She reached into her bag, pulled out the recorder and inserted a tape. "Third, since you like extortion, Mr. Sikes, please listen to this recording and ponder its meaning."

NINE

Saturday: March 29

Frances had been awarded a bachelor's degree in sociology from the University of Santo Domingo. The title of her honor's thesis was "The Role of Commercial Propaganda in Mass Communications," focusing particularly on the national television networks in the United States. She had recorded and analyzed hundreds of hours of programming offered by these networks, categorized the programs according to theme and content, and concentrated on the advertisements.

She had argued that television was supported by a corporate structure dedicated to sales and profits. Thus, it was in the media interest, and certainly within its power, to create "stars" – public personalities who attracted the attention of millions. These stars enticed viewers to watch programs supported by slick sales pitches.

Corporate promotional departments employed statisticians, psychologists and sociologists to study the TV audience, breaking it down according to age group, education, income level, geographic location and myriad other factors. Commercials were then tailored carefully for the interests and tastes of all likely audiences.

It was not surprising, therefore, that commercials tended to reflect prevailing attitudes, prejudices and stereotypes. For example, products and services related to the kitchen almost always featured a conservatively dressed woman, since this was her place or "role" in the home. Commercials for cars, beer or tools – designed to appeal mostly to men – also featured women, but nearly naked.

Further, Frances believed that television not only reflected popular culture, but created it, shaped it and reinforced it. For example, promotional departments seized the symbols and language of emerging social movements and turned them into sales strategies. In this way, cultural quirks became cleaned-up, sanitized and no longer quirky. Frances had called it "homogenizing the culture."

However, the most sinister element about television, according to Frances, was the encouragement of a lifestyle dedicated to *consumption*. In fact, consumption has become the mainstay of the world economy and US citizens were regularly referred to as "consumers."

Frances believed the meaning of life in the US was to work hard, make money, then spend it. Further, one's personal identity was connected directly to ownership; *what you own defines who you are, and the more you own the more you are*. Unfortunately, in this great game of consumption, huge swathes of the earth have been ravaged and whole populations displaced or held hostage.

This Saturday morning, Frances followed closely the intense reporting on Fari. Although most of the hoopla still centered on historic, ethnic and sexual issues, the videos taken on Thursday demonstrated clearly that Fari was also a superior baseball pitcher. This delivered an extra kick to the reporting; former pitchers and coaches were asked to give their opinions of Fastball Fari.

Frances knew, however, that if a celebrity refused to cooperate or, even worse, committed some social sin or scandal, the media – with the public support – was likely to strike back. In this regard, she was keenly aware that Fari has not yet granted an interview or said more than ten words in front of the cameras. Now, two days after her last public appearance, Frances noticed a new tone creeping into the reporting.

For example, one local channel ran videos of fans complaining about Fari's refusal to appear in public. Then several reports surfaced from "reliable sources" claiming that Fari spoke perfect English and avoided the fans and cameras by traveling in disguise, usually hidden inside different vehicles. These escapes often involved the Twins' pitching coach, Chet Macquire.

Most of these stories simply reported that Mr. Macquire accompanied Fari, but the tabloids and gossip columns expanded on this aspect of the story. They noted that Mr. Macquire had recently become a widower, and he and his daughter no longer lived in their Richfield home. Could they be staying with Fari? One big, happy family? Was there Sex and Romance?

Television gossip programs also focused on Fari. Frances had seen one program that presented a slow motion, enlarged image of Fari's chest as she pitched. At the bottom of the screen was the question, "Does she or doesn't she?" The young, good-looking couple hosting the show made jokes about the advantages of "braless pitching."

Frances laughed with wicked sarcasm. Well, no matter, she thought, at eleven o'clock today there would be the annual spring ritual to kick off the season—a press conference to introduce the Minnesota Twins team to the media and fans. This should reduce much of the pressure that had been mounting for access to Fari.

Then, tomorrow, on Sunday, Fari would be the starting pitcher in the Twins' season opener against the Chicago White Sox. The crowd would surpass forty thousand, and the frenzy to secure tickets had reached the level of desperate and insane. Alfred told her he had seen offers on the Internet for up to eight thousand dollars!

The game would be televised worldwide and the publicity and promotion were getting ferocious: "Tune in tomorrow at three in the afternoon to watch *Fastball Fari* in her rookie debut with the Minnesota Twins, brought to you by *Dodge Trucks!*"

Frances appreciated the bitter irony of exploiting Fari's image in the interest of profit. Fari, former pitcher for the Baltimore Bananas, was entirely oblivious of this "stardom" conferred upon her, yet her identity had already generated huge amounts of revenue.

In this regard, Frances remembered a provision in the contract with the Twins; if Fari appeared in a promotional event "for monetary remuneration" while wearing a Minnesota Twins uniform or anything with a Twins trademark, the Twins were entitled to a royalty payment.

Frances believed this offered another way to squeeze Howard. She'd have to think about it.

Yesterday afternoon Howard had made two wire transfers into separate bank accounts and Fari had signed the contract. Howard had not been happy, but he had no choice. Further, he hated the stupidity of getting beat by his own big mouth.

Yesterday evening's news programs reported that Fari Madrigal had signed a contract with the Twins: "Howard Sikes announced that

Fastball Fari Madrigal signed a one year contract with the Minnesota Twins. Mr. Sikes refused to disclose the terms of the contract. However, Channel Four News has learned that, incredibly, Fari Madrigal signed a standard, *minimum wage* contract!

"The Twins have not confirmed or denied this report, and efforts to contact Fari Madrigal or her agent, Frances Madrigal, were not successful."

This news caused another media firestorm, but Howard replied "no comment" to all questions. However, he had told a few members of the board about the contract, so the news was bound to get out, just as he'd hoped it would. He was anxious to demonstrate his deft negotiating skills.

Nevertheless, there was an immediate backlash from women's groups and civil rights groups, complaining that a pitcher of Fari's caliber ought to be paid more than the minimum. Maybe there was a little discrimination going on?

This reaction had not been anticipated and Howard shut up and laid low. However, the media exposure had lifted his identity to a new high, and he was so pleased he didn't care if he became a hero to some and a villain to others.

*   *

Sweat tickled Doc's lower back and his bowels rolled. He hated these Saturday sessions with his psychologist, Herman Schumacher. For one hour he had to sit and subject himself to the humiliation of confession. In retaliation, he "confessed" only lies. In preparation, he had taken a hit of speed before arriving at Herman's office and now his heart banged furiously. He knew Herman wanted to "read" his body language and he willed his body to relax.

Herman saw Doc's edginess and tiny, bottomless pupils. He wondered if Doc had gotten into his own drug supply. He made a note to have Sherry insist on a toxicology exam.

Skipper "Doc" Harris was proving to be one of Herman's more difficult clients. Doc had done well in medical school, which included a few classes in psychology that allowed him to prepare defenses against Herman's inquiries. Also, Doc exhibited the traditional attitude of superiority assumed by most medical doctors toward psychiatrists and psychologists. Moreover, Doc was not a willing participant; he had been forced into Herman's tender care by Sherry.

Under these circumstances, it was too much to hope for Doc's co-operation, but Herman had expected this. He found Doc to be entertaining and occasionally surprising; also, intelligent, depraved and a bit of a sociopath. He began with innocent chit-chat. "Well, the Twins have a new pitcher."

"Yeah. Fastball Fari."

"Remarkable. And not bad looking either."

Not bad looking? Doc thought Fari was absolutely stunning. But he didn't like the salacious glow in Herman's eyes, as if they were buddies sharing a dirty secret. He would not be Herman's buddy. "She's got a super fastball and great control."

"What's she like? I heard she has something like autism." Herman set down his little innocuous verbal bits.

"Asperger's Syndrome." Doc breathed a little easier. "It's a mild form of autism. She acts a little strange, but she's sharp and lucid." He almost said more, but shut his mouth abruptly. The speed gave his mouth a motor of its own.

Herman saw Doc had relaxed slightly. Now he fired a question from a different direction. "How's it going on the trip with Sherry?" He noted the sudden twitch around Doc's eyes and knew he had hit on target.

Doc's heart jumped. He hated the idea of a trip with Sherry, and why did Herman keep bringing it up? It was Sherry's great idea; leave the kids with their grandparents while she and Doc took off on a "vacation." The idea was to "make up," and find some way to live with each other amicably. Sherry had alerted Herman to this vacation idea, and now Doc had no choice but to acquiesce. However, he would *never* go on that vacation. "We've decided to postpone it for a few days," he said, lying through his teeth. "Debbie isn't feeling well."

Herman wondered about this; it was the second postponement in a month. He felt sure Doc was lying, but he'd check later with Sherry. "Then you and Sherry are getting along better?"

Doc felt a stab of anger. He gave Herman a flat look. "Why don't you ask Sherry? You talk to her more than I do. She's got *spies* everywhere."

Spies? Was this paranoia, or the truth? Herman suspected it was partially true; Sherry had "spies," but they weren't "everywhere." For that matter, Herman's secret consultations with Sherry could be called a form of espionage. In this sense, Doc's paranoia might be warranted.

"You know I don't talk to Sherry." Herman lied more smoothly than Doc. "It's just you and me."

"Yeah, right. You, me and Sherry's army. You know why I'm here, Herman. My wife is blackmailing me, and *you're* her accomplice." Doc no longer cared what he said to Herman, or what Herman reported to Sherry. If he was supposed to be "sick" or "perverted," then he would damn well be as deviant as possible. He had only one more session with Herman, and then *adios*. It didn't matter what he said anymore. Maybe he would even tell the truth.

*   *

For the past two days Fari worked hard on fielding drills. Mac had been horrified to learn she had very little experience fielding batted balls. He had known several pitchers whose careers had ended with injuries sustained by a hard linerl. In Mac's case, he'd had a broken toe and a broken nose. The toe was no big deal, but the broken nose had been scary. A line drive had zoomed straight toward his head and Mac just managed to get his glove in front of his face. Even then, the force of the ball slammed his glove into his nose and broke it. If he had been a split second too late, he might've been hurt seriously or even killed.

Fortunately, Fari exhibited excellent hand and eye coordination and quick reactions. Mac had put her together with Cleo and Brent Shiner, their second baseman, one of the best fielders in the league. Soon, under Cleo's constant chatter and laughter, Brent had loosened up and taught Fari how to handle hit balls. In any case, Mac didn't really care if she caught the ball or not. If the ball came hot and hard, he wanted her to jump out of the way.

"But it will be a hit," Fari had protested.

"Better they get a hit than the ball hitting you."

Cleo hit another grounder, harder this time. Fari quickly shifted sideways, crouched with the glove down below her knees, and snared the hot shot. She spun quickly and threw the ball to Mac, who stood at first base. She felt pleased with herself and inhaled deeply.

She loved the sounds, smells and sights of this baseball field. Papa had taken her to her first baseball game when she was only three. At that time in Costa Rica – a country wild about soccer – baseball had few followers and players. The huge Sabana Park in southern San Jose had two baseball diamonds with a few outdoor bleachers.

Fari had become fascinated immediately. Papa had been a pitcher, and she saw that it was the pitcher who set the tone and pace of the game. The pitcher and the batter held everyone's attention; it was a personal duel in front of an audience – until the ball was hit, then all attention followed the ball.

It wasn't until they had moved to the Dominican Republic that Fari attended her first professional baseball game. She had been shocked at the size of the stadium and the thousands of strangers. At this point in her life – she was sixteen – Fari had learned to venture safely into public areas by wearing "disguises,";baggy clothes, oversize hats, big sunglasses. These disguises were not intended to protect her identity – no one knew who she was – rather, they provided a barrier, an obstacle, between her and the world.

She loved the hot dogs at the baseball stadium, and she, Mama and Papa ate hot dogs and drank strong coffee. Fari cheered for every player from each team, and did not care who won or lost. The excitement for her was in the total experience of the game – the movement of the ball and the players, the green grass of the field, the plump white bases forming a diamond, and the crowd. When there was action on the field, there was action in the stands. The passion – either jubilant or disgusted – flashed around the stadium in an instant, uniting thousands of strangers into one common identity. These were sublime moments for Fari, who could not connect socially any other way.

For Fari, the purity of baseball begins with the ball, the most natural shape in the universe – moons, worlds, stars and solar systems all assume a spherical shape. The ball flies through space and demands the total attention of the teams and spectators. The teams are coherent social units consisting of separate parts, each with a different, vital role to perform. This too is consistent with universal principles, and reveals the necessity and beauty of diversity. It was this social unity that Fari found so difficult to realize.

Papa had explained the baseball team concept like this: "The manager is the head, the pitcher is the heart and the fielders are the limbs, bone and muscle." He told Fari to pace her pitches with a steady rhythm, like a heartbeat – not too fast and not too slow. In this way, she would control the pace of the game and force the batter to come forward into the batter's box – into the target zone.

On the "Baltimore Bananas," Fari's imaginary team, her teammates stood behind her, ready to catch the ball, but they were only ghosts, mere concepts. She had badly wanted to become part of a real flesh and blood team, but the social phobias always seemed stronger.

When Fari was younger, before they moved to the Dominican Republic, she took "anti-anxiety" drugs for a few months. Her entire personality seemed to collapse into a state of calm repose. The phobias receded a bit and she actually managed to join a little league baseball team. The boys were all Costa Rican and not very good, but they liked to play the game. However, they weren't too sure about having a girl on the team. Although Fari felt thrilled to be a teammate, her teammates did not feel the same toward her.

Even here, now, in Target Field, she felt the isolation and segregation; the only woman in North American major league baseball, the only woman on this baseball field. She and her teammates hardly knew each other, and their relations were further complicated by sex and tradition. She yearned to be "normal," just another teammate, and not a sports enigma or pornographic celebrity.

Cleo hit a particularly vicious line drive, straight toward Fari's head! She dropped quickly and fell back on her butt laughing. "Dios mio!"

"Sorry!" Cleo yelled.

"That's it for today," Mac called out. He strolled over and helped Fari to her feet. "Quick reactions," he said with a smile.

Fari dusted off her uniform and smiled back. "Gracias. Cleo es peligroso."

"He sure is. JD wants to know if you'll throw batting practice. He figures it will help get you accustomed to the mound."

Fari's heart lit up. This exercise offered an opportunity to interact with her teammates in her *formal* identity – as a baseball pitcher, a teammate – rather than as a woman.

"It's an easy job," said Mac. "Just lob the ball into the sweet zone.

Let the boys hit it." He looked her over; she breathed a little hard, a shine of sweat on her face, wet in the armpits, but still awesomely gorgeous.

Fari looked toward home plate. "Me gustaría mucho."

"Just throw for fifteen minutes or so, give everyone a chance to take a few swings, then we'll break for lunch."

Fari nodded and smiled, still not looking at him. "Okay." She trotted toward the mound.

The stadium was empty, except for the players and coaches, and Fari could relax a little. Also, pitching batting practice did not require retreating into her cocoon. The grounds crew had set up the pitcher's shield and she didn't have to worry about hot grounders or liners. A group of players gathered around the dugout and the batting cage. A few fielders stood in small groups around the field, their postures casual and loose, ready to catch the hit balls and await their turn at bat. The focus on this exercise was not fielding, but batting.

Doug Patterson, a utility player – pinch-hitter and pinch runner – stood in the batter's cage and waved his bat. Fari nodded at him and he nodded back. She threw a few soft pitches to Doug, who smashed the ball in all directions, including a few home runs. She liked the sharp crack of bat on ball, and the grounders and liners zooming past her, sometimes smacking into the shield, making her jump. A bag of balls lay next to the pitcher's mound and Fari simply picked up balls and threw them over the plate.

Now Jeff Jensen, another utility player, stepped into the batter's cage. As Fari bent over for another ball she saw Donnie standing at his position at first base. He stood crouched over, looking serious, as if ready to play. *Why? What's he doing?* She looked behind her and saw Brent Shiner standing at second, pounding his mitt, grinning at her. She turned further and there was Tony Rikes deep at shortstop, looking at her, laughing. Phil Jackson stood at his position at third. Cleo stood in center field.

Fari's heart soared and tears stung her eyes. *Oh Papa*, she cried in her mind. *We are the Minnesota Twins!*

The fielders – her teammates – broke into loud chatter and laughter: "C'mon, Fari, blow him away." "Let's go, baby, strike out this guy!"

Fari bounced on her toes and laughed at the sky. She looked at Jensen, reared back and let fly a fire ball. Jensen saw it coming and jumped back quickly. "Hey!"

*   *

In the afternoon, the pitching staff assembled in their conference room to review their strategy for Chicago. Later, at three o'clock, all players would attend a press conference to kick off the season.

Mac liked to talk over the game plan for their next opponent. He and the pitching crew sat around an oval table facing a large screen TV, watching several video clips of Fred Robbins striking out. Robbins was Chicago's top hitter and they had put together a profile of his batting habits.

Mac huddled off to one side with the starting pitchers for their first two games, Fari Madrigal and Doug Ferguson. Joining them was their catcher, Charlie Rice, also a rookie. Charlie had been called up last year from the farm team and had played in only a few games, but JD had decided that Charlie would start on Sunday.

Charlie was shaped like a fire plug; short, stout and well-grounded. A thatch of red hair burst from the top of his head. His eyes reflected the deep, guileless blue of the sky above Iowa farm country.

Of course, the media made much of this rookie pitching combination for the Twins' season opener. They had checked the record books and sure enough, it had happened only twice before, but never with the Minnesota Twins.

JD did not explain publicly why he wanted Charlie Rice to start this Sunday, but he told Mac privately that their regular catcher, Brock Schmidt, had been overheard making dirty comments about Fari. Also, Schmidt was suspected as the main source of the "Fari stories" leaked to the media. "Besides," JD had said, "Charlie's got good karma."

Fari wore her cap and sat back from the table, her back against the wall. She had crossed her legs and crossed arms, one hand holding the baseball. She listened and nodded, but kept her face hidden.

Mac explained about their computer analysis of Chicago's batting habits. "We track the batters over time as they face different pitchers, right-handers or left-handers. We know how many times they swing and miss at any particular pitch, like a fastball, curve, or whatever." As he talked, he held up a printout and pointed with his finger. "Think of the strike zone as a clock. At the top is twelve, at the bottom is six. A twelve o'clock pitch would be letter high, right over the plate. A plus twelve would be within the strike zone, and a minus twelve outside the zone, or too high. Got it?" He looked at the faces staring back at him (Fari had her head turned, but watched from under the cap). Fari and Doug seemed to understand, but Charlie presented a troubled expression.

That's all right, thought Mac, he's got good karma. Besides, the catcher played a limited role in the outcome of a pitch. However, it was necessary for pitchers and catchers to go over the strengths and weaknesses of each batter. He encouraged Charlie to look on and listen, but he concentrated on Fari and Doug.

Doug took over the lecture and showed Fari how to read the printouts. Mac sat back and thought about their dinner the other night. For the first time, Fari had talked about her late father, Jose. She had talked about his accident and the shock and sorrow of his sudden death. She had talked more directly to Kim, making a personal connection.

"At first, I was angry," Fari had told Kim. "Angry at world, or at God. How could He take such a good man before his time?"

Kim had nodded emphatically, understanding perfectly.

"But no answers to these questions," Fari had continued. She had flashed her eyes at Mac, then back to Kim. "Do you know physics?"

This question had surprised Kim. "What do you mean?"

"There is law about universe called law of thermodynamics. You know it?"

"It sounds familiar, but I'm not sure."

Fari had reached out and held Kim's hands. "The law says energy can be created or converted, but never destroyed. The spark of life from your mother is still around somewhere. She is not really gone, Kim, just like my Papa is not gone. They simply converted to different form of energy."

Mac had thought about this from time to time, wondering if Jenni's spirit was close by, listening and watching. Sometimes he called her name, or talked to her, and felt her presence almost as substantial as his own.

Later that evening, after dinner, he and Kim had talked about this new idea. Kim had become frustrated by the shifty ground of religious doctrine, and especially troubled by the notion of "faith." But Fari offered science – *physical laws* – providing an alternative foundation for understanding and coping. Mac didn't know what to think, but he was ready to accept anything that promised closure to an irrational and painful event.

Meanwhile, Fari was astonished at all this information about the Chicago batters. She remembered her father had told her about these analyses, but she had never imagined such depth and detail. If she knew what kind of pitch to throw and where it should go, how could those Chicago batters stand a chance?

As the others argued about the peculiar stance of one of Chicago's batters, Fari withdrew briefly into her cocoon. She stared at the floor until everything went silent. A shadow moved inside her mind and her father appeared before her. He wore his old Baltimore Orioles uniform.

Oh, Papa, she said in Spanish. *I'm starting in the season opener!*

I know, Fari. I'm so proud of you.

You'll be with me during the game, on the mound?

Of course, honey. I wouldn't miss it for the world.

I feel so good about this game, Papa. We know the details of each batter. If I work steady and throw real hard . . .

You'll blow 'em away, he said, completing their ritual joke.

With you by my side, I know I can win this game.

I know you can too, honey. I can help. I'll be here, waiting for you.

"Waiting for you."

Fari blinked and looked around. Mac stood next to the table, looking down at her.

"Perdón?" she asked.

"The media hullabaloo is about to start and JD wants to talk to you." He noticed Fari's eyes appeared unusually bright and clear.

"Okay. Vamos!" She jumped to her feet, and because she felt confident about pitching against Chicago, and still warm from her visit with Papa, she leaned over and kissed Mac lightly on the cheek.

Fari's lips scorched Mac's skin like fire. He drew back quickly and looked around. No one saw the kiss and thank God she didn't wear lipstick.

Fari laughed at this goofy reaction and ran out the door. Mac stood motionless for a moment, savoring the burning sensation on his face and wondering what it meant. Fari was a total mystery.

*   *

Along the third base line, the grounds crew had set up a wooden platform with a speaker's podium. Apparently, there were too many journalists for the press auditorium, so they held the press conference inside the stadium. This was part of the preseason ritual, a media pep rally for the upcoming season.

There were twice as many journalists as there had been two days earlier. They covered the whole seating area between home plate and third base, standing in the aisles or on the chairs. Those in front looked in danger getting pushed off.

Most of the players had already gathered on the wooden platform, while JD and Fari stood off to one side. Mac wondered what they talked about, but JD had wanted to talk to Fari, not him. He stuck his hands in his pockets and watched the shouting, undulating mass of media.

"Your father was no good with the media either." JD's lips underwent a smooth, synchronized motion, and the cigar flipped from one side of his mouth to the other. "In private, he was smart and articulate, but in public his lips froze together."

Fare nodded and studied the grass. The baseball spun rapidly in her right hand. She heard the general noise of the journalists, but she couldn't bring herself to look. Her abdomen had tightened into knots and she felt her teeth grinding.

"Are you comfortable living with Mac, Cleo and Kim?"

Fari pulled herself together, blocked out the Eyes and Ears and unclenched her jaw. "Yes. We have good time together."

JD watched her carefully and knew she spoke the truth. "Yes, you seem more relaxed now."

Fari nodded, looking again at the ground. "Yes. Do you know what?"

"What?"

"Thirty-four years ago my Papa opened his professional career against Chicago White Sox."

JD tilted his head and screwed one eye shut. "That could be right. When Jose first came up, he was in the American League." The cigar bounced up and down. "So we're making *more* history!" He laughed, then composed himself quickly. "You know, it *is* true we're making history here. You're the first woman to play professional baseball in the major leagues, and tomorrow you'll be our starting pitcher."

Fari looked down and nodded.

"That's why these journalists are here. To see *you*. This is their job. They've traveled far and they're spending a lot of money. Plus, they're our connection to the fans, not only here, but baseball fans everywhere." He paused and waited until she flicked her eyes at him. "I think you should say something to them."

Fari sighed and looked toward the outfield. "I know. It is considerate thing to do. After all, they are human too."

JD jumped back and waved his hands. "Wait a second. I wouldn't go *that* far."

They laughed together and JD almost lost the cigar. "This is how it'll go: Howard will say a few words and introduce the team. Then I'll say a few words about the upcoming season, whatever. Then I'll announce that you'll take two questions."

Fari listened carefully, chewing her lower lip. "Only two questions?" She glanced at the journalists. "Hay muchos."

"Only two questions. It doesn't matter what they ask, or who asks it. All they want is to see and hear you talk."

Fari sighed and nodded. "Okay."

He squeezed her arm. "Thanks. We won't have another press conference until after tomorrow's game." He looked at her over the tops of his glasses. "Are you sure about this?"

"Yes."

"Okay." He turned toward the platform. "Let's get the show on the road."

The team assembled on the platform, the shorter players in front, taller ones in back. Fari stood toward the back center, in front of Cleo and Donnie, the first baseman. She bent her knees and hid behind the man in front of her. The journalists crowded together only twenty yards away, their cameras clicking and whining.

Howard Sikes jumped on the platform and stepped to the podium. While he waited for the journalists to quiet down, he smiled and waved as though riding in a parade. Finally, he leaned toward the microphone. "Ladies and Gentlemen!"

There followed a lull in the noise and Howard filled it. "Welcome to Target Field, home of the Minnesota Twins." He introduced the coaches and players, and when he mentioned "Fari Madrigal," the journalists cheered and buzzed for almost a minute. Howard went on to recount all the hard work they'd performed during the past year to put together a good team. He expressed optimism and promised the fans a winning season. Finally, he introduced Jack Daniels Johnson, general manager.

JD stepped up to the podium and calmed the journalists with a few jokes and sly remarks. He talked for about five minutes, explaining how they mixed technical improvements with what he called "positive energy." He paused and said, "I know that most of you would like to ask a question of Fari Madrigal . . ."

An answering roar drowned out his voice. JD waved his hands in the air and spoke loudly into the microphone. "Fari has agreed to answer two questions." This triggered another exuberant reaction. JD turned and held out his hand toward Fari. After a second's hesitation, Fari stepped down and let him guide her to the podium. She kept her face lowered, the baseball spun quickly in her right hand.

Mac was aware of Fari's phobia about appearing before a crowd of strangers. Why did she agree to do this? What would she say?

The journalists cheered and carried on. The mechanical noises of their cameras reminded Fari of a forest of mad crickets. She hunched her shoulders and tried to offer a smaller target, but the podium was short and narrow. Slipping into her cocoon was not an option; she needed to be conscious and alert. *Now is the time to change my behavior.* She took a deep breath, straightened her shoulders and looked directly at the journalists. *You can take my image, but you will never touch my soul.*

JD asked one of the grounds crew to point to someone in the crowd. The selected journalist pushed his way to the front of the squirming mass and yelled out his question, but the shouted suggestions of his colleagues drowned him out. Finally, JD got everyone to shut up for a second.

"How do you feel about pitching in the major leagues? How do you . . ."

Again the reporter was drowned out by groans and shouts. What a stupid question!

Fari leaned toward the microphone, her head tilted down and her cap hiding her face. She spoke softly with a thick Spanish accent. "I like it. I love to pitch and Minnesota Twins have good team." She paused, glanced at JD, then looked directly toward the journalists. "For me is like fireworks. I feel like colorful explosions." She shut her mouth abruptly, looked away and stepped back.

The media took a moment to absorb this, but immediately shouted more questions. The grounds worker singled out another journalist, this time a woman, and they all waited until she could be heard.

"Did you really sign a minimum wage contract, and if so, why?"

This was greeted with loud shouts and whistles; apparently, this question had more meat to it. Fari leaned toward the microphone. "Yes, I signed minimum wage contract." She was about to say more, but the woman interrupted her.

"But *why*? You know you could have gotten more!"

Fari realized there was more to the question than simply confirming a fact. She spoke more confidently. "I do not need more. I am single person." Her face turned darker, as if she had become too personal.

The journalists regarded Fari quietly, with a new evaluation. She took this to mean they waited for more, so she spoke again. "Mr. Howard Sikes *did* pay more." She turned and looked for Howard, but he had jumped off the platform. "Mr. Sikes donated eight million dollars." Fari stepped away from the podium.

This declaration was followed by dead silence, everyone staring at Fari with shock. The silence lasted only two seconds before the journalists shouted louder than ever. Meanwhile, Howard Sikes had disappeared.

*   *

Doc Harris sat in a corner booth in Dominique's Bar & Restaurant and sipped from a chunky glass of scotch and ice. Two days ago, he had bribed one of the security guys to tell him which vehicle carried

Mac and Fari from the stadium. He had followed the delivery van into downtown, where Mac and Fari jumped into the skyway system. He had managed to follow them for fifteen minutes, but then lost them. However, they had been heading south, toward the condos and apartment buildings around Loring Park. Today, he would find out which condo they're staying in.

He took another sip of scotch, but cautioned himself about his alcohol intake. He had taken a "relaxer" not too long ago and if he drank too much, he'd have to crawl out of the place.

Sherry's parents had never approved of Doc; they *tolerated* him. If Sherry should ever be granted a divorce, they'd sigh with relief. But Sherry had made it clear there would be no divorce, mainly because their two daughters were still young; ten and thirteen years old.

At that moment, the effects of the relaxer kicked in. Doc's heart slowed and he levitated two inches above the chair. His eyes rolled toward the window. *Fari, where are you?*

*   *

"I wouldn't walk around in here by myself," said Mac. "Too many crazies."

"Yeah," answered Cleo. "They've had a few incidents in this park."

Mac, Cleo, Kim and Fari walked through Loring Park, four blocks from the condo. Lighted walkways circled the ponds, but most of the park remained hidden in darkness. Along the west side, Hennepin Avenue presented a constant parade of light, traffic and noise. On the north side, jazz clubs and yuppie bars offered funky atmospheres and high prices.

Mac had heard that thousands were already descending on the Twin Cities to be close to history, many hopeful of somehow procuring a ticket to attend tomorrow's season opener. He amended that; they were coming to see Fastball Fari. He turned around and looked at Fari and Kim walking behind them. He winked at Kim.

"How ya doin, Dad?" she called.

"I'm okay. And you?"

"Estoy tuanis!"

"What?"

"C'mon, Mac." Cleo pulled Mac forward. "Fari's teaching Kim dirty words in Spanish."

"Talking dirty in Spanish?" Mac looked at Fari. She flashed her eyes at him.

They walked slowly around the ponds. The cool night was not silent; insects buzzed, tires swished on concrete and occasionally they heard a scream or a siren. It was Saturday night and the moon was full.

"Hey, how about some ice cream?" Cleo pointed across the park to a Baskin & Robins.

"Quiero helado," answered Fari.

"Vamanos!" shouted Kim.

They walked off the sidewalk and into the shadows. Picnic tables and benches were scattered here and there. They saw a solitary silhouette sitting at a far table and the glow of a cigarette.

The Baskin & Robins was deserted. The girl behind the counter sported spiky, blue hair and one pierced eyebrow. She smiled sweetly. "Hi. Can I help you?"

Cleo ordered a banana split. Mac and Kim wanted double chocolate cones. Fari was undecided. She walked beside the glass case, inspecting the buckets of ice cream from under the bill of her cap. "Something tropical."

The girl worked fast, making the banana split and the cones. Now she walked down the counter to face Fari. "You wanted something tropical?"

"Yes." Fari looked into another bucket.

"We have pineapple or papaya or mango." The girl smiled happily and bounced on her toes.

Fari glanced at her from under the cap. "Pineapple?"

"Si. Hay pineapple sherbet, or pineapple helado con pedacitos de piña." The girl spoke in a breathless rush, her cheeks flushed. "Me gusta Español. Usted esta Fastball Fari, verdad?"

Fari glanced at the girl and noticed two more employees standing just inside the storeroom. They were boys not much older than the girl. "Si, pero es secreto, por favor."

The girl giggled and shook her hands as if they were on fire. "No problem! Secret! Oh my God! Fastball Fari!" She looked behind her at the two boys. "Is it all right if they meet you?"

Fari nodded and looked away.

Fari doesn't mind this personal attention, Mac noticed. Of course, they weren't really in public and this place was deserted other than the three employees. Still, Fari seemed willing to tolerate more social contact. And what about that astonishing performance this afternoon at the stadium?

Mac had talked to a few of the local journalists afterwards. They had been ecstatic about Fari. Despite her "movie star looks," her manner did not appear self-conscious or contrived – indeed, she came across as authentic and spontaneous. However, most of the excitement centered on what she had said. The revelation about Howard Sikes' donations had hit them, in the words of one reporter, "Like a bolt of lightning."

"This is Matt and Ringo," said the girl. "I'm Melanie."

The boys stood stiffly with trembling smiles. Fari shook hands with each one and repeated their names. She asked Matt what he did during the day.

"I . . . we're in school!" he shouted, indicating Ringo.

"What about you, Melanie?"

The girl bounced on her toes and clutched her chest. "I go to school too. I'm tops in my class. I'll finish the year with a four-oh average." She turned and buried her face in Matt's chest, her shoulders shaking.

Maybe she laughed or maybe she cried, Mac couldn't tell. Fari asked Ringo for a double pineapple cone. "Yes, ma'am!" Fari followed him to the pineapple bucket and watched him work.

"What about tomorrow, Fari, with Chicago?" Ringo asked. He expertly laid one scoop on top of the other.

Fari accepted her cone, took a quick taste, and then laughed. "We gonna blow 'em away!" The others smiled and laughed politely. But then Fari said something amazing. "I might even pitch no-hitter."

Mac doubled over, gagging. Cleo jumped away from Fari and looked back at her like she must be crazy. "Damn, girl, don't *ever* say that!"

*　　　　　*

Across the street, within the shadows of the park, Doc Harris sat at a picnic table and watched them eat their ice cream. They were good friends having a good time, while he was alone out in the dark.

Doc knew which condo Fari lived in. This discovery had brought an instant rush of elation, but had worn off quickly, like a drug. Now he felt preoccupied with how he should exploit this information. He watched Cleo pay the bill and they left, still eating their ice cream.

Good night, Fari. I *do* love you, and I know you won't let me down.

TEN

Sunday: March 30

Howard Sikes sat on the toilet in his bathroom, bent over with his chin resting on his hand, not unlike the famous statue of *The Thinker*. Indeed, Howard was thinking and not taking care of waste business. The bathroom was the one private place where his kids or wife wouldn't suddenly bother him. The drawback, however, was that he couldn't stay in there forever.

Yesterday, as a result of Fari's startling announcement about the donations, he had been immediately assaulted by all sides to confirm or deny. He had rushed home and turned off the phones, but the calls had piled up like angry bees in a bottle.

Today was the Twins' first game of the season. Soon, in a few minutes, he would have to leave this bathroom and confront the world. What would he say to the Board of Directors? He had emphasized his negotiating skills in announcing Fari's contract and the Board had responded with the proper gratitude. But there was also surprise and a little suspicion. Now what would they think?

Yesterday, Howard had been surprised that Fari agreed to address the media, but then what she said! His heart had almost stopped. Frances had promised to say nothing about the donations, but he never imagined Fari might say something.

Were they working together? Did Frances orchestrate this announcement? Fari did not seem as though she followed a script. On the other hand, maybe they *were* manipulating him. Look what happened in his office on Friday – they choked him with his own words!

He could deny the donations and try to stonewall; or he could admit it and endure the embarrassment before the Board.

Howard groaned again and looked at his watch; twenty minutes past seven. How could he appear at the stadium with no plan or no idea of what to say? He had to talk to Frances *now*. He took out his phone, hit the speed dial and inhaled deeply.

*   *

Frances walked along the shore of Lake of the Isles. She preferred to walk on the grass rather than the asphalt and her tennis shoes were dark with dew. A phone went off from inside her shoulder bag and she fished it out. It was Howard Sikes. "Good morning, Mr. Sikes. How are you today?"

"Good morning, Mrs. Marchena. I'm not feeling too good."

"I'm sorry to hear that, sir, and today is the big day. Aren't you excited?"

Howard didn't answer for a moment. "Yes, it's a big day. For the Twins, for Fari and for me." His voice sharpened. "Now I have to comment on these *donations* I supposedly made."

"And what will your comment be?"

"I'll have to deny it." His voice lost some of its steel. He felt compelled to say this, but there was little confidence behind it. "I kept my part of the deal. I didn't mention the Red Gang."

Frances cringed again at this crude description. From the very beginning, the name "Red Gang" had been pure journalistic fiction. Well, no matter; she had already decided to let Howard off the hook. She had come up with a compromise that would advance their relationship and allow him to save face. If she let him escape with a little dignity, he could be a useful friend.

She saw a bench up ahead and sat. The early sunlight pierced the foggy mists covering the lake and the islands settled comfortably on the water. She began. "Mr. Sikes, you can admit to the donations, but deny they had anything to do with Fari's contract." She paused to let that sink in. Here was the compromise she proposed; he would admit gladly to the donations, and they would both insist it had nothing to do with the contract. Of course, this wasn't true, but when she weighed the lie against all the lives this money would improve, she found the lie easier to handle. For Howard, the lie would save his reputation, maybe even improve his image.

"That's an interesting idea, Mrs. Marchena," Howard said carefully. "Since you suggest it, I assume you'd back me up?"

"Yes, sir, I would."

"But what about yesterday? Fari implied that it *was* related."

"Don't worry about that. Fari will release a statement clearing up that misunderstanding. By the way, do you mind if I call you Howard? Please call me Frances."

*   *

When Frances returned from her walk, she took a shower and changed clothes. She and JD would join the condo dwellers for Sunday morning breakfast. JD drove on a long, circuitous route toward Loring Park, keeping an eye out for any possible journalists, but he never noticed the black motorcycle trailing along a block behind.

They parked at the designated place, on the south side of the park, where they met with Kim and Mac. With the excitement of game day and the thrill of meeting secretly, everyone exhibited a high, confident mood. JD led the way across the park, moving at a brisk pace. Mac had questions, but JD wasn't in the mood for business. "We'll work it out later, Mac. First things first. I'm hungry!"

Frances and Kim lagged behind. Kim studied the huge stone church across the street. A brilliant, stained-glass mosaic of holy images provided a glimpse into paradise. Above the stained glass, two tall, narrow towers pointed the way to heaven. The doors stood open and people gathered on the steps and sidewalk. Kim turned to Frances and asked if she knew anything about physics.

They arrived at the condo just in time to offer advice to Cleo on the ingredients of a Spanish omelet. Cleo offered to let them make the breakfast. JD backed down saying, with a straight face, "At my age I can only *think*, I can't *do*."

Betsy, Cleo's girlfriend, was also there, and they all greeted each other. Betsy was nuts about baseball and had first met Cleo when she begged him for his autograph. She was tiny, at least compared to Cleo; only five feet tall and weighed about one hundred pounds. She worked as a physical therapist in the children's ward at the University of Minnesota Hospital. Her movements were graceful, her smile full of sustenance and Cleo Hagerty loved her madly.

"Where's Fari?" asked JD.

"Next door," answered Betsy. "She'll be over soon."

JD wandered around and finally settled on a stool at the kitchen counter. "How does Fari seem, Cleo?"

Cleo stopped chopping onions and stared into space, recalling the incredible scene last night at the ice cream shop.

"Well? Does she seem nervous? Scared? What?"

"Scared?" Cleo snorted. "Shit, man, she ain't scared. Last night she said we were gonna blow 'em away." His smile appeared halfhearted because he knew what *else* she had said.

"Good for her," said JD. "A positive attitude."

"That's not all she said." Cleo stepped closer and poked JD in the arm. "She said, 'maybe I'll throw a *no-hitter.'*"

JD leaned back in surprise. "She said that?"

"Yeah, man. Mac almost choked to death!" Cleo smiled, glad to be rid of his burden.

JD knew how superstitious baseball players could be. Some went to ridiculous lengths to ensure a good performance. He regarded it as a sort of mild form of witchcraft. However, one particular taboo seemed general and traditional: If a pitcher has a chance at a no-hitter, everyone on the team must never mention it, or even think it.

JD remembered occasions when the pressures of a no-hitter had threatened to blow a team apart. A player who dropped the ball, or fumbled a play and spoiled a perfect game, cried like a baby. Sometimes they never recovered.

JD did not share this superstition, but he had to respect it in his players. What they believed influenced how they played.

At that moment, Fari entered from the garage next door. She wore a long-sleeved, flannel shirt tucked into a pair of jeans. Her hair hung loose and slightly curly, and she carried a baseball.

Immediately, JD noticed something different about her. The jeans and shirt fit more snugly and there was something joyous in her expression. She had the look of a woman learning to fly and loving it. They all greeted each other and JD led Fari into the living room. They sat in matching armchairs next to a bookcase. Fari took an interest in the books, tilting her head and reading the titles.

"Do you like to read?" asked JD.

She glanced at him and smiled. She held the baseball cradled in both hands. "Yes. On the farm, yo leía todos los días."

JD wondered if she referred to the time when Jose had died. "You lived on the beach?"

"Yes." She reached out and touched a book. "I read this one three times."

"What's that?"

"Tolstoy. *War and Peace.*"

How strange, thought JD; that book happened to be one of his all-time favorites. "You must like it, I guess."

"Si." Fari crossed her legs, the right hand took charge of the baseball and spun it quickly. Her body shifted back and forth in short, precise movements. Her voice issued high and breathless. "His style is straight-forward and direct. Like Solzhenitsyn. Russians are good at that."

Yes, they are, thought JD. He studied the smooth sweep of her forehead and cool brightness in her eyes. Yes, there was something different about her, including more direct eye contact. For a moment he forgot what he wanted to say, but then he remembered that this amazing woman was today's starting pitcher! "Cleo said you mentioned something about a 'no-hitter?'" He smiled when he said this, but Fari cringed.

She stopped moving, the baseball stopped spinning and she looked away. "I am sorry about that."

"Well, between you and me, it might not mean much, but to them it means quite a lot."

"Yes. *Kim mi dio la cuenta.* I must be careful what I say."

He noticed the double meaning in that statement, accompanied by the look in her eyes. She referred to the media storm stirred up by her announcement about Howard Sikes and the donations. JD did not want to get into that subject. He stood up and reached for her hand. "Let's go help Cleo. I'm hungry!"

The omelets were filled with chilies, onions, tomatoes, mushrooms and cheese, accompanied by a plate of big, fluffy pancakes. After a round of applause for both cooks – Cleo and Betsy – everyone dug in. Amidst the clink and clatter of silverware, a brisk conversation bounced around the table.

No one mentioned baseball. JD talked about the wine he made on his farm during the off season. He had a small apple orchard of fifty or sixty trees and several honey bee stands. He collected the honey himself, wearing a bee suit and carrying a smoke machine. He mixed the honey and apple juice together, added a touch of sugar, let it ferment, and produced a clear, golden cider.

The smooth taste and high potency of this wine was legendary. Cleo picked up the story and told about a time when he visited JD's farm during "siphoning day." They used plastic hoses to siphon the wine from twenty-gallon barrels and into one-quart, glass bottles.

"Oh, *man.*" Cleo rolled his eyes. "This stuff tasted *good,* and you couldn't help but take a few swallows every time you siphoned. And we're talkin about *hundreds* of bottles." He waved his hands and laughed. "By the time we finished, everyone was on the floor!"

They all laughed. Mac also noticed something different about Fari, a more direct intensity in her eyes, a bolder attitude. This confused him even more – not only did she seem mysterious, but now she was *evolving.*

Breakfast was over and now they would go to Target Field and step into the annals of history. Fari especially felt the psychic force of this event – a feeling so marvelous she wanted to prolong the moment. She closed her eyes and saw her father immediately.

Papa! The game starts in five hours.

Yes. His face twisted with concern. *How do you feel?*

Fari wrapped her arms around herself and shivered. *Oh, Papa, I see everything with great clarity. I feel strong in my mind and my body.*

Yes, I see that. We've worked long and hard to get to this point. And now we're here.

Yes.

This is your moment, my love. This is your moment.

"Come on," said Mac. He laid his hand lightly on Fari's shoulder. "We'd better go to the stadium."

*   *

The rental office for the townhouse complex was just up the street from Fari's condo. Doc Harris sat in the cool interior of the reception area, watching the front of Fari's condo. He had just popped a little hit of speed – his morning "eye-opener," he called it – and the drug raced through his bloodstream.

The sales representative, Myrtle, asked what Doc might be interested in. They offered a variety of different styles and accommodations, short term and long term. Myrtle was an attractive, older woman with a hard, caved-in body and eyes like stones.

Doc went into a long spiel about being a "visiting professor." He was in Minneapolis to conduct a series of seminars and required a comfortable residence for only two or three weeks. No maid service. Also, he wanted to be close to this area right here – he stabbed the map with his finger – near the entrance to the complex, so he could get in and out quickly. He heard himself babbling and shut his mouth. Get a hold of yourself!

Myrtle suggested he look at photos of the insides of the town-houses, along with a list of the amenities and services available. She indicated on the map which townhouses were vacant. (She never once used the word "condo.")

Doc noticed immediately there were three vacant townhouses close to Fari's. One was almost directly across the street from Fari, but off to one side. He could see why this might not be such a desirable location; the back of the condo was exposed to the traffic along Nicollet Avenue. But if someone wanted to spy on Fastball Fari, then it was perfect.

Doc filled out the forms and paid the deposit in cash, plus three weeks rent in advance. Myrtle asked for some ID; maybe a driver's license? Doc smiled and reached for his wallet, but then froze in sudden panic. His license had a Minneapolis address! How could he be a professor from out of town?

His hand jerked in midair erratically, like a machine receiving conflicting messages. Then he remembered his passport. He switched on a smile and tried to keep his teeth from chattering.

He dug out his passport and handed it over. His driver's license was in his luggage, he told Myrtle, which somehow got rerouted to Chicago, can you imagine, and he had to fill out all those forms, but luckily they found it, I mean, O'Hare is so big and crazy, you know, so many people you can't move . . . He snapped his mouth shut.

Myrtle didn't know what to think of Doc. He looked good and wore expensive clothes, but there was something unsettling about his eyes. This made her hesitate, but he was obviously well-off, so she decided to accept his deposit. She promised herself to keep a close eye on this strange bird.

Doc floated out the door happy and content. At least something in my life is going right. Hey, look at this! I'm the only person in the world who knows where Fastball Fari lives, and now I live right across the street!

He looked at his watch. It was almost time for the Fari Madrigal show.

ELEVEN

⁓

Good afternoon, ladies and gentlemen. This is Herb Karnak of WCCB radio, coming to you from Target Field near downtown Minneapolis, home of the *Minnesota Twins!* It's a big day here at Target Field, the opening game of the Twins' 2014 season. Also, of course, today's game will go down in history. Fari Madrigal, the Twins' rookie pitching phenomenon, will become the *first woman ever* to play professional baseball in the major leagues.

Joining me in our play-by-play presentation will be Bob Weir and Chuck Forbes. Bob is with me here in the WCCB sports booth and Chuck is outside the stadium, roaming through the crowds. We'll hear from him later, but, Bob, I have to say that *in here* the excitement is electrifying.

Hi, sports fans. You're so right, Herb. This stadium is packed! Forty thousand plus in here today and several thousand more outside the stadium. Also, sports fans around the country . . .

Around the world!

Around the world will watch Fari Madrigal take the mound in her *first professional appearance.* You know, Herb, Fari came up to Minneapolis only six days ago and already the whole sports world is turned upside down! I talked to some of the Twins players earlier and virtually all agreed that Fari Madrigal has the best control of any pitcher they've ever seen. And these guys have seen the best. Yet she's a rookie, Herb, and a woman!

And what a woman, Bob. They're still talking about that press conference yesterday. We were both present for that performance and, speaking for myself, Fari took my breath away.

Oh, she's absolutely gorgeous. But what she *said* has the sports community in an uproar. She said she signed for minimum wage because she doesn't need any more money than that! When, Herb, have we ever heard a major sports personality say something like that?

Never!

Never. And then she said that Mr. Howard Sikes, owner of the Minnesota Twins, made an eight million dollar donation!

Well, in all due respect to Mr. Sikes, he hasn't been known to make donations of any amount. Last year he gave fifty thousand dollars to the Republican Party.

In any event, eight million dollars is serious money. Earlier this morning, Mr. Sikes announced that the donations went to programs for the homeless and drug treatment, but were *not* related to Fari's contract.

Well, we applaud Howard Sikes for these donations, however they happened, but Fari's first public appearance created a firestorm. When I looked at her and listened to her, I could not believe that she's a baseball pitcher.

And what a pitcher, Bob. Apparently, she started throwing balls at age three or four. Her father taught her how to pitch. But get this; her father, Jose Madrigal, pitched his first pro game in 1975 against the *Chicago White Sox!*

Wow, Herb, where did you hear that?

One of our statisticians just handed me a note. That was Caroline. Thank you, Caroline. At the time, Jose Madrigal was a rookie with Kansas City. He was called in as a reliever in the seventh inning and saved the game. Well, there ya go. *More* history, folks, in case you're counting.

That's just amazing, Herb. These strange twists of fate are finally culminating here, today, with the Twins' first game of the season. Also, of course, we have to mention that with Charlie Rice starting as the Twins' catcher, we have another one for the history books. It's the first time for the Minnesota Twins that a rookie pitcher and catcher have started on opening day!

As I said earlier, Bob, the atmosphere in here is *electrifying*. All private boxes are jammed and every seat and square inch of this stadium is filled!

And the place is shakin, Herb. We're rockin and rollin!

Excuse me, Bob, but we've got Chuck Forbes on the line now. He's outside the stadium. Chuck? Can you hear me? Sounds a little crazy out there, Chuck.

Hi, sports fans, Chuck Forbes here, in the parking lots outside Target stadium. You're right, Herb. It *is* crazy out here. The police estimate the crowd at about twenty thousand. The Twins have set up two giant TV screens so the fans can watch the game. Can you hear me, Herb? They're cheering wildly because the screens have just been turned on. Can you hear me?

Thanks, Chuck, we'll check back with you later. That was Chuck Forbes reporting from the parking lots outside Target Field. Well, Bob, it sounds just as crazy outside the stadium as inside.

The enormous interest in Fari Madrigal is hard to believe. Apparently, she appeals to all kinds of people, young and old, male and female. Also, she has an ethnic appeal.

What about sex appeal, Bob?

Now, Herb, behave yourself.

Okay, I'll be a good boy. Hey, I see the players beginning to appear in both dugouts.

That's right, Herb. Ladies and gentlemen, we are about to begin the Twins first home game of the season! At this moment, we'll take a short commercial break before we come back and *play ball!* This is Bob Weir, along with Herb Karnak, coming to you from the sports booth of WCCB radio, the voice of the Minnesota Twins! Don't go away, sports fans, we'll be right back with *Fastball Fari!*

*   *

"What about national anthem?" Fari asked.

"What about it?" Mac felt hot standing this close to Fari inside the dugout tunnel. Most players had passed through and were out on the field. The doorway led to bright lights and the noise of thousands of people.

"I do not know words." Fari stood in front of him with her head tilted down, the cap hiding her face.

"That's okay," he said. "You don't have to sing. Just look respectful."

She nodded and smiled. "I will pray, for proper expression."

"And everyone will be watching."

"Yes."

The crowd sounded louder and Mac remembered what JD had once said: "The noise of a big crowd sounds exactly like the roaring winds of a hurricane." JD should know; he had grown up in Florida and had seen a few of the big storms. "Are you all right?" he asked.

Fari turned to look out the doorway. Her face appeared calm, but her eyes sparkled and snapped. "Not really." She glanced at him briefly. "But Papa will be with me."

Mac didn't know how to respond. Sometimes he talked to Jenni and summoned her presence, so he understood what she meant.

Fari looked down at her glove and picked at it. "I want to pitch complete game, Mac."

"So do I! We all want to pitch a complete game." He smiled, but his stomach fluttered and lurched. "Just keep your eyes on me and Charlie. If there's any question or doubt, don't hesitate to talk to Charlie or call me out to the mound."

She reached out with her right hand and placed it against his chest. Her long, thick fingers played with a button on his uniform. She spoke softly, just above the noise of the crowd. "When I pitch in game, I cannot talk. I am by myself." Her fingers went still and she looked straight into his eyes for one full second. "Comprende? It is ritual I have."

Mac felt himself falling into those golden portals, but her hand on his chest kept him upright. He opened his mouth and stammered. "Sure, I understand." Many pitchers had rituals they went through on game day.

"Hey, Mac!" Stew shouted from the dugout. "They're gettin ready out here!"

"Well, here we go." Mac wanted to hug her, but he hesitated, afraid it would seem too intimate. He stuck out his hand. "Good luck!"

Fari nodded and shook his hand. "Okay!" She bounced on her toes, turned and trotted into the dugout. Mac heard the crowd roar even louder. He followed her into the dugout and the noise overwhelmed him.

The players jumped around, letting off tension, slapping high fives with each other and with Fari. They felt pumped up by the crowd, by the first game of the season, and by their starting pitcher, Fari Madrigal. Several times a voice bellowed over the loudspeakers, but the words were swept away by hurricane winds.

The screams from the throats of forty thousand people was the loudest thing Fari had ever heard. The noise stayed suspended in the air – one, long continuous roar. As she understood it, first they sang the national anthem, then the governor of Minnesota, Wendell Hind, threw out the first ball. A month earlier, the Twins' management had invited the governor to perform this traditional spring ceremony, an honor for any Minnesotan, and he had graciously consented. (Privately, Mr. Hind didn't give a damn about the Twins, but that was before Fastball Fari. Today he had arrived at the stadium an hour early in hopes of meeting her. The governor carried a lot of clout, but JD wasn't impressed. "Not before the game. Maybe after.")

The packed stadium was an enclosed system, Fari noticed. The electromagnetic field of each person coalesced with the electromagnetic fields of thousands of other people and produced one gigantic wavelength. Fari felt the pressure like a vice around her chest. She gasped for breath, her heart thumped.

Finally the crowd noise settled into the constant chatter of excitement. The loudspeakers blared again and this time they were heard: "WELCOME TO TARGET FIELD!" The scoreboard exploded with blinking lights and fireworks. Huge letters splashed across the giant screen. PLAY BALL! The crowd roared again with renewed vigor and Fari felt swept away by the force of the noise. The ground shook!

Players from both teams lined up on the third and first base lines, getting ready for the national anthem. Fari stood between Brent and Cleo. She reached out in both directions and grabbed their hands. In a few minutes, she will walk out to the mound and become a professional baseball pitcher. Her skin tingled with electric chaos and she squeezed Brent and Cleo's hands with considerable strength. The crowd stood and the national anthem issued from the loudspeakers.

Fari stared at the vast expanse of green grass. The grass was the same dark green color as the ocean after a morning rain. The waves rose, curled and smashed against the sand. She saw movement and white spots before her eyes. The governor had thrown the ball and the Minnesota Twins had taken the field.

Fari stepped toward the mound. Adrenaline pumped hard and fast and she saw the sharp, blunt tops of each blade of grass. Suddenly, she was startled to see another pair of shoes. It was Cleo. He stood on the grass just off the mound, rubbing a baseball in his big hands.

Fari stopped and smiled at the contrast. Her cocoon had filled with the raw force and lonely mystery of Mother Nature – and here, a friend.

Cleo placed the ball gently in her right hand. "I put a special mojo on this ball." He shouted above the noise of the crowd. "I'll put a mojo on *all* the balls. Every time you get a new ball, wave it toward centerfield. Okay?"

Fari came halfway out of her cocoon and concentrated on what Cleo had said. He sounded serious, but she couldn't talk. She nodded once.

"Blow 'em away, Fastball Fari! I'm right behind you!" Cleo squeezed her arm and trotted into center field.

Fari examined the ball. Cleo had already scuffed it and it would fly snappish and lively. As she stepped up the mound, she noticed there were no marks or footprints; the dirt was as smooth as the beaches at home.

Just like the beaches at home, said Papa.

Papa! Look where we are!

Inside Target Field. A full house!

She heard his voice plain and clear above the roar of the surf.

Remember the basics, Fari, he said. *Down and in on any batter is the hardest place to hit the ball.*

Yes. Mac says the same thing. We have a plan, but I need your advice and strength.

You have it, my love. You always have it.

She nodded and looked toward home plate. Charlie Rice had put on his mask and a batter stood off to one side, swinging his bat. This would be Chicago's second baseman, a right-hander, batted .296 last season. As Papa had mentioned, he was vulnerable to fastballs and breaking balls low and inside.

Charlie looked over at Mac, got the signal, then passed it on to Fari; a fastball at four o'clock. The batter stepped into the box and looked at her. He wasn't big, but he looked powerful. Fari stared at home plate until she saw the line of the pitch, but then she hesitated, surprised. The line had never appeared so bright! She took this to be a good sign. She inhaled deeply, went into her delivery and let fly.

"Strike!" The umpire shouted, and Target Field tilted and rocked in a gale force cheer.

*   *

We're back, baseball fans, with the top half of the fifth inning. The Twins lead the game two to zip. In the bottom of the first, the Twins earned their first run on a walk to Billy Shots, who stole second, then scored on a single by Cleo Hagerty. This was Hagerty's first at-bat this season and he connected with a hard liner to left-center. In the third inning, Harmon Kobrouski smashed a solo homer over the left field fence for the Twins' second run. But for Chicago, Bob, it's been all zeros.

That's right, Herb. Fastball Fari is *blowin 'em away* here today in Target Field, and that's been the big difference in this game so far. Chicago has no hits and, of course, no runs. Fari has pitched flawlessly except for two walks, one in the second, then one again last inning. They were the only Chicago batters to reach first base, and there they stayed. Fari has faced fourteen batters and struck out *nine!*

Fari Madrigal is putting on quite a show, that's for sure. She's burning in those fastballs at over *ninety miles an hour.*

Okay, we're ready to go, Herb. Robbins steps up to the plate and Fari immediately looks in for the sign. She goes into her delivery and here's the pitch. *Ooooh! A blazer!* Called strike one!

Again, Bob, Fari's putting those pitches right on the money, keeping them low and inside. And she works quickly, with no wasted movements or walking around. She delivers the pitch, then goes right back to the rubber and waits for the batter.

Okay, fans, Robbins is ready now and Fari goes into her windup. Here's the pitch. *Swing and a hit!* The ball bounces foul down the third base line. Strike two!

Fari threw a change-up that time, Bob, mixing her pitches. Robbins was way out in front of it. He's spooked by the speed ball.

Yeah. Did you see the way he banged his bat on the ground? He's losing his cool. Okay, sports fans, here we go. It's two strikes and no balls on Robbins. Fari goes into her wind up, delivers the pitch. Robbins *swings* and hits a weak grounder toward the mound. His bat breaks! Fari picks up the ball barehanded and throws to first. One out!

We heard the crack of that bat all the way up here. Fari jammed him with a fastball and Robbins connected near the handle. A piece of the bat flew over by O'Brien, the third base coach!

That's one down here in the top of the fifth and Buster Holly approaches the batter's box. He struck out in the second inning, went down swinging at a Fari fastball.

Two years ago Holly led the league in RBIs, but last year he was troubled by a hamstring injury. He's been working hard during the off season and now he says he's ready to play.

Holly steps into the box and Fari goes into her wind up. Here's the pitch. *A swing and a miss!* Strike one. Boy, Herb, he took a vicious cut at that one.

He sure did! He was aiming for the fences. When he led the league in RBIs two years ago, he had forty-two home runs.

I think he'd be happy with just a piece of the ball. Okay, fans, Holly is ready and Fari is set. She goes into her wind up and here's the pitch. Holly *swings* and hits a high foul ball behind first base. Strike two.

Fari has amazing poise for a rookie, Bob. She works quickly and always seems in control. Here on the TV monitor, we see close ups of her face and she looks . . . serene, almost without expression.

You're right, Herb. She's all business and never seems to get rattled or shook. But I've noticed something strange in her routine. Whenever she gets a new ball from the umpire, she waves it toward centerfield. What's *that* all about?

Who knows? Some Caribbean ritual, maybe.

Whatever it is, it seems to be working. Okay, the count on Holly is two strikes and no balls. We're in the top of the fifth, with one out and no one on base. Fari looks in for the sign, her face *serene*, then goes into her wind up. Here's the pitch. Whoa! The ball sails inside and Holly has to jump back quickly. Ball one. Look at that, Herb. Holly is saying something to Fari. He didn't like that pitch.

No, he didn't, Bob. The pitch was a breaking ball, low and inside. Holly likes to crowd the plate and Fari moved him back a little.

She may look sweet, folks, but Fastball Fari is *tough*. Right now, she's ahead of Holly on the count, two strikes and one ball. Okay, here we go. Fari goes into her wind up and here's the pitch. Holly swings and hits a high foul ball! Reynolds trots over by the Twins' dugout, waits and catches the ball. Two out!

Listen to that crowd, Bob. They *love* it! Fari had Holly rattled with that inside pitch, then caught him flat-footed with a fastball. Look at that, Bob; Holly's throwing things around in the Chicago dugout.

That pitch was clocked at *ninety-five miles an hour!* That's two out here in the top of the fifth. And now Jim Stice, Chicago's shortstop, steps up to the plate. Stice struck out in his first at-bat and we'll see what happens now.

A ball traveling at ninety-five miles per hour takes only a split second to cross the plate.

That's right, Herb. If they blink, they lose it. Okay, sports fans, Stice steps up to the plate and Fari immediately goes into her wind-up. She's working fast today. Here's the pitch. The ball hits the dirt in front of Charlie Rice! Ball one.

They've just announced the official attendance for today's game, Bob. *Forty-two thousand, five hundred and fifty.* A *new record* for attendance here in Target Field!

More for the record books, Herb. And I'll tell ya, folks, there might be over forty thousand here, but they sound like *millions*. Okay, Stice is ready and Fari goes into her wind up. Here's the pitch. *Swing and a miss!* Another fastball, Herb, and Stice was *way* behind it.

That's right. Fari is working that inside corner like a *master*. Her control seems consistent and very accurate. Unusual in a rookie.

Unusual for anyone, Herb. Of course, we've all heard the stories about how Fari Madrigal started pitching at a very young age, around four or five.

And threw baseballs at a *dummy*, Bob. Frances Marchena, Fari's mother, described how Fari grew up pitching to a department store dummy!

Well, she's pitching here, now, inside Target Field, and putting on an unforgettable performance. Stice steps into the box. The count is one and one, with two outs and no one on base. Fari looks in at Stice, who is not a dummy, and goes into her wind up. Here's the pitch. Stice *swings* and misses again! This time he swung so hard the bat flew out of hands!

It sure did! I think he was lookin for a fastball, but that pitch dropped at the last second and Stice hit nothing but air. The bat flew halfway to third base!

Fari stands patiently on the rubber while Stice retrieves his bat. As you mentioned earlier, Herb, she never seems to change expression. Now, for instance, as she waits for Stice, she stands motionless, facing home plate. Meanwhile, Stice is taking his time.

You're right, Bob. He's stalling. Fari is working fast today and Stice wants to break up her rhythm.

Stice is finally ready and steps into the box. The count is two strikes, one ball. The crowd is cheering with every pitch. Fari goes into her wind up and delivers the pitch. Stice lets it go and the umpire called a ball! That was *awfully close*, Herb.

Stice got a break on that one! Fari came in a little too low, so says the ump. Although with two strikes, I'm surprised Stice didn't swing. No one on, two out – he's got nothing to lose.

All right, sports fans, we're in the top of the fifth inning, with two out and nobody on. The Twins are leading two to nothing. Chicago's shortstop, Jim Stice, is at bat and the count is two and two. Forty thousand people are on their feet, screaming for a strike out. Fari goes into her wind up, here's the pitch. *Swing and a miss! She struck him out!*

*   *

They were in the bottom of the seventh inning and the Twins were at bat. There were two out, but they had one man on first. Tim O'Brady, the Twins' right fielder, was at bat. The Twins had scored twice in this inning on a walk, a stolen base, a single and a double. Chicago changed pitchers and now their reliever pitched to O'Brady.

The home team is leading four to nothing, thought Mac, but the cheering is all for Fastball Fari. It seemed that no matter what happened on the field, there was a constant roaring from the crowd. And why not? Through seven innings Fari has pitched beautifully. Her control and accuracy were phenomenal. It was no wonder Chicago has no hits.

Seven innings and no hits. Mac wouldn't let himself speculate further, or even *name* the thing. He stood where he always does, in the corner of the dugout, where he could watch the pitching action without people standing in front of him. Also, he could see the whole bench lengthwise. He liked to watch the players' expressions, gestures and postures. He believed these were keys to knowing their state of mind.

Fari sat in the opposite corner of the dugout, with her glove resting on her lap, her hands folded on top of the glove. Her hat was pulled low and her eyes hidden. He could see no clue as to what she might be feeling. No one sat within five feet of Fari, no one even *looked* at her. Mac smiled; it's happening already. Seven innings and Chicago has no hits. Two more innings, six more batters to go.

Sitting closest to Fari was Charlie Rice, her catcher. The muscles in his jaws bulged as he chewed a huge wad of gum. The rest of his face remained motionless, even his eyes were rigid. After the second inning, Charlie had come up to Mac and told him that Fari threw the ball *exactly* where it was supposed to go. "I've never seen anything like it!"

Neither had Mac. He wanted to say something to Fari, but she hasn't looked at him or come near him the entire game. True to her word, she hasn't spoken to anyone, not even JD. Although Mac had advance notice about this, he still felt a little sorry for himself. She pitched with no expression on her face, throwing with speed, power and precision. Almost like a machine, he thought, like a robot. But she didn't look or smell like a machine!

Crack! O'Brady hit a high fly ball toward center. Mac backed away from the wall and bounced on his toes. At first, it looked like a home run, but the ball died in the dead air and the centerfielder caught it on the warning track. Three outs.

Now Chicago was up to bat and the crowd roared. Mac had never heard it so loud in here and he wondered if they all sustained hearing damage. He watched Fari put on her glove and trot out to the mound. He looked at JD, who sat on the bench a few feet away. The cigar jumped up and down furiously and his eyes were closed. Mac knew this was some sort of meditation. He heard a sudden cheer and turned to see a new Chicago batter at the plate. Mac remembered Jeff Rose and his vulnerabilities.

Charlie Rice looked at Mac and Mac gave him the sign; breaking balls down and out. Charlie squatted behind the plate and gave the sign to Fari. She nodded, went into her smooth, coordinated wind up and delivered the pitch. Mac saw it break halfway to the plate and Rose swung and missed. The crowd erupted with a thunderous cheer.

Fari threw two more breaking balls and now the count was two strikes and one ball. She moved halfway down the mound and kicked at the dirt, softening up the "sweet spot" – that hollow place on the mound where she planted her left leg and the body's momentum transferred into the forward movement of the delivery. Fari liked a soft, slightly tilted sweet spot.

When she was satisfied with the sweet spot, she moved up the mound and glanced toward the Chicago dugout. Mama sat somewhere behind the dugout, wearing a disguise. She had told Fari earlier that she wanted to be in the best position for "putting *the eye* on Chicago's batters."

Fari smiled and looked toward center field. Mama put the eye on the batters and Cleo put a mojo on the balls.

Yes, and it's working so far, said Papa.

It is. They both have strong karma.

So do you, my darling. I can feel it. You've been holding back, haven't you?

Yes. I still feel fresh and strong.

And do you see what's happening?

Yes, Papa. Chicago has no hits.

No hits, my love, over seven innings. It's now or never.

I know.

C'mon, Baltimore Bananas! Blow 'em away! Throw fastballs, honey.

Fari set her left foot on the rubber and looked in toward home plate. The count was one ball, two strikes, and Charlie signaled for another breaking ball. She shook her head and gave him a sign; get ready! She filled her lungs with air, reared back and hurled forward with a grunting exhale.

The ball hit Charlie's mitt. Rose swung hard. Strike three. One out.

*   *

Mac stepped away from the wall and looked closely at Fari. What had just happened? This was the first time she waved off a signal. Instead of a breaking ball, she threw a snappy fastball. Mac looked at Charlie, who stared back at him with his arms held out, as though asking, what should I do?

What could he tell Charlie? It was obvious Fari had her own game plan. He waved Charlie off and shouted, "Get ready for anything!" He saw Charlie nod and shrug his shoulders. He was a shy kid who worked the fields around his family's farm in early spring, but here he was now, with more eyes on him than he had ever imagined.

And Chicago has no hits with five more batters to go.

Mac looked at the bench, but no one sat on it. All the reserves and pinch hitters were on their feet, their faces a study in stone cold control, but all were moving or jerking in some way; chewing gum or tobacco, clapping hands, snapping fingers, bouncing up and down, vibrating in place. The only sign of excitement from JD was the cigar, which moved faster than Mac had ever seen it. Just then JD turned to look at him. "She's gonna do it, Mac. She's gonna do it!"

Mac looked away quickly, pretending not to hear. He watched as Fari threw another fastball. The batter swung and "crack," the ball bounced sharply toward second base. Brent Shiner moved over two paces, caught the ball and threw it softly to first base. *Two outs.*

The stadium exploded with noise.

*   *

Far above the Minnesota dugout, inside the Lansing private suite, Doc Harris told the "blonde bombshell" a dirty joke. He couldn't remember her name, but she sported a riotous, platinum hairdo. She worked as secretary to one of the glittering group of entrepreneurs gathered inside the Lansing suite.

The blonde clutched a glass of champagne and appeared a little drunk. Doc couldn't help but admire her splendid cleavage. Under different circumstances, he might have been interested, but not here and not now. The people crowded inside this luxurious cave represented the top elite within the social and business communities throughout the Midwest. Also present, of course, were several members of the Lansing family, including Doc's wife, Sherry.

Doc stood inside the lair of the tiger that was about to devour him. He knew he didn't belong here and so did everyone else. He hadn't wanted to watch the game from here, but Sherry had demanded.

The "blonde bombshell" held her glass at a tilt and champagne dribbled onto her lap. She didn't belong here either, thought Doc. It occurred to him that maybe she was attracted to him in some *kindred* way; they were both corrupt lowlifes.

He told the blond he had to get to the bathroom and he pushed off through the crowd. At once, a tunnel opened before him, as if these people had radar. He worked his way to the other corner of the suite and pressed himself against the glass.

There were two out in the top of the eighth inning. A batter stepped up from the Chicago dugout and walked toward the batter's box. Another pinch-hitter. They were trying everyone, hoping to get a hit. But Fastball Fari still pitched hard and fast.

Doc felt the press of bodies behind him. Everyone wanted to watch the lovely Fari as she pitched her way into legend. He liked that image. The blonde had said that: "Fari Madrigal is pitching her way into legend today." He knew it was true. He could see it in the way she moved on the mound and the lively pop of the fastball.

He looked around at the rich, beautiful people inside the Lansing suite. How many of *them* are having a fantasy about Fari? *All* of them! But only *I* know where she lives.

Fari wound up, threw the ball and the batter hit it! Doc watched the ball fly high into foul territory. Charlie Rice ran down the first base line, leaned into the crowd and caught the ball! Three outs! The eighth inning was over! The stadium irrupted with wild cheering.

My Fari is going down in history and we are here to watch it.

*   *

Mac knew he stood in the eye of a hurricane. All around him swirled the lusty winds stirred up by the screams of forty-two thousand people. Inside the Twins' dugout, there was no movement and no talking. Fari sat alone in her customary spot in the corner, no one near her. She sat as before, with her hands folded in her lap and her cap pulled low.

My God, thought Mac, we're going into the ninth inning and Chicago has no hits! His heart pounded wildly and he tried to relax. He breathed slow and deep. The Twins were at bat, but the players behaved as if in shock or stupefaction. Only JD still moved with an easy, fluid motion, as he walked back and forth in front of the bench, as was his custom when he took in a game there. The cigar had been chewed to a tiny stub.

Charlie Rice was up to bat this inning. He walked toward the bat rack and paused next to Mac. "Mac?"

"What?" Mac kept his eyes on the field.

"My whole family's here today. My Mom and Dad, brothers and sisters, aunts, uncles, cousins. Hell, the whole population of Helmsville, Iowa"

Mac looked at him. Charlie's face had turned pale. "Are you all right?"

"No!" Charlie stepped quickly into the tunnel and vomited violently.

Surprised, Mac stepped back. Charlie coughed and heaved. Mac put a hand gently on his back. "You all right?"

Charlie nodded, still coughing.

Mac felt a tug on his sleeve. "Where's Charlie?" JD shouted. "He's up!"

Charlie emerged from the tunnel and wiped his face with a towel. He picked up his bat and looked at Mac. "This is the best day of my life!" He ran onto the field.

Mine too, thought Mac. Fortunately, I don't feel like throwing up. He looked at the scoreboard and saw the Twins had two outs already! He hadn't paid attention to what the Twins were doing. So what? We have four runs and Chicago has no runs. And no hits.

Crack! Charlie hit a long fly ball, but it didn't look long enough. The Chicago centerfielder ran off to his left a few steps and caught the ball. Three outs.

Oh no, thought Mac, his stomach flipping, here we go. *The ninth inning!*

*   *

Fari slipped on her glove, jumped up from the bench and trotted onto the field. A storm raged out here. Thunder rolled and the winds whipped the surf into gigantic waves. Suddenly, she was jostled and bumped. She looked up and saw Charlie Rice standing in front of her. Where did he come from? She saw terror in his eyes. She wanted to help him, but she couldn't speak. She leaned over and kissed him gently on the cheek. A deafening clap of thunder shook the sky.

Charlie disappeared and Fari walked calmly toward the mound. The thunder echoed back and forth, gathering strength and volume with each reverberation.

I've never seen or heard anything like this in my life, said Papa.

I feel the energy and heat of thousands of people.

Papa laughed. *The hot air will slow down the fastballs.*

Fari nodded. *Then I'll throw harder.* She bent down, picked up the new baseball and waved it toward center field. This time Cleo jumped straight into the air and turned in a complete circle. It must have been a special mojo.

It was a special mojo, said Papa. *After all, we're in the ninth inning, honey, and you've got a no-hitter going!*

She heard the awe and pride in Papa's voice. He had never pitched a no-hitter, although once he had pitched a one-hit game.

It's hard to believe, Papa. It feels like a dream, a dream I've had all my life.

It's both, my dear. It's a dream and it's real. It's a dream come true.

She looked toward home plate. Charlie Rice stared back at her with his mask held over his heart, a message of some kind. She inclined her head in acknowledgment. He put on his mask, squatted down and the first batter stepped up. Charlie had wanted to stop giving signals to Fari, but Mac told him to signal anyway: "To keep the opposition on its toes." Now Charlie made some nonsense movement with his fingers, but Fari noticed they were crossed.

She laughed. Look at all the magic I have! She didn't recognize the next batter, a right-hander. He must be another pinch-hitter. He was tall and thin and stood well back in the batter's box.

Throw him junk, suggested Papa.

Fari nodded, saw the pitch in her head, then wound up and threw. The batter swung and hit a hard grounder toward Fari's right. Tony Rikes ran down the ball, pivoted and threw a soft liner to first. One out!

Thunder rolled and crashed.

Fari closed her eyes, inhaled deeply.

Take it easy, my love, said Papa. *Only two more outs. You're pitching a no-hitter, honey!*

I know, Papa. I can feel it.

*   *

Listen to that crowd, Bob!

It's absolutely incredible, Herb! This stadium is *shaking!*

That's one out here in the top of the ninth. Mark Myers jumped on Fari's first pitch and hit a sharp grounder. Rikes ran it down, and did you see how deliberately he threw to first base? These guys are playing *careful.*

Of course they are! We're in the ninth inning and Fari is pitching no-hit ball! No one wants to make a mistake. The pressure on that field right now is *enormous.*

And the pressure and excitement here inside Target Field is boiling over. Okay, sports fans, the next batter is approaching home plate. It's Gianfranco, Chicago's first baseman. He struck out in his first at-bat, then went down on a caught fly ball in the sixth.

As we reported earlier, Bob, only once in the last one hundred years has any rookie pitcher ever pitched a no-hitter in his – or *her* – first big league game. In 1902, a rookie by the name of *Ambrose Wheelock* pitched a no-hitter in his first pro start for the old New York Highlanders.

So they say, Herb. We'll check that further. There's no doubt, however, that we are witnessing history unfold right here today! And Fastball Fari has a bigger audience than Ambrose Wheelock ever imagined. Okay, fans, there's one out here in the top of the ninth inning with no one on base. Gianfranco steps up to the plate. He's a left-hander and batted three oh three last season. The crowd is on its feet, cheering, screaming. Fari goes into her wind up and here's the pitch. *A fastball right down the middle! Called strike one!*

Oh, *man!* A lightning fastball! And listen to that crowd! They *love* it! Fari has put on a sterling performance so far this afternoon. Over eight innings she's has *fifteen strikeouts* and only two walks. Chicago has hit the ball *once* out of the infield. And, of course, the overriding factor inside this stadium right now is this: *Chicago has no hits!*

Okay, fans, Fari and Gianfranco are ready. Fari goes into her delivery and here's the pitch. Gianfranco *swings* and hits a high foul ball out of play. Strike two!

In case you've just joined us, or you've been on a different planet for a while, we're in the top of the ninth inning here at Target Field in Minneapolis, Minnesota. The Twins have four runs, seven hits, no errors. The Chicago White Sox have no runs, no errors and, listen to this; *no hits!* There's one out in the ninth inning and Fastball Fari is two outs away from pitching a *no-hitter!*

And that great, roaring noise you hear is the delirious cheering of forty thousand people! Okay, here we go. The count is oh and two on Gianfranco. Fari winds up and delivers the pitch. Gianfranco *swings* and hits another foul ball off to the left this time!

Gianfranco is hanging in there. He's got two strikes on him, so he's got to protect the plate. Fari has demonstrated she can throw strikes when she wants to.

Charlie Rice throws out a new ball and again Fari turns and waves it toward centerfield – some kind of secret ritual going on there. Gianfranco steps up to the plate and we're ready. The crowd is going wild now, screaming with every pitch. Fari sets, goes into her wind up, kicks and delivers. *Swing and a miss! She struck him out!*

*   *

Mac was blown backwards by the sudden gust of cheering. JD slid an arm around his back and held him to the ground. Another batter approached the plate, but Mac didn't care who it was. Top of the ninth inning. Two outs. Chicago has no hits.

Fari stood on the mound with both feet on the rubber, facing home plate, her cap tilted low, but Mac knew she looked out from the shadows. My God, he wondered, what was she feeling right now? Just then, Fari lifted her head and looked directly at him. He saw she was *laughing!*

"What's wrong with Charlie?" JD shouted. "He's pukin in the dirt."

Poor Charlie Rice. The anxiety was tearing him apart. The whole town of Helmsville was here!

Mac saw Fari settle her left foot on the rubber and look toward home plate. He assumed Charlie felt better and they were ready to go. He watched as Fari leaned back, lifted her arms and flew forward in that explosive delivery. He squeezed his eyes shut and tightened his belly. A second later the crowd erupted wildly. He looked up at the scoreboard. Fari had thrown a strike!

JD grabbed Mac and shook him like a rag doll. The winds rushed and roared. Mac's head swam, his ears flapped. Fari wound up for the next pitch! He shut his eyes and screamed as hard as he could.

Crack! The bat met the ball solidly. Mac's heart skipped, his eyes snapped open.

The white baseball floated slowly through the heated and clamorous air. A sudden hush fell over the crowd as they watched the ball fly toward history and legend – a small cowhide sphere caught in the grip of gravity, in the gaze of millions. Down and down it fell, until it disappeared into the baseball glove of Cleo Hagerty.

TWELVE

They held the press conference in the spacious ballroom of a nearby hotel. The whole team was there, transported by bus from the stadium, one block away. The bus could hardly move through the crowds filling the streets. Most of the forty thousand fans from inside the stadium mixed with the twenty thousand in the parking lots and flooded the nearby neighborhood, blowing away police barricades.

Journalists fought their way through the crowds and arrived at the hotel breathing heavily, producing an atmosphere laced with giddy hysteria. When the team walked out on the stage, the room burst into cheers and applause. The players grouped around Fari, congratulating her, pushing her to the center of the stage. She laughed and cried, unable to speak, hiding her face behind her hands.

A microphone had been set up and Howard Sikes said a few words, a few of the players spoke, but the crowd chanted, "Fari!" "Fari!" "Fari!" Finally, JD took Fari by the arm and drew her gently toward the microphone. She stood slightly crouched, her hands covering her face, as the cheering continued. After a moment, she leaned toward the microphone and spoke through her fingers. "Quiero decir gracias a mis companeros." She turned and bowed to her teammates. "Muchas gracias, muchachos."

The crowd went wild and wouldn't let up. Frances finally organized the pandemonium into a semblance of a press conference. Although Fari was unable to face the crowd directly, Frances persuaded her to answer a few questions.

Mac and Cleo knew they'd have trouble leaving the hotel. Yes, the crowd was joyous, but also hungry, *ravenous* for Fastball Fari. They decided to spend the night in the hotel. They sent Stew to rent two connecting suites in his name. Fari was held captive by the tumultuous crowd for nearly an hour. Finally, Cleo escorted her off stage and into the freight elevator.

Fari felt weak and exhausted from holding together her cocoon. She sagged against Cleo. "Thank you." The silence and safety of the elevator allowed her a few moments to recover, and soon she regained the glorious rush of winning the game, pitching a no-hitter! She had a hard time grasping the reality of it; she could only *feel* it.

JD, Frances, Mac, Kim and Fari assembled in Cleo and Betsy's suite, which provided a large, formal dining room. The mood was subdued, languorous. Fari appeared lethargic and giddy. Since the end of the game, she had managed only occasional bursts of Spanish. The others felt limp and speechless, immersed in the deep, empathetic connection that comes from sharing a profound experience.

After dinner, Fari came out of her trance and said a few coherent sentences in English. Cleo rose from his chair, walked around the table and stood next to Fari. He bowed deeply from the waist. "Thank you, Sister Fari, for the most glorious day of my life."

Fari stood up and bowed back. "Thank *you*, Cleo, for mojo."

Cleo fell into her arms and buried his face in her shoulder. Kim and Betsy walked over and they all rocked together in a group hug, emitting a low, keening noise.

Mac had the silly sensation of floating inside a thick cloud of cotton candy. He had never seen such a beautifully pitched game in his life. And it was her major league debut! *A no-hitter!* Even now, at the mere thought of it, his spine shivered.

Frances and JD announced they were leaving. Frances knew the Command Center must be swamped by correspondence, and she wanted to review it before Alfred arrived the next day. JD and Frances embraced Fari, congratulated her again, then left.

Kim and Mac escorted Fari toward their own suite, but detoured for another round of hugging with Cleo and Betsy. Finally, they were alone in their own private space. The suite had two bedrooms; Fari would stay in one, and Kim and Mac in the other.

Mac drifted toward the wall of windows and drew aside the curtains. Crowds of people still hung around the intersections, yelling and whooping. You'd think we won the World Series, he thought. A no-hitter! He had never pitched one. The fewest hits he ever gave up in one game was three. Ah, but he had dreamed, of course, as every pitcher must dream about pitching a no-hitter. Just then he felt two thin arms encircle his waist and he looked down at Kim.

"Good night, Daddy," she said. "I'm so proud of you and Fari." She buried her face in his chest.

He stroked her silky, blond hair. "Good night, honey. I hope you remember this day the rest of your life."

"Oh, I will!" Kim jumped back, smiling. "Fastball Fari is snap, crackle and pop." They laughed and Kim turned to Fari. They hugged and whispered, then Kim skipped off to the bedroom.

Fari sat in an armchair facing the window, staring into the night. She felt exhausted from the earlier high-charged, adrenaline rush. When Cleo had caught the last out, she and Papa had lost themselves in a wild burst of joy. She cried and screamed, only vaguely aware of wetting her pants! Thank God she was immediately swamped by her teammates and no one noticed.

Now she drifted on the velvet sensation of deep contentment, not unlike the drained euphoria after an orgasm – the same lavish exhaustion. Her cheeks flushed and she became aware of Mac standing next to the window. She believed she had a psychic and emotional connection with both Mac and Kim. They had all lost someone dear to them and yet had summoned the strength to carry on.

"Mac," she said softly. She gestured with one hand and indicated the floor next to her. "Venga, siéntese."

He moved closer and sat on the thick carpeting. He drew up his knees and hugged them to his chest.

"Papa taught me to conserve my strength," said Fari. She continued to stare out the window. "I am sorry I ignored your signals. I should have explained earlier."

Mac thought about it; she's apologizing for ignoring my signals? He had an urge to laugh, but stopped himself in deference to the serious tone in her voice.

Fari sat up straighter and spoke with a sharper edge. "When Papa died, I lived alone on beach. I read books." She sighed heavily and pounded one thigh with her fist. "I read so much my dreams were in *narrative*."

Mac held his breath as Jenni crossed his mind. He kept his mouth shut, realizing Fari had chosen this moment to say these things. He listened with his eyes, ears, heart and soul.

Fari lifted her head and glanced at Mac. "Papa is still with me and always will be." Her voice sounded lighter and he heard a smile. "He was with me today, Mac. He told me to throw fastballs."

Mac smiled, recalling how she had reared back and fired hard during the last two innings.

Fari shifted in the chair, glanced at him and spoke quietly. "Papa and I pitched fantasy games together, surrounded by jungle."

Mac sat motionless, breathing quietly, not wanting to distract her. She set a new record tonight for talking.

"Jungle is order, but is also unpredictable. Random movement is part of universal mechanism." She paused and asked, "Le gusta el mar?"

Mac hesitated, thrown off slightly at the sudden change in subject and language. "Yes, I love the ocean."

"Tides go up and down, according to moon. You see? This is assurance and security." She leaned down and brought her face close to his. "But people can be unpredictable in bad ways."

Mac knew she tried to tell him something, but what was it?

Fari reached out and laid one hand gently on his shoulder. She *did* try to tell him something, but without actually saying it. She liked Mac, she might even love him. He had always treated her with respect and kind regard. She felt an urge to tell him her secret.

But she held back, unable to find the words. Or the courage, she thought, disappointed with herself. She didn't want to hurt Mac or Kim, but someday she knew she would have to. On sudden impulse, she put her hand on the back of his head, pulled him forward and kissed him quickly on the lips.

Mac felt Fari's mouth make a dry, soft contact against his lips. For a second or two they kissed, then she withdrew and sat up in the chair. "Usted mi cae bien, Mac," she whispered, running her fingers through his hair. "I hope you visit our farm. You and Kim. Les invito."

Mac nodded silently, unable to speak, his lips welded shut.

*   *

Doc Harris slipped out of the arms of Janice, the blonde bombshell, swung his legs to the floor and walked over to the window. Fari's condo remained dark and silent and now he was sure they weren't coming home tonight. He turned and looked at the pale, naked form lying on the bed. Janice's ass was flat and round, a little bigger than he preferred. But she proved to be an enthusiastic lover, even drunk as she was. To him, it was just another screw, and now he felt disgusted with himself. He had not wanted to do this again, mainly since he was sure Sherry still had private detectives watching him.

After the game, he and Sherry had gotten separated. He figured he could pull a fast one and disappear for a while. He made arrangements with Janice to meet at a bar not far from the townhouse complex, and she left before he did. Doc had plunged into the crowds around the stadium and skipped into the nearest skyway system. No one could have followed him. He met Janice at the bar, they had a drink, then walked to the condo.

Doc looked at Fari's condo again. He imagined the lights on, the shade up and Fari naked. Her body would be firm and strong, yet curvy, *luscious*. He laughed and slapped his bare thigh, feeling good about himself again. Earlier, inside the Lansing suite, he had felt suffocated and squashed by the combined arrogance of all those rich people.

Janice turned on her back and cocked one leg in the air, her breasts lying flat against her chest. Doc felt his penis stirring and glanced at his watch. They had time for another quick one before he dumped her at her hotel.

*   *

The Command Center was dark and quiet. Frances leaned back in her chair, her hands behind her head, staring at the computer screen. She loved the solid, secure feel of JD's house. It was one hundred years old and still felt firm and strong. This old house has sheltered many lives and will shelter many more. Or maybe it would rot from within, weakened by years of personal failings and private shames.

At this moment, however, during the residence of Jack Daniels Johnson, the house absorbed a *positive* energy. Also, of course, with all the plants, it was an oxygen factory.

Beep! The corporate email went off again. This was number six hundred! Before this afternoon's game, it was a little over three hundred. Tomorrow morning, on Monday, she expected a flood more.

At that thought, Frances felt a sudden gush of love for Fari. She had been so nervous about this first game that Frances had to help her get dressed. Then she went out and pitched a no-hitter! Frances had sat in amazement during the last two innings, caught up in the general excitement. (But she never missed putting *the eye* on every Chicago batter.)

Frances skipped through the corporate messages. Most of the big, multinational companies begged Frances to allow them to buy (or rent) Fari's glittering identity. They wanted Fari associated with *them*. Why? For profit.

Well, thought Frances, that's all the better for me. As the Devil knows, there's nothing easier to manipulate than a motive driven by greed.

She leaned over the keyboard and typed in a name. This time she got a response! United Brands had sent an e-mail! Did they want Fari to wear a grass dress and a hat festooned with fruit? The new Miss Chiquita Banana?

"Ha!" Frances shouted. They've got a surprise coming! She had waited forty years for this moment. She retrieved two letters she had previously written especially for this occasion. One letter was addressed personally to the CEO of United Brands; the other was sent to the hundreds of other corporations interested in Fari.

As she worked, she recalled the horror of that day so long ago. She saw the white, bloodied sheet with Felipe's boots sticking up from one end; she saw other covered bodies and families crying and pounding the ground.

As the tears gathered and rolled down Frances' cheeks, she remembered to sit back from the keyboard. *Maybe nothing will come of this, but I made a promise and I have to try.*

When she had sent the messages, she leaned back in the chair and tried to still the disturbance inside her chest. Fari had done her part of the deal; indeed, she had performed above and beyond the call of duty. Now it was up to Frances to properly exploit this opportunity. Tomorrow morning she will have to be sharp, clever and swift.

This attack against United Brands will surely stir up the media and they'll discover the saga of the "Red Gang." Frances' name will be featured in a drama of romance, violence and murder. The media will love it and the public will be appropriately aghast and titillated.

She heard music coming from the kitchen. Suddenly, all her cares and worries disappeared before the prospect of a late-night snack and someone to talk to. She turned off the phones, left the office and walked toward the light and music. She found JD bent over the stove, waving a spatula in time with Mozart. "Hi," she called.

He turned around. "Hi. How about a piece of grilled cheese sandwich?" He stepped aside and revealed a plump sandwich roasting on the grill. "I figured the smell might get to you."

She smiled back at him. "It was the music. But that sandwich smells and looks lovely."

JD covered the sandwich and joined Frances at the breakfast bar. He wore a long-sleeved, green robe, trimmed with colorful material he had picked up in Guatemala. "You must be very proud of Fari. I sure am."

"Oh, yes. So is Jose."

"Yes."

They were silent for a moment. The violins wept soft and low, as if on cue. "I've never seen any pitcher with such control," said JD. "It's scary, almost supernatural." He smiled to let her know he was kidding.

But Frances wondered; where did Fari get this phenomenal talent if not from God?

"Or maybe it's something psychic," JD said. He stood up, stepped over to the stove and turned the sandwich. "The trick is to get the cheese soft, partially melted, but not gooey."

Frances had focused on the word "psychic" and thought it was as good an explanation as any. "You may be right," she said, as JD returned to his stool. "It might be something telekinetic."

He stared at her for a moment. "Are you serious?"

Frances laughed and sat up straighter. "Fari used to tell us she saw the pitch in her mind *before* she threw the ball. She described it as a 'mind picture.'"

They thought about that. Finally JD asked, "What does she see in these 'pictures?'"

"She sees the line of the pitch, like a white line, where it's supposed to go. Then, according to her, her body moves automatically."

JD believed this was entirely possible. In fact, he was convinced there were many things going on in this universe we can't imagine. The idea that Fari can somehow influence the trajectory of her pitches seemed easy to accept. He recalled her behavior during the game and wondered if she went into some sort of auto-hypnotic trance. "When was she diagnosed with Asperger's?"

"When she was five. But Jose and I knew something was strange before then." Frances paused and stared at the far wall for a moment, watching something in her memory. "Jose built a pitcher's mound in the backyard and liked to throw the ball a few hours every day. Fari, even as a baby, was completely fascinated by this activity. She'd sit on the grass and watch him for hours.

"When she was around three, she tried throwing the baseballs, but they were too big. Jose brought home a few racquetballs and they fit her little hands perfectly."

JD shook his head and laughed. "And now look at her. Throwing ninety-mile-an-hour fastballs."

Frances laughed with him. "Yes. It's amazing." She looked into her wine glass and nodded to herself. "Asperger's Syndrome is rarely diagnosed in girls. Fari is a special person."

A faint whiff of burnt bread passed under their noses. JD jumped up quickly and skipped to the stove. "Damn!" he said and Frances laughed.

The sandwich wasn't burned all that badly, but it was a bit gooey. Nevertheless, they shared a few delicious mouthfuls of warm bread and cheese, accompanied by a glass of wine. When they had finished the sandwich, they carried their wine into the dark living room and sat on the sofa. Far off flashes of lightning provided brief, stark snapshots of the lake. It also illuminated a truck with a microwave dish on its roof.

JD decided to keep to the back rooms and leave the front of the house dark. Also, he realized that with Fari's marvelous performance this afternoon, the public's interest in her had gone beyond fever pitch. He looked at Frances. "I want to ask you a personal question, and if you can't answer I'll understand."

She nodded. "Go ahead."

"What really happened between you and Howard Sikes?"

Frances laughed and almost spilled her wine. "That's highly confidential, JD."

"Yes, I know."

Aside from her own intuition about JD, Frances knew that Jose had loved him. Besides, she was dying to tell someone! "Howard and I sat on a bench not too far from here. When I told him he had to give up eight million dollars, he jumped up so fast he stepped in the water!" She bent over laughing and related the rest of the story.

JD thought it over. "Five million to local charities and three million to the Madrigal Foundation. What's that?"

"A nonprofit institute that donates money and material to rural school systems in the Dominican Republic. We solicited money, and Jose donated his time and part of his pension. Also, local businesses contributed."

"And now you've got three million dollars. Since this is an overseas donation, I suppose Howard can't claim it on taxes?"

"I don't think so."

"Ha! That's good."

"Yes. And the money is good for us. We'll be able to provide hundreds of kids in the rural areas with a primary education."

"Really? That's remarkable."

"A dollar goes a long way down there. We'll use half the money to build prefab school rooms and train teachers. The local communities will help with labor and material. The other half of the money goes into a special trust and the interest pays the teachers' salaries."

JD shook his head in admiration. "Three million means nothing to Howard, but look what you can do with it."

Frances sat up straighter. "Yes, it's amazing, isn't it? It reminds me of what Churchill once said."

This caught JD by surprise and he looked at her over the tops of his glasses. "How's that?"

She raised her glass and spoke in a British accent. "Never have so many owed so much to so few!"

They laughed together.

Twenty-five years ago, JD had spent five days with Frances and Jose at their home in San Jose. He had enjoyed himself immensely. Every night they had built a fire, drank "guaro" and talked. "Remember when I came down for your wedding?" He laughed. "I think we got drunk every night."

Frances laughed with him. "I think we did." She spoke again more softly. "Jose always appreciated your help, you know."

"Yes, I know. And he was worth it a hundred times over." They remained quiet for a moment, then JD deflected the conversation. "We used to talk about the 'paradigm of human behavior.'"

Frances laughed. "Jose thought the industrial revolution provided the opportunity for a new paradigm. The human race had moved from agriculture to manufacturing, and since resources are limited, we had a chance to adopt a paradigm of cooperation. Instead, we embraced *competition* and something called 'national interest.'"

"Ah, yes." JD sighed. "The age-old question: Where did we go wrong?"

She glanced at him to see if this was a joke, but he looked serious. "All I'm doing, JD, is rearranging the resources a bit."

"Yes, I see what you're doing, and I think it's highly admirable. But you know what it means? Fari will have to endorse hamburgers and shoes."

"Yes. We know we'll do things we don't like. Compromising our values." She paused and looked into his eyes. "But the *benefits*, JD. The benefits will far outweigh any shame or discomfort for me and Fari."

He smiled. "I respect what you're doing and I back you all the way."

"Thank you, JD. That means a lot to me. I've been working secretly, but I'm glad you know. I'm glad we can talk about it."

"Anytime. As I said before, you and Fari are a delightful surprise in my life. And at my age that means a lot!" He laughed.

"Thanks. But it *is* hard. I've never handled such huge sums of money, nor dealt with so many people. The plan seemed fine in my head, but the reality is almost overwhelming." She fell back against the sofa and looked out the window. "I'm afraid Fari and I have taken on more than we can handle."

"I should remind you of something Churchill once said."

She smiled and looked at him. "How's that?"

JD raised his glass and spoke in a deep British accent. "Never give up, I say. Never give in. Fight on to victory!"

They laughed, clinked glasses and tossed off the wine.

THIRTEEN

Monday: March 31

At seven thirty in the morning, Frances sat at her post in the Command Center, rested, showered and fed. Alfred would show up after school, at about two in the afternoon. Meanwhile, she watched the computer and TV for any response from United Brands.

In her letter to the CEO of United Brands, Frances described an incident that occurred in March 1980, during a strike on the banana plantations of United Fruit Company in Palmar Sur, Costa Rica. Twenty-two workers had been killed in a confrontation with police and the company's security guards. Shortly after this incident, in June, a civil suit was filed on behalf of the families and eventually a court in San Jose issued a ruling condemning United Fruit for "acting in bad faith" and "with reckless disregard for human life."

Frances demanded that United Brands take out half-page advertisements in various editions of national and international newspapers (these she listed), including all the principal dailies in Costa Rica. These announcements should display the names of the dead, along with an apology from United Brands and condolences to the families. Further, she suggested that they appear in tomorrow's editions.

In her letter to all other corporations, Frances informed them of her demand to United Brands and included a copy of the civil court's decision. She went on to say she would love to discuss endorsement possibilities, but, regrettably, she could not talk to them until United Brands had printed the announcements.

Frances watched the business channel, waiting to see if someone might leak this news. If someone didn't leak it fairly soon, then she would. If she called a press conference right now, fifty journalists would be outside the house within fifteen minutes. Such was the power of national celebrity. Look at what she was doing now, for example – setting in motion a corporate whirlwind!

"Hey, Frances!" JD called from the front hall. "You've got a package."

Frances made her way to the front door, where she found a young man holding a long box and a clipboard.

"Someone sent you flowers," said JD. "A nice way to start the day. Well, I have to take off. Will you be at the stadium later?"

"I don't think so." Frances signed her name to the receipt. "Alfred and I have lots to do today."

"Okay, I'll see you later. Give 'em hell!"

"I will. Good luck against Chicago."

Frances gave the young man a tip and he blushed and smiled. "Say 'hi' to Fastball Fari."

Frances carried the box into the kitchen and unwrapped it. She found a dozen red roses lying in a bed of white tissue paper. On top was a small envelope. She opened it to find a card that read, "Thank you for your support. H.S."

She smiled and smelled the roses. Lovely! She found an empty vase and set the flowers on her desk in the CC. Yesterday, she had confirmed Howard's version of the donations, and since then the tone of reporting on Howard had shifted slightly. Now he was regarded as something of a corporate maverick, a hard-headed capitalist with a soft heart.

Frances had seen an interview with Howard last evening. He had acted humble and embarrassed, but managed to accept all the credit. He even explained the social programs that would benefit from his donations. She wondered how much was public posturing and how much was real interest. Wouldn't it be amazing, she thought, if this experience forced Howard to start listening with his heart?

She decided to help him in this noble endeavor by demanding that he donate even more.

Someone mentioned United Brands on the TV! A young woman sat at a desk with stock market symbols flowing above her head. Frances grabbed the remote and turned up the volume.

"Carl Prescott, a Pepsi vice president, confirmed the report. Apparently, Mrs. Marchena has demanded that United Brands publish the names of twenty-two workers who were killed in 1980 during a strike on a plantation owned by United Fruit Company, now known as United Brands.

"Pepsi spokesperson, Marcy Williams, said that Mrs. Marchena's statement included a copy of a court decision issued in Costa Rica regarding this incident. Apparently, this decision condemns United Fruit for, quote; 'exhibiting reckless disregard for the lives of the workers and their families,' unquote. The document is in Spanish and they're having it translated.

"Meanwhile, we have no further details about Mrs. Marchena's statement, except that Ms. Williams did imply that other US corporations also received the same message. We've been unable to confirm this and United Brands has not returned our calls."

Frances recalled that PepsiCo was one of the first companies to send a message. It was unusual in that it was a personal communication straight from the Chairman, Mr. Rodney McNulty. She found the message and wrote down the phone number. Mr. McNulty might be a good mediator in her negotiations with United Brands. Also, she liked the fact that his company was the underdog in the global soda pop wars.

The story on United Brands broke quickly as several more corporations admitted receiving the same declaration from Frances Marchena. Half an hour later, a spokesperson for United Brands issued a statement: "The current management of United Brands does not recognize responsibility for what might have happened in a foreign country thirty-four years ago. Unfortunately, labor unrest can sometimes lead to violence, injury, and even death. However, this is a general condition and not specific to United Brands.

"Furthermore, we regard Mrs. Marchena's statements as hypocritical, since she was arrested and convicted of second degree murder during the same strike. Mrs. Marchena was a member of the 'Red Gang,' a group of young communists found guilty of killing a security guard.

"We believe this is a publicity stunt staged by Mrs. Frances Marchena for reasons only she knows. Her statements are damaging to the good name of United Brands and we regard her actions as irresponsible and possibly litigatory."

Frances listened with a smirk on her face; the "Red Gang" indeed! No one ever heard of the Red Gang, but in Central America the name United Brands still evoked the lingering stench of corruption. Remember the *banana* republics, with their "ruling military juntas?" Remember the coup d'état against Guatemalan President Arbenz in 1954? To this day, Guatemala has not recovered! In a fury, Frances whirled around, picked up her red phone and dialed the personal number of PepsiCo CEO, Rodney McNulty.

"Hello?" A deep male voice answered.

"Hello. This is Frances Marchena. I would like to speak with Mr. Rodney McNulty please."

"Mrs. Marchena! This is Rodney. Please call me Rod. I'm glad you called. Interesting things are happening this morning, aren't they?"

"They sure are, Rod. Please call me Frances."

"Pass on my congratulations to Fari for such a wonderful performance yesterday. Absolutely amazing. You must be very proud of her."

"Yes, I am." Frances made a snap decision based mainly on the sound of his voice. "We've been considering an association with Pepsi."

"Oh, yes? Well, I hope so. We're prepared to do whatever it takes to welcome you into the Pepsi family."

"Thank you. But at the moment there's a little snag."

"Yes, we're all hung up on United Brands." McNulty was silent for a moment. "Are you serious about this? You won't talk to us until UB prints those ads?"

"Yes, I'm *very* serious." Frances decided to use a little trump card on Rodney, even though it bordered on crass manipulation. "I've been researching Pepsi this morning. You've been doing a fine job at turning the company around, but you could use extra help in Latin America, right?"

McNulty seemed to hesitate, then answered. "Yes, you're right. We have a lot of ground to make up south of the border."

Frances appreciated his restraint for not snapping at the bait like a shark. In the corporate reports she had read, McNulty was described as a "gentleman with a sharp, keen mind and a hands-on style."

She tried to sound casual. "Well, I believe we can work out something, Rod. As you know, Fari is fabulously popular in Latin America."

McNulty made no comment, so Frances continued. "In any case, it was nice talking with you, Rod. Maybe we can do business soon."

"Uh, yes, I hope so. Could you call me back in an hour, please? I might have more news about United Brands."

"Of course, Rod. Thank you." She cut the transmission and threw the phone in the air. "Vamos hasta el cielo!"

*   *

Last night, Mac had promised Fari he'd take her to a nature reserve. Today's game started at two in the afternoon, so they had plenty of time. She told him she wanted to go to a place "completely surrounded by natural things."

They sneaked out of the hotel and into a rental car. Mac drove to the condo and they changed clothes. The nearest nature reserve he knew was on Diamond Lake in south Minneapolis. The reserve featured paths and wooden walkways through the swamp and forest.

Fari dressed in her usual outfit; hiking shoes, jeans, bulky sweater, cap and dark glasses, but this time, no baseball. When they were safely on the highway, she took off the cap and glasses. Although Mac pronounced the traffic as "light," she thought there were quite a few cars and trucks. She studied the high walls constructed along either side of the highway. "Why are those walls, Mac?"

"Sound barriers. It's a courtesy to the people who live along the highway."

She smiled. "Muy considerado."

Mac glanced at her. He admired the lovely symmetry of her face and the bold, honey-colored eyes. This morning, however, he had learned something about Fari that scared him. JD mentioned that she might have telekinetic powers. Mac thought he referred to television, that she was tele-genic.

"No, Mac. *Telekinetic.* Look it up."

Mac did look it up and almost dropped the dictionary. The power to influence material objects with the mind!

Fari sensed the stiffness in Mac. Last night he had been relaxed and easy, but this morning he acted nervous. Maybe it was the kiss, she thought. She wasn't skilled in social intercourse and sometimes committed terrible blunders. Part of the problem was the confusion between their professional and personal identities. Mac was the pitching coach and she was a pitcher. This relationship was clear and straightforward. But who are we right now inside this car?

Mac left the highway, followed Minnehaha Parkway to Diamond Lake and parked the car. The wooden sidewalks were built on posts driven into the marshy ground. The trees and bushes looked bare, but green glowed everywhere as the buds of spring emerged. The air felt cool and smelled of swamp and organic rot.

Mac and Fari walked slowly, Fari with her hands in her pockets. Their footsteps echoed hollowly off the wooden sidewalk. At this early hour, the reserve was deserted. For the first time in days, Fari felt completely surrounded by nature. No houses were visible, but they heard the distant, dull mutter of the city.

Fari closed her eyes and inhaled deeply. The natural smells ignited a feeling of longing. She thought about home, the safety and familiarity of it. She shivered, shook off the homesickness and focused on Mac. "You come here often?"

"Yes. I used to come here a lot. Kim likes it and, uh, Jennifer liked it."

Fari wondered if this was another blunder on her part, making him come to a place where he has to confront painful memories. But it was his choice.

"It's nice in here," he said. "We should come back in two weeks when all the leaves will be out." He looked at her and smiled. "But in the summer, the mosquitoes would drive you crazy."

She smiled back and looked away quickly. "Hay mosquitos en la jungla, but not many on beach."

"Really?"

"Yes. I think too much breeze."

The wooden sidewalk carried them over a stretch of water. Water lilies floated here and there and a forest of cattails waved in the wind. Fari laughed and pointed. "Perros calientes!" She looked at him. "Hot dogs on sticks."

Mac felt a lurching pressure inside his chest. Cattails as hot dogs.

That had been a favorite joke between he and Jennifer, part of their private, coded language. A lump formed in his throat and they walked on silently.

Mac remembered the day when they told him he had to quit playing baseball. He and Jenni had come out to this reserve to be alone and talk. Mac had felt betrayed by his own body. His whole adult life had been built on his performance at sports, and now he couldn't perform anymore. He had lost his life and didn't have another to replace it. Jenni had stuck by his side all the way, offering encouragement and love. A few years later, they came out here to the reserve and Jenni told him she had been diagnosed with cancer.

These memories stirred up a steaming magma deep in Mac's bowels – a hot, poisonous brew. He recognized an old twisted oak tree along the trail and stopped, only vaguely aware of Fari stopping next to him. He and Jenni called this their "magic tree." They'd linger at this spot – kissing, laughing, crying.

Fari moved off one side, her eyes on Mac. His face had paled and his eyes went dark and distant. "Mac?"

The last time Mac and Jenni had been in this reserve, Jenni was in a wheelchair. She had been drugged heavily, but she knew they were in their favorite place; her hands had stopped shaking and her eyes had focused. Earlier that day, the doctors had told him they could do nothing more for Jennifer.

Jennifer was fading before his eyes and he couldn't stop it, he couldn't save her!

The volcano erupted. Mac's spine snapped backwards, his face lifted to the sky and a long howl issued from his throat.

Fari stepped back, astounded, then realized Mac was in anguish. She hugged him tightly, turned her face toward the sky and howled with him.

*   *

Alfred wore bright yellow tennis shoes and Frances teased him. "My God, Alfred, turn off those shoes!"

Alfred laughed in his shy way. "You're just jealous."

Frances laughed with him, happy at his arrival, and happy with the problems of United Brands. The red phone rang; it was Rod McNulty.

"Hi, Rod. How's it going?"

"Hello, Frances. I took the liberty of talking to Don Fredricks. I told him I was in contact with you and if he had any private suggestions, he could pass them on through me. I assume this is okay with you?"

"Of course." Donald Fredricks was Chairman of United Brands!

"He called me back a few minutes ago. He says they'll print the names and condolences, but no apology. And only in international papers, not in the US. That's his suggestion."

A rush of relief washed over Frances. She had been worried about their first foray into Corporate America, but now she knew the power was real and these people took her seriously. She even has a *friend*; Rodney McNulty, Chief Executive Officer of PepsiCo!

She looked at the clock. Events will have to happen quickly if United Brands is to get the announcement in tomorrow's editions. She had won the battle and could afford to be gracious. "Okay, Rod, please tell Mr. Fredricks that his proposal is not quite satisfactory. Tell him it's okay on the international editions, but in the Costa Rican newspapers they *must* include the apology." Fredricks had offered a compromise and she offered another.

"All right, Frances. Speaking for myself, I think you're being very fair. I'll try to convince Fredricks, but we don't have much time."

"Any help will be greatly appreciated and we have a little time yet."

"By the way; is it true, what they said? You were convicted of murder?"

His voice carried a tone of awe. "Yes, Rod. Second degree murder. We didn't intend to kill anyone. It's a long story."

"Okay. Maybe someday you'll me that story. I'll call Fredricks and talk to you later."

"Thank you, Rod." Frances laid the phone on her desk, sat back and closed her eyes. She saw all the things she wanted to do – the possibilities were as endless as the extent of poverty and suffering. One person, Fari Madrigal, can help improve the lives of thousands, maybe millions!

She leaned over and turned off her phones except the red one. The little skirmish with United Brands would soon be over; a promise made and delivered. Now it was time for the main event! Her eyes strayed to the vase of red roses and she thought about Howard Sikes.

She picked up the red phone and punched his office number. "Hello. This is Frances Marchena. I would like to speak to Mr. Sikes please."

"Just a moment, Mrs. Marchena."

Howard came on the line in less than three seconds. "Hello, Frances. How are you?"

"Fine, Howard. Thank you for the roses. They're beautiful."

"You're welcome. I appreciate what you did."

"I wonder if it's time for you and I to meet by the lake again." She listened to his response, then laughed. "This time I suggest you wear *boots.*"

*　　　*

Later that evening, Fari sat at the desk in her bedroom and wrote in her journal. The experience with Mac that morning in the reserve had exhausted them both, yet they had to rush back to the condo and get ready for the game. Fari wouldn't be pitching, but she was on the team and wanted to be at the stadium. It was Mac's job, of course, and he had to pull himself together.

After the game, Mac had been quiet during their walk through the skyways. When they had said their goodbyes at the condo, they laughed at their hoarse voices, a shy recognition of their shared experience on the field of grief.

Fari stood up and stepped over the window. She shoved aside the curtain, bent over and pulled up the inside window. Immediately, she heard a low rumble and looked toward the street. A motorcycle passed beneath the glow of a streetlight, a black shadow that disappeared into the darkness. A sudden shiver ran up her spine, but it wasn't the cool breeze. It was the motorcycle; something about the motorcycle touched a nerve.

A horn honked and Fari returned to the desk. She liked to hear the sounds of the city, sounds of life beyond this room. Sirens were the sounds she heard most often. She wrote in the journal about their visit to the nature reserve, including a description of the "magic tree." Mac had told her later about the significance of this old, gnarled oak tree.

A puff of cool air blew across her back. She wore only a bra and panties, but even then she felt constricted. When she had lived on the beach, she rarely dressed in anything more than sandals or boots. She

169

had lived alone with the ocean in front of her and rainforest all around her. She liked the touch of the breeze on her skin, and the cool, wet kisses of raindrops. Now, however, she had left on her underwear, which seemed symbolic of how she felt in the city – vulnerable, spied on, confined.

She re-focused on the journal. Mac had told her about the hospital psychologist he'd been seeing, but nothing seemed to happen. He had never imagined there could be something called "proper grieving." He confessed he hadn't been to Jennifer's grave since the funeral, afraid of what kind reaction it might provoke.

Fari had been surprised by Mac's outburst, but even more surprised at her own. For a moment she had gotten lost in the screaming, really feeling the anger. Afterward, her heart had felt lighter, cleaner.

She wrote in the journal. "The magic tree really works."

Tomorrow, Tuesday, the Twins had a day off. Chicago was here for only two games and the Twins began another series on Wednesday against the Kansas City Royals. Fari was scheduled to start the third game, Friday evening, the Twins' first night game of the season.

Fari loved pitching in the big leagues, and now she and Mama were in a perfect position to solicit funds. These were the two overriding reasons for her presence here. Beyond them, she saw no future for her here; not in this city, not in this culture. Her life outside of baseball had been squeezed downto the size of this condo, this room. Outside these walls, she was a wanted woman, a target for the Eyes and Ears, a star in pornographic fantasies.

Now she understood the anger she had felt that morning in the reserve.

Another siren whooped nearby, a car door slammed, someone shouted. Fari smiled. She can endure the silence within these walls and the city noises from without. And to maintain her strength, she would always remember this: The little cottage on the beach was hers now, and someday she would live there.

She heard a soft knock on the door. "Fari? Are you still awake?"

It was Kim. "Yes, Kim. What is it?"

"Uh, my Dad's here. He wants to talk to you."

"Okay. I will be right out." She jumped up from the desk and pulled on pants and a shirt. She felt better now, at least about her own personal program, but what about Chet Macquire?

*   *

Doc danced and laughed inside his new condo, celebrating the photo opportunity of a lifetime. He had waited for over three hours, and finally his patience was rewarded. The curtains had parted and Fari appeared at the window wearing only a bra and panties! She had bent over, jerked up the window and disappeared. It happened fast, but he had managed to get off three quick shots. He had zoomed in close and nearby streetlights helped. He had no trouble making out Fari's facial features.

My God, these photos are worth *thousands*.

He had made this part of his plan. He knew Fari would help him. The extra money would kick up his level of retirement considerably. He had contacts in the media and they would help him sell the photos. But it had to happen fast. Friday was his day of departure. The money he'd received for his "stolen" car had already been wired to his account in Canada, and now the tabloids would outbid each other at the chance to publish these photos! Fifty thousand? A hundred?

He shouted, laughed and stomped his feet. It's good-bye Sherry and hello to a new life!

FOURTEEN

Howard Sikes felt in a good mood this morning. The concession receipts from Sunday's game had broken all previous records, and yesterday's game was the second highest. At the same time, the story broke about his charitable donations and his image soared to heights he never thought possible. Now he worried about *next* year; Fari signed a one year contract. Meanwhile, gotta make hay while the sun shines!

The limo arrived at Lake of the Isles and Howard saw Frances walking along the water's edge. He told Pedro, his chauffeur, to stand by, then walked briskly toward the lake.

Frances threw pieces of bread on the water and watched the ducks and geese swim in to snap it up. She admired their colorful feathers and graceful movements. The cool, morning air carried a moist tingle and colors appeared sharper, clearer.

"Good morning, Frances."

She turned and saw Howard standing next to a bench. He held a white a paper bag in one hand. "Good morning, Howard." She walked over and they shook hands.

He had brought Costa Rican coffee and bagels with cream cheese. They sat on the bench together, nibbled at the bagels and sipped the steaming coffee. Howard chatted about the inquiries he'd received from all over the world, people wanting to talk to him about Fastball Fari.

Frances saw he was pleased with himself. "I hope you mentioned the donations."

He gave her a sharp look. "Well, if they ask me, I'll talk about it."

"I was thinking you might bring it up in the context of asking other people in your position to do the same."

Howard smiled. Not many women rose to his level in the corporate elite, but Frances was a different character altogether. She was not from the corporate world. He didn't know *what* world she was from. "I wasn't exactly a willing donor," he reminded her. "I don't think I'd be very convincing as a crusader."

"You sounded pretty good in the local interviews. But you're probably right. You won't be convincing unless you actually *believe* it." Give him time, thought Frances. Howard was not stupid, he was merely blind, and she had thought of a way to open his eyes. "In the contract we signed, there's a clause about promotional activities. I have some questions."

Howard nodded, trying to keep his face straight. In the projections for this year, the accountants had figured in about one million in royalties from Fari's promotions. This figure was based on what they received from two other players active in promotion, one of whom was Cleo Hagerty. "What would you like to know?"

"The percentage is eight percent?"

"Yes, that's right."

"Okay. If Fari receives so much for a promotion where she appears in a Twins uniform, or anything with 'Twins' on it, she's obligated to pay the Twins eight percent of that amount. Is this correct?"

"Essentially, yes."

"Well, then, tell me this, Howard: How much would the Twins get if Fari receives nothing?"

Oh God, thought Howard, *now* what? He knew he didn't understand Frances because she continually surprised him. He had brought bagels and coffee, hoping to set a friendly tone, but things have already gone haywire. He decided to be patient. "If Fari receives nothing, then the Twins would get nothing."

Frances admired his self control. "Here's the problem we have, Howard. Fari has decided to donate *all* her promotional revenue. In fact, it's not even revenue; she won't receive a dime."

Howard wished he had an accountant with him, but it seemed reasonable to define Fari's activity as "donating her time;" that is, without payment. In that case, what would the Twins get? Frances has him just where she wanted him – staring at a big loss. "What do you suggest?"

"I suggest, Howard, that you and I have dinner together this evening."

He leaned back and looked at her. "Are you serious?"

"Yes. I'll make a deal with you. I can guarantee you a percentage of Fari's promotions, but it all hinges on your personal participation this evening."

Howard continued to stare at her, his face blank. They were making some kind of deal, but what was this about dinner?

Frances smiled sweetly. "I hope you don't have anything important scheduled for this evening."

Howard finally found his tongue. "And what if I did? Does it matter? Do I have a choice?"

"Not unless you don't want the money."

He rolled his eyes, irritated she was so crass as to declare the obvious. "Okay. Where and when do we eat?"

*   *

Doc Harris spent the morning in the basement of his home, printing the photos of Fari. The image remained a little dark, but there was no doubt that it was Fastball Fari. He'll try other techniques to lighten it a bit, but it helped that she had worn a white bra and panties. The contrast appeared very erotic. It might even be art!

The Twins were off today, the kids were in school and Sherry attended her Tuesday morning breakfast club. Doc trotted upstairs to the kitchen and rummaged in the fridge. He heard the garage door open and close! He froze, listening. Footsteps moved through the hallway and headed toward the kitchen. Although Sherry was never home this early, he knew it was her.

Doc closed the refrigerator door, moved over by the breakfast bar and assumed a casual pose. Sherry stepped into the doorway and looked at him calmly. "Hello."

She wasn't a bit surprised to find me here! Those detectives are still following me! Doc put on a smile, but his spine itched with sweat. "Hi. You're a little early." Quickly, he thought over his movements during the last few days.

Sherry wore a pale pink suit with a white scarf. Her lips shone bright red, her eyes flat and focused sharply on Doc. "What is that strange car in the driveway?"

Doc's stomach lurched, but he forced a laugh. "You wouldn't believe what happened this morning. My car was *stolen!*"

Sherry stepped back, her eyes wider. "Your *car* was stolen?"

"Yeah. Can you believe it? I went to Rosedale Mall to pick up a prescription and when I got back to the lot, the car was gone! At first, I thought I had the wrong lot, but after ten minutes, I realized it must've been stolen."

Doc said this in a fast, breathy voice, smiling all the while. This was his automatic response whenever faced with Sherry – smile and lie. It didn't occur to him that a smile might not seem appropriate while reporting the loss of his most prized toy.

Sherry noticed this. Doc loved that car. It was a special edition and had cost eighty-five thousand dollars. "You reported it?"

"Of course. I had my phone and called the cops. After that, I went into the mall and rented a car."

"What did the police say?"

He assumed an expression of regret. "They weren't too hopeful. They said a car like that was usually a target of *pros.*" He shrugged his shoulders and flicked a hand. "They gave me copies of the report and I called our insurance people." The car had theft insurance, but Doc would never collect.

Sherry stepped over to the sink and washed her hands. Doc moved back toward the table in the corner, maintaining the same distance between them. "Of course, I'm sorry about the car, but insurance will cover most of it and I'll just get another one." He smiled brightly.

Sherry moved away from the sink and trapped Doc in the corner. Her eyes bored into his like screwdrivers. "Well, that's good. You'll need transportation to and from your new condo."

This declaration punched Doc squarely in the solar plexus. His eyes glazed, his mouth went slack. Finally, his brain kicked into gear. "You weren't supposed to know about that."

Sherry's eyes narrowed. "Is that right?" Her voice cracked like a whip.

Doc stepped backwards and hit the wall. "It was *Herman's* idea. It was a plan, part of my recovery plan. He encouraged me to do it." He put the blame on Herman, his psychologist.

Sherry looked at him from a different angle. "Herman?"

"Yes. He said I should have a place for myself, to get away from everyone, to meditate, to be alone." He was thinking quicker now and wondered if she knew about Janice.

Sherry tried to reconcile the strange creature in front of her with the nice young man who had courted her all those years ago. For her own sake, she found it hard to accept the idea that his love had always been a lie. She hated to think of herself as being so foolish. But Doc had broken her heart and she would never forgive him. She tolerated his presence because he was a good father and the kids still needed him. She decided to back down and let it go.

Doc felt impatient to get out of the house. He smiled with practiced sincerity. "Sherry, it's just a place I go to be alone for a while, and it's only for a few hours."

She wondered what could be happening behind those beady, rat's eyes. "When you're home, you're always alone anyway. Why pay for a fancy, fully furnished townhouse?"

Doc felt himself sink further into his own crap. "The condo is *my* place." He looked at her from under his eyebrows. "This house is *yours*."

Sherry stared at him for a moment, then turned and walked away.

Doc listened to the receding footsteps, then skipped into the basement, retrieved the prints of Fari and ran out the house.

*   *

Mac stood on a narrow asphalt road winding around the top of a hill. From here he looked far into the distance. In one direction, he saw houses and shopping centers. In the other direction, he saw farmland and silos. He loved the sight of those silos; they always evoked memories of farm life and family.

He and Jenni had grown up on farms. One spring, during his senior year in high school, he helped Jenni and her family work up six hundred acres of fields. Mac and Jenni drove the tractors all day; they plowed, diced, harrowed, planed and planted.

It was hard work, but they loved it. Every noon they'd eat lunch in a grove of oak trees next to a small stream. Before returning to the fields, they'd lie back on the blanket and make love. "Having dessert," they called it.

Mac stepped off the asphalt and sat on the soft, brown grass. A stiff breeze blew over the hill and shook the flowers. Of course, it was too early in spring for flowers, but in a cemetery flowers could appear at any time.

"Are you at peace?" Mac asked Jennifer, who lay next to him.

The grass over her grave was brown, but patches of green had sprouted. Mac thought about Fari's view of death, about spirit and energy. In that case, Jenni's spirit could be anywhere. But the earthly remains of the woman he loved lay in this little patch of ground.

"Remember working on the farm?" he asked. He broke off a stem of grass from her grave and stuck it in his mouth. "God, I thought those times would never end." He looked down at the gravestone and traced her name with his finger.

Four months ago, during the funeral, he had been paralyzed with sedatives. He had stood like a wooden statue next to the coffin, staring into nowhere, listening to the breeze. Kim had clung to him, sobbing. Now, this morning, he had a clear mind and a clean heart and realized this was a quiet, beautiful place.

That amazing outburst yesterday in the reserve had been a purge of some sort. Part of the anger was directed at Jenni: *She* was the one who got sick; *she* was the one who died. But there was also self pity; the woman he loved, his wife, has left him to face the world alone.

Yesterday, when he had screamed at the top of his voice, he had learned a simple, but profound truth: Death is a natural part of life. Death happens. Death is happening everywhere all the time. The trap comes from trying to understand it.

He will not hold Jenni accountable for her death, he thought, or God, or fate, or karma, or whatever. In fact, he forgives everyone and everything, including himself. Jenni is gone, but the memories would live as long as he would.

Mac turned on his butt and faced Jenni's grave. He told her how he felt about Fari Madrigal. You'd like her, Jenni, he said. You both have a fierce sense of independence, dignity and grace.

A sudden gust of wind lifted the flowers from a nearby grave and deposited them in Mac's lap. He looked down and laughed. The flowers were dry and brown, dead. He laid them gently on Jenni's name, then reached over and grabbed a handful of her grave grass.

"I'm going on with life, Jenni, and it doesn't hurt so much anymore."

*   *

Herman noticed Doc's eyes resembled bullet holes and his clothes were disheveled. Was Doc grieving over the loss of his favorite toy? Herman had talked to Sherry just before Doc arrived for this appointment, and she had told him the incredible news about Doc's car. She had not related the details, but she sounded skeptical. Also, she said Doc had found himself a new hangout, but claimed it was Herman's idea.

Herman felt slightly alarmed that Doc has strayed so far off the path of reality. Doc suspected that Sherry and Herman communicated, so why tell an obvious lie? Was there another motive in telling the lie? A message?

"Amazing game, huh? A frickin no-hitter!" Doc crackled with energy. He felt high and confident. He had the money from his car, he had the photos of Fari and he would soon be free. This was his last session with Herman and they'll never see each other again. "I never saw anything like it. Pure art."

Pure art? Herman recognized the sudden shift in Doc's mood. He took it for granted that Doc was high, but usually he appeared high and morose. Now he seemed high and happy. Was this evidence of a manic phase? In eight previous sessions, Doc had not mentioned art, music or culture. Herman tried for anger. "She moves like a dancer. I'd love to see her naked."

Doc's face flushed, as if he'd been slapped. Herman wants to see Fari naked? I've got photos of Fari in her underwear! "Speaking of Fari naked, I had a dream the other night." Doc often deflected their conversations with "dreams."

Herman almost rolled his eyes. Doc used these "dream stories" to stall and pass the time. On the other hand, Herman found these dreams (or lies) valuable in what they revealed about Doc's mental condition. "Was it a long dream or a short dream?"

Doc ignored Herman's sarcasm, crossed his legs and began his story. "It was a flying dream. God, I love those dreams. I wore a backpack and floated in the darkness above the trees. I was out in the country somewhere. There were no houses, no lights. A full moon was the only light."

When Doc paused for breath, Herman wanted to ask if he had ridden on a broomstick.

"Then I saw a light in the distance," Doc continued. "Like a window, rectangular. I flew closer and guess what? I saw Fari Madrigal in her *underwear*. She was absolutely stupendous.

"But that lasted for only a second. I kept on flying and finally landed in some place I didn't recognize. The language was different, people looked different, even *I* was different. When I looked in the mirror, I saw a stranger." He sat back with a satisfied sigh; this "dream" was safely boring, but carried a kernel of truth.

Herman remembered what he had read in Doc's file; while an undergrad at college, Skipper Harris had been arrested twice for "loitering" outside the windows of the girls' dormitory. Was he also a peeping Tom in his dreams? "What was in the backpack?"

Doc lost the smile. "What?"

"The backpack. What was in it?" Herman focused deliberately on an obscure detail.

Doc looked stunned for a second, as if he had forgotten everything he'd just said. Then his face broke into a happy grin. "Money, Herman. There was *money* in the backpack." He laughed in harsh, staccato yelps.

To Herman, it sounded like the bark of a lunatic.

*   *

Frances met Howard Sikes at the stadium at six in the evening. She told Pedro the chauffeur the address of their dinner date. "St. Elmo's Church on eighteenth and Chicago."

Pedro knew this was a dangerous part of town, but she did say "church," so how bad could it be? They cruised slowly, in harmony with the rhythm of rush-hour traffic. Frances told Howard more about the Twin City Home and Help Program. His donations would make it possible to set up an educational and training center. Their goal was to re-train the homeless and help them find jobs. She looked him in the eyes. "Thank you, Howard. Your donations are making it possible for many people to escape from poverty and state dependence. This is a noble cause and I endorse you for it."

Howard stared at her, astounded. He waited for the laughter, but she remained serious. "As you well know, I was *forced* to make those donations. Not exactly a noble gesture."

"It's true your motives were elsewhere, but your donations will be regarded as noble by the people you're helping."

Howard looked out the window. He thought of those donations primarily as money down the drain, but the whole event turned into a great public relations coup. It was true he hadn't thought much about the actual destination of those funds. He presumed it had to do with some reality far beyond him. Howard had been born with a silver spoon in his mouth – *two* silver spoons.

Old, brick apartment buildings lined this part of Chicago Avenue. Toys lay scattered on bare patches of yard. People sat on the front steps and stared at the limo as if it might be a mirage – visible, but way out of reach.

"Here we are," announced Pedro. The car glided to a stop in front of a small, elegant church building.

Frances leaned forward and addressed Pedro. "You'd better not park around here. Go somewhere and wait. We should be finished at around seven thirty or eight."

"Just call me."

"Okay."

Howard leaned back and made no move to leave the limo. People walking on the sidewalk stopped and waited to see who might emerge from this long, pretty limousine.

"What is this, Frances?" Howard gestured at the church.

"St. Elmo's serves dinner to the homeless. You and I have volunteered to help serve dinner this evening. I thought you'd like to see where your money's going."

Howard groaned and covered his face with his hands. "Do I really have to do this?"

"Howard, look at it this way; you've made an *investment,* and, like all your investments, how can you ignore it?" She smiled brightly, as if this made perfect sense. She pulled him by the arm. "Come on. It's time to eat."

Frances led Howard around the side of the church, down narrow stairs and into a large basement area filled with tables and chairs. The air felt instantly warmer and smelled of food. Four people worked in the kitchen; three women and a man. Frances introduced Howard to the women, two of whom worked at St. Elmo's, while the other introduced herself as a volunteer. Frances introduced Howard to Ramon, the project director, whom she had arranged to be present this evening.

Frances identified Howard as "the man who made the donations." The women crowded around him, hugged him and planted kisses on his cheek. Howard shrugged and laughed, his face flushed. My God, thought Frances, he's *blushing*.

Ramon and the women recited a list of the many things they would do with Howard's money. They wanted to improve the church's wiring and plumbing, bring it up to code and turn the upstairs into a dormitory. Now they could finish the work quickly and provide shelter for thirty people!

Frances recognized the sincere admiration of these people and so did Howard. He seemed genuinely pleased. He caught her looking at him and smiled with a touch of irony.

"Mrs. Marchena, we should get ready," said Ramon.

"Okay." Frances took off her jacket. The women moved into action, carrying trays of food to the warming tables. Howard jumped out of the way.

"We're about to serve, Howard," Frances told him. "Maybe you could take off your jacket and tie, huh? Look a little less formal for our humble clientele."

Ramon hung Howard's suit jacket and tie in a nearby closet. Howard rolled up his sleeves as Ramon showed him his place in the line. Howard would butter the bread and give each person one slice.

"Spread the butter like this," said Ramon, demonstrating. "Not too thick, but enough to cover the bread." He smiled apologetically. "We try to be a little conservative with the food. There're a lot of hungry people out there."

Ramon would be next to Howard, serving potatoes. Frances stood at the end of the line filling Styrofoam cups with coffee. They were ready. The volunteer opened a door at the back of the room and a line of people walked quickly toward the serving counters.

Howard regarded these men and women with intense curiosity, as if discovering a previously unknown species. He noticed a different smell now – the sharp, pungent odor of damp, dirty clothes and unwashed bodies. They picked up a tray and a plate and moved down the line. Howard handled the bread with great care, as if unfamiliar with his new job.

A few people in the line exchanged greetings with the women and Ramon. Ramon had worked in shelters for years and most of these people knew him as a friend and protector. Howard became engrossed in his observations and the line stalled.

"Who's the new guy?" A cracked voice shouted.

"He's a good friend," Ramon answered. "He's helping us."

"Oh, yeah? Well, he ain't helpin so fast, is he?"

There was scattered laughter. Howard looked up into the biggest, blackest eyes he'd ever seen. The woman looked seventy, with a maze of wrinkles covering her face. She was tiny, but stood with her back straight and her head held high. Howard saw she had lost most of her teeth. "What's your name?"

Her lips folded inward and she exhaled a blast of sour air. "Agnes. Gimme my bread!"

Howard had seen such people only in the movies, or TV, but here they were right in front of him. They wore all manner of clothing, none of it too clean or spiffy. Some showed cuts and bruises, some had kindly eyes, others exhibited anger, some seemed blank and lost, but most displayed the wary aspect of the abused. This was real life tragedy, Howard realized – a flesh and blood horror story.

Something heavy shifted inside his chest.

An older man stepped in front of Howard. He wore a soiled, double-breasted suit coat, but no shirt. He accepted his slice of bread and touched his fingertips to one eyebrow. "You are a gentleman and a scholar, sir." His voice issued deep and robust, like an actor on stage.

The next person was a young man dressed in rags, with one eye completely closed by a giant purple swelling. The other eye was also swollen, but a glittering pupil peeked through the bruise. The man accepted his bread and smiled. The pupil focused on Howard. "Thank you," he said softly.

This injured man felt grateful to *him* – to Howard – for his one slice of bread with the butter spread evenly but not too thick. Howard wanted to say "You're welcome," but he couldn't talk. He wanted to tell this young man to get to a doctor, but he couldn't say that either.

Howard's ribcage tightened, his hands shook.

Now a woman passed in front of Howard, her hands resting on the slim shoulders of a young girl. The girl held a tray with two plates. Howard thought this had to be some mistake. He turned to Ramon. "She has a little girl."

"Yes. That's Monica and Alice. They sleep in parked cars. We help with meals and make sure Monica sees a doctor."

Howard turned back to the little girl and her mother. Monica and Alice. They sleep in parked cars. The pressure in his chest burst and his vision swam. He gave *two* pieces of bread to each one and layered on the butter pretty thick too. What the hell, he thought, if we run out, I'll buy more!

*   *

Mac visited with Kim and Fari in their condo. Kim had asked them to review the paintings she did for art class. She liked to paint landscapes, which were hard to find in the city. There were several renderings of Lake of the Isles and one depicting JD's office, which looked like a park.

Fari pointed to the painting of JD's office. "Me gusta. Indoor landscape."

Fari told Kim about living on the beach. "Talk about landscapes!" She described the deserted beaches, the piles of volcanic rocks, the tall, stately palm trees and the ocean. Kim listened with her eyes wide. Like Mac, she loved the ocean.

Fari invited them to their farm. "We have horses."

"Horses?" Kim perked right up. She loved horses and had been begging Mac to buy one.

Fari nodded. "Sometimes, I travel by horse. No roads."

"Wow. That's fantastic." Kim looked at her father. "Let's go!"

Mac laughed. "Maybe some time when you don't have school." He looked at Fari. "Some time when we can stay for a while."

She returned his look and held his eyes for two seconds. "Tu promete?"

Mac knew this was a promise he'd be held to. "Yes, I promise."

Fari and Mac said good night to Kim and moved off down the hallway. Their arms and shoulders touched and the bumping was not casual -- Mac felt every contact like fire. Abruptly, he pulled away from her, afraid of invading her space.

Fari sensed waves of warmth emanating from Mac and they exerted a gravitational effect; she was attracted. This set off another conflict between her head and her heart, a conflict she had yet to resolve. If she didn't maintain control, something crazy might happen.

They went downstairs in silence and stopped at the doorway leading to Mac's condo. It occurred to Mac that Fari hadn't touched him yet today. Usually, she acted free and spontaneous with her gestures, but now he detected a cool detachment in her demeanor. Or was this his imagination? He looked at his feet and reached for the doorknob. "Well, thanks for dinner. It was great. We have a big day tomorrow and . . ."

"Mac, stop."

Mac stopped. Fari pushed away from the wall and crossed her arms. The hallway was dark, her eyes were lowered. "I tell you something." She whispered and Mac leaned closer. "I do not belong here."

He felt instantly relieved. He was worried she might tell him something *bad*. "I know you can't live here. You're not meant for this place." He took a deep breath. "Look, you're a phenomenal pitcher. The best I've ever seen. You're good for baseball and great for the Minnesota Twins."

That was not what he wanted to say. He held out his hands and Fari took them. He said the first thing that came to mind. "I've never known anyone like you. I think you're a very special person. I have a powerful intuition about you. You're okay, you're all right, you're *good*. You intrigue me. You drive me crazy."

"Hush." Fari reached up and laid a finger against his lips. "I am leaving."

"I know." He smiled. "But not tonight."

She looked away and smiled. "No. Este noche no." She noticed the sudden, far-away look in his eyes. Poor Mac. She had created another *departure scenario* for him. But he has to know, she told herself.

Mac heard the message: Beware of loving me because someday I'll be gone. He tried to catch Fari's eyes and she gave him a brief glance. He saw the lovely, secret person looking back at him and he knew why she had said this; she wanted to protect him. But he had already been through the hell of a love cut short and he had survived. What's more, he had learned that the love was worth the pain.

FIFTEEN

Wednesday: April 2

Cleo and Frances shopped at a Latino market and Frances bought a kilo of cooked rice and beans. She and Fari yearned for a traditional Caribbean breakfast; gallo pinto con huevos y tortillas. Cleo dropped Frances off at Fari's condo, then continued on his errands.

Fari had just stepped from the shower. She wore a thick, white robe tied loosely around her waist and blue bath sandals. Her hair hung wet and curly. Frances wore her customary power suit, but she took off the jacket for cooking.

Fari mixed the rice and beans together and added a touch of coconut oil. Frances talked about Howard Sikes, but Fari's mind roamed elsewhere, enjoying a rerun of last night's dangerous encounter with Mac. For a moment, when they hugged goodnight, their bodies had pressed together so hard . . .

"Fari, you're burning the pinto."

Fari withdrew from the daydream reluctantly, not really caring about the food. "Sorry, Mama." She turned off the flame. The eggs and tortillas were ready.

"Fari?" Frances had noticed the languorous expression on Fari's face and the bright, jitterbug quality of her eyes. "What do you think about Howard Sikes?"

Fari didn't know what to think about Howard since she hadn't heard a word. Passion was a selfish thing; it invaded your whole person and everything else paled in significance. "Let's eat first," she said, trying to deflect Mama a while longer. "We'll talk later."

Meanwhile, Frances entertained her own recollections. She and

Howard had spent two hours at St. Elmo's Church last night. When they had run out of bread and butter, Howard had called Pedro and told him to buy more and pick up twenty ice cream cakes.

Howard and Ramon had talked for an hour about the training program. Ramon had worked for years as a social worker, but Howard, as a businessman, had brought a different perspective and suggested a few good ideas. Ramon had almost cried when Howard mentioned he owned an old warehouse that might be perfect for the training center.

Frances felt awestruck at how small, subtle twists in life could yield such momentous consequences. She said a prayer to all the gods of fate and coincidence.

She said the same prayer now as she sat across from Fastball Fari, who had lately experienced a few twists in her own life. Fari still appeared gripped by a dreamy aspect, but Frances decided to wake her up. "I've made an agreement with the Pepsi people." She stood up and cleared the table. Fari had barely eaten. "They promise to donate *twenty-five million dollars!*"

Fari snapped out of her daze. "Really? *Twenty-five million?*"

"Yes. It's fantastic. They're already involved in several charitable programs. They donate rebuilt and used computers to schools here in the States. We'll introduce a similar program in Central America, starting with Costa Rica, Nicaragua and Honduras. The opportunities are mind boggling, especially for learning and job training."

Fari jumped to her feet and clapped her hands. "That's wonderful, Mama! Congratulations!" This was their first major conquest in the corporate world and proof that their dream was working.

"Now here's the bad news." Frances smiled brightly. "They want to start immediately. McNulty is sending in a team today and they want to start filming tonight."

Another shock wave hit Fari, driving her further away from the Mac feelings. "*Tonight?*"

Frances nodded. "Yes. They'll make their donation today to a special 'Fari Fund,' as they call it. The only condition being that you agree to start now, this evening."

"Who are they?"

"It's a film team. Director, technicians, make-up people. They've rented a local sound stage."

Fari's face paled and Mac vanished quickly from her mind. The Eyes and Ears had invaded her space and now they advanced even closer. She had known this moment would arrive, but now she felt unprepared.

Frances saw the discomfort on Fari's face, but she expected it. The plan had become reality, and now they had no choice but to go forward. This would mean pain and embarrassment for Fari, but a major step forward in social relief. Rod McNulty told Frances that this donation could provide one computer for every five kids in the target areas. Further, they had set aside funds for solar-powered internet connections in rural areas.

Imagine what might happen when those kids see the whole world open up before their eyes? At least a few will break out of the cycle of poverty. For Frances and Fari, this gave their project substance, meaning and urgency.

Fari knew this, and knew that a few hours in front of the camera was a price she would pay; not gladly, but willingly. She saw it as a duty, like an appointment with the dentist, and her reaction was similar; a mixture of fear and dread.

Frances soothed her daughter's anxiety. "I made a deal with McNulty. They won't ask you to do anything crazy. Just act natural, say a few lines in English and Spanish."

"No striptease?"

Frances laughed. "No strip. He said they'd do the commercials 'with dignity.'"

Fari nodded and returned to the more pleasant sensations associated with Mac. She remembered how his arms felt, and those big hands with the long, strong fingers.

"Fari."

"Yes, Mama?"

"Look at me." Frances studied her daughter's face. "Are you all right? You seem, uh, distant." She didn't want to explore this other agenda she saw in Fari's eyes. "I have another job for you."

Fari focused on her mother and locked Mac into his own little room. "Yes, Mama?"

"I talked to a local news woman and met with her briefly." Frances paused and held Fari's eyes. "Are you willing to give an interview?"

Fari felt herself shrink again, but the swelling in her heart gave her strength. "What do *you* think?"

Frances smiled. "As your agent, I recommend it."

Fari nodded and looked away. "One woman in front of a camera? I can do that."

"Yes, well, maybe a cameraman or two. They want at least thirty minutes of film time. It's perfect timing. You've said nothing since the game on Sunday and Farimania is peaking."

"Farimania?"

Frances laughed. "Yes. We need to stir the pot, keep the interest boiling. I suggested Friday morning for the interview, before pitching your second game. What do you think?"

Fari knew the game started in the evening. "What time?"

"Early. She said she could do it here, or at her studio."

Fari's forehead cleared. "Yes, Mama. Let's do it here."

Frances smiled and nodded. "The reporter's name is Evelyn Harris. I told her you'd meet with her in someone else's condo."

Fari sat up straighter. "I have seen her on TV. She can ask anything?"

"Anything she wants. That's the deal. Why? You have deep, dark secrets?"

Fari smiled. "Yes. If I don't like the questions, I won't answer."

"That's what I told her. She can ask what she wants, but the answers are up to you."

Fari closed her eyes, lifted her face to the ceiling and wrapped her arms around herself. "Oh, Mama, life is amazing."

Frances studied her daughter, this big, beautiful baseball pitcher. She had a sudden vision of Fari as a baby, streaked with blood and birth debris, a tiny, brown, screaming creature, helpless and utterly stupid. Indeed, the look on her face at this moment was very similar.

Frances walked around the table and wrapped her arms around Fari. They rocked together silently, mother and daughter. Frances found Fari's ear and whispered. "You're right, honey. Life *is* amazing."

*   *

Doc relaxed on the sofa in the living room of his new condo. A journalist friend would arrive shortly, and Doc would peddle the photos of Fari. His friend told him that if the photos were recognizable, they'd be worth around one hundred thousand dollars! Doc tingled with excitement; only two more days and *adios!*

His cell phone buzzed. He looked at the caller ID, but didn't recognize the number. "Yes?"

"Dr. Skipper Harris?"

"Yes, this is Dr. Harris."

"Dr. Harris, how are you? This is Dr. Conners from Southdale Fairview Hospital. You had a check-up scheduled for Monday, but you didn't show up."

"Yes, that's right. I had an urgent meeting." Doc wondered what this was about.

"I'm sorry to bother you, Dr. Harris. I've left messages for you, but maybe you didn't get them. Your wife gave me this number."

Sherry again! Doc tried to figure this out. It didn't sound like an emergency. "What did you want, Dr. Conners?"

"We were hoping you'd make the appointment. We wanted to talk to you. When is the soonest you could come to our office?"

Doc had gone into the hospital diagnosed with a kidney stone. They had scheduled him for surgery, but the next day he passed the stone. He had spent only one day in the hospital.

"I suggest tomorrow morning if that's possible," continued Dr. Conners.

What the hell was he talking about? "Excuse me, Doctor, but what's the problem? Something wrong with my kidneys?"

Dr. Conners sighed. "We took various tests, including a blood test, which is standard in these cases. We would like you to come in for another blood test as soon as possible."

"Could you be a little more specific, please?" Doc's voice rose, beads of sweat pricked his scalp. "What exactly is the problem?"

"I didn't want to tell you this over the phone, Dr. Harris, but it's better you should know. Your blood tested HIV positive. As you know, this is the virus that carries the auto-immune deficiency syndrome, or AIDS. We have a program here at the hospital that deals exclusively with HIV positive people. This is an educational and treatment program . . ."

"Wait a minute!" Doc jammed his jaws together and shoved his words through clenched teeth. "Are you telling me that I have *AIDS?*"

"No, Doctor, you do *not* have AIDS. You have the virus which may cause AIDS. There's a big difference. That's why I wish you'd come in to talk about it. Many HIV positive people are . . ."

Doc squeezed the phone until he heard it crack, then threw it against the wall. It blew up with a bang and a shower of sparks. He ground his teeth so savagely he tasted blood.

Blood!

He ran to the kitchen sink, filled a glass with water and washed out his mouth. He gagged into the sink, knowing his actions were madness because the poison was *in his blood*. Foreign biological bodies, tiny time bombs, rushed through his bloodstream!

His knees buckled and his face pressed against the drain hole. He screamed and vomited.

* *

Mac opened the door and heard screams, laughter and the pounding rush of hundreds of shoes. Whenever he visited Kim's school, it was always the same; kids yelling and running around. Yet, this was one of the best schools in the Twin Cities and Kim loved it.

"Mr. Macquire?"

Mac turned and recognized one of Kim's teachers, but he couldn't remember her name. "Oh, hello. I'm here for the speech competition."

The teacher, a thin, gray-haired woman, guided Mac toward the auditorium. The sounds and smells transported Mac backwards in time. His sixth grade teacher, Mrs. Reading, had dragged him toward the principal's office because little Mac had stuck a dirty drawing on the back of Mary Lou O'Hanlon, his first love.

He suddenly remembered the teacher's name: Mrs. Pickberry! How could he forget a name like that? It's easy when your mind is elsewhere and you're in love.

"Here we are." Mrs. Pickberry ushered him into the big room. "I think we're almost ready. I'm so glad you could make it. Not many parents can get here at this hour." She lowered her voice. "How's Fastball Fari?"

"She's fine, Mrs. Pickberry. She'll be pitching this Friday. Do you follow the Twins?"

"No, sir, I do not." She punched her arm into the air. "But I do like a girl with spunk!"

The auditorium was shaped like a theater, with semicircular rows of seats descending toward a small stage. Most of the seats had been taken, but Mac saw very few people his age. They were mostly students. They waved and asked about Fastball Fari. After a moment, he stepped into the shadows and became invisible.

Kim had joined the speech club last year. She told him it had been her mother's suggestion. Jenni thought it would help Kim build up her confidence. Mac couldn't argue with this. In any event, Kim became quite good at it. The first time he had watched his daughter speak in front of an audience, he had been shocked and impressed. Here was his daughter, the little girl he sees every day, commanding the attention of all these strangers.

Mac had admired the poise and self-possession of this girl, his daughter, and became engrossed in the story she told. When she finished, he had clapped just as enthusiastically as the others.

This morning they were holding the regional speech finals among the area's private schools. Kim was one of five finalists. Each finalist would give a fifteen minute presentation, and a panel of judges decided who would go on to the state finals.

Kim liked astronomy and she drew most of her speech material from the strange phenomena discovered in space. She had done speeches on black holes, comets, asteroids and the big bang. However, Mac had detected a difference in her last two speeches. One had been about "sono-luminescence," and the other had described how a particle accelerator worked. Not exactly astronomy; more like pure research.

Nevertheless, Mac had been impressed with the way she had taken a complex subject and presented it in clear language. At least, she made him think he understood it. The judges had also been impressed. However, for today's competition, he had no idea what Kim's subject would be. She had kept it secret.

The students around him wore everything from suits and ties to jeans and t-shirts. This school had no dress code, except that students should appear "presentable" and "decent." These kids looked decent, clean and well fed. The tuition was quite high, so Mac assumed most came from comfortable backgrounds. The boys seemed quite young, but some of the girls could pass for twenty.

Mac remembered when he was that age, fourteen or fifteen, and his whole life lay out in front of him. He had an abundance of time, of *future*, and so, like all young people, he concentrated on the present, *this moment*, because he knew he wouldn't stay young forever.

"Hey, Dad!" Kim ran up the steps, followed by a boy her own age.

"Hi, honey. What's up?"

They hugged and Kim introduced her friend. "Dad, this is my friend, Zero. He's one of the finalists."

"Zero?"

"Pleased to meet you, sir" said the kid and they shook hands. Zero's hair fell halfway down his back and one fine eyebrow was decorated with a silver bar. He resembled more of a *one* than a *zero*; tall and skinny. He wore a plain black T shirt, black jeans and black tennis shoes.

"Is your name really 'Zero?'" Mac asked.

The boy rolled his eyes. "Both my parents are mathematicians. What can I say?"

"Isn't that cool, Dad?"

Mac was shocked to see his daughter's eyes goggling at Zero. My God, was this her *boyfriend*?

"His subject is Einstein." Kim punched Zero on the arm. "Tell him about it."

"I'll try to explain Einstein's theory of relativity in fifteen minutes."

Mac didn't know a thing about Einstein's theory, but Kim obviously found it very cool. "It has something to do with energy, right?"

Zero looked him in the eyes. "Not really. It's more an explanation of the relationship between time and space. But it was these theories that led him to his famous equation for energy."

Mac wondered if it was related to the law of thermodynamics, energy and death. He tried to regard Kim as a sexual being, but she seemed so young. However, her body was changing; he could see it. He looked at Zero. Do I have to talk to Kim about sex? Yes. When? Soon.

"We gotta go, Dad." Kim grabbed Zero by the hand. "They're about to start. I'm up third and Zero's up fifth."

"Okay, honey. Good luck." Mac looked at the kid. "And good luck to you too, Zero. You seem like anything but."

"What?"

"C'mon." Kim pulled Zero down the stairs and they disappeared behind the curtain. They were still young, but their hormones were raging. Love and sexual awakening loomed just around the corner. Mac wished he had some sage advice for Kim, but he didn't know anything more about love now than he did at her age.

He had known Jenni from grade school, but they started going steady in high school. Love wasn't complicated at that age; it was easy – kissing, dancing, touching, and yielding to the unbearable excitement of delicious and mysterious sensations. Now, twenty years later, Mac had the same wild feelings for Fari Madrigal.

This time, however, love was complicated.

The lights dimmed, leaving only the lights above the stage. A middle-aged man in a brown suit approached the podium and introduced himself as "Prof" Johnson. He welcomed everyone to the regional finals. He went on to explain the format, and introduced the judges and contestants. Kim looked for Mac and blew him a kiss.

First to speak was a young man wearing a white shirt and red bow tie. He announced his theme as "Were Dinosaurs Killed by an Asteroid?" He started by describing the origin of asteroids.

Mac tuned out. He had heard this story several times on the educational channels. Besides, Fari Madrigal offered a more attractive daydream than this kid talking about mass death. He recalled hugging with Fari last night in the hallway. At first, he had felt uncomfortable with the different bumps, curves and smells. Plus, it amazed him that he should be in a passionate embrace with someone other than Jenni. Just in time, however, he realized that his needs had gotten ahead of his responsibilities.

This was what made love complicated; age and experience.

Mac heard applause. The dinosaur story was over. Prof Johnson introduced the next finalist, a girl this time; Kerry O'Brien.

Kerry wore a simple skirt and blouse. Her hair had been chopped short and dyed black. She announced her theme as "Physiological Reactions to Emotional States."

Here was something Mac might get interested in. He sat up straighter and tore his mind away from Fari. The girl spoke in a clear voice, her enunciation perfect. She began by saying she would examine "fear" and "love," which, surprisingly, shared very similar physiological reactions.

Mac didn't think it was surprising; didn't love and fear go together?

Kerry went on to explain how these physical reflexes had evolved as survival tools. Fear, for example, triggers chemicals that sharpen our reactions and strengthen our muscles. It was the same with love, she said, which also fulfilled a biological necessity; procreation.

Mac lost interest in Kerry's presentation. It sounded too technical, as if she described how farm animals mate. There was more applause and Kerry went back to her seat. Prof Johnson thanked Kerry and introduced Kim Macquire. This time the applause sounded much louder and Mac realized the other contestants were probably from different schools. Kim was the favorite here among her classmates. This gave him hope; maybe Zero attended a school on the other side of town.

Mac forced himself to forget Fari for a moment and concentrate on Kim. She would quiz him on every detail of her speech. She approached the podium, made eye contact and began speaking.

She described how she sometimes climbs out her bedroom window at night, sits on the roof and stares at the stars. One night, a particularly bright light appeared on the horizon. It shone brighter than any star and hovered above the roofs of far-off houses. At first, she thought it was an airplane or helicopter, but it made no noise.

She described how the object moved closer slowly until it stopped directly above her. She had felt terrified, but unable to move. Suddenly, a beam of light appeared and lifted her into a strange craft. There were other beings present, but she couldn't see them clearly because of the lights in her eyes.

Mac felt spellbound by this story, not only the words coming from Kim's mouth, but the expressions on her face and the way her voice cracked at certain terrified moments. His daughter was an actress! Her delivery carried a powerful conviction and Mac could almost believe it happened. She finished with a catch in her voice – the aliens had delivered her back home.

The audience broke out in cheers and applause. Mac clapped hard and tried to catch Kim's eye. She looked in his direction and he gave her a thumbs-up. He thought she performed better than the two previous contestants.

Next up was a young man dressed in a sweater and jeans, his

hair white and spiky. His subject would be "Tiny Farmers of the Rain Forest." Mac imagined mystical creatures like trolls or leprechauns, but the kid referred to the amazing leaf-cutter ants of Central and South America.

Mac listened for five minutes, but it would take more than rainforest ants to fend off thoughts of Fari. He remembered her skin didn't smell like lilacs, but a deeper, thicker odor, similar to mushrooms fresh from the earth.

He heard another round of applause and the rainforest ants were over. Mac had heard enough to realize the kid had a good delivery and great diction. Now it was Zero's turn. Mac listened carefully to the applause as he was introduced. It sounded muted and hesitant, from which he concluded Zero was from elsewhere.

Zero began by asking the audience to imagine that space and time were two sides of the same coin and the name of that coin was "motion." Motion implied duration, and duration implied space and time.

In our universe, time appears uniform and sequential. If it weren't, everything would happen at once. Obviously, this is not the case. Therefore, time has encountered *resistance*, time has a limit, and that limit corresponds directly to the velocity of light.

Mac found himself absorbed in the complex ideas of Einstein and the strange phenomenon we call "time." Mac had always regarded time as a malevolent force threatening all living things with death and decay. However, Zero made it sound like time was a harmless component of nature and itself vulnerable – jerked around by gravity and devoured by black holes.

It was an interesting theme and Zero delivered it with robust enthusiasm. Mac had to admit that he was as good as or better than Kim and the others. He clapped loudly for the friend of his daughter.

There followed a fifteen minute recess while the judges made their decisions. The auditorium broke out in bright chatter and laughter as the lights came up. Mac sat back, pleased with the speeches and the positive energy inside this room. Maybe this was the attractive ingredient in falling in love, he thought; the excitement of new discovery.

"Mr. Macquire?" Mrs. Pickberry leaned over Mac with a troubled expression.

Uh, oh, thought Mac, she caught me thinking dirty thoughts! He slumped further in the seat.

"I'm sorry to bother you, sir, but I thought you should know. There are several journalists outside, asking about you."

*   *

Doc sat on the floor of the shower, his head bent under the hot blast of water. A debate raged inside his head about what to do next. What about Sherry?

"Oh, God," he groaned again. During brief moments of lucid thought, he had recalled that the HIV virus remained undetected for the first six months or so after the moment of infection. He had been infected at least that long. He had had sex with Sherry on an average of three or four times a month. Was that enough? Shit, it only takes once. Besides, who knows how long he's had the virus?

What about Janice, for whom he had no last name or phone number? Did he infect her, and then set her loose in the world to infect others? What about the people he had met at the "paper bag parties?" They were usually careful about protection, but sometimes the drugs and booze led to loose maintenance.

The depth of the disaster had no bottom.

He imagined fifty different variations of how to tell Sherry and the kids. One example:

A blood test, Daddy? Why?

Well, kids, your old man has the HIV virus. You know, the virus that causes AIDS? It's just possible that you're infected. Of course, your mother is most at risk. Right, Sherry? What do you think?

This scene was so horrid, Doc stood up abruptly and banged his head against the shower head. He reached up and looked for blood.

Blood.

He cried again. With each convulsion he saw different scenes from his life; at home with Mom and Dad; Dad drunk and hitting Mom; Dad hitting *him*; the virulent silence of his mother's shame; working three jobs to stay in school.

Then along came Sherry Lansing who allowed Skipper Harris to sink in his claws. Sherry lifted Doc to a level of consumption he never dreamed he'd see; mansions, jets, butlers, maids, cooks, chauffeurs! However, from the first time Doc entered the front door of the palatial

Lansing mansion, the inhabitants, even the servants, treated him as if his presence was accidental.

None of that mattered anymore. The severity of his situation had forced him to abort his escape plan and make a new plan, but the new plan was merely an acknowledgment of the only alternative available to him.

When there was only one way to go, nothing else mattered except the details.

*　　　　　*

Target Field was packed again for this first game against the Kansas City Royals. Bradd Johnson was scheduled as the Twins' starting pitcher. Most fans had arrived early to the stadium to watch the pre-game warm-ups, hoping to see, film and photograph Fastball Fari.

Mac had arrived late to the stadium, only an hour before game time. He had come straight from Kim's school. The winner had been Kerry, and Zero was runner-up. They would go on to the finals next month. Kim wasn't too bothered by this, as she had been rooting for Zero.

Mac felt anxious about encountering Fari at the stadium. The contrast between last night's intimacy and the loud, brash baseball park was startling. But more than this, he wondered if last night night's passionate embrace might have been a sudden weakness in both of them, a momentary loss of control, and now, in the cold light of day, they should make a rational assessment of their behavior.

Was this crazy thinking? He forced himself to concentrate on his job and went through his game-day routine.

Meanwhile, Fari walked through the outfield and allowed the public a good look at her. Mama had suggested she do this and Fari had agreed; it seemed the safest way to show herself to the fans. These people, and the millions watching on TV, made it possible for her and Mama to solicit huge sums of money.

Fari walked slowly, never moving closer than twenty yards to the outfield fences. As she moved, whole sections of the stadium, thousands of people, jumped to their feet, shouting and waving, holding up signs, cameras and kids. Fari regarded the crowd as one giant organism with thousands of tiny mouths, emitting delirious emotions.

She would walk through left field, then headed for the bullpen, where she would spend the game. She didn't expect to see much of Mac this afternoon, and for this she felt relieved. She had second thoughts about him and about the reality of their lives. She had come here to pitch and squeeze corporations, and after one year she would leave.

Yet, she had allowed herself to get involved with Mac. Well, not involved exactly, but almost. Further, Mac and Kim were still recovering from a terrible loss, and now she had complicated their lives even further. Did she have a right to do this?

But what about love?

Love wanted only free expression and reciprocity. It didn't care about the practicalities of one's life. That's where the mind comes in, arguing for common sense and responsibility, keeping a lookout for traps and minefields, warning one's heart that it's not safe to lie out in the open like that.

Fari had had a few boyfriends. Like any normal person, she was attracted to affection and intimacy. However, she experienced trouble with romantic commitments, or "going steady." Her first two boyfriends had told her they were "in love" with her, but this "love" was expressed as an attitude of possession; they *belonged* to each other.

Such responsibility terrified Fari. After messy endings to these early relationships, she regarded romantic love as a scary mystery, to be approached with caution. She found it safer and more convenient to remain single.

The level of cheering increased as Fari approached the bullpen. People in the bleachers leaned over the railings, screaming and waving their arms, but Fari was through displaying herself. She walked with her head down and her eyes on the grass. As she approached the bullpen, she almost collided with Mac! He and Bradd Johnson were just leaving for the dugout.

All motion and sound faded as Mac and Fari stood face to face. Mac reacted first. He stepped aside and told Johnson to go on, he wanted to talk to Fari. He looked at her and smiled. "Hi."

She studied his shoes. "Ola. How was speech contest?" They shouted above the crowd noise.

Mac had to think for a moment. "Kim gave a great speech, but didn't make the finals."

"Too bad. I helped her."

He tried to catch her eyes. "She doesn't mind. She loves doing it and she's good at it."

Fari glanced at him, brought her hand to her mouth and laughed.

Mac smiled back. "What?"

"It is strange talking to you here."

"Yes, I know. Everyone is watching. We're on TV right now." He looked toward the dugout and saw JD waving his arms. It was time to go.

Fair's eyes sparkled. "Can we kiss goodbye?"

He saw mischief in her expression, but something else too. "We're teammates. We slap each other on the butt."

Fari laughed into her hand, and the crowd laughed with her. She looked around at the multitude and the multitude looked back.

"I'd say we're standing right under the magnifying glass," said Mac. He had wanted to give her some sign and receive a sign in return, but now it was too late. He started to move off. "Well, I'll see you after the game."

"Mac, stop."

He stopped. Fari let her eyes linger on his for almost second and he thought he saw almost to the bottom, to a brilliant white glow.

"I invite you to dinner tonight."

Mac was stunned by what he had just seen in her eyes and could only stutter. "Uh, sure."

Fari turned and trotted away, accompanied by the furious screams of thousands of fans.

*   *

That evening, Mac dressed casually for dinner; jeans, a flannel shirt and a little cologne Kim had given him for his birthday. Kim was spending the night at a friend's house and planned to return to the condo tomorrow after school. The Twins had won again that afternoon, seven to two, on the strength of good pitching by Johnson. Fari had inspired the pitching staff and the whole team seemed to work harder.

Mac looked at himself in the mirror and made lastminute adjustments. Fari had asked him to accompany her to a sound stage after dinner. She was making commercials! This seemed to run counter to the "real" Fari. However, he didn't know all the details and she would explain later. He checked his watch and it was still only five to six.

He wondered if Fari had put a spell on him. Who knows what powers she had with this "telekinetic" business? Could she read his mind? Read his heart? Manipulate his emotions? He took a deep breath, walked through the garage to Fari's condo and knocked on the door.

The door opened and Fari stood in the doorway. "Hi, Mac. Entre, por favor."

"Hi."

She wore a loose, sleeveless top and a short, pleated skirt. It was the first time Mac had seen her in a dress. Her brown legs were long and shapely. She led the way into the dining room and Mac willed his eyes to stay steady. Her hair hung down her back in a single, thick braid. Also, of course, there was the maddening, ubiquitous scent of lilacs. No baseball in sight. This was not Fari the baseball pitcher; this was a different Fari.

The lights in the dining room had been dimmed and several lit candles sat on the table. As Mac entered the room he felt a soft "click." Colors blurred, sounds muted, motion slowed. He stood by the table and stared at the candles, waiting for the next move.

"Siéntese, Mac. Le gusta vino? Blanco o rojo? It is Chilean."

Mac sat and nodded, his eyes still on the candles. "Yes, thanks. White."

Fari twirled around and skipped into the kitchen, enjoying the freedom of movement afforded by the skirt. Most of her clothing conformed to one rule; nothing constraining or confining. She carried the glasses of wine into the dining room and handed one to Mac.

"Thank you."

"Con mucho gusto." She almost laughed at their formal manners, but Mac's face remained solemn. "I have Chinese food." She had heard from Kim that Mac loved Chinese food and Fari knew about their favorite restaurant.

He looked at her and raised an eyebrow. "You didn't cook dinner?"

She looked away and smiled. "No. Fan Woo cooked it."

Mac sat up and smiled. "Hey, they have great food." He looked at her from the corners of his eyes. "You had inside information."

Fari lifted her glass. "We make toast?"

Mac raised his glass toward hers. "To Fan Woo and the here and now."

She nodded. They clinked glasses and sipped the wine, Mac with his eyes on Fari, and Fari with her eyes on the candles. The flames burned in her pupils, dancing, twisting, illuminating secret corridors and a maze of identities. Mac blushed and looked away.

That's another thing I like about Mac, thought Fari; he has a sense of propriety. Yes, he was a good man, but there could be no romance between them. He might become "un amigo con permiso," but she doubted it. He seemed the kind of person who wanted commitment and security.

"You look different tonight," Mac said with a smile. "You look very nice." He laughed and blushed again. "Excuse me. You look nice all the time. It's just that I've never seen you in a dress."

"Gracias. I like dresses, but never in public. I thought you might wear suit and tie."

He started to laugh, then looked at her more closely. "Really?"

"No. I am kidding." This was a different Mac, not the easygoing, good buddy she was used to. However, she wasn't acting as a good buddy either and wondered if this was another social blunder.

Mac relaxed in his chair and sipped the wine. As he watched the candle flames, a deep sense of contentment folded over him, like a thick, warm blanket.

"Mac?" Fari's voice came from far away.

He looked at her and saw the same deep clarity in her eyes he had seen earlier at the stadium. He felt a faint tug at the back of his brain.

"We eat soon." Her words reverberated hollowly as if they were inside a tiled room. "They send car at seven thirty." She paused, wavering on the fragile line between wanting and choosing, and then she chose. "For tonight, tengo un plan."

Mac leaned toward Fari unconsciously, like metal toward a magnet. "What's the plan?"

"We have dinner, go to sound stage, then come here and sleep together."

Mac's eyes flew open and he jerked backwards. "What?"

Fari smiled and slapped him on the arm. "Estamos buenos amigos, verdad?"

He hesitated only a second, then nodded emphatically. "Yeah! Sure!"

SIXTEEN

Thursday: April 4

At seven thirty in the morning all seemed quiet in JD's house. JD was still upstairs, but Frances had already arrived at her post in the Command Center. She expected a call from Rod McNulty, who was in New York. He and his promotional team had received the "rushes" of Fari's performance from last night.

The sound stage had been constructed inside a large warehouse on the outskirts of downtown Minneapolis. Blocky scaffolding rested against the walls, slender towers of lights crowded the corners and narrow tracks crisscrossed the floor. There were objects that resembled giant umbrellas and other objects that didn't resemble anything.

Frances had been impressed. Fari had been shocked. She stood behind Mac, clutching the back of his shirt with both fists. There had been about twenty people in the room, engaged in various activities. A tall, impeccably groomed woman had peeled away from a nearby group and introduced herself. "I'm Jill Cassidy, Mr. McNulty's on-site assistant." Jill was a handsome woman of indeterminate age. Her pale skin stretched tight over her cheeks and jaws, and her eyes appeared unnaturally round. She wore a white silk blouse, loose black trousers and spiky high heels.

"Everything's ready," she told them. "We've worked out several different angles, positions and action sequences."

Fari had worn her Minnesota Twins uniform and tennis shoes, but balked when Jill declared that make-up was first on the agenda. Jill explained patiently that because of the lighting and the cameras, it was necessary. "This is for *television*, honey."

For four hours, Jill and the director had moved Fari through several "scenarios." Fari spoke one or two lines of dialogue in each scenario, in both English and Spanish. At one point, after two hours, Jill had asked if Fari would dance for them. By this time, Fari had become accustomed to the cameras and the brash, frantic behavior of everyone around her. She might dance, she had said, but not by herself. Immediately, several men and women had volunteered.

Fari had pointed at Mac. It had taken ten minutes of coaxing, but Mac agreed finally and only on the condition he would not appear on film. After one minute of dancing, Mac and Fari had seemed to forget everything but each other.

Frances smiled now as she recalled that scene; Mac and Fari dancing for each other, not for the cameras. And why not? Mac was highly regarded by JD as a baseball confidant and good friend, and this was recommendation enough for Frances. Besides, she and Fari expected to live here for at least a year – a long time for Fari to remain shut up and alone inside her elegant prison.

For the first time since her father's death, Fari has had to step out of herself and face the world – a young woman in the midst of self-discovery, conquering corporations, saving lives, fulfilling dreams. She deserves love, and Mac would be a steady, loyal companion.

The blue phone rang: Rod McNulty. "Good morning, Rod. How are you today?"

"Fine, Frances. Fantastic, in fact. These rushes of Fari are great. Have you seen them?"

"Yes. I was there last night. She looks good on camera, doesn't she?"

"Oh, yes. She's got an extremely powerful presence. I'm very impressed. Please pass on my appreciation to her."

"I will. And we appreciate Pepsi's donations. By the way, I talked to our lawyer in Costa Rica and we're forming a non-profit institute."

"That's great. Let me know if you run into trouble. I have contacts in the State Department."

Frances smiled. Ah, the trappings of power and connections. "Thank you, Rod. When will the commercials be ready?"

"They start editing today. It's amazing what they can do. They can put Fari in any setting you can imagine – in the middle of a city, a crowd of people, or in the desert. In a few days we'll have various versions ready for your inspection. We want to work closely with you. With Fari as our spokesperson, we expect a huge jump in sales."

"Well, that's what it's about, isn't it? Everyone comes out happy."

"What about you and Fari? What do you get?"

She saw a long, politically twisted explanation and decided against it. "Personal satisfaction."

"Well, I respect you for your work and what you're doing. You're certainly a breath of fresh air in my life, where greed is the norm."

McNulty's voice carried a slightly sardonic tone. Imagine, thought Frances, a top corporate executive saying something like that! She chose a light response, remembering he had grown up in Montana cattle country. "We all need a breath of fresh air, sir, in this world filled with cow pies."

They laughed together.

"Well," he said. "If there's anything more you want, any help or introductions, please ask."

"Thank you. Now that you mention it, there might be one or two things."

"You got it."

"Are you acquainted with Mr. Bradley Piper, CEO of McDonald's?"

"He's a friendly acquaintance. McDonald's is a big customer, so I talk to him frequently."

"McDonald's is huge. They're all over the world."

"Yes. Does Fari like Big Macs?"

Frances laughed. "She might. It depends on how much they like her."

"Oh, I think they would like Fari very much. Ronald would be *ecstatic*."

Frances wanted to tackle the next target on her list, but McDonald's was a corporate giant of awesome size and scope. "I wonder how much they might like her."

"I should think they'd like her as much as fifty million, at least."

Frances almost dropped the phone. *Fifty million dollars!* She waited for her throat to clear before choking out a response. "Are you kidding? That much?"

"As you said, they're huge. McDonald's could be very helpful to your project. Especially with tax-free donations."

"I agree, Rod. Thanks for the advice. I have to think about this, but I'd like to talk to you further about it."

"Of course. Call anytime."

Frances turned off the phone and sat back. She had trouble trying to imagine one million dollars, but fifty million? When she and Fari had formulated their plan, they had no idea how much money they might solicit. Jose had told her once that top players were paid half a million a year for product endorsements, but that was in the seventies. They figured such fees were higher these days, but they never imagined numbers in the tens of millions!

They'll have to revise the plan, *expand* it. Their plan involved investments in two general categories; one, helping those most in need; two, helping Mother Nature. There didn't seem to be much sense in saving lives if we go on destroying the Earth.

* *

For Doc it was a big day, his last full day in this city. Last night he had taken three sleeping pills, but slept only intermittently. His thoughts sliced across each other like arrows in a medieval battle. He had nightmares in his sleep and nightmares while awake.

Towards dawn he retreated to the shower for the hot and cold treatment. Forty minutes later he emerged white and wrinkled. Various details needed his attention today, but he could hardly move in this near-catatonic state. He popped a hit of speed. As he waited for it to kick in, he thought about his father. Daddy had died disgraced and drunk when Doc was ten years old. Daddy had never called him "Skip" or "son." It was always "dunderhead" or "dim bulb."

Well, Daddy, here I am, just about as low as I can get. Satisfied?

The initial rush of speed touched Doc's spine like a hot wire. He jerked upright and the daydreams vanished, along with the depression. He felt lighter, almost floating, and soon he would zoom through the atmosphere.

He got to his feet gingerly, his arms held out for balance. The sky appeared brighter now, turning blue, but clouds hovered on the horizon. He picked up his "To Do" list, stuck it in his pocket and straightened his jacket and tie. During his last day in Minneapolis, he wanted everything to go perfectly.

*   *

Mac opened his eyes and saw gray light. He and Fari lay together like two spoons. Fari breathed evenly and he assumed she still slept.

The small clock next to the bed said seven thirty. He remembered they had set the alarm for eight fifteen. He snuggled closer and rubbed his bare legs against hers. They still wore their underwear; Mac in his shorts and T-shirt and Fari in T-shirt and panties.

When they had gotten home last night it was almost midnight. Fari had apologized for spending so much time filming, but Mac had enjoyed watching her move and speak in front of the cameras. The make-up didn't seem to add or detract from her beauty, but Jill, the executive assistant, had been very impressed. She commented several times on what she called "Fari's natural photogenic aura." When they had arrived back at the condo, Fari still wanted them to sleep together, but she emphasized *sleep*. She had been exhausted by the filming.

Mac pressed his nose and lips against the side of her neck. Her skin felt smooth and warm, the mushroom odor stronger than ever. Her heart beat slowly and powerfully against the palm of his hand, in time with the tiny pulse he found at the side of her neck. It seemed like a miracle, this small, delicate movement sustaining such a big, lovely person. There was a sudden commotion inside his shorts and his penis popped up.

He fell in love with her constantly, from moment to moment. Last night, she and Frances had explained about the donations from Howard Sikes and PepsiCo. When Frances described Howard's conversion at St. Elmo's, Fari had tears in her eyes. What sports hero had ever done anything like it? He hugged her closer.

Fari felt Mac's erection against her butt and his hand cupping her breast. "Buenos días, Mac," she whispered.

He wondered how long she'd been awake. He moved his lips against her ear. "Buenos días. Did you sleep well?"

She nodded. "Yes. Y tu?"

"Great." He sighed and nestled closer, forgetting about his erection. He felt her shaking and realized she was laughing. She took his hand, put it to her lips and kissed each fingertip. "You have been awake long?"

"A little while," he breathed.

She turned over on her back and smiled up at him, her eyes soft and warm, almost a palpable touch. "Perdón, Mac, but I have to pee and brush teeth."

"Okay. Me too."

"How about breakfast? Would you like that?"

"Sure."

She turned into him, buried her face in his neck and laid one leg over him. The feeling was intensely erotic and Mac wanted to experience this woman from every possible perspective.

Fari groaned, rolled over and sat up. "Hasta la vista, Mac. Don't go anywhere." She jumped out of bed. The white T-shirt hung high and wrinkled, exposing a flash of red bikini panties. She ran into the bathroom and closed the door.

Mac lay back and hugged Fari's pillow to his face. Her pheromones invaded his sensory system and triggered another erection. What did he expect this morning? Did he expect to make love with Fari? Was he thinking with his penis, or his brain? Was he in love, or was he *enchanted*?

The bathroom door opened and Fari stepped out naked. Her face was turned away, but Mac saw she was smiling. His eyes traveled down the full, lush figure covered in brown velvet skin. His breath caught deep in his throat and blood rushed into his groin.

Fari sat on the bed and glanced at him. "Go to bathroom and come back. I left out spare cepillo."

Mac whipped off the sheets, jumped into the bathroom, peed and brushed. As he took off his underwear, he flashed briefly on Jennifer. He apologized silently, certain she would understand. He felt butterflies in his stomach and his lungs seemed on the verge of hyperventilating. He had made love with only one woman in his life, but aren't all women the same physically? Yes, but this woman was Fari Madrigal – the same physically perhaps, but different in all other respects.

Fari sat on the bed and stared through the thin slit between window and shade. She saw a piece of concrete sidewalk and black asphalt. She hadn't made love in almost five years, and fewer than ten times in her life. But now her blood pumped passion and her skin felt like fire. Still, she worried about her lack of experience. Surely, Mac would help her.

Mac crawled back into bed and Fari joined him. Immediately, sexual attraction and animal frenzy took over. They kissed wildly, their mouths wide open, trying to devour each other. Their hands traveled quickly to all the warm, secret places, blazing trails of fire. They locked together and rocked the bed in hard, jackhammer intercourse. Five minutes later they shook together in a massive orgasmic earthquake.

*   *

Doc had not talked to Sherry in two days, but he had left a message asking her to meet him at the house at nine thirty this morning. He had no clear agenda about this meeting, except to tell Sherry about his blood test. This would be his final duty to his wife.

The speed raced nicely through Doc's system, keeping him on an even keel. He approached the house slowly in his rental car, noting that the driveway was clear and the garage door still down. He had arrived early, hoping Sherry would be still upstairs getting dressed.

He walked through the backyard and opened the door to his study. He moved directly to the closet, bent down and carefully inspected his safe; two small slivers of paper still lay delicately on the hinge and door. He dialed the combination and opened the door. There were secrets in this safe and a ticket to ride.

"More dirty little secrets?"

Doc almost fell backwards. Sherry stood in the doorway, perfectly coiffed, ready to sail forth on the society luncheon circuit. He gave her a sneer. "We all have our dirty little secrets."

Doc's shirt and suit appeared slept in, but Sherry was shocked at his face; his cheeks hung loose and pale, blue shadows circled his eyes. She had been about to reply sharply, but something in his expression stilled her tongue. She looked closer at his eyes; the pupils resembled pinpoints.

Doc sucked in air and willed his heart to slow. He regarded Sherry silently, waiting until he could talk without stuttering. "I have some news for you." The words burst forth in one explosive breath.

The force of his voice and the twisted look in his eyes caused Sherry to step back a few paces. She felt pressure in the air around her and the hairs on the back of her neck stiffened.

The speed delivered a screaming edge to Doc's nervous system. He spoke as if wielding a hammer – loud and violent. "Dr. Conners called me. He did a blood test on me. On my *blood!*" He reached out with one arm and swept everything off the top of his desk. Objects and papers flew and crashed against the wall.

Sherry stood frozen before this sudden violence. Doc's face shined with mania. He pointed a finger at her. "Get yourself tested, Sherry. I have the HIV virus. Do you hear me? My blood tested positive for HIV!"

The world tilted and Sherry fell back against the wall. When her vision cleared she saw Doc smiling at her. Was this a joke? She opened her mouth and moved her jaws. "Are you serious?"

Doc's eyes stared over her left shoulder. "Get a blood test, Sherry. Call Dr. Conners. He'll tell you all about it." He whirled and headed toward the door.

Sherry pushed away from the wall and looked in all directions, as if wondering which way to run. "*Wait a minute.*" She shouted at Doc's back. "*Are you serious?*"

He reached for the doorknob, then paused. "We could have had a good life together, Sherry, but you got too nosy. Good luck to you and the kids. Get a blood test. Goodbye." He opened the door, stepped through and slammed it shut.

*　　　　　*

Target Field was again filled to capacity for the afternoon game against the Royals. Most had come to see Fastball Fari, but she appeared only before or during the game, never after. The general mood was festive, but there was also frustration at Fari's reluctance to appear in public. The media highlighted this attitude as they moved through the crowd. There were those, however, who appreciated Fari's decision to remain secluded in the face of such rabid interest.

Frances recognized this negative slant on the reporting and allowed Evelyn Harris to announce tomorrow's interview with Fari (which would be broadcast locally at five thirty p.m.). Evelyn's station released commercials they had already prepared and the news flashed quickly across the country. Snagging Fastball Fari for an interview was regarded as a major news coup for the station and Ms. Harris.

In the best tabloid tradition, Fari's life was closely investigated and examined. Reporters were dispatched to Costa Rica and the Dominican Republic, in search of more "news." Fari's former teammates, classmates, teachers and neighbors were interviewed, and former residences of the Madrigal family were photographed and filmed. They even filmed Sabana Park in San Jose, Costa Rica, where Fari pitched in her first league game at fourteen years old. All this, however, shed little light on the true personality of Fari Madrigal. The people they interviewed reported that Fari had always kept to herself, rarely appeared in public, and sometimes wore "disguises."

They had discovered a few facts; Fari earned a degree at a university in Santo Domingo; she lived alone for two years in the rain forest after her father had died; the last time she was involved romantically was five years ago. Beyond this, not much else was known about Fari, and this only increased the mystery, which intensified the interest.

The media had also been busy looking into the life of Frances. She had grown up on a banana plantation in southwestern Costa Rica, attended the University of Costa Rica and the University of Santo Domingo, where she earned an advanced degree in sociology. In 1985 she married Jose Madrigal, former pitcher for the Baltimore Orioles, who died in a farm accident in 2012.

A cloud of controversy surrounded Frances. First, there occurred the test of willpower with United Brands, then the little flap with Howard Sikes about donations. In regards to this, the announcements printed by United Brands in Costa Rican newspapers had been discovered and reported in the US (much to the amusement of Frances). However, the media concentrated most of their attention on the trial and conviction of the "Red Gang." Frances was often portrayed as a fiery revolutionary. In this regard, the US media was similar to the Costa Rican media; they both injected their "stories" with drama and exaggeration.

However, the facts were simple: Frances and her family had belonged to the local communist party, as did virtually all the plantation workers. She and her family participated in the strike in which twenty-two workers were killed, one of whom had been Frances' fiancé.

Five days later, the "Red Gang" attacked and killed a security guard. Ever since this news surfaced, broadcasters assumed dark looks and lowered voices whenever reporting on Frances Madrigal.

Shortly after these stories appeared, a popular radio "talk show" host speculated that Frances (with Fari's help) may have "brainwashed" Howard Sikes and "induced" him to make donations to the poor. To lend credit to this story, he referred to a report about Mr. Sikes's recent volunteer service at a local "soup kitchen." Was the great capitalist turning "pinko?"

Chet Macquire was often referred to as "Fari's companion," but the precise nature of their relationship remained unclear and the ambiguity fueled wild speculation. The local media had heretofore ignored Mac, but now they desperately wanted to talk to him. What was he like, this Chet Macquire, "companion" of Fastball Fari?

Mac had experienced a brief flash of fame during his high school and college days, but those were casual encounters with local sports reporters. Now, however, the attention was from every direction, even the foreign media, and with an in-your-face quality he had never experienced.

Kim, too, had to be careful. There had been directives circulated at her school asking the students to respect and protect Kim's privacy. However, any time Kim left the school she was open game for reporters and gawkers. In this regard, Mac felt immensely grateful for Cleo's involvement. He picked up Kim at her bus stop and brought her home safely.

*　　　　　*

Mac walked through the tunnel and entered the dugout. The stadium was packed and noisy, but it was still thirty minutes before game time. He saw eyes and cameras pointed at him and he stepped back into the shadows.

Evidently, Fari didn't mind the eyes and cameras. As she had done yesterday, she walked slowly around the outfield, accompanied by JD. She had told him earlier that this was the only safe way to show her appreciation. Also, it figured into her mother's strategy in allowing only brief, tantalizing glimpses of Fari, which increased her "promotional value."

Mac leaned back against the cool cement wall and watched as Fari and JD walked across centerfield together. Occasionally Fari waved to the crowd, which produced an instant reaction and a higher noise level. He flashed briefly on that morning's sexual encounter. It had been intense and frantic, as if they were starving people suddenly presented with a banquet. They had talked and laughed about it afterwards, both of them surprised and delighted. They promised to take it slow next time, pace themselves and draw-out the pleasure.

"Your arm feels all right?" JD asked Fari, shouting above the crowd noise. "You're okay for tomorrow?"

"Yes." Fari took off her cap and wiped her brow. The crowd let loose with a husky cheer.

JD had seen an extra spark in her eyes and wondered about it. "You feel okay in your heart?"

She flicked her eyes at him, then back at the crowd. "Yes. I am good in my heart."

"Okay." He walked with his hands clasped behind his back, occasionally looking up at the raucous crowd. "Is Frances really a communist?"

Fari laughed and the crowd laughed back.

JD leaned toward her. "I visited Jose's farm once. Did you know that?"

She shook her head.

"This was just after he came up to the majors, long before he met your mother. He had some trouble." He wondered if he should mention the trouble, but if she already knew then he wouldn't have to, and if she didn't know, then he wouldn't tell her. "Anyway, I stayed for about week. I loved it. It was beautiful, especially the beaches." He hooked his arm through hers. "Is that where your cabin is? On those beaches next to the jungle?"

"Yes."

He nodded. "Wow. I'm impressed. It's really isolated there."

They approached the bullpen and stopped. Fari looked toward the dugout, but Mac was not visible.

"Your Papa was a good man." JD's voice barely carried above the cheering. "I knew him well." He tried to catch her eyes. "I know Mac pretty good too. What do you think of him? Is Mac okay as a coach?"

Fari felt a sudden commotion inside her chest and looked away. "Yes, he is okay. I mean, as coach."

JD laughed happily and the crowd cheered wildly. "Oh, yes he is!" He spun around and trotted across the field toward the dugout. He hopped down the steps and roamed around as he always does, talking to the players and slapping high-fives.

Mac kept to himself, studying the Royals' batting line-up, keeping his head down and face hidden. Suddenly, someone tapped the bill of his cap. He looked up and straight at Fari. She stood in centerfield, staring back at him. He looked around quickly, then back at Fari. She smiled and waved, and the stadium shook in a strong gust of cheering.

*　　　　*

Doc Harris moved into a downtown hotel. The suite had been leased by his clinic for visiting doctors and important (wealthy) patients. What he "moved" was himself, the clothes on his back and one briefcase. He'd been wearing the same clothes for two days and didn't even carry a toothbrush, but these little details were no longer part of his life's routine. All his routines were finished.

He had taken a "relaxer" earlier and it smashed his brain flat, offering very little surface area for thought. Yet, there existed a small corner of his mind that remained lucid. Occasionally, he found himself in that corner and was able to think clearly. Even then, he couldn't think too far ahead for fear of thinking all the way to the end, and if he thought about the end, he'd never have the courage to get there.

He saw himself as a passenger inside someone else's nightmare machine. He was a *victim* – hounded by Sherry, humiliated by her parents, infected with a deadly virus. Therefore, whatever he did to fight back was not only fair, but *their* fault. They deserve what they were going to get.

*　　　　*

Mac sat alone in the living room of his condo and thought about the game that afternoon. The Twins had won again, beating Kansas City six to two. They got good pitching from Sandy Wilson, and, for the second game in a row, Cleo went two for four with two runs batted in.

The whole team was lifted by the excitement and pride of having

Fastball Fari as their teammate. Also, the wild crowds packing Target Field had encouraged them to kick up their performance. This would be happening all season in every city the Twins visited!

JD told Mac there were already several press conferences scheduled in each city, hoping Fastball Fari would appear. Also, security had become increasingly important, not only because of the crowds attending the games, but because of housing and transportation for Fari. In this regard, JD mentioned there had been threats directed against Fari. Apparently, not everyone loved her.

When Mac heard this, he immediately called Stewart, from the communication department. Stew described several faxes and emails, which he called "nuisance mail." According to him, they were "mostly racial or sexist in nature."

Mac demanded that Stew read him an example.

"'You Goddamn black bitch,"' Stew read. "'Go back to the jungle! Baseball is a man's game!'"

That didn't sound too good, yet it wasn't particularly dangerous.

"It came from a public library in Boise, Idaho," Stew said.

This surprised Mac. "How do you know that?"

"They're investigating."

"Who's investigating?"

"The security guys. Anytime we get threats or wacko shit, they take a look at it."

"You got something threatening on Fari?"

Stew hesitated and Mac growled.

"Alright," Stew admitted. "Some threats. They sent emails."

"*Who* sent emails?"

"Something called 'The Men's Baseball Militia.' They sent a 'manifesto' that says, quote, 'one of the last American male bastions, baseball, has been breached, we mean *bitched*, by a black girl.' They go on to say they must 'repel this invasion.'"

"'Repel this invasion?'"

"Yeah. Screwy, huh?"

"The security guys take this seriously?"

"This 'militia' sounds crazy, but the last email was traced back to Des Moines, Iowa."

Mac knew there were "crazies" loose in the world; people who seemed normal, but harbored murder in their hearts. For example, almost every week some random act of violence occurred in the nation's secondary or primary schools.

Last year, Kim's school had installed metal detectors and hired two full-time security officers. Mac had attended several parent-teacher meetings to discuss what they called "security concerns." He was shocked. When he was a kid in school, the most serious incidents were playground fights among the boys, and sometimes the girls. No knives or guns. He had been introduced to drugs in high school, but it was mostly alcohol and marijuana.

Things had changed quickly, with metal detectors at the doors and cops roaming the hallways. Soon they'd hand out helmets and flak-jackets and line the walls with sandbags. And now the white baseball militia – crazies for sure – had declared war on Fastball Fari.

Mac heard the garage door slam and Kim ran into the room. They hugged each other and Mac held on to her long and hard.

"You all right, Dad?" Kim detached herself and sat on the floor in front of the cold fireplace. She wore sneakers, jeans and a flannel shirt. Mac noticed this was more Fari's style than what Kim usually wore. He couldn't think of a better role model than Fari Madrigal. However, the way Kim looked at him right now reminded him of Jenni; the same posture and expression, the same eyes. A hot wave of affection swept over him. "I love you, Kim."

She smiled at him. "I love you too!" She continued to study him, her head tilted to one side. "What's this about, Dad? Why'd you want to talk to me?"

Mac sat back and gathered his thoughts. Since Jenni died, he and Kim had become soul-mates, confidants. Whenever they were alone like this, the silent ghost (or energy) of Jenni became a lingering presence. It was the reverse of the birth process; he and Kim's identities combined to give life to Jennifer. But now Mac was about to introduce a fourth party to their intimacy and he worried about Kim's reaction.

Mac drifted for a moment, recalling Fari standing in centerfield this afternoon. His spine tingled when he thought about that touch on his hat. It scared him. He hadn't had a chance to ask her about it and he wasn't sure if he should. Maybe it was his imagination, but he didn't think so. She had anticipated his reaction.

At that moment, Fari was next door with her mother, preparing for an interview. Mac had been invited to this interview, but he felt it was time to slow down a little. He still worried about this telekinetic stuff and the possibility he could be hypnotized or enchanted. If she could touch his hat, why not his brain or heart?

"Earth to Dad, Earth to Dad," sang Kim, waving her hands in front of his face. "Jeez, what's wrong with you?"

"I'm in love," he answered silently. He wasn't usually this nervous with Kim, but he had never found himself in this situation. He felt obligated to say something, but couldn't think of how to say it.

Kim scooted across the floor and sat in front of him. "Okay, we'll play twenty questions. Is it something with your job?"

He smiled and nodded, recognizing their "truth or dare" game. They used it sometimes to pry each other open.

"Okay. Something with the job." She leaned forward and studied him. "Does it have to do with Fari?"

He nodded and his eyes lit up. Kim saw this and noted the intensity. My God, she thought, he's really in love. "Okay," she said, continuing the game, helping him along. "It's something to do with the job and Fari. Is it on a professional level or personal?"

"Both," he whispered.

Kim nodded. "Maybe because she likes you so much?"

Mac leaned back and looked at her. "You think she likes me?"

Kim saw her father as just another kid confronting love for the first time; nervous and insecure. Here was a side of him she'd never seen before; her father vulnerable, unsure of himself. This endeared him to her even more and she loved him in a new way.

She didn't mind him loving Fari. She had reconciled herself to the fact that her mother was gone forever, a shadow from the past that existed now only as a memory or a spark of energy. But more than that, Kim had seen the depth of this loss in her father, the loss of his first and only love. And if he had a chance to love again, wouldn't that be good for him?

Yet, there existed a flip side to this sentiment – it brought a sense of closure or finality to the experience of her mother. Now, however, in the face of her father's tender condition, Kim resolved to save her tears for later.

She stood up and sat on his lap. "How do you feel about Fari?" She felt his muscles jerk.

"I don't know, Kim. But it's something strong and you should know about it because I can't hide it." He buried his face in her neck. "I'm sorry. I didn't know this would happen."

Kim patted him on the shoulder. "Don't be *sorry*, Dad. It's nothing *bad*. You and Fari are good people. Go ahead and be in love."

He drew back and looked her. "Really?"

"Sure." She laughed at his expression; just like a little kid! "Fari and I talked about it."

"You *talked* about it?"

"Hey, Dad, she's a good friend. We're roommates. We talk." She was amused by the goofy look on his face. "By the way, Fari invites you for breakfast tomorrow morning."

SEVENTEEN

Friday: April 5

Grey light filtered into the hotel room. Doc Harris watched the new dawn from his chair beside the windows. The TV was turned on, but the sound was muted. The large screen displayed the bright, cheery colors of a golf tournament; sunny fairways, blue sky, multicolored crowds of people. Compared to Doc's world of cold shadows, the TV offered a glimpse into paradise.

Doc couldn't be sure if he'd slept or not; he'd had no dreams and no nightmares, which seemed a good sign. He pushed himself out of the chair, shuffled into the bathroom, popped a hit of speed, then took a cold and hot shower. Fifteen minutes later, dressed in his wrinkled suit, he rode the elevator downstairs and walked out of the hotel.

The day had begun cloudy and dark, with a stiff wind blowing from the north. Bits of paper, leaves and other debris blew down the street. Doc walked with the wind, going south. He inhaled deeply in short, powerful breaths, in time with the banging of his shoes on the concrete. He held his head high and swung his left arm smartly, holding the briefcase in his right hand. The speed expanded his chest and he fought the urge to break into a run.

The glass and concrete canyons channeled the wind and a sudden gust pushed Doc forward, almost blowing him off his feet. He laughed. Fate was impatient this morning! The air around him crackled with electric madness.

* *

Fari's dream exploded into thousands of colored pieces. Her eyes snapped open and she lay still, opening herself to the dawn. A sense of doom scored across her psyche. She shuddered and looked at the clock; seven a.m. A gray haze crept around the edges of the window shade.

It was too quiet. She missed the songs of birds in the morning. In the jungle, dawn was always greeted with a full symphonic celebration, led by birds and monkeys. But here it was silence, or sirens, or tires on asphalt.

Kim had told her about an alarm clock programmed with different natural sounds. Maybe she and Mac could find such a clock somewhere and she'd buy two; one to play the sound of ocean surf, the other bird songs. It might make her feel more at home, especially during the all-important moment when a new day begins.

Thinking of Mac made her smile and stretch luxuriously. Last night they had decided to sleep in their own condos; Mac was still concerned about Kim's reaction. Fari could respect this. Besides, Kim would be staying at a friend's house this weekend and she and Mac would have plenty of time to explore and experiment with each other.

They had to be careful, however. They were breaking the team rules. They were teammates and promised not to "get involved."

On the other hand, Fari remembered her conversation with JD the day before. He had almost endorsed some sort of relationship with Mac. In fact, JD had orchestrated their living arrangements, with Kim as a roommate and Mac and Cleo next door. How should she interpret this? As tacit approval of a clandestine relationship?

Yes, she answered. But what about Mac? He would have to decide for himself, but she would plant a few ideas in his head. She knew one thing, however, in regards to the feeling of doom, she wanted Mac close to her for the next few days.

The dark feeling persisted. She tried to imagine trouble on the horizon, but could think of nothing. Maybe it had something to do with the interview this morning? It was useless to speculate. Her intuition had been attuned to the natural rhythms of nature, but here, surrounded by steel and concrete, such rhythms became smothered and distorted.

Fari turned her mind to more pleasant business; breakfast with Mac. She threw off the covers, peeled off her underwear and marched into the shower.

*   *

Doc slowed as he approached the townhouse complex. He had put on dark glasses and a checkered cap. He didn't expect to see detectives hanging around at this time of the morning. Still, he acted with caution.

Across the street from Doc, a woman walked her dog. She was dressed elegantly in a black suit and high heels. The dog, a tiny white poodle, pranced at the end of a rhinestone leash.

Doc wondered if she could be a watcher, but then he noticed she carried a plastic bag containing dog crap. He laughed. By God, no detective would go that far!

Doc entered the complex and turned right. He opened the front door to his condo and stood motionless for a moment, listening. He had placed several little clues here and there to let him know if anyone had entered, but none had been disturbed. Satisfied, he ran up to the bedroom and sat at his observation post.

He would be safe here until it was time to go. His wife or her detectives couldn't break into the townhouse and there was no way to contact him. So far, everything had gone according to plan.

Fari would be the starting pitcher tonight and everyone looked forward to seeing her pitch again. He had heard about tickets going for thousands of dollars! Of course, the game would be beamed around the world. Just think of it; all those people bursting with excitement and anticipation.

The end was near now and he had to operate on a moment-to-moment basis. No more forward thinking or backward thinking, no more regretting, no more trying to figure out what went wrong.

He stomped into the kitchen, made a mug of instant coffee, stirred in milk and sugar, and added a generous shot of vodka. He took a sip; a little strong, but not bad. He threw a "relaxer" into his mouth and washed it down.

As always, the mere act of taking the medicine produced an immediate response. He skipped over to the windows and sat where he could see the entire front of Fari's condo. Her front door was separated from the street by a short sidewalk leading to an iron gate.

Whenever Mac and Fari left the condo, Mac locked the front door behind him, while Fari waited by the gate. Then Mac opened the gate with a different key. Doc had never seen them use the garage door. It was a short walk to Nicollet Mall and the skyway system, and, as far as he knew, they seldom used a car.

He sipped the coffee and vodka. Mac and Fari were scheduled to meet this morning with Howard Sikes, and they would have to leave soon. Doc would wait here until departure time. He closed his eyes and drifted on the warm, rolling waves of vodka and drugs. His chest felt stuffed with sawdust and his heart thudded like a sticky piston. His head drifted toward the tabletop.

He heard a motor, tires on asphalt, doors slamming. He lifted his head, opened his eyes and focused on the street. A car had parked in front of Fari's condo!

Doc blinked several times, clearing his vision. It was a black utility vehicle with four people standing around it; two men and two women. They opened the back door and pulled out lights, suitcases and cameras.

Doc panicked and pushed himself upright. It was a news team! Sherry ordered a press conference to denounce him right here on the street! But then he recognized Frances, Fari's mother. She and the others disappeared inside Fari's condo, carrying their equipment.

Doc leaned back in the chair. His hand wandered for a second, made contact with the coffee mug and lifted it to his mouth. He drank and the liquid dribbled onto his shirt and pants. He laughed so hard he choked. He cried again. His thoughts moved slowly, blindly. What had just happened down there? A car on the street.

*   *

Mac sat in the living room of Fari's condo and watched the technicians set up their lights and cameras. They used the fireplace as a backdrop, with two armchairs angled toward each other. One camera sat on a tripod; the other was a portable video cam.

Evelyn Harris sat with Fari and Frances in the kitchen and explained the format and agenda for the interview. Mac had seen Ms. Harris several times on TV. She had a reputation as a competent reporter, specializing in community issues and local politics. He was surprised to discover she seemed much younger in person than she appeared on the screen.

Fari stood next to the breakfast bar, wearing jeans and a turtleneck sweater. They had had breakfast together that morning. She had been lively and talkative, but reserved, avoiding his eyes more than usual and had not touched him.

Just then Fari turned, flicked her eyes at him and winked. Mac's heart skipped. Once again, he wondered if she bewitched him. How would he know?

He turned his attention to his current preoccupation – the crazies in this world. He realized he had inherited something else from Jenni's passing; a deep-rooted horror of sudden death. Accident, illness, natural disaster, madness; the evening news was full of any number of ways one might die suddenly.

The spirit of malevolence lurked everywhere and was liable to strike from any direction. In this regard, Mac and Fari would meet this morning with JD and Howard Sikes. The agenda was personal safety. Mac had told them about Fari's concerns and he wanted the Twins more involved in her protection. They all appreciated Cleo's role as bodyguard, but they had been worried about journalists, or overzealous fans. Now they confronted serious crazies with twisted morals.

A technician stepped in front of Mac and looked into the kitchen. "Excuse me, Evelyn, but we're ready out here."

"Okay, Frank, thanks." The three women filed into the living room, which suddenly seemed very crowded. Fari had begged Mac to remain for this interview, even though it had nothing to do with him. His presence would only provoke more rumors and speculation.

While Frances and Evelyn talked together, Fari glanced at him again, another quick wink. He was stunned momentarily at the depth of feeling he saw in her eyes.

Evelyn and Fari took their places in the armchairs before the fireplace. Evelyn wore a charcoal gray pants suit with a white blouse and no jewelry. She was tall and good-looking, with tough eyes and a strong jaw. Her voice sounded melodious, her diction and delivery perfect.

The lights came on and the cameras rolled. Evelyn looked straight into one of the cameras and began her introduction, gesturing toward

Fari. Mac noticed that one camera focused on the two of them, the other was a close-up of Fari. He saw that Fari held a baseball in her right hand, which lay beside her leg, off camera. Under the bright lights her brown skin glowed, her eyes sparkled.

Evelyn explained this was an exclusive interview and she thanked Fari and Frances for the opportunity. "Well, Fari," she began. "I guess we should start with the beginning. Could you tell us a little about where you grew up? When and how you started pitching?"

Although Fari avoided eye contact, she apparently had no problem looking directly into a camera. Her face held a captivating expression; a blend of animation and sincerity. Her manner seemed relaxed, but, off camera, the baseball spun furiously. She spoke English with a strong accent, her voice soft and musical.

She talked about growing up throwing baseballs at dummies, how her father had taught her to pitch and how both her parents had supported and encouraged her pitching. She gave a short, chronological report, spoke for less then two minutes, then stopped. She sat back and waited for the next question.

Evelyn seemed caught off guard. She glanced at a clipboard resting on her knee. "It must have been hard playing baseball in Costa Rica, where the national sport is soccer. I understand at one point you were prohibited from playing? Could you tell us about that?"

Fari glanced at her mother, who was the likely source of such a question. She didn't mind that Mama wanted to help Evelyn Harris, but she wondered what other clues she may have passed on. Fari told the story quickly, without emotion, as if it had happened to someone else. Again, she finished abruptly and waited for the next question. She didn't look at Evelyn directly, but stared at the floor or into the cameras.

Evelyn led Fari through their move to the Dominican Republic when Fari had been sixteen. She made a little joke about Fari's degree in philosophy; it seemed an unusual pursuit for a girl obsessed with throwing a baseball.

Fari tilted her head and looked into the distance. "I am solitary person and philosophy is solitary activity. I like to observe and wonder."

Evelyn laughed politely. "Any answers?"

Fari's eyes shifted nervously. "Only to me."

"Well, let's hear it, Fastball Fari, baseball pitcher and philosopher. What's your perspective on life?"

Fari held herself motionless, even the baseball, and, for the first time, looked directly at Evelyn. "I wonder if human beings are indigenous to this planet."

Evelyn blinked and her smile froze. "Excuse me?"

Fari looked into the camera. "Humans are only species that commits systematic genocide, not only against other humans, but against every living thing."

A few seconds of silence followed this remark, with Evelyn staring at Fari as if waiting for more. But Fari had finished. Evelyn turned to one of the cameramen. "Cut for a minute. Let's take a break."

*   *

Doc opened his eyes. He saw a cloth-covered, flat surface. Where the hell was he? His head felt like a cannonball and it took a great effort to lift it. He pushed himself upright and cringed at the bright sunlight blasting through the window. He made an assessment of his mental and motor capabilities. The speed felt like high, screechy violins, while the relaxers contributed a deep, humming bass. The vodka flowed somewhere in between. He looked at his watch, closing one eye to see clearly. Eight fifteen. It must be close to departure time and he was already hammered.

But not hammered enough, he decided. His mouth felt like burnt fuzz. He reached for the coffee, but it was cold and stale. He stood up, waited for his legs to steady, then lurched toward the kitchen. He heated water in the microwave and made another instant coffee. This time he added a generous shot of one-fifty-one rum, which he thought would go better with the coffee.

As he stirred the coffee and rum, he felt a little better, a slight rise in mood. He remembered he had two extra hits of speed. There was no turning back and he was never coming back. He pulled out his pill bottle, shook out two black and yellow capsules and swallowed them with the coffee and rum. He staggered back to the table and looked into the street. A bright, eerie light reflected through the curtains of Fari's front windows. He assumed this meant they were still filming, but soon Mac and Fari would have to leave for the stadium.

What if they leave with the news people? This thought caused a momentary surge of alarm, but Doc immediately suppressed it by denying the possibility; there was not enough room in the car. He had to believe this because any other course of action was unthinkable. He *had* no other course of action.

A bolt of anger swept through him. His cheeks flushed and his jaws tightened. *Those bastards.* He turned, opened the briefcase and pulled out a bulky manila envelope. He threw the envelope on the table, where it landed with a dull thud.

You think I'm kidding, you bastards? You think you can step all over me, crush my life and get away with it? You think I'm a little bug that can't hurt you or fight back? He pointed at the envelope. There's our ticket to ride, you arrogant sons-of-bitches!

He swung around and looked at Fari's condo, angry at *her*. What right does she have, a black girl from a foreign country, coming up here and immediately grabbing the spotlight and having the whole world on a silver platter?

The first tickle of speed clawed at the back of his skull. He closed his eyes and pulled it along, trembling at the initial surge of power. Watch out, you bastards, that little bug you squashed is about to bite back.

*   *

Frances and Mac served coffee to the camera crew and Evelyn Harris. Mac could tell Ms. Harris was curious about his presence. She watched him, especially whenever he addressed Fari. Fari and Mac had decided earlier to conduct themselves cautiously, but Mac had been caught off guard by Fari's secret looks.

Evelyn announced she was ready to begin again and the cameramen turned on the lights and cameras. Mac had noticed Fari kept shifting the conversation away from herself, then ambushed Evelyn with a powerful declaration. He glanced at Frances and knew she and Fari had rehearsed this conversation.

Fari remained outwardly calm, but the baseball continued to spin rapidly. She had revealed a little more of the inner, hidden Fari, which proved to be as mysterious as everything else about her. Although she appeared remote, in control and almost majestic, Mac recalled fondly yesterday morning's frenetic sexual encounter when Fastball Fari was revealed as a natural woman capable of losing all control.

Evelyn asked Fari to comment on the no-hitter she pitched and Fari's face turned dreamy. She talked about how it felt to pitch in front all those people. She mentioned the presence of her father, Jose Madrigal, and insisted he had "helped" her on the mound. It was evident by her expression that pitching a no-hitter in the majors had been the most marvelous moment in her life.

Evelyn related her own feelings about watching Fari pitch in her first game. Then she mentioned Fari's "value" to the game of baseball and to women and minorities in general. However, said Evelyn, Fari was also enormously valuable to the Minnesota Twins.

Ms. Harris paused and looked at her clipboard, but Mac knew where these statements headed; she hoped for controversy and drama.

According to advance ticket sales, said Evelyn, every game the Twins would play this season had been sold out. Further, the cost for commercial time for the games had skyrocketed. And yet Fari signed for only minimum wage. "Why did you accept those terms? What was the real story behind your signing for the Minnesota Twins?"

Fari glanced at her briefly. "The real story?"

Evelyn leaned toward Fari. "You admitted to signing for minimum wage, then immediately said that Howard Sikes had paid more. You said he donated eight million dollars."

"Yes. But these things were not related." Fari lied without batting one lavish eyelash. She knew the question was coming and had no choice but to backup her mother.

"Your presence on the Twins will generate millions in revenue, yet you'll be paid about four hundred thousand dollars this year. You don't feel like you've been taken advantage of, or slighted?" Evelyn's voice carried a sharp edge, as if *she* was being slighted.

Fari talked toward the baseball in her hand. "I do not value myself and other people in terms of money. I want to survive, but why want more?"

Evelyn stared at her for a moment. "Are you saying you *deliberately* took a lower salary?"

Fari looked directly into the camera and smiled. "If we all work half as hard spiritually as we do trying to be millionaires, we would live in a world of saints." Although she made it sound like a joke, her eyes flashed with serious intent.

Evelyn Harris studied her clipboard, as if searching for the next scene in the script. Fari sat quietly, a small smile on her plump, curvy lips. The baseball lay motionless in her hand.

Frances stood up and addressed Evelyn. "Uh, excuse me. We're already past our deadline. Do you have enough, do you think?"

Evelyn apparently found nothing more on the clipboard. She told the camera crew they were finished and to pack up. Evelyn turned to Fari, thanked her and they shook hands. In the sudden movement and activity, Mac kept to his chair in the corner. At the outset, they had made it clear that there would be no photos or video of Mac, nor any indication he was even present. Still, he thought it odd that Evelyn Harris had not asked Fari about this "companion" business with Chet Macquire.

While the news team packed their gear, Mac met Fari in the kitchen.

"How was I?" she asked.

"Marvelous!"

She kissed him softly on the lips. A sharp sensation sliced through his pleasure center and his knees buckled.

*   *

Doc made another cup of coffee, adding more caffeine to the ocean of speed already rushing through his veins. The one-fifty-one rum tasted like tropical alcohol, but he added another shot to the coffee.

He heard a car door slam. He carried his coffee and rum to the window. The news team was leaving! As they loaded their equipment, Mac and Fari stood in the doorway talking to Frances and another woman. The other woman looked familiar, but Doc's vision was impaired.

Frances disappeared inside the car with the others, and they left. Mac and Fari went back into the condo and the door closed. Doc looked at his watch. They were supposed to be at the stadium within half an hour. Almost time to leave.

He picked up the manila envelope and carried it downstairs, along with his coffee and rum. He made his way to the front hallway, unlocked the front door and leaned against it. Narrow windows to either side of the door gave him a good view of the front of Fari's condo, only seventy feet away.

He heard a motor and backed away from the window. A black motorcycle passed by slowly with one rider dressed in black leather. The bike kept going and disappeared around the bend.

Doc took a long swig of coffee. The rum scorched his throat and he coughed and shouted. "Here I am in the departure lounge!" He laughed breathlessly, the speed squeezing his chest like a vise. He held the manila envelope awkwardly in his left hand, his body swaying from side to side. His eyes closed. Scenes from his life flashed by like the windows of a passing train.

His heart shook and stars exploded. He fell backwards against the wall, the coffee mug dropped from his fingers and smashed on the floor. He grabbed the wall with both hands, trying to remain upright. Loud drums pounded inside his head and chest. In one, tiny lucid corner of his mind he thought this was a heart attack.

After a few seconds, however, his vision cleared. Gradually he came back into most of his senses. He saw broken pieces of mug strewn across the floor. His shoes squished with hot coffee and rum. He pushed away from the wall, holding out his arms for balance.

He caught movement in the corner of his eye and looked out the window. Fari's front door had opened. They were leaving! Doc stuck his right hand into the manila envelope. The bass drums in his head beat harder. *It's time to go! It's time to go!*

His chest convulsed and he spat out a sob. Mac and Fari appeared in the doorway, wearing their hats and sunglasses. Doc watched his left hand reach out and open the front door. He stepped outside, his feet sloshing in his shoes.

Although Doc was gripped in the twitching fist of speed, everything shifted into slow motion. His legs swept out in front of him with difficulty, as if walking through water. The drums in his head beat with a frenzy, his heart banged with the same rhythm.

Fari stood on the short sidewalk between the front door and the gate, while Mac closed the condo door and locked it. They had their backs to the street.

*　　　　　　*

Mac turned from the door and walked toward Fari. From the corner of his eye he saw someone moving toward them, a man in a suit carrying an envelope. The man resembled Doc Harris, but this guy was dirty and rumpled.

*　　　　　　*

Doc saw Mac staring at him with a blank look, as if he didn't recognize him. He kept moving, but it proved difficult. He put his head down and leaned into the growing pressure, pointing himself toward Fari, his right hand still hidden inside the envelope. Despite the riotous maelstrom inside his head and chest, he had the presence of mind to remember his shaking hand. He'd have to get close.

*　　　　　　*

The man walked toward them with a purpose, looking straight at them. Mac felt a sudden chill. Then he recognized Doc Harris! My God, he looked terrible. Was he in trouble? He reached for Fari and pulled her closer.

"It's Doc," he whispered.

*　　　　　　*

Doc made it halfway across the street; only a few more steps to Fari. The blood roared through his temples like a freight train. But no; the noise came from *behind* him. He felt a breeze tug at his clothes as a black motorcycle sped by him and skidded to a stop in front of Fari's gate, smoke rising from the wheels. A black leather-clad figure spread his legs and lifted his arms.

Doc stopped, momentarily paralyzed, his feet stuck to the asphalt.

*　　　　　　*

Fari heard the deep rumble and knew the dark trouble had arrived. She saw the motorcycle screech sideways toward the gate, gravel and dust flying. She was barely aware of Doc Harris standing in the street, but he was not the danger. She closed her eyes and concentrated.

Mac jumped back and pulled Fari with him. His hand fumbled in his jacket pocket, searching for the keys. He grunted, hyperventilating, the panic building. He saw the black figure raise his arms, holding a pistol. "No!" Mac backed up against the door, hugging Fari, trying to protect her.

*   *

Doc saw the black figure point a finger at Mac and Fari. Doc blinked and saw the finger was a pistol! For a split second, despite the drugs and drums, Doc saw the bitter irony in this situation. He almost laughed. His right arm lifted and the manila envelope lined up on the black figure. He pulled the trigger. POW! The envelope flew away and the black figure staggered backwards.

BANG! The black figure fired his pistol. Doc heard a scream. He lined up the sight and squeezed the trigger again, and again! The black figure flew backwards to the pavement and lay still.

The gunfire echoed for a second, then all was silent. Doc stood in the street, the pistol held straight out in front of him. He watched the black figure, making sure he was down for good. He heard a shout from far away and turned his head.

"Doc, help! Fari's shot! Doc!"

Fari lay face down on the sidewalk. Mac jumped up, opened the gate and pulled Doc over to Fari. Doc moved in a stupor, still holding the pistol. Mac shouted for Doc to help Fari, then ran into the condo.

The black, bloody hole in Fari's back was obviously an exit wound. Upper right side, Doc noted, so the heart should be okay. But maybe the lung was clipped. He flexed his hands and realized he still held the pistol. He looked into the condo and heard Mac screaming for an ambulance. He turned and saw four or five people standing outside their condos, staring in his direction.

Let's give them the last act, he thought. He lifted the pistol and stuck the barrel in his mouth. He tasted oil and cordite.

Will I hear anything? Will I feel it?

He jerked the trigger. Click.

EIGHTEEN

"About what time was this?" asked Detective Falk.

"Nine fifteen." Mac sat on a stiff wooden chair inside a small office reserved for the police, just off the emergency room at Hennepin County General Hospital. Detective Amos Falk was with the Minneapolis Police Department, Homicide Division.

"Okay. You opened the front door. Then what?" Falk exercised patience with Macquire, respecting his grief and shock. Sudden violence was an awesome experience and often hit people to their core. Amos had been a cop for twenty years; five years on the streets, fifteen as a detective. He wore his toughness and cynicism like the shell of a turtle. Indeed, he resembled that animal; small, elongated head, thick, oval body, short arms and legs.

"We stepped outside," answered Mac. "I turned to lock the door. Fari stood behind me on the little sidewalk." Mac's voice faded as he looked into the corner of the room. In his mind's eye he could see her; she smiled at him, her eyes blazing in the morning sun. "She stood by the gate."

Amos cleared his throat. "And at this time you noticed nothing strange?"

Mac looked back at him. "No. Not at first. Then I saw Doc Harris. He was in the street walking toward us."

"When you first saw him, how far away was he?"

"About fifty feet, maybe. At first, I didn't recognize him, but as he got closer I saw it was Doc." Mac had to tread lightly here, talking about Doc Harris. "He didn't look too good."

"Naw, he's a real mess." Amos pulled in his turtle head. "He's got all kinds of stuff in his blood. Prescription drugs, alcohol. He's lucky to be alive."

We're all lucky to be alive, thought Mac, except for the bastard on the bike. He looked at Falk. "Who was he?"

Amos hesitated. They had an ID on the dead man, but it hadn't been released yet, pending notification of the family. But he figured Macquire deserved an answer. "His name was Rupert H. Day, from Hutchinson, Idaho."

"Rupert H. Day," Mac repeated slowly, trying to get a feel for the man through the name.

"The 'H' stands for Hitler."

"What?"

Amos smiled. "Rupert's father was a great fan of the Fuhrer. He gave his son Hitler's name." He was about to say more, then thought better of it. Mac deserved a name, but not the preliminary findings of the investigation. This was going to be a very sensitive and well-pub-licized case. On one hand, Falk was pleased with all the attention, since he was chief investigator; on the other hand, he hated to make a stupid mistake in the glare of the public spotlight.

"The Men's Baseball Militia." Mac's voice issued sharp and thin.

Amos thought he'd better set Mac straight on this. They didn't want any conspiracy rumors flying around. He waved his small hands like flippers. "Naw, there was nothing like that. Our boy Rupert was the founder and sole member. According to all indications so far, he acted alone in this. Just your average, garden variety wacko."

Falk said this as though such "wackos" walked around everywhere, nothing special about this one. An angry depression bubbled up from Mac's guts and he felt a sudden stab of white-hot hatred. But what did he hate, who did he hate? Is it possible to hate a dead man?

"So you saw Dr. Harris walking toward you," prompted Amos, try-ing to speed up the interview.

Mac stood up and paced in a circle. "Yes. I thought nothing of it at first. But just then this other guy, Rupert, pulled up on his motorcycle."

"Pulled up? Just like that, nice and easy?"

"No. He came up fast and braked hard. I knew something bad was happening, but I couldn't get the key." Mac stopped pacing and stared at the floor. He whispered, almost to himself. "I couldn't get the key out fast enough."

Amos looked away and kept his mouth shut. The victims always think they should have done something, some heroic action, to save themselves or their loved ones. Then the guilt would set in. Ordinarily, this never bothered Amos, but this was not an ordinary case.

"Mr. Macquire, I've been a cop for twenty years and I still get surprised once in a while. No way to anticipate something like that and it happens so fast."

Mac looked at him, tears sliding down his cheeks. "But we *knew*. They sent emails, for Christ's sake!" He wiped away the tears. "But somehow we just couldn't *believe* it. It's hard to believe people could be so crazy."

Amos almost laughed, but caught himself in time. He knew very well how crazy people could get, and that's why he wore this hard turtle shell. On the other hand, the shell couldn't protect what the eyes could see or what the ears could hear. Amos felt filled to his eyeballs with the vicious, crazy shit people did to each other. Sometimes he wondered if his shell was misplaced; he was starting to rot from the inside.

Mac fell back on the chair and looked at the opposite wall, the scene playing in front of him. "We backed up to the front door, Fari and I. Rupert pulled out a gun and pointed it straight at us. I thought we were dead for sure." He swallowed and continued in a softer voice. "I remember looking into the barrel. It was huge. But I couldn't move." He looked at Falk. "I literally could not *move*. I was paralyzed. Maybe it was terror, I don't know, but I was frozen." Mac paused again, recalling the feeling of total helplessness.

Amos listened and waited.

Mac continued. "Still, the guy didn't shoot right away. It seemed like he hesitated. Doc fired first. By that time, he was only about ten feet from the guy. When we heard the shot, we screamed." He clamped his teeth together against the bile rising in his throat. "I heard a second shot and Fari shouted and fell. I jumped on her, covered her, and we both screamed. I heard more gunfire. Two more shots, I think."

This agreed with what Amos already knew; that Dr. Harris had shot first, hitting Rupert in the shoulder; then Rupert's gun went off and the bullet hit Fari; then Dr. Harris fired again twice more. One of those bullets went straight through Rupert's cold and crazy heart, killing him instantly. Amos asked Mac, "I understand you opened the front gate for Dr. Harris?"

"Yes. He was a *doctor*. I wanted him to help her. I ran into the house and called 911. When I got back, he was tending to her."

There was silence for a moment as they thought about that, each in his own way. Amos was continually astonished at the freaky things he sometimes encountered out here on the edge, where the absurd meets the tragic. For example, he believed Doc Harris was there to kill Fari Madrigal, but he had to ask. "Did Doc save her life?" Amos savored this question, wondering if the paradox could become even freakier.

Mac thought about it. Would his answer matter in a court of law? Some day it might. He decided to relate only what he saw, not what he thought. "He shot the guy who was about to shoot Fari or me, or both of us. Then he helped her. He took off his shirt and pressed it against the wounds, turning her to one side so she breathed easier." Mac stopped again as he remembered squatting next to Fari, his shoes splattered with her blood. He closed his eyes against this horrible scene.

Amos relished the complex currents swirling through this case. The neighbors at the condo complex reported that Dr. Harris had stuck the pistol in his mouth, but didn't pull the trigger. The cops discovered the pistol was empty. Amos believed that Doc *did* pull the trigger, but had run out of ammo. "Had you seen Dr. Harris around there before? Around the condo?"

"No. We were always very careful about coming and going. But he worked at the stadium. It's possible he could've followed us one day."

Not only that, thought Amos, but he rented the townhouse right across the street! Mac apparently didn't know this and Amos would keep it to himself. Further, they had found photos featuring Fari Madrigal in her underwear. According to Amos' partner, who had seen the photos, there were enough background details to provide a positive ID as to where they were taken.

Amos smiled. It wasn't often he came across a case that offered so many little mysteries. He dearly wanted to talk to the good Dr. Harris, but he would wait awhile longer; Dr. Harris was still incoherent. However, difficulties were already appearing. They had one person dead and one gravely wounded. Would there be an arrest? Would they charge Dr. Harris? With what? He had a permit for the gun, and he shot a wacko who wanted to shoot Fari and Macquire, maybe saving their lives. Amos sighed and his smile grew broader. He loved it!

The phone on the desk rang and Amos snatched it up. "Yes?" He listened for a moment, then held it out to Mac. "Dr. Smith."

Fari's surgeon! Mac grabbed the phone. "Yes?"

*   *

Frances sat alone in the corner of the waiting room. The emergency room was fairly quiet this morning, but business would pick up as the day wore on; it was Friday and they expected the usual weekend rush. At the moment, however, the only pressing emergency was Fari Madrigal.

Ever since she had heard the news about Fari, Frances had been plagued by the image of Felipe lying dead on the ground, his blood soaking the earth. The rage of that moment so long ago had struck her again thirty-four years later. And was this situation all that different? No. Fari, like Felipe, had been fighting for social justice and the common good. Like Felipe, she was shot down.

Frances stood up abruptly, feeling the need to do something, but she didn't know what. For a second, she felt the panic of being surrounded by all those weirdoes who inhabit the edges, like the one who shot Fari. "He was crazy," they told her. But she knew better. It was the *culture* that was sick and crazy.

"Mrs. Marchena?"

She turned and recognized Dr. Smith. She clutched her chest.

"Fari came through surgery in good shape. She's going to be fine."

Frances slumped toward the floor. The doctor stepped forward quickly and caught her. He was accustomed to the raw emotions of the waiting room. "She's in recovery right now," he said softly. "We'll let you know as soon as she wakes up. Are you all right? Would you like something?"

Frances shook her head, unable to talk, hanging on to the only thing that mattered: Fari was alive and all right!

*   *

The news spread through the country like a shock wave. Fastball

Fari has been shot! The details were sketchy. Apparently, she was shot as she left her house this morning in Minneapolis. According to police, there were several shots fired, with one person confirmed dead. Chet Macquire, the Twins' pitching coach, was with Fari when she was shot, but was not injured.

Fari was rushed to Hennepin County General Hospital and into emergency surgery. The hospital spokesperson reported that she arrived in critical condition with a bullet wound in the chest. The police released no further details, but witnesses at the scene say that a fourth person was present and also involved in the shooting. However, police refused to confirm or deny this version of the incident.

Alarm and sadness were evident on the faces of announcers around the country. Many stations sent out news teams to record the reactions of the public. These scenes ranged from deep, quiet sorrow, to loud, shouting fury. There appeared renewed calls for a saner gun policy; here was another tragedy involving two hand guns! Women's groups and civil rights organizations released statements condemning violence against women and minorities, describing Fari as one more ethnic hero cut down in her youth. The most profound reaction, however, occurred quietly within the hearts of all Americans, where the knife twisted a little deeper, causing internal bleeding and black despair.

*   *

Mac and Amos heard a soft knock on the office door and it opened. Dr. Smith stuck his head inside. "Fari's awake, Mr. Macquire. She asked about you."

Mac raised his eyebrows to Amos and Amos jerked his thumb. "Go."

As they walked down the hallway, the doctor told Mac that Fari had opened her eyes about twenty minutes ago. Frances was with her right now. They stopped at a door and the doctor stepped back. "Don't stay too long, Mr. Macquire, and don't get her excited. She needs rest."

Mac nodded, composed himself for a moment, then opened the door. The bed was to his right. Frances stood on the other side of the bed, facing him, holding hands with Fari. He stopped just inside the door, distracted by the machines, noises and lights. Bottles hung above the bed with thin tubes running down and disappearing beneath the sheet. Finally, he looked at the bed, at the black hair sprayed out on the pillow. Fari looked straight at him and smiled. "Ola, Mac."

He lost it. He fell to the floor on his knees and buried his face in the sheet between her feet. The vicious horrors of sudden loss gripped his chest and he shook with wracking sobs. Oh, Jenni, I'm so sorry! Oh, Fari!

"Venga, Mac."

Mac allowed himself a good cry, remembering that Fari was alive and well. He wiped his face, stood up and shuffled toward the head of the bed. He had always been squeamish about needles and tubes and hospitals. He felt weak in the knees, but when Fari looked at him, his legs felt stronger. Although she lay in bed weak and wounded, her eyes had lost none of their power. She lifted her hand and he took it. She tugged weakly and pulled him closer. He bent over and put his ear to her mouth.

She kissed his ear, her lips dry and cracked. "I am glad you are okay."

Another blast of rage shook Mac, but he bit his lip and controlled the urge to scream. What Fari needed now was a solid presence, not emotional outburst. He looked at her, at the brave smile and bottomless eyes. "I'm glad you're okay too." He was fully aware of how absurd this sounded under the circumstances, but they all knew what he really meant: We're glad you're alive.

"The doctor says no broken bones, no lung damage," said Frances from the other side of the bed. She wanted to reassure Mac and herself that Fari was not truly crippled by this incident, not physically anyway. Besides, it was easier to focus on the technical details rather than the how and the why. How could anyone possibly explain in rational terms what had just happened to her daughter?

Fari felt the hole through her chest like a cool, empty tunnel, from one side to the other. It was already healing, she could tell. She closed her eyes and thought about the people and places she loved, drawing strength and energy.

Yes, her chest was healing, but what about her soul? Here the wound festered and burned. She also detected an element of shame.

However, she didn't have the strength to think about it. Not now. All she could think about was how to get home.

Mac felt another tug on his hand. He leaned down and laid his head next to Fari's. "Yes, my dear?"

"Promete me algo, Mac." Her voice sounded stronger.

He nodded. "Sure. What is it?"

She squeezed his hand with surprising strength. "Help me get home."

*   *

People felt drawn to the drama of a fallen hero. Hennepin County General Hospital covered two city blocks near the heart of downtown, astride the intersections of several arterial streets. Traffic became snarled by the influx of media, sports fans and curious citizens. They congregated on the sidewalks and spilled into the streets.

Police arrived to clear the streets. Crowds of media gathered around city hall, two blocks away, where they beseeched the police department for more details. Finally, the police released the name of the dead man, but that was all. However, it was enough to get the media off their backs. Now the focus of reporting shifted to Rupert Hitler Day and Hutchinson, Idaho.

Rupert's father was serving time in a federal prison on weapons charges. He and Rupert were active in the local white militia movement. Rupert had been recruited by the Detroit Tigers several years ago and played with their minor league team in Nebraska. He was a pitcher. However, after reports of fights and racial incidents, Rupert had been released. One reporter with connections into the Idaho police department tumbled onto the name "Men's Baseball Militia," and this was reported gleefully. Next, several reports and commentaries appeared about the white militia movement in general, who was involved, and their activities.

Meanwhile, reporters pestered the Minneapolis police for the name of the person who shot Rupert. Who was this heroic mystery man? Finally, the police announced that Dr. Skipper Harris, forty-nine years old, shot and killed Rupert H. Day. Police had recovered a pistol at the scene registered to Dr. Harris, for which he had a permit.

This set off a fresh round of feverish reporting, especially since Dr.

Harris was connected to one of the most prominent families in the Midwest. Doc's clinic and residence were filmed, but his family was not at home and could not be located. It was presumed that Sherry Lansing Harris and her children were staying at the Lansing family compound in Wayzeta. A family spokesperson would not confirm or deny, and the family declined to issue a statement.

At first, this news was reported in an upbeat manner, as if Dr. Harris played the hero in this drama. Soon, however, rumors circulated among the journalists that Dr. Harris had also tried to kill himself. This indicated more pieces of the puzzle were missing. From then on, the reporting on Doc Harris became subdued, pending further investigation.

Of course, the greatest concentration of media was at General Hospital, where journalists and the public gathered in a noisy vigil, clamoring for more information about Fari, Mac and Frances. The hospital had a small press room, but it was jammed and overflowing. Security guards kept order and told people to shut up, this was a hospital!

*　　　　　*

Mac and Frances sat together in the police office, while Amos Falk talked to Fari. JD had visited the hospital a short time earlier, but Fari had been sleeping. JD told Mac that Major League Baseball had canceled tonight's game. The game would be re-scheduled for a later date.

Howard Sikes had also stopped by and talked with Frances. "Howard offered to have Fari moved to a private hospital," Frances told Mac. "He'll pay all costs not covered by insurance."

Mac barely heard her. He felt exhausted and couldn't stop thinking about those long seconds staring into the barrel of Rupert's gun. He couldn't tell exactly who Rupert had aimed at; he and Fari stood close to each other. But the round, black hole had been pointed head high. Oh my God, he thought suddenly, Kim almost became an orphan!

Jenni was taken from him not too long ago and now Fari was almost killed. The only two women he had ever loved! Did he have some kind of jinx? A bad karma? Not from this life, he was sure. Although he had made mistakes and blunders, he never deliberately set out to hurt anyone. Then *why?*

"The doctor said she was very lucky." Frances was about to describe how lucky, an inch either way, but judging by the look on Mac's face, it would only pull him deeper into his funk. She looked at him from a different angle, remembering that this man loved her daughter.

"Mac," she said softly, getting his attention. "I'm trying to concentrate on the only positive outcome of this incident: Fari's alive. That's all that matters." She looked at him through her tears. "Instead of moving Fari to another hospital, I'm taking her home to the Dominican Republic, to the farm."

Mac nodded, not trusting his voice. He had been prepared to hear this, but the words hit hard. Yes, Fari was alive, but soon she would be gone. He agreed with Frances; we have to get Fari out of here. He remembered her talk about unpredictable human behavior. It was almost as if she had forecast her own encounter with tragedy.

*　　　　　　*

Amos sat in a chair toward the foot of the bed, his stomach full of butterflies. He was star-struck, he admitted it. He had seen ugly people and he had seen beautiful people, but he had never seen anyone like Fari Madrigal. She appeared calm and dignified, despite the obvious weakness of her body. Her eyes, when she looked at him, penetrated to the back of his skull. The doctor told him she had refused painkillers, preferring a clear mind. Was she in pain? If so, she didn't show it.

Amos pretended to consult the notebook in his hands, taking time to gather his thoughts. Finally, he asked, "Did you see if Dr. Harris was carrying anything?"

"No. I saw only person in black."

Amos had interviewed thousands of people over the years, most of them strangers. That was the nature of being a cop; you spent all day dealing with strangers. Like all good cops, Amos had developed an inner radar system that gave him clues to someone's character or "profile." But now, as he studied Fari Madrigal, he ran up against a blank wall. "You knew Dr. Harris from the stadium, I guess. Did you know him well?"

"No. We talked only once."

Amos thought he heard a trace of bitterness or anger, but her eyes remained steady. Although his intuition failed him, his built-in lie detector told him she spoke the truth. Apparently, whatever motives had driven Dr. Harris had originated inside his own head. Amos would soon find out. Doc was next on his list.

However, as long as Fari appeared strong and alert, he would linger by her side. It felt good sitting next to her. She radiated a clean, warm energy, like a burst of sunrays. He drifted on this pleasant current for a moment, then pulled his eyes back to the notebook. He slipped out a small photograph, leaned forward and showed it to her. "Can you see this okay?" She nodded. "Do you know this man? Have you ever seen him?"

Fari studied the photo. It was an unremarkable face; pale, chubby cheeks, flat chin, a white, jagged scar under one eye. She shook her head and looked away. "No. I never saw him."

Her voice sounded weaker and Amos thought he'd better leave soon. "This is a fairly recent photo of Rupert Day." He was about to say more, but he looked at her and asked, "Do you want to know about him?"

She shook her head. "No."

Well, that was that, Amos thought. We know about Rupert, we know about Macquire and we know about Fari. What about Dr. Harris? Doc seemed to be the linchpin in this mystery. Amos studied Fari's eyes and saw the dullness setting in.

"Just a couple more questions, then I'll leave." He asked the magic question. "Why do you suppose Dr. Harris walked toward your condo with a pistol in his hand?"

Fari stared into the far corner for so long Amos thought she hadn't heard him, but then she turned her face toward him and spoke with a shadow of a smile. "He was there to save my life." She said this without a trace of irony.

Amos stared at her until he was sure she was serious. "You really think so?" He allowed a bit of disbelief to creep into his voice.

Fari smiled. "I do not know *why* Doc was there, but he was at that place at that time, yes?"

"Yes, ma'am, he was."

"And he did shoot that man, didn't he?"

"He surely did."

They stared at each other for a second, until Fari looked away. Amos shook his head and looked back at his notebook. He drew a big question mark.

"Can I see him?"

Amos looked up. "See who?"

"Doc Harris. I want to talk to him."

Amos wondered what this could mean. Should he regard Dr. Harris as a suspect? Was he dangerous? Yes, he killed someone, but to save another life. He then tried to kill himself, but he didn't. Is *that* against the law? He had the pistol inside a manila envelope – carrying a concealed weapon?

Amos shook his head and blew out a long sigh. To his delight, this case was getting more complicated. He knew in his heart that Doc Harris wanted to kill Fari and maybe Mac too, then commit suicide. Was Dr. Harris dangerous? Did he still want to kill Fari? "I want to talk to him first. Also, I'll talk to Dr. Smith. We'll let you know."

Fari nodded and closed her eyes.

Amos sat a while longer, watching Fari as she fell asleep, her chest rising in slow, regular breaths. Her head had tilted to one side, presenting Amos with her splendid profile. He admired the long, thick eyelashes and the clean, smooth sweep of her jaw and neck. Her arms lay straight at her sides, palms up, intravenous tubes in both forearms.

Amos was a great fan of the Twins. He went to games whenever he could, and rarely missed opening day. He had been there for Fari's no hitter. He recalled the excitement and awe he had felt, not only at her pitching, but for the privilege of participating in history and legend. Goosebumps tingled across his body.

He stood up, bent over and kissed her lightly on the forehead. Take care, Fastball Fari. God bless you.

*   *

Frances sat quietly as Fari slept. She worked on a statement she would read later to the media. There had been enormous pressure from all sides, including the police, for her to give a first-hand report about Fari.

She oscillated between inflammatory outburst and a calm recitation of the facts. She had seen some of the public's reactions on TV. Most people were outraged, but there was also frustration because there seemed to be no clear target for their rage. Yes, Rupert Day was dead, but there was a feeling that other, darker forces had somehow conspired to create someone as twisted as Rupert.

This wasn't too far from the truth, as Frances saw it, but such forces were not dark or hidden; they were out in the open for all to see and emulate – the obsession for power and control; the fear and hatred for anyone different or strange; the propensity to settle disputes with violence; the desperate need for attention and recognition.

Frances forced herself to leap beyond these social realities and think about the future. Fari was alive, but what about her pitching? The bullet went through the upper right part of her chest, tearing muscles and ligaments. No one has mentioned what effect this might have on her pitching, but it might be all over for her, at least in the major leagues.

Thank God Fari had been able to satisfy her deepest wish and dream – she pitched as a professional baseball player in a major league game and pitched a no-hitter! The memory will last a lifetime.

And what of their plan? Frances had talked to Rod McNulty, who had thought of holding back on releasing the commercials. Frances told him to go ahead; she and Fari wanted the commercials to appear. The bitter irony was that Fari had become even more famous after being shot.

"Hi, Mama."

Frances looked up and saw Fari awake and groaning. "Hi, honey. How do you feel?"

"Okay, but sore. It itches."

"That's a good sign. You're mending already."

"Yes. Did the doctor say when we can leave?"

"Howard Sikes talked about renting a hospital plane. It will have a doctor, two nurses and all the equipment of an emergency room. The doctor said if you go in this plane, you could leave sometime tomorrow."

Fari's eyes lit up. "Really? Tomorrow? Let's go, Mama."

"All right, honey. I'll talk to Howard. I think it's costing a lot of money, but he has learned to give."

They laughed together and Fari's face twisted with pain. "Ouch!" She laid one hand on her chest. "It hurts."

Frances almost shouted. *Alleluia! Fari is alive and laughing and it hurts.*

"I am sorry, Mama. About the plan. What now?"

"I don't know. McNulty is going ahead with the commercials, which is good. We'll set a precedent and prove your value." Her face softened. "I don't know about pitching again, honey."

Fari looked away and shook her head. "It is over." She stared at the tubes in her arms, then flicked her eyes at her mother. "I could make movies."

Frances leaned back and laughed. "Are you serious?"

Fari nodded. "Yes. You said I had offers. Lots of money in Hollywood, Mama."

Frances stared wide-eyed at her daughter. "You *are* serious."

Fari shrugged her shoulders and immediately grimaced. She had to be cautious with body language. "While I am still famous, I have to find something else to keep me famous. Then we go ahead with the plan."

"Hollywood is dangerous. The US is dangerous."

"Anywhere is dangerous. Maybe the movie people will come to Santo Domingo, or somewhere else."

Frances felt a chill. "I don't know, Fari. I'm scared for you. Maybe we should think of something else. When you're famous, you draw the attention of millions of people and some of them are crazy."

"I'll have bodyguards, live in seclusion."

Frances smiled. "Maybe. But first, let's go home. Then we'll talk about it."

"I talked to Papa. He suggested Hollywood."

Just like Jose, thought Frances, to make Fari pick herself up, dust herself off and keep going forward. She felt a deep, solid love for both of them.

They heard a soft knock on the door and Dr. Smith looked in. "Am I disturbing anything?"

Frances stood up. "No, of course not. Please come in." He was the doctor!

Dr. Smith walked to the bed and took Fari's hand. "How are you feeling?"

She flicked her eyes at him. This man's manner was gentle and confident. "A little sore, but it itches."

"Already? That's good news. But we'll keep an eye out for infection for the next few hours."

"Excuse me, doctor," said Frances. "Could we leave tomorrow? If we left on that hospital plane Mr. Sikes talked about, would you allow us to leave?"

The doctor's eyebrows rose and he looked from mother to daughter. "Tomorrow? You want to leave?"

Fari looked into his eyes for two seconds. "Yes."

The doctor shrugged his shoulders. "Let's decide tomorrow morning. If no infection develops, then I don't see why not."

Fari squeezed his hand. "Thank you."

"By the way, there's a young lady out there asking about you. I don't know how she got through security. Her name is Kim."

"Please let her in."

"You said only family and Chet Macquire and we're being strict about that. This place is a madhouse." He smiled. "Sorry, but you're quite famous."

Fari nodded. "Please let Kim in. She is my sister."

His eyebrows rose again, no doubt recalling Kim's pale skin and blond hair. "Okay, but only a few minutes." The doctor checked Fari's IV bags and the needles in her skin.

"I'll leave now, honey," said Frances. "They're reorganizing a press conference." She kissed Fari on the cheek and started for the door.

"Wait, Mama," Fari called. "Have you seen Evelyn Harris?"

"No, but I talked to her on the phone. She's outside with the other media people."

"What about the interview? It goes on this afternoon?"

"She said they'd delay it until she hears again from me. What should I tell her?"

"Ask her to please wait until tomorrow, after we have gone. And tell her I want to tape another message. It should be just her alone with a camera."

Frances stared closely at her daughter. "What message?"

Fari smiled. "I want to say good-bye."

Frances laughed. "Good-bye? What will you say?"

"I do not know yet." Fari nodded at the clipboard tucked under Frances' arm. "What will *you* say?"

Frances shook her head. "I don't know either. I have three different versions."

"Be calm and conciliatory, Mama."

Frances heaved a sigh and rolled her eyes. "Okay, honey. I'll try." She left the room.

Dr. Smith checked Fari's pulse and temperature. "You're doing fine. Quite good, in fact."

"Thank you. I have good doctor."

"Flattery will get you everywhere." He lost the smile. "Amos Falk tells me you want to talk to Skipper Harris."

"Yes."

He studied her for a second, but could read nothing in her expression. "Well, it's all right with me, but under certain circumstances." Now he smiled. "Falk is not happy with Dr. Harris. I guess he's got a lawyer and he's not talking."

Fari nodded and smiled back. "He will talk to me."

*　　　*

Mac sat in a pew in the hospital chapel, which was off limits to journalists. Kim ran into the chapel sobbing and buried her face in his chest. He stroked her hair and kept his mouth shut.

Finally, Kim turned her head sideways and wiped her face. "Goddamn maniacs," she whispered.

Mac patted her on the shoulder. "Hey, we're in church."

"I know. I don't like church."

"Yeah, well, happy things happen in church, you know. Like weddings, baptisms."

She gave him a sour look. "Yeah, right. If I ever get married it'll be outside, in a garden, or on the beach."

"Good idea."

She rested her head on his shoulder. "How could someone *do* that?" Her body shook and she hugged him harder. "And you too!" She cried again.

Mac felt bad for Kim. She had just lost her mother and now almost lost her father! And her good friend Fari was shot. He tightened his arms around her and whispered in her ear. "Everyone's all right, honey. Fari will be okay."

She nodded and said something into his chest.

"What's that?"

"She's leaving tomorrow. They're renting a hospital plane."

So soon? Mac's stomach dropped. Events moved quickly and he could only sit and watch. He felt greatly relieved that Fari would recover completely, but now he would lose her to geography. She would be alive and well, but living elsewhere.

Kim leaned back and caught his eyes. "I wonder if they need pitching coaches in the Dominican Republic."

*　　　　*

Doc Harris stood in the middle of the room, his clothes wrinkled and stained, his face dirty and unshaven. The door to the room was open and Amos Falk and two uniformed policemen stood in the hallway, watching anxiously. Doc stared at Fari, but when her eyes turned toward his, he looked away quickly.

"Thank you for saving my life," said Fari.

Doc barked out a short laugh. "Yeah, right."

"You need help, Doc. You are sick."

He snorted and rolled his eyes. "You bet I am! Mentally, morally and physically." He glanced at the doorway and whispered. "Do they have a recorder in here?"

She shook her head. "No."

He thought he could believe her. This was a hospital room, not a police interrogation room. He had just gone through half an hour of questioning by Amos Falk, but never said one word. Sherry's family had sent one of their high-powered attorneys to make sure Doc didn't say anything foolish, or embarrass the Lansing name any further.

The lawyer advised Doc not to answer the detective's questions and demanded to know if they had read him his rights. No, they hadn't, said Amos, because Doc hadn't been charged with anything. Still, the lawyer refused to let Doc talk to Amos. Finally, Amos charged Doc with carrying a concealed weapon, discharging a weapon in a public place, manslaughter and jaywalking.

This was exactly what the lawyer had hoped for and he would spring Doc quickly on bail. The Lansing's wanted Doc shut up and isolated. Now, as Doc stood before Fari, he felt stupid and out of control, like a feather on the breeze.

"You are hero, Doc," said Fari.

Doc glanced at her and this time her eyes locked on and bored deep into his brain. His head jerked back, his heart fluttered.

"Is your life so bad, Doc?"

Doc tried to answer, but his mouth wouldn't move. A vision suddenly invaded his brain – sunrays ripped through storm clouds, a rainbow bloomed and splashed brilliant colors.

"Think up a story, Doc. You are hero."

He wanted to tell her the truth, but what *was* the truth? That man had wanted to kill Fari and maybe Mac too, but Doc had killed him. That's what happened, but that wasn't his *intention*.

"You and I and Mac are reborn," said Fari. "We faced death, but we were spared. Now we start over." Her voice turned soft and melodic. "You are hero, Doc. You are changed man."

Doc could hardly believe what he heard. Fari told him to keep on living and he had wanted to kill both of them! He saw the sincerity in her eyes and he felt it – a warm touch on the side of his heart.

For some reason, he thought of his daughters, their lovely faces and fresh, clean smell. He did love them; they were his little girls. He blinked away tears and moved his mouth.

Fari held up one hand. "Do not talk, please. I am tired. Leave now."

*　　　　　　*

At noon the next day, Saturday, Fari Madrigal was wheeled out of her hospital room, down the hallway and into a freight elevator. She and her entourage were in disguise; Fari's face was covered by an oxygen mask; Dr. Smith, Frances, Mac and a nurse dressed in hospital whites and wore masks.

"I told the head nurse and the administrator," said Dr. Smith. "But no one else. They'll be awfully surprised to find that room empty."

The elevator bumped gently and stopped at the basement garage, where a private ambulance waited. They wheeled Fari to the back doors and prepared to slide her in. The doctor bent over and moved

Fari's mask to one side. She smiled up at him.

"It was a privilege to meet you, Fari Madrigal. Please take care of yourself."

She shook his hand. "Thank you, doctor, for letting me leave."

Fari said goodbye to the nurse and they pushed the gurney into the ambulance. One paramedic rode in the back with Fari, but she insisted that Mac also ride in back. Frances sat up front with the driver. When they had buckled in, the driver, a young African-American woman, held out her hand toward Frances. "I'm Robin. Where we goin?"

Frances shook hands with her. The ambulance was a private rental, all arranged by Howard Sikes, but the crew had not been told their destination. "Midway airport," answered Frances.

"Midway airport?" Robin shifted into gear and eased toward the exit ramp. She glanced at Frances. "You know where that is?"

"God, no! Midway Airport, the doctor said. You don't know where it is?"

"No, ma'am, I don't." They cruised up a ramp to street level and shot into traffic. Robin leaned forward and picked up the radio transmitter. "Hey, Stan. Where's Midway airport?"

There followed a few seconds of static, then a voice came back loud and clear. "It's near downtown St. Paul. Take 94 East and get off at the Capitol Street exit."

"Got it. Thanks."

"Does this ambulance have a siren?" Frances asked.

Robin looked at her. "Sure it does. Are we in an emergency situation?"

Frances smiled. "We might be."

Robin smiled back. "In that case." She leaned over, flicked a switch and the lights and sirens came alive. Nearby cars scattered like cattle before a freight train.

Mac groaned. They moved faster with the siren and he wanted them to go *slow*. He looked down at Fari's lovely face. Her complexion was darker today, her eyes more lively. She said she had slept well. Mac had not. He and Frances had slept on cots in Fari's room.

"Do not look sad, Mac." She reached up and grabbed a handful of his hair. "Recuerda, Fari y Mac están buenos amigos, verdad?"

His throat swelled and he nodded. "Right."

"You and Kim will visit."

Mac kept nodding his head, biting his lip, trying not to act like a baby. He knew Fari would be all right and they would see each other again. He was just too weary in his heart to see something like this happen. Fari was a good person and one of the best baseball pitchers he had ever seen, and she should not be lying here with a bullet hole in her chest.

"Mac?"

Fari flicked her eyes at him and his chest loosened immediately.

"I will heal," she said. "No daño permanente." Her lips trembled. "But I will never pitch in majors again." Tears seeped through her eyelashes and she squeezed his hand. "I am hurt, Mac. I am hurt bad."

Mac knelt on the floor and laid his head next to hers. He knew she wasn't talking about the gunshot wound. He put his lips against her ear. "When you get to the farm, look for a magic tree."

Fari remembered that day in the forest reserve with Mac. Yes, she thought, Mac is exactly right. "Help me find one, Mac?"

"Of course."

"Okay. I wait then. When do you visit?"

"JD says next month. Maybe. We'll see. Everything's happening too fast."

Fari closed her eyes. She felt better when problems were put in their place, awaiting the proper administration of the antidote or solution. Once again, life was just beginning. And maybe that's all life is, she thought – a series of beginnings and endings.

The workings of the universe had put her in harm's way, but then saved her from death. This experience changed her and set her on a different path with an unknown destination. She knew well what she had left behind, but had no idea where she was going. Meanwhile, she would convalesce in the little cabin on the beach.

As they approached Midway Airport, Robin turned off the lights and siren. There could be no doubt about their destination; waiting on the tarmac was a sleek, white jet with a big, red cross on its side.

"That's it!" shouted Robin. She was excited at this secret transfer. Frances had told her they were transporting Fastball Fari Madrigal!

After a brief inspection by security guards, the ambulance drove directly onto the tarmac. A door on the side of a nearby building opened, and JD, Cleo, Howard Sikes and Kim ran toward the ambulance.

Mac knew the real journey was about to begin, and the real goodbye. He and Fari looked at each other, knowing their time together was almost over – until next time. And that made this goodbye a little easier to take; knowing there would be a next time. Fari pulled Mac's head closer and kissed him hard and quick.

He kissed her back, his heart breaking.

The back doors of the ambulance flung open and JD, Howard, Cleo and Kim crowded forward, everyone smiling and talking at once. They helped slide Fari's stretcher out of the ambulance and wheeled it over to the jet. The crew was aboard and they could leave at any time.

Mac stood next to Fari's stretcher while the others loaded suitcases and bags. He held Fari's hand tightly. The cool, empty ache of loneliness crept across his belly and curled around his heart. He had gotten used to being in love again, and now the person he loved was leaving again. This time, however, instead of the devastation and turmoil of Jenni's departure, Fari's departure filled him with a sense of relief and hope. *She will be safe and I'll see her again. But when?*

Their luggage was aboard the jet and they were ready. The others stepped up to Fari one by one and said their goodbyes. Mac was surprised at Howard and Cleo; they both had tears in their eyes and trembling smiles. Not exactly a buoyant farewell. Also, Howard's tears almost certainly included the pain of losing a great source of profit. Then, for a moment, Mac and Fari were alone while the others said goodbye to Frances. Mac stood awkwardly next to the stretcher, feeling wooden and stupid, squeezing Fari's hand. The ache in his heart welled up and tears stung his eyes. *Fari's leaving!* He could hardly believe it; it was all happening too fast. She tugged on his hand and he bent over her face. One of his tears landed on her lips and she licked it, swallowed it.

"I invite you to breakfast, lunch and dinner," she whispered.

He smiled and nodded. This was their new private joke, referring to gobbling each other.

"What about late night snacks? Or afternoon delights?" She smiled and blinked both eyes at him.

A faint electric current shot through Mac's insides and triggered a jolt of sexual energy. He saw the lovely, secret person inside her eyes

– the "real" Fari – the one who transmitted gentleness, intelligence and natural mysticism. Whether bewitched or beloved, he needed to spend more time with this woman. "I'll see you soon."

She nodded. "Yes. Soon.."

The plane's crew wheeled Fari toward a platform, which lifted her toward a wide doorway in the plane's side. Frances and Mac hugged good-bye.

"We'll be okay," Frances whispered. "Please visit soon."

Mac smiled, nodded, kissed her on the cheek. Kim ran over, stood by him and took his hand. They watched as Fari and Frances disappeared into the plane and the doors closed.

The closing of the doors was like the closure of a new chapter in Mac's life – in *all* their lives. He and Kim had learned that life sometimes delivers great random events, good and bad, and that these events change us and push us back into life as a different person.

The engines increased in volume as the jet cruised slowly toward the runway. There were a few windows along the side, but Mac distinguished nothing through the flood of tears. He waved anyway, in case they were watching. The jet's pure white paint and big red cross was reassuring – an airplane dedicated to saving lives, carrying its precious cargo, Fari and Frances, to safety.

My God, thought Mac, Fari left just as quickly as she arrived! In only two weeks, this woman had captured his heart and the hearts of millions, pitched a no-hitter in her first (and only?) major league game, forced big corporations to hand over huge donations and survived an assassination attempt. And now she was gone. They heard a sudden roar and the jet took off down the runway. In the pale air it looked like a giant white dove, the dove of peace, undertaking a mission of mercy and evacuation.

Mac closed his eyes and held his breath. His heart felt tied to the jet and about to get ripped out of his chest. A lump caught in his throat and he could only squeak. "Fari."

He felt a light touch on his lips, warm and sweet, unmistakable. Lightning bolts and rainbows burst inside his brain and showered his neurons with colorful electric confetti.

He smiled. See you later, Fastball Fari.